PRAISE FOR

Zoli

"Soaring and stumbling over decades of midcentury Eastern Europe, *Zoli* is a riveting novel. . . . [It has] an inner reality so authentic it could only have come from the matrix of the novelist's imagination. . . . Colum McCann is blessed with an unlikely mix of an adventurer's spirit and an introvert's compassionate eye. His fiction reflects this sweet incongruity, roaming among life's dispossessed with heartfelt ease. . . . [*Zoli*] gives us a tapestry of an entire culture, one shrouded and then marginalized into near extinction."

—GAIL CALDWELL, *Boston Sunday Globe*

"Beautifully written . . . Beautifully conceived, wonderfully told, the story is proof of an indomitable spirit. The elusive character of Zoli, the brilliant artist, is unforgettable."

—*The Washington Post Book World*

"McCann affirms with *Zoli,* his fourth novel, that he is a writer with a method and a mission. . . . The Roma hardships under the Nazis, their hopes and cruel disillusion under Communism, are grittily conveyed in scenes well researched and often gripping."

—*Los Angeles Times*

"As Zoli sets off across Europe on foot, stripped of not only the potency of her Romany heritage but the promise of a utopian future, each new encounter is charged with both futility and wonder."   —*The New Yorker*

"Lyrical . . . as rich and sensuous as loamy, freshly turned soil . . . McCann's research and lustrous prose bring Zoli vibrantly alive."   —*Entertainment Weekly*

"As assured as anything McCann has ever written, rich in vivid detail but wise, too, about the cruelty of the world . . . McCann allows us to enter a world few of us know anything about. . . . his prose is just plain gorgeous."   —*San Francisco Chronicle*

"Astonishing . . . a carefully crafted and subtle portrait of one woman's rich and troubled relationship with her people, and with her own Gypsy heart . . . With a subtle and nuanced appreciation of a culture far different from his own, McCann offers us a place at the Gypsies' campfire and gives us compelling reasons to stick around and warm up."   —*The Philadelphia Inquirer*

"With a poet's language, McCann creates a haunting story about the pain of exile."   —*People*

"Mesmerizing . . . McCann artfully weaves Romani traditions, superstitions and expressions into a vibrant tableau, vividly rendering Zoli's conflicting urges to flee and stay."
                                                   —*Kirkus Reviews* (starred review)

"McCann vividly animates an insular culture different from our own. Full of dense descriptions of everything from the intricately carved caravans to the Gypsy women whose hair is sewn with gold coins, [he] tells a very convincing and very powerful story about the strength of community and the burden of exile."   —*Booklist* (starred review)

By Colum McCann

FISHING THE SLOE-BLACK RIVER

SONGDOGS

THIS SIDE OF BRIGHTNESS

EVERYTHING IN THIS COUNTRY MUST

DANCER

ZOLI

LET THE GREAT WORLD SPIN

TRANSATLANTIC

Zoli

RANDOM HOUSE TRADE PAPERBACKS

NEW YORK

ZOLI

A NOVEL

COLUM McCANN

2008 Random House Trade Paperback Edition.

Copyright © 2006 by Colum McCann
Reading group guide copyright © 2008 by Random House, Inc.
All rights reserved.

Published in the United States by Random House Trade
Paperbacks, an imprint of The Random House Publishing
Group, a division of Random House, Inc., New York.

RANDOM HOUSE TRADE PAPERBACKS and colophon are
registered trademarks of Random House, Inc.

RANDOM HOUSE READER'S CIRCLE and
colophon are trademarks of Random House, Inc.

Originally published in Great Britain in 2006 by
Weidenfeld & Nicolson, an imprint of the
Orion Publishing Group, London.

Originally published in hardcover in the United States by
Random House, an imprint of The Random House Publishing
Group, a division of Random House, Inc., in 2006.

LIBRARY OF CONGRESS CATALOGING-IN-PUBLICATION DATA
McCann, Colum.
Zoli : a novel / Colum McCann.
p. cm.
ISBN: 978-0-8129-7398-3
1. Irish Travellers (Nomadic people)—Fiction.
2. Women poets, Irish—Fiction. 3. Journalists—Fiction.
I. Title
PR6063.C335Z42 2007
813'.54—dc22   2006042922

Printed in the United States of America

www.randomhousereaderscircle.com

9 8 7

For Allison, Isabella, John Michael, and Christian

Much of this novel was written and
researched while I was a fellow at the
Dorothy and Lewis B. Cullman Center for Scholars
and Writers at the New York Public Library.
It is dedicated to all of those at the library
and to librarians everywhere: thank you.

If you keep quiet, you die. If you speak, you die.
So speak and die.

> —*Tahar Djaout*

But in our century, when only evil and indifference are
limitless, we cannot afford unnecessary questions; rather,
we need to defend ourselves with whatever there is to
hand of certainty. I know that you remember. . . .

> —*John Berger*
> AND OUR FACES, MY HEART,
> BRIEF AS PHOTOS

To get back before dark is the art of going.

> —*Wendell Berry*
> THE COLLECTED POEMS OF
> WENDELL BERRY 1957–1982

Slovakia

2003

He DRIVES ALONGSIDE the small streambed, and the terrible shitscape looms up by increments—upturned buckets by the bend in the river, a broken baby carriage in the weeds, a petrol drum leaking out a dried tongue of rust, the carcass of a fridge in the brambles.

A dog, all bones and scars, noses out in front of the car, and within moments the dog has brought children, crowding up against the car windows. He tries nonchalance as he snaps down the locks with his elbow. One boy is agile enough to jump onto the hood with hardly a noise—he grabs the windshield wipers and spreads himself out. A cheer goes up as two other kids take hold of the bumper and skate behind on the bare soles of their feet. Teenage girls jog alongside in their low-slung jeans. One of them points and laughs, but then stops, still, silent. The boy slides off the hood and the skating kids let go of the bumper, and suddenly the river is in front of him, swirling, fast, brown, unexpected. He yanks the steering wheel hard. Brambles scrape the windows. Tall grass crunches under the wheels. The car swerves back towards the mudtrack, and the children run alongside again in uproar.

On the far bank two old women stand up from where they're washing bedsheets using riverrock and lye. They shake their heads, half-smile, and stoop once more to their work.

He steers around another tight corner, towards a blind line of trees, past the remains of a shattered lettuce crate in the long grass, and there, across a rickety little joke of a bridge, is the gray Gypsy settlement, marooned on an island in the middle of the river, as if the water itself has changed its mind and flowed either side. Shanty houses. Windowless huts. Jagged pipes and mismatched wood. Thin scarves of smoke rising up from the chimneys. Each roof pockmarked with a satellite dish and patched with scraps of corrugated iron. Far off in the distance a single blue coat flaps in the branches of a tree.

He guides the car into the long weeds, stops, pulls the hand-brake, takes a second to pretend that he's looking for something in the glovebox, searches deep, though there's nothing there, not a thing, just a chance to get a small respite. The children crowd the windows. He pushes open the car door, and all he can hear from the settlement across the water is a dozen radios blaring all at once, songs Slovakian and American and Czech.

Instantly the children thumb his sleeve, knuckle his ribcage, pat his jacket pockets. It's as if he has become a dozen hands all at once. "Quit!" he shouts, swatting them away. One boy hops on the front bumper so that the whole car bows to the rhythm. "Okay," he shouts, "enough!" The older teenagers in dark leather jackets shrug. The girls in unbuttoned blouses step back and giggle. How immaculate their teeth. How quick the silver of their pupils. The tallest of the boys steps forward in a muscle-shirt. "Robo," the boy says, puffing out his chest. They shake hands and he pulls the boy aside, has a word, face close to his ear. He tries to block the deep smell of the boy, wet wool and raw smoke, and within seconds a deal is struck—fifty krowns— to bring him to the elders and to keep the car safe.

Robo shouts out a warning to the others, backhands the

child who is tiptoe on the rear bumper. They make their way towards the bridge. More children arrive from along the river, some naked, some in diapers, one in a torn pink dress and flip-flops, and the same girl seems to appear from all angles, but in different shoes each time; beautiful, coal-eyed, hair uncombed.

He watches the kids cross the bridge like a strange line of herons, one foot heavy on the solid planks, high-toed and light on the rest. The metal sheets vibrate under their weight. He totters a moment on a piece of plyboard, sways, reaches for a hold, but there is none. The children put their hands to their mouths and snigger—he is, he thinks, every idiot who has ever walked this way. He feels the weight of what he carries: two bottles, notepad, pencil, cigarettes, camera, and tiny recorder, all hidden away deep in his clothes. He pulls the jacket tight and leaps the final hole in the bridge, lands in the soft mud on the far side, just twenty yards from the shanties. He looks up, takes a deep breath, but it's as if a thousand chords have been struck all at once, his ribcage is thumping, he shouldn't have come here alone, a Slovakian journalist, forty-four years old, comfortably fat, a husband, a father, about to step into the heart of a Gypsy camp. He takes a step forward through a puddle, thinking how stupid it was to wear soft leather shoes for this trip, not even good for a quick retreat.

At the edge of the shacks he becomes aware of the brooding men leaning against woodpole doorways. Women stand with hands folded across their stomachs. He tries to catch their gaze, but they look beyond him and away with thousand-yard stares. Strange, he thinks, that they do not question him; maybe they've mistaken him for a policeman or a social worker or a parole of-ficer or some other government fuckwad here on an official visit.

He feels briefly powerful as Robo leads him deeper into the warren of mudroutes.

Doorframes used as tables. Sackcloth for curtains. Empty čuču bottles strung up as windchimes. At his feet, bits of wood and porridge containers, lollipop sticks and shattered glass, the ground-down bones of some dead animal. He catches glimpses of babies hammocked from ceilings, flies buzzing around them as they sleep. He reaches for his camera but is pushed on in the swell of children. Open doorways are quickly closed. Bare bulbs switched off. He notices carpets on the walls, and pictures of Christ, and pictures of Lenin, and pictures of Mary Magdalene, and pictures of Saint Jude lit by small red candles high above empty shelves. From everywhere comes the swell of music, no accordions, no harps, no violins, but every shack with a TV or a radio on full volume, an endless thump.

Robo leans over and shouts in his ear, "Over here, Uncle, follow me," and it strikes him how foreign this boy, how distant, how dark-skinned.

He is led around a sharp corner to the largest shanty of all. A satellite dish sits new and shiny on the roof. He knocks on the plywood door. It swings open a little further with each knuckle rap. Inside there is a contingent of eight, nine, maybe ten men. They raise their heads like a parliament of ravens. A few of them nod, but they continue their hand, and he knows the game is nonchalance—he has played it himself in other parts of the country, the flats of Bratislava, the ghettos of Prešov, the slums of Letanovce.

In the far corner of the room he notices two women watching him, wide-eyed. A hand pushes him at the small of his back. "I'll wait for you here, mister," says Robo, and the door creaks behind him.

He looks around the room, the immaculate floor, the ordered cupboards, the whiteness of the one shirt hanging on a nail from the ceiling.

"Nice house," he says, and knows immediately how foolish it sounds. He flushes red-cheeked, then draws himself tall. In the corner sits a broad-shouldered man, tough, hard-jawed, gray hair tousled after a bad night's sleep. He steps across and announces quite softly that he's a journalist, he's here on a story, he'd like to talk to some of the old folk.

"We're the old folk," says the man.

"Right," he says, and pats his jacket. He fumbles in his pocket and breaks open a pack of Marlboros. Stupid, he knows, not to have broken the seal already. In the silence the others watch him. His hands shake. A bead of sweat runs down his brow. He can almost hear the chest hair rustle under his shirt. He unwinds the plastic, lifts the cellophane, and shoves three cigarettes up like peeping toms.

"Just want to talk," he says.

The man waits for a light, blows the smoke sideways.

"About what?"

"The old days."

"Yesterday was long," says the man with a laugh, and the laughter ripples around the room, tentatively at first, until the women catch it and it builds, unraveling the tension. He is suddenly slapped on the shoulder and his grin breaks wide, and the men start to talk in an accent that starts low and ends high, musical, fast, jangly. Some of the words appear to be in Romani, and from what he can make out, the man's name is Boshor. He reaches past Boshor, throws the cigarettes on the table, and the men casually reach for them. The women step across, one of them suddenly young and beautiful. She bends for a light, and he looks away from the low swing of her breasts. Boshor points to the cards and says: "We're playing for a little food, a little drink too." The man pulls again on the cigarette. "We're not really drinkers, though."

He takes his cue from Boshor, opens a button, slips back his shirtfront, exposing his flabby chest, and removes the first bottle like a trophy. Boshor picks up the bottle, turns it in his hands, nods approval, and rattles off a salvo of Romani to more laughter.

He watches as the young girl reaches into a cupboard. She takes down a mahogany box with a silver clasp, opens it wide. A matching set of china cups. She puts them on the table, unscrews the bottle. He is given, he notices, the only china cup that is not chipped.

Boshor leans back and gently says: "Health."

They clink cups, and Boshor leans forward to whisper: "Oh, it's for money too, friend. We're playing cards for money."

He doesn't even flinch; he slaps down two hundred krowns. Boshor takes it, slips it into his trousers, smiles, blows smoke towards the ceiling.

"Thank you, friend."

The cards are put aside, and the drinking starts in earnest. He is amazed how close Boshor sits to him, their knees touching, the dark of the hand on his jacketsleeve, and he wonders now how he will navigate their secrets—even their Slovak is a little difficult to understand, their country dialect—but soon enough the second bottle is on the table. He does it calmly and quickly, as if to suggest it's always been there. The drinking unfolds, and they begin to talk to him about crooked mayors and bent bureaucrats and subsidies and the dole, and how

Kolya was beaten with a pickaxe last week and how they are not allowed into the pubs—"We're not even allowed within fifty fucking meters"—all the things they know a journalist wants to hear. Even the Gypsies have soundbites, he thinks, as if he should be surprised, all the words down pat—*racism, integration, schooling, Roma rights, discrimination*—and it's all horseshit really, though he's getting somewhere; they become more talkative as the bottles drain, the voices rise to a clamor, and they fall into a story about a motorbike taken by the cops.

"Everything that gets stolen is what we steal," says Boshor as he leans forward, his eyes slightly bloodshot and tinged with yellow. "It's always us, isn't it? We're prouder than that, you know."

He nods at Boshor, shifts in his chair, seeks a pocket of silence, passes around more cigarettes, and flicks the matchstick to extinguish the flame.

"So," he says, "are motorbikes the new Roma horses?"

He's briefly proud of his question until Boshor repeats it, not once, but twice, and then there's a giggle from the youngest girl and the men slap their thighs in laughter.

"Shit, friend," says Boshor. "We don't even have bridles anymore."

Another round of laughter goes up, but he pushes his question harder, saying surely horses are part of the ancient Gypsy ways. "Y'know," he says, "pride, tradition, heritage, that sort of thing?"

Boshor's chair scrapes against the floor and he leans forward. "I told you, friend, we don't have any horses."

"Different times?"

"It was better under the Communists," says Boshor, flicking ash towards the doorway. "Those were the days."

And that's where his heart surges, he's momentarily high on the lift of it, and just by leaning forward, ever so slightly, he has Boshor by the neck-scruff, a newsman's trick.

"Yeah, back with the Communists we had jobs, we had houses, we had food," says Boshor. "They didn't knock us 'round, no, friend, may my black heart stop beating if I tell a lie."

"Is that so?"

Boshor nods, and from a battered wallet takes out a photograph of a traveling kumpanija long ago in which the men are elegant and the women long-skirted. They are out on a country road, and a red flag with a hammer and sickle flutters from the caravan roof.

"That's my Uncle Jozef."

He takes the photo from Boshor, turns it in his fingers, and wishes to Christ in the clouds above that he had clicked his tape recorder on, for now it has begun, but he wonders how he will reach into his pocket without attracting too much attention, if the small red light will shine through his jacket, and where he should begin his real questions. He wants to say that he is here about Zoli, do you know about Zoli, she was born near here, a Gypsy, a poet, a singer, a Communist too, a Party member, she traveled with harpists once, she was expelled, have you heard her name, did you hear her music, *We sing to sweeten the dead grass,* did you see her, is she still talked of, *From what is broken, what is cracked, I make what is required,* was she damned, was she forgiven, did she leave any sign, *I will not, no, never call the crooked finger straight,* did your fathers tell stories, did your mothers sing her songs, was she ever allowed back?

But when he mentions her name—leaning forward to say, "Have you ever heard of Zoli Novotna?"—the air stalls, the drinking stops, the cigarettes are held at mouth-level, and a silence descends.

Boshor looks towards the doorway and says: "No, I don't know that name—do you understand me, fat-neck?—and even if I did, that's not something we would talk about."

Czechoslovakia

1930s–1949

THERE ARE THINGS ABOUT youth that only youth knows, but what I recall most clearly was sitting in the back of the caravan, wearing red, staring out at the roads going backwards.

I was six years old. My hair was cut short. I'd hacked it off with a knife. I tell this to you directly, there is no other way to say it—my mother was gone, my father, my brother, my sisters and cousins too. They had been driven out on the ice by the Hlinka guards. Fires were lit in a ring around the shore, and guns were pointed so they could not escape. The caravans were forced to the middle of the lake as the day grew warmer. The ice cracked, the wheels sank, and the rest followed, harps and wheels and horses. I did not see any of it happen, daughter, but I could hear it in my mind and, although there was great music to come along later, sweet sounding moments when our people were raised up and strong and valued, that will always be a time of looking backwards, listening and waiting for my dead family to catch up.

Only Grandfather and I escaped—we had been out beyond the lake, traveling three full days. We came back to silence. He clapped his hand over my mouth. The horse reared and the caravan shuddered. Ash from dead fires ringed the lake. Grandfather jumped to the ground. Wait here, he said. He was not a man with whom you could dispute. He thought that places were good and most people were good, but the rules they put on the places were vile, and that people became vile with them.

He did not wait to shed a tear, nor did he pick up the hats and scarves and boxes that were floating among the shards of ice. Instead he walked across to me, his hair at his shoulders, and said, Quick now and silent, Zoli, don't say a word.

We pulled the curtains on the windows and wrapped the sharp knives in towels so they would not clink. He draped the mirror in a shirt. All the dishes were put in cloths. The road we took was small, with a line of green down the middle, two mud-tracks worn on either side. It was already spring, which was why the ice had cracked. Small buds were beginning on the trees. Birds whistled and the sun was bright as tin. I shut my eyes against it. I kept waiting for my mother to appear, my father too, my brother and my two sisters, all my cousins as well, but Grandfather pulled me close, looked over his shoulder, and said, Listen here, child, the Hlinkas are still out there, you must not make another sound.

I had seen the Hlinkas, their leather boots that wrinkled below their knees, the billyclubs that slapped along their thighs, the rifles across their chests, the roll of fat at the back of their necks.

Grandfather guided Red along until dark, then pulled us into a grove of trees. The stars were like clawmarks above us. I sat in the corner and rocked back and forth, then chopped my hair off with a very sharp knife. I hid the braids in my pillow. When Grandfather saw me, he slapped my face twice and said, What have you done? He took one of the braids, put it in his pocket, pulled me close, and whispered to me that my mother had once done the same when she was a child, it was not a good thing, it was against our laws.

When we woke, there were dark marks in a line down my grandfather's cheeks. He went outside, plunged his face in a stream, fed some snowmelt to Red, and we went on.

For days we traveled, first light until last. We went through a village where the four-faced clocktower told three different times. The shops were open and the market was bustling. When we entered the square Grandfather's shoulders went stiff.

Some Hlinkas were gathered around the church steps, laughing and smoking. They fell silent when they heard the clopping of our horse. An armored truck came from behind the clocktower. Quiet now, said Grandfather. He whipped Red's rump and we left quickly, out past the church and into the countryside, far away.

Fascist snakes, he said.

We knocked on every door, looking for food, and late in the evening we came upon a laneway with high brambles. A stone house sat surrounded by high trees. A cat watched from a windowsill. Grandfather bartered with a peasant to repair a gable wall in exchange for some soup and a little money. The peasant said, Go ahead and fix the wall first. Grandfather said, I can't with the child so hungry, look at her, we need money for food. The peasant said, If I give you money you'll run off and gyp me. Grandfather held his tongue and said: I'll build the wall if you give the child food.

The peasant came out from the house, balancing a small bowl of borscht for us to share. We drank from the same side of the handle-shorn cup. The soup was measly and watery.

There are times in a fountain's life, Grandfather said, when even it must learn to swallow piss.

We stayed that night in the weedy field behind the peasant's house. The peasant had a radio, and we heard it faintly but there were no reports on the killings. I leaned in close to Grandfather and asked why my family had not bolted across the ice, and he said to me that my father was strong but not strong enough to escape the fascists, and my mother was strong but with a different strength, and my brother surely attempted but was probably beaten back. He looked away then and said: The Lord or whoever have mercy on the soul of your youngest sister.

When the dark was fully down, Grandfather pulled hard on his tobacco and said: When ice breaks it sends out a warning, child. The Hlinkas ringed the lake with their fires and waited for the day to get warmer. We were lucky they never found us.

He ran the blade of his knife along his thumb. I asked how deep the water was and what happened when the ice got thinner, but Grandfather said no more questions, they would be *mule* soon, spirit, they did not want to be disturbed. Maybe they were able to swim away, I said, under the ice. He looked at me and sighed. I asked if the horses were spirit too and he said no more questions, girl, but later in the evening, when the night had fallen upon us, he lay down beside me and said that he did not want to think about what the first crack was like, nor the screaming of the horses, nor the creak of the wheels, nor the breath of the soldiers, nothing at all. He pinched my cheek and told me a story instead about nails and a forge and a sky that was pushed into place with strong hands, and he finished it off by saying that good things would be built in the long days to come.

In the morning the peasant came out of his house and said, Away with you.

Grandfather slapped Red on the rump and asked her to

leave a big steaming one for the peasant outside his house, but she did not. We went on, but that became his favorite saying, and then his never-ending joke, whenever we got somewhere he did not like: Go ahead, horse, and shit.

~

No small turn of my grandfather's head was lost to me. He was made up of elaborate things. He had three shirts and he did not believe a man should have more. The open collars were folded down outside the lapels of his black jacket. His enormous mustache curled and the hairs on his chin were long. His nose was bony and it had been broken many times. He wore a Marx pin on his hat, but he always removed the hat before we got near a village, stuffed it in the waistband of his trousers where it made his jacket bulge. The pin would only bring trouble, he said.

He liked to smoke very thin rolled cigarettes, he held them between the fourth and little finger of his right hand. The grapevine turned his fingers green, and the smell of the tobacco drifted back over the air.

As far as he knew, Grandfather was thirty-nine years old. My grandmother had escaped this world years before I entered it. He kept a photograph of her inside his jacket, but half of her was worn away from forever coming in and out of his pocket. They had been mother and father to many, but all except one were already buried. The last one still alive had taken gadžikano ways, which meant he was dead too. Nobody said anything about him anymore, not even his name. From my earliest days Grandfather had called me Zoli, a boy's name, after his first son. Sometimes, when I was called Marienka, I would not even turn to answer. He said that the most important thing about names were the namers, to hell or high water with what anyone else said. We are full of names, he said, we always will be, that's our way.

We drove on, Grandfather and me, we left it all behind: the chocolate factory, the tire plant, the rivers and the mountains. We called the mountains the Shivering Hills, though of course they were the Carpathians. He wore shiny knee-boots with concertina creases at the ankles and the right boot was split at the back seam. I liked to lean out from the back of the caravan to watch it, it looked like it was speaking, open and closed, open and closed, though there were long stretches of road where it didn't say much at all. I was not old enough yet, daughter, to know why my family had been driven out on the ice.

~

The spring before, I remember waking early one morning, me, my brother, and my older sister. My mother and father were sleeping, the baby, Angela, too. I peeped into the zelfya, which was hung from the ceiling, and watched her little chest rise and fall. We tiptoed out, down the three steps. The sun had not yet fully risen. Outside the fields shone green and white. Most of the other children were already playing outside. There were twenty of us, maybe more, making a lot of noise. Father came to the door and threw his slipper at us to make us quieten.

Shut up! he shouted.

We hushed and went towards the fields, near the factory, and crossed the low wall, made of tires. It gave a tiny bounce. My shoes were made from rubber too and they squeaked when I landed. We looked out over the field of frosty grass.

The game we played was to see who could find the longest

sleeve of ice. The greenest blades were best since they stood tall and straight and did not bend over with the weight. Slowly we went through the field, over the hard muddy ridges of ground, searching. I could hear my brother shouting how he'd found a sleeve, possibly the biggest sleeve ever, you could fit your finger in it, maybe even your arm. We pushed and shoved and yelped and laughed and laid the ice out on our fingers to measure it before it melted.

I loved the feel of the frost and I stayed in the long grass, looking. The trick was to hold the bottom of the blade steady and then to coax the ice along—too slow and it broke, too fast and it fell. The most perfect sleeve came off almost whole and you could see down its sparkling length. I put it to my mouth and blew air through. I could feel my own breath at the other end and then the ice dissolved on my tongue.

I stayed in the field until the sun rose over the trees and the others were gone. The shadows grew long and then sprang back all of a sudden. The sun topped the highest branches and soon everything began to melt. My socks were soaked through. I ran back over the field and over the bouncing tire wall, towards the caravans, just beyond the edge of the cypress trees. The fire was already lit, and my father had his hands cupped around the first smoke of the day. Everyone else had already eaten, and they had run off towards the chocolate factory. My mother banged the last of the kasha out of the pot and said: Zoli, we thought the gadže got you and took you away, where in the world were you? My father said: Get over here, you little pup. He grabbed my ear, pulled it hard, took a piece of bread from his pocket, and gave it to me. How was the ice? he asked. Delicious, I said. Was it not cold? he said with a laugh, and I said, Yes, it was cold and delicious together.

~

My grandfather once said, Show me a child of ours who is not happy and I will show you a gadžo dwarf.

~

We went down the road, Grandfather and I. My days were spent still staring backwards, waiting for my dead family to catch up, though of course I knew then that they never would.

We ate from the forest: boiled leaves, pine cones cracked open in a fire, wild garlic grass, and whatever small animals he'd caught in a trap the night before. We could not eat birds, we were not allowed, it was ancient law, but we ate rabbit and hare and hedgehog. We filled our canteens from the taps of houses where they welcomed us, or from the fast-running streammelt that came down from the mountains, or from wells abandoned in the fields. Sometimes we stopped with the settled ones who lived in tin huts and underground hovels. They opened up with great friendliness, but we did not stay, we kept moving on, there was no time for that, Grandfather said we were meant for skies not ceilings.

In the evenings Grandfather sat and read—he was the only person I knew who could read or write or count. He had a precious book I did not know the name of and in truth I did not care, it sounded strange and ridiculous and full of huge words, nothing like his stories. He said that a good book always needed a listener, and it sent me to sleep quickly—he always read from the same pages, they were heavily thumbed and they even had a tobacco burn in the bottom left corner. It was his only book and he had stitched another cover on, a brown leather one with gold lettering from a catechism to fool anyone who questioned him. I found out years later that it was *Das Kapital*—the notion still makes me shiver, though in truth I'm not sure, čhonorroeja, if he ever got a lot of meaning from the pages, they confused him as much as they finally confused others.

Why didn't Mama read? I asked him once.

Because.

But why?

'Cause she didn't want to feel the weight of my hand, he said. Now run along and stop asking me stupid questions.

Later he gathered me up in his arms and I snuggled against his long hair and he said it was tradition, it had always been so, only the elders read, and that one day I would understand. Tradition meant sticking with old ways, he said, but sometimes it meant making new ways too. He sent me off to bed and tucked the blanket around me.

On our slow trip eastward, under the shadow of the mountains, he promised that if I kept quiet he would teach me to read and write, but I must keep it secret, nobody else could know, it would be better that way, it would cause a fuss among those who did not trust books.

He unbuttoned the breast pocket of his shirt where he kept his eyeglasses safe. The glasses were broken, wrapped in bits of wire and tape. The cross frame was held together with a supple twig. I laughed when he put them on.

When he began he did not start with A, B, C, but with a Z, although my other name was Marienka.

We slept under the sky, the weather was fine and the nights were full and soft, except of course for our yearning for those we'd left behind. We had little left to remember them by, but there was an old song my mother had sung: *Don't break bread with the baker, he has a dark oven, it opens wide, it opens wide*. There were times I would sing it for Grandfather while he sat on the low steps and listened. He closed his eyes and smoked his tobacco and hummed along, and then one day he stopped me cold and asked, What did you say, Zoli? I stepped back. What did you say, child? I sang it again: *Don't break bread with the Hlinka, he has a dark oven, it opens wide, it opens wide*. You changed the song, he said. I stood there, trembling. Go ahead, sing it again, you'll see. I sang it over and he clapped his hands together, then rolled the word *Hlinka* around in his mouth. He repeated the song and then he said: Do the same with the butcher, precious heart. So I did the same with the butcher. *Don't chop meat with the Hlinka, he has a sharp knife, it slices deep, it slices deep*. He said: Do the same with the farrier. *Don't shoe horses with the Hlinka, he has long nails, they'll make you lame, they'll make you lame*. I was too young to know what I had done, but a few years later, when we found out what the Hlinkas and Nazis had done with ovens and nails and knives, the song changed for me yet again.

In fact when I see myself now from a distance, when I look back on it all, I was just another girl in a polka-dot dress on the backroads of a country that seemed strange to me at every turn.

Once, a motorcar passed us, and a man in a rich brown overcoat wanted to take a photograph. Grandfather turned his head. This is not the circus, mister. The man held out a few hellers. Grandfather said: I'd rather skim stones. Then the man took out a crisp note from his wallet and pulled it tight so that it made the noise of a drumskin, and Grandfather said with a shrug: Well, why didn't you say so? I was made to stand still on the steps and I held the flare of my skirt. The man put his head under a black sheet. He looked like a hooded bird. A bulb flashed and I jumped. He did it six times. Grandfather said: All right, mister, that's enough.

He was quiet when we clopped away again under the trees, but in the next village he bought me a peppermint stick. He slapped the whip at Red's rump and said: Don't ever give them something for nothing, Zoli, you hear me?

They documented me when we got to Poprad because all Romani children had to be examined by the age of five and I was already seven. The building was grand and white, with statues outside and a row of gray steps leading up to a huge wooden door. Inside there was a curving staircase, but we were told to go to the small squat cabins in the back courtyard.

The clerk examined Grandfather's papers for a long time, looked him up and down, from his hair to his boots, and said: Is she yours?

My daughter's daughter, he said.

She's surprisingly tall, you know.

I heard a creak of leather and noticed Grandfather had stretched up on his toes.

She took me into an office, closed the door on my grandfather, turned my face back and forth in her fingers. Your left eye's lazy, she said. She pulled my head down and checked in my hair for lice and then asked where the bruise came from. What bruise? I said. My hair had begun to grow and my grandfather had sewn a single coin at the fringe, where it bumped against my forehead. She pulled back the coin, pressed her finger against my forehead. It's ridiculous to have money in your hair, she said. Why do you people insist on such things?

I watched the bob of silver at her neck. She put the cold round metal of it against my chest and listened through tubes.

She shone the flashlight into my throat, put me up against a wall, and mumbled something. She gazed at me and said I was very tall for my age. I was indeed tall, even for seven, but now I had to be five once more.

The clerk said: Five, my holy eye.

She measured my nose and the distance between my eyes, even the length of my hands and wrote it all down carefully. She took my thumb and rolled it back and forth on a soft pad of black ink and pushed my other fingers down hard onto the page. I liked the little patterns my fingers made, like bootprints down by a river. She asked me lots of questions, where I was born, what was my real name, if I went to school, where were my parents and why weren't they with me. I told her they had fallen beneath the ice but said nothing about the Hlinka guards. She said: What about your brothers and sisters? I said, Them too. She raised her eyebrows, looked at me sternly, and then I blurted: My brother, Anton, tried to break away. Break away where? she asked. I looked at my fingers. Break away where, young lady? From the lake by the forest. Who in the forest? she asked. The wolves, I said. Lord above, she said. And what did these wolves look like? I didn't say another word but she said, Oh, you poor thing, and then she touched me on the side of the face with a gentle stroke of her finger.

She took me out to where my grandfather was waiting. She looked around quickly, then leaned in close and whispered something. Grandfather stepped back and swallowed hard. The clerk looked over her shoulder again.

Do you want to make a complaint? she said.

About what?

I'll make sure it gets to the right people.

I don't know what you're talking about, said Grandfather.

The little girl told me, she whispered.

Told you what?

You don't have to worry, she said.

Grandfather flicked a quick look at me, then started talking a long line of gibberish about a pack of wolves and men who were hungry and wheels that leave a mark in the forest and birds flying above the trees. It made no sense at all, not even to him.

The clerk stared at him: I'll ask one last time. Do you want to make a complaint or not?

Grandfather went off on another long kite line of gibberish.

The clerk sighed and her voice became stern and loud again. I've had enough of you people, she said. One day you want help, the next you just spout nonsense.

She slapped her hand down on a desk bell. Another official came out from a back office. He wore black elastic bands on his sleeves. He raised his eyes to heaven when he saw us. Christ, he muttered. He shoved the papers across the wooden counter without even looking at them.

All right, she must come in and register every three months.

What about the other children? asked Grandfather.

All the Gypsy children have to do it.

And the other children?

Oh, them? he said. No, why?

Grandfather made a rattling sound in his throat and signed the papers with an XXX. On the way out I asked him why he didn't write using the letters he'd taught me, but he turned and pinned me with a look. Halfway down the steps he caught me by the ear and said: Never tell them that story, never. Do you hear me?

He almost lifted me in the air by my ear.

They'll make it twice as bad, he said. And then they'll just shove us under again. D'you understand me, child? Never.

The pain shot through me. We walked down the last of the steps. I looked at my hands. They were black with fingerprint ink. I sucked at my fingers, but he slapped my hand.

A respectful girl keeps her insides clean, he said. Don't bring that ink down into your belly.

The wagon was listing sideways on the cobblestones. I went up and held on to Red's reins, rubbed against her, my ear hot against her pulsing neck. Grandfather climbed up and sat a long time, staring at the building. Finally he said: Come up here, precious heart. He lifted me up with one hand and sat me on the board beside him. He sat quiet a long time, then he spat sideways, put his arm around my shoulder, and said to me that one of the reasons he wrote XXX was that he would not let them make an idiot of him with their rules.

He took the reins in his hands and was about to slap them down on Red's rump, but then he looked back over his shoulder and whispered: Go ahead, horse, and shit. And as if by the very string of heaven, Red lifted her tail and left two steaming loads on the cobbles outside the grand white building, and we drove away laughing, we never laughed so hard. At the end of the road we looked back and saw a man lifting the clumps up on a shovel with a scrunched red look on his face. We laughed even harder until the building was out of sight and we went out on the country road with the trees in bloom and the midges rising and blue dragonflies on the air, the kind that leave the shine from their wings on the glass once you put them in a jar.

Grandfather put his hat back on his head and wound his curling mustache around his finger and said very loud again to the road: Go ahead, horse, and shit.

We followed signs—a knotted wishbone to turn left, a broken twig for a right fork in the road, a white cloth for a friendly farmhouse where we could water Red and fill our canteens.

It was late summer and the cherry trees were heavy and drooping. We crossed a lovely clean river and went deep into the forest where we were shielded from view by thick lines of yew, green oak, sycamore. Among the wiry grasses grew wild orchids and dandelions. Grandfather brought me into a clearing where fourteen caravans stood, they took my breath away, beautifully colored and carved. Water came up from the ground around a piece of swampy grass. A tin cup was upended on a nubbed pole. A girl came towards us with a drink. It ran cool against the back of my throat. I watched as Grandfather took giant strides across the camp and put his arms around the shoulders of his very own brother who he had not seen in years. He shouted at me to hurry up and come meet my cousins, and cousins of cousins, and cousins of other cousins. Soon we were surrounded, and I was scooped up immediately into a new life which was so much like my old life.

A few of them had strayed down from Poland, carrying harps. I had never seen instruments so tall, beautifully carved and strung with catgut. They stood twice my height. Even when I stretched on my toes I could not reach the top of the strings. They were varnished and carved with wheels and griffins and birds. The plucked sound carried through the trees. There was nothing so lovely. The women who played the harps had very long fingernails. They painted their nails every night, using whatever colors could be found, boiled up from animals and red riverstone and some from bird eggs, light blue. The colors were brushed on with tiny brooms made from weed-grass. Eliška, a Polish woman with hair black as thumbprints, owned a very fine enamel brush—she had found it at the back of a theater in Krakow, she said it belonged to a famous actress who could be heard on the radio. Who needs a radio when you have Eliška! she shouted.

She took my arm and walked me across the camp: You have the eyes of a little devil, she said.

She laughed and spun me round in the air and later told me to sit with her as she brushed the color onto her fingernails. Her words were quick and clipped. Eliška had fallen in love with a young man named Vashengo and soon she would marry. She said she would teach me an old song that I could sing at their wedding. Hers were the old laments I already knew, but then she taught me a new one. *I will fill the empty cup, it is not so hollow anymore, I will fill it with wine, it will come from the palm of your hand.* I learned it quickly and wandered around the camp singing it, until Vashengo said: Please shut up, you'll drive me to the nuthouse. I sang another verse and he clipped me on the ear. Eliška whispered to me that I was all right, not to worry, pay no attention to the men, they wouldn't know a good song if it kissed them on the lips. Come here, she said, and I'll braid your hair like your mother used to. How do you know how my mother braided my hair? I asked. It's a secret, she said. I began to cry, so she said: Oh your mother was famous for many things, most of all she was a great singer.

She leaned down to my ear and sang, and the songs grew and grew, and she took my face in her hands and kissed my forehead. Pity about your eye, said Eliška, otherwise you'd be as pretty as she was.

It was my talent that I could remember words and phrases, and so I was kept up late at night to listen to the songs. Sometimes they shifted and rolled and changed. If the women were swaying with čuču, they could not remember where the song had led the night before. They said to me: Zoli, what did I sing? And I would say: *They broke, they broke my little brown arm, now my father he cries like the rain.* Or I would say: *I have two husbands, one of them sober, one of them drunk, but each one I love the same.* Or I sang: *I want no shadow to fall upon your shadow, your shadow is dark enough for me.* They smiled when these words came out of my mouth and told me again that I had the look of my mother. At night I fell to sleep thinking of her. I pictured her in my mind, she had a row of perfect teeth except for a bottom one missing.

It is strange now to talk of such things, but these are the moments I remember, čhonorroeja, this was my childhood, I try to tell it to you as I saw it then, and as I felt it then, when I was not yet shunned, when it was all still free and open to me, and for the most part it was happy. The Great War hadn't yet begun and, although the fascists sometimes hunted us to give us another dose of their hatred—we were no more than wild animals to them—we settled as far away from them as possible, kept to our own ways, and made music where we could. That, back then, was enough.

~

In the new camp there was another girl the same age as me. Conka had red hair and freckles in a band across her nose. Her mother had sewn a string of pearls in her hair. Her dresses were threaded with silver, and she had the most beautiful voice of all, so she too was kept awake at night to sing. The canvas flap of the singing tent was pulled back for us. We stood on buckets so we could be seen. Grandfather shoved his hat back on his head and lit up a smoke. Everyone gathered in a half circle around us. The women played the harps at a furious pace, once or twice they bent a fingernail backwards in the strings, but still they kept going.

My voice was not as sweet as Conka's, but Grandfather said that it hardly mattered, the important thing was the right word, to pull it out, or squeeze it short, and then dress it up with air from my lungs. When we sang, Conka and I, he said that we were air and water in a pot and together we boiled.

In the nighttime, we tried to fall asleep by the fire, but our favorite stories kept us up late and when a story was really good we had no legs to hold us up. Her father slapped us and told us to go to our beds, we'd waken the dead. Grandfather carried me and put me beneath the eiderdown where my mother had once stenciled a harp using thread that came from cottonwood trees.

One evening, Grandfather carried home a carpet of a man's face, and he hung it on the wall above the drawer full of knives. It was a portrait of a man with a gray beard, a strange gaze, and a high forehead. It's Vladimir Lenin, he said. Don't tell a soul, you hear me, especially the troopers if they come along. Later that week he bought a second carpet—this one was the Holy Virgin. He rolled the Virgin into a tight circle with string, and positioned her above Lenin, so that if a stranger came into the caravan, he could reach up with his knife and cut the string and the Holy Virgin would come down on top of Lenin in a rush. Grandfather thought it hilarious and sometimes he cut the string just for fun, and if he was drunk he would talk to their faces and call them the greatest of bedfellows. If there was a rumble outside in the camp, he would quickly cut the string and shove his leather-bound book into a hidden pocket at the back of his jacket. Then he stood outside with his arms crossed and a scowl on his face.

He would sooner have invited in typhus than a trooper.

If they forced a check on us they pushed their way past him without asking, stomped their boots on the floor, but they never found Lenin or the book. They tore the place up and tossed teacups to one another. From outside we could hear the smashing, but what was there to do, we just waited until they came out, down the steps, their boots shiny at the knees and scuffed at the toes.

When they were gone, we cleaned the mess, and Grandfather rolled up the Virgin again, let Lenin look out once more.

Grandfather went to the Poprad market one day and didn't come back for four more. He had built a wall for a man who had given him a wireless radio. He carried it into the camp with great fanfare, put it down by the fire, and music jumped out. Vashengo's father came to look at it. He liked the music indeed and everyone gathered around and fiddled with the knobs. But in the morning, a group of elders came and said they didn't like the children listening to outsiders. It's only a radio, said Grandfather. Yes, they said, but the talk is immodest. Grandfather took Vashengo's father by the arm and they walked down by the river and worked out a plan: he would only listen to music and not the other shows. Grandfather took it with us to our caravan, turned it very low, and listened anyway. It's my duty to know, he said, and he ran the little yellow dial along the glass panel, Warsaw, Kiev, Vienna, Prague, and the one he loved the most, though it didn't get any sound: Moscow.

One day I heard him slam down the wooden backing on the ground: This bloody thing needs batteries, can you imagine that?

He came back a couple of days later with a sack full of batteries over his shoulder and his clothes covered in flecks of gray. He told us that the gadže now wanted walls held together with cement—all his other walls he had built with rocks and air—but if that's what he had to do for batteries, that's what he had to do.

Soon everyone grew to like the radio. Mostly we listened to music, but every now and then government voices came through. In the caravan, Grandfather tuned it in to whatever he could find, all the different languages. He spoke five—Romani, Slovak, Czech, Magyar, and a little Polish—though Eliška said he should forget all that red gibberish, he sounded the same in every language, he should come back in the next life as a loudspeaker strung up on a lamppost. He said that loudspeakers were fascist and just you wait, you black-haired chovahanio, you witch, when the good ones, the Communists, finally get power. She shouted at him that she couldn't hear him, that she must have been asleep when he was talking. He shouted back: What the hell did you say, woman? I thought that Eliška might lift her skirt to shame him, but she did not, she just turned away. She got a lash of his tongue, and he said something rude about her little enamel brush and where she could sweep it. Soon everyone began laughing and joking and it was forgotten.

Still, Grandfather got in fist-thumping arguments about the book he carried. He sat with the elders around the fire and tried to talk to them of revolution, but they said that our men were not meant for such things. Petr the violinist nodded in agreement with Grandfather, and Vashengo too, but Conka's father was loud against him.

Did you ever hear such nonsense! If Marx was a worker, how come he never worked? How come he just wrote books about working? Tell me, did he just want to keep pissing on a hot stove?

Grandfather clicked his fingers, stood up, and shouted: Whoever is not with us is against us!

He and Conka's father stepped across the pots and came to blows.

In the morning, they drank their coffee and began all over again.

So you never answered my question, said Conka's father. If Marx loved the poor so much, how come he had time to write books?

Grandfather took me down to the river. He tipped his hat and brought me across a fallen log, and he held my hand as we balanced near the edge. Listen to me, Zoli, he said. The river here, it doesn't belong to anyone, but some of them say they own it, they all say they own it, even some of us say we own it, but we don't. Look there, see the way the water is still moving underneath? It'll keep on moving. Only inches below, girl, the owning is gone, even ours, and you have to remember that, otherwise they will make a fool of you with their words.

The next day he led me to the schoolhouse.

I had heard about schools and did not want to go, but he pulled me under the green overhanging roof. I tried to run away but he caught me by the elbow. Inside, the desks were arranged in neat rows. Strange pictures with lots of green and blue hung on the walls—I did not yet know what a map was. My grandfather talked with the teacher and told her I was six years old. The teacher arched her eyebrows and said, Are you sure? Grandfather said, Why wouldn't I be sure? The teacher's hands trembled a little. Grandfather leaned forward and stared at the teacher. The teacher went white in the face. Bring her here, sir, she said. I'll gladly look after her.

I was put in the corner with the youngest of all, dribbles from their noses, one even wore diapers. The older children giggled when I sat on the tiny seat, but I stared at them until they were quiet.

That night, when it was raining, and the sound of it was drumming off the leaves outside, there was an enormous fight in the singing tent. Stay where you are, said Eliška. But I want to sing, I said. Stay where you are, she said, if you know what's good for you. I huddled up under the eiderdown. There was screaming and shouting. Then it stopped and the music started and I could hear Conka's voice drifting out under the rain. *They broke they broke my little brown arm*. She got the words wrong, muddled them up, and I wanted to run through the wet grass to tell her, but I heard some more shouting and the whip of a tree branch, so I pulled the eiderdown over me and stayed quiet. Grandfather came in with his hat dripping wet. He didn't seem to notice a cut on his cheek, by his eye. He sat by the window and smoked some grapevine, looking out.

No matter what, he said, it's my choice.

He kissed me goodnight on the forehead and he turned on the wireless radio and it played a polka. In the morning I was caught by the oldest woman, we called her Barleyknife because of the scar on her breast. She slapped me nine times. I walked over to the fence, my face stinging. She tied back her hair with a clothes peg and shouted after me: You'll learn to marry the butcher's dog, wait 'til you see, mark my words, you'll marry the butcher's ugliest dog.

Rain dripped off the slanted school roof, down the window-pane. The teacher smelled of lye. Her neck was goose-white and she wiped chalk from the board with her elbow. My knees kept bumping against the top of the desk. I wore a blue skirt with white polka dots and a frilled hem. Across the room, the older gadžo boys were able to spit silently through the gaps in the front of their teeth. Soon one side of my hair was soaking wet with spittle, but I did not turn. I think they expected me to shout, but I did not. They whispered an old rhyme at me, say-ing: *Marienka sold a horse for a dog, she ate the dog with rotten haluški.* I said nothing, just stared ahead. I hated the way that the chalk rubbed the blackboard, it squeaked and made me feel cold. They laughed at me and the way I talked, but the school-teacher could not believe that I already knew the ABC's and, after a week or two, she gave me a book about a prince who turned into a lion.

The older children shouted at my back and threw bird eggs at me. I picked up the shells and put them in my dress pocket. I tucked the book in the hedges near the school and covered it with leaves. When I got back to camp I held out my hand full of birdshell. The women were delighted, even Barleyknife, she said that maybe school wasn't so bad after all, and she went off to paint her fingernails blue, though she also painted the nails on her feet—that was one difference between the Slovaks and Polish, we kept our feet unpainted and never wore rings on our toes.

One day I forgot about the rain, and the book in the hedges

was ruined, all the pages were stuck together. They tore as I opened them. The schoolteacher said that I should have known better, but still she gave me another one, wrapped this time in oilcloth.

She insisted I take a bath in her house, close to the school, every morning, though I washed in the river with Conka every day. I told her that a Gypsy girl will bathe in running water, but not in a bath and she laughed and said: Oh, you people. She fiddled with my clothes, even gave me some she pretended were new. They were wrapped in brown paper, but I could tell they had been worn before—I saw the roll of paper and twine in the corner of her desk.

She ran her fingers hard through my hair, looking for lice, then combed paraffin through my braids and wrote a long letter to my grandfather: *Sir, Marienka needs to take proper care of her hygiene. Her mathematics and wordcraft are up to standard, especially given her circumstances, but it is imperative that the highest levels of cleanliness be maintained. Please ensure that the proper steps are taken. Yours, Bronislava Podrova.* Grandfather rolled a grapevine leaf around the note and smoked it.

She talks more shit than a factory outhouse, he said.

After that, I didn't go to school for a while. Everyone was delighted, especially Barleyknife who made up her very own song about a black girl who goes to a green schoolhouse and then becomes white, but finally on the road home she turns black again. I thought it was a stupid song, and so did almost everyone else, but Barleyknife sang it whenever she had climbed down into the bottle.

There was still talk of punishment for my grandfather because not only did he send me to school, but sometimes he sat in the open now, reading his book. The punishment never happened, though. Vashengo's uncle stood up for him and said it was all right for one child to go to school because then we would know what was going on, not to worry, it was time to stick together, we would use it for our benefit, one day, just wait and see.

Petr, an old man with a soft handsome face, played his violin and Grandfather stood clapping his hands in the middle of the big canvas singing tent, and it seemed like everything was going to be all right.

The teacher gave me more books. Conka loved the pictures of wild animals and we snuck off and put the jaguar, the dolphin, the tiger up in the stars beside the badger and the wagon, the hen and the wheel—I had no idea then that others had different names for the stars, the plow, the hunter, the seven sisters. There was so much I had yet to see. Bit by bit, the stars turned on their sides and fell below the line of the earth.

～

I began at an early age to like the feel of a pencil between my fingers. Days in the caravan, I sat in silence with Grandfather as he spread his playing cards on the table. Red limped past in the muddiness outside. One morning, Grandfather sat beside me at the diamond window and looked outside and said he thought of that horse as a sickness he was catching. He had ridden the animal many times, and in his voice he said that he might not be able to do so too much longer. That was the way of things, he said, it was all right, he would still always catch the sound, all he had to do was open his ears and listen, that was enough.

Red disappeared into the trees by the water. We listened to the shake of her mane and the whinny of her throat and the dip of her flank in the water. The bushes bent and the stems snapped as she returned through the mud. We harnessed her up. I stayed in the caravan as we went down the roads. I sat with my pencil, sharpening it, and I shaped to a stillness the sound of Red's hooves in the muck outside: *dloc dloc.*

Gray meadows rolled past. Dark squares of plowed earth. Faint sounds came from the harps when we went over a bump. At night we jumped down from the carriages and swung open whatever gates we could find. Everyone gave a coin for the kerosene and Conka's uncle told great Romani tales. Often they would not stop until well into nightfall, long ramblings about twelve-legged horses and dragons and demons and virgins and cruel aristocrats, about how the gadže blacksmiths tricked us with their molten buttons.

This I tell you, daughter: they were warm nights even when they were cold, and I recall them dearly and perhaps, in truth, they were warmer because of those that were yet to come.

We moved our kumpanija near the smaller town of Bánksa Bystrica, and we were allowed to stay in the field of a man we called the Yellow Farmer. The farmer had huge yellow boots that went up to his waist. He stamped around in them and sometimes went fishing down by the river. Janko was four and he was found one day on the riverbank, hiding in the boots, his little head popping out of the top rim. Nearly all of him was tucked inside, only his grin could be seen, and after that we called him Boot.

They were quiet moments in the Yellow Farmer's field, but

bit by bit we began to hear that terrible things were afoot in the country. The Germans didn't take over as they had in the Czech lands, but Grandfather said it hardly mattered, the Hlinkas were just like Gestapo, except they wore different badges. The war was coming our way. New laws were brought in. We were only allowed in the cities and villages for two hours a day, noon until two, and sometimes not even then. After those hours, no Roma man or woman was allowed in public places. Sometimes even the purest woman was charged with spreading infections and was thrown in prison. If a man was caught on a bus or a train, he was beaten until he couldn't even crawl. If he wandered the streets, he was arrested and sent to a workcamp to chop logs. We learned the sound of military vehicles the way we'd once learned the sound of animals—jeeps, tanks, convoys of canvas-covered trucks, we could tell which was coming around the corner. And yet we still thought ourselves to be among the lucky ones—many of our Czech brothers streamed south with terrible stories about being marched down the many-cornered road. Everyone now listened to my grandfather at the fire. He knew what was happening from his radio, and even Conka's father went with him to the millhouse where they were allowed barter for batteries.

Grandfather didn't have time to build any more walls, he said that now everything was held together by factory cement, but if he ever built another wall he would do it his own way, and hold it together with what he called cunning.

At night he turned the radio to polkas again, away from news of the war. Someone called Chamberlain had become a doormat, he said. Grandfather sat on the roof of our caravan and drank until he fell asleep under the stars. I whizzed the radio away from polkas and heard a man announce in Polish about what was happening, the same thing in Slovak too. Of course there was no Romani radio, there was not even a half-hour show, and we didn't hear news of our own people.

Who needs news, Grandfather said, when it's all around us? A pig doesn't need a gold ring in its nose to know where it is sleeping, does it?

Conka's mother went to Poprad but she got lost in the backstreets near the promenade, by the fruit market. Everyone searched for her, but she was picked up by the Hlinkas. They took her to the back of a bookshop, pushed her down on a table. They laughed at her long fingernails, said they were so lovely. One said he liked her fingernails so much that he would like to bring one of them home, maybe his wife would like to see such fine artistry. They held Conka's mother down by her shoulders. All she could see was a very dark patch of ceiling above her head and then the room began to spin. One held her arm. Another held the pliers. The nails came out one by one, though they left one little finger alone—they said it was so she could please herself if she got a Gypsy itch.

They strung her nails on a little chain around her neck and sent her out of the bookshop into the street, where she fell. The troopers came out of the bookshop and brought her to hospital because, they said, she had grazed her knee. They said to the nurse: Take care of this woman's knee, it's very important that you fix her knee. On and on they went about her knee. The nurses lifted Conka's mother from the ground. Her hands were streaming blood.

They tried to heal her but she left as quick as she could. None of our people wanted to remain in a hospital amongst sickness and death, it was not a good place to be. Conka's father drove her home, and she lay crying in the back of the cart. Her hands were huge with white bandages that soon turned brown no matter how much she boiled them. She stayed in her caravan. Every day she took off the bandages and bathed her hands in water mixed with dock leaves, and then she pasted the stumps of her fingers with woodsap and chamomile. She stared at her hands as if they did not belong to her at all. Conka said it was not the pain that made her mother wail, but because she would never be able to pluck the harp again. She tried the catgut strings with the stumps of her fingers, but her hands bled once more and that was it—the owls were in the sycamores, and things would never change.

The bookshop burned down. My grandfather and Conka's father came back smelling of petrol. A feast was held. The tent rippled in the wind and my grandfather sang "The Internationale"—it was not the first time I had heard it, but now even Eliška joined in. She made a song up too: *There are good rocks to throw and better roofs to burn,* even Grandfather liked it, and I recall the last verse was that thorn trees would learn to grow from Hlinka hearts.

We were in the thick of things. The axles were packed with grease and we got ready to leave our Polish brothers and sisters, although Eliška was coming with us. She had married Vashengo. Before we split, we gathered in a circle at the tent, and Grandfather told us the news: there was a new law out that said we needed licenses for any type of musical instrument, and so that would have to be the end of the harps for a while. The harps were buried in huge wooden containers that the men made out of maple trees from the Yellow Farmer's forest. The men dug huge pits and laid the harps in the ground. We covered the ground with brambles and switched plants in the soil so that nobody could find them. Conka and I ran to the place of the burial, and she started a game where she jumped up and down on the ground and we pretended that music was coming out from the earth and that's when I put together a song in my mind, about down in the ground where the strings vibrate, I can still to this day recall every word, the harps listening to the grass growing above them, and the grass listening back to the sounds two meters below.

~

We went that night from the Yellow Farmer's place, sloshing down the bowerpaths through a mudstorm. The wheels got stuck in the puddled roads. We lifted them out and walked bowlegged for a better grip, following the notched bones and bundled straw and other signs. A boy my age, Bakro, the cousin of Conka, walked alongside me. I think he already had the desire for me. He squandered his time in the mirror at the back of the caravan, fixing his black hair. A line of tanks went past and the last one stopped to search us, they didn't even clean their boots on the steps. Conka and I hid under an eiderdown, but the Hlinka who came in lifted it immediately and prodded at our dresses with his boot, then spat at us. Nothing could be worse for a Romani girl. When they left, we called them pigs, lizards, snakes. They were unclean, the last of the last.

On we went, walking at the paced hollow clop of the horse's hooves. Bakro whispered to me that he would protect me, no matter what, but my grandfather fixed an eye on us and I did not feel a sway in my belly for Bakro the way I did for other boys.

At night, Grandfather released Red and stepped between the tongues of the carriage, hoisting it with his bare hands. He turned it slightly while I slipped small rocks under the wheels, and in the morning we moved on again.

The radio reports came in from across what we now called, once more, Slovakia—it was confusing with Bohemia and Moravia and Germany and Hungary and Poland and Russia, and so Grandfather stood up one night and said that one day it would all soon be Rromanestan or the Soviet Russia, but someone else said that it might be America, where a very blue lady would hold a torch for us and everyone was created equal. We were moving around the country then, every week a new place, but someone, usually Boot's father, always returned to the forest and stayed with the harps. At night he slept near them. He swore there were restless spirits who came to play.

I soon reached womanhood and had to burn the red rags. It happened in a forest of white poplars and Conka knew what was going on, she had already been through it herself. She gave me a strip of cloth to clean myself up. I was careful now where I stepped, the touch of my skirt could dirty a man. She said no matter, but be careful not to go behind the hedge with a boy, they might take advantage. Together we sewed pebbles in the hem of our dresses to weigh them down. Nine days later Grandfather said that I had to learn to call him Stanislaus now; he did not want to be grandfather to a grown woman. I blushed and knew that soon it would be time to walk under the linden blossoms with a husband.

Stanislaus, I said, go ahead, horse, and shit.

It was the first time I had said such a word in his presence, and he squeezed my shoulder and pulled me to his chest and laughed.

Bakro gave me a silver chain and, although I didn't wear it around my neck, I kept it in my pocket and wound it around my fingers. The next day he came along and put a gingerbread heart in my hand. I was quite sure we were to be married and I begged Stainislaus not to let it happen, but he looked away from me, said he had other things to worry about, and walked off through the mud to talk to Petr.

Grandfather pointed over at me, and Petr nodded. I put my head down, kept my paths to myself. In my mind the old songs repeated themselves, took a new direction, turned, swerved.

We went further east and, by the banks of the Hron River, on a muddy morning, Red died. She was found on the ground with a single eye open. Grandfather lifted her with ropes and took her off to the glueyard. The blood sloshed in her as she was dragged along. I would never forget the sound. She was hoisted onto a cart. The body thumped, her eye still open. Grandfather came back with a bottle of fine slivovitz and offered me some, but I turned away and said no. He said, These things happen, girl. No they don't, I said. He grabbed my braids and said to me: Do you hear me, girl, these things happen, you're no longer a child. He let go of me and I watched as he stamped away through the bushes.

A couple of years later, čhonorroeja, when so much of my life was taking place in the city of Bratislava, and in the printing mill, using words that had come from the songs, I asked Stránský and the Englishman Swann not to put the few pages of my first poems together with glue, rather to stitch them with thread. I thought the glue might have come from the same yard. They didn't know what I was talking about, and, in truth I don't know why I expected them to. I could not stand the notion of the glue of Red traveling along the spine of the book, leaning down to things so foreign to her, who would want their own horse in their book, holding it together?

I was writing things down then, on any paper I could find, even the labels from bottles. I dunked them in water, dried them out, and filled the emptiness with ink. Old newspapers. Brown butcher sheets. I dried them out until the bloodstains were faint. It was still a secret, my writing. I pretended to most that I could not read, but, I thought, then, surely it could do no harm? I said to myself that writing was no more nor less than song. My pencil was busy and almost down to a nubbin.

Wash your dress in running water. Dry it on the southern side of the rock. Let them have four guesses and make them all be wrong. Take a fistful of snow in the summer heat. Cook haluški with hot sweet butter. Drink cold milk to clean your insides. Be careful when you wake: breathing lets them know how asleep you were. Don't hang your coat from a hook in the door. Ignore curfew. Remember weather by the voice of the wheel. Do not become the fool they need you to become. Change your name. Lose your shoes. Practice doubt. Dress in oiled cloth around sickness. Adore darkness. Turn sideways in the wind. The changing of stories is a cheerful affair. Give the impression of not having known. Beware the Hlinkas, it is always at night that the massacres occur.

~

There are things you can see and hear, nowadays, long after: the way the ditches were dug, and the way the ground trembled, and the way birds don't fly anymore over Belsen, about what happened to all our Czech brothers, our Polish sisters, our Hungarian cousins, how we in Slovakia were spared, though they beat us and tortured us and jailed us and took our music, how they forced us into workcamps, Hodonin and Lety and Petič, how they placed a hard curfew, and even that curfew had curfews upon it, how they spat at us in the streets. You can hear stories about the badges that were sewn on the sleeves, and the Z that split the length of our people's arms, the red and white armbands, and the way there were no lean dogs near the camps, the way Zyklon-B turned all the hair of the dead brown, and how the barbed wire flew little flags of skin, the slippers that were made of our hair. You can hear all this and more. What happened to the least of us, happened to us all, but little will ever bring it back to me in quite the same way as the day when my grandfather, Stanislaus, was stopped by a tall fair-haired soldier in the little gray streets of Bratislava.

We had gone, on a coal train, all the way through Trnava, beyond the lake, to the thick air and stinking puddles of the city. Grandfather was carrying six homemade toothbrushes to sell at a house where it was reputed there were streetwalkers: it was the only way in those days to make a little money.

Thirteen years to heaven, I had grown curious about the life beyond. What a sight the city was for me—the laundered shirts on strings across the streets, the fancy paper wrappers on the ground, the tall cathedral, the bony cats staring out from windows. Grandfather said to keep close by his side—there were a lot more Germans around now the resistance was stronger, they were helping the Hlinkas with reinforcements, and it was best to keep out of their way. There were rumors of what they would do to us if we took a wrong step. Still, I fell behind. He called at me: Come on, you lanky camel, keep up. I hurried and linked my arm in his. We came to a narrow alley in a hundred narrow alleys, up on the hill, near the castle. I stopped a moment and watched a child playing with a paper kite. Grandfather turned a corner. When I caught up, he was standing boardstiff, next to a kiosk. I said: Grandfather, what's wrong? Say nothing, he said. His eyes had grown huge and he began to tremble slightly. A German soldier was coming towards us. He had fair hair, like so many of them. We had not broken curfew and I said to Grandfather: Come on, don't worry.

The soldier's uniform was crisp and gray. He had not yet seen us, but Grandfather couldn't help staring, watching his manner—a Rom knows another anywhere.

Grandfather pulled hard on my elbow. I turned away, but just then the young German soldier saw us and his face slid like snow from a branch. He could, I suppose, have walked away, but he hitched his rifle to his chest, cocked it back, stepped across and ignored, with no great difficulty, the pleading of my eyes. He stared at Grandfather, picked the toothbrushes out of his pocket one by one, and then replaced them just as slowly. A dog loped away to the side of us and the soldier aimed a kick at it.

And what is it you have to say? said the soldier.

What is it you want me to say?

The soldier prodded him in the chest, hard enough that Grandfather took a step backwards.

It was demanded of us that we give praise to Tiso and then, if required, to say Heil Hitler with a snap of the hand. Grandfather let the first of the salutes out easily. He had learned to say it so often that it had become as easy as a simple hello. Good, said the soldier, and then he stood waiting. The bobble in Grandfather's neck grew. He sucked in the skin of his cheeks, leaned towards the German soldier, and whispered in Romani: But you are one of us, you have colored your hair, that is all. The German soldier knew exactly what he was saying, but he thumped Grandfather on the cheek with the butt of his rifle. I heard the jawbone crack and Grandfather went down to the ground. He rose and shook his head and said: Bless the dear place your mother came from.

He was knocked down a second time.

On the third time, he rose again and said Heil Hitler and his boots snapped together smartly at the heels.

Do it again, said the soldier, and this time click your heels together better and while you're at it, salute.

This happened eight times. In the pocket of my grandfather's jacket, the toothbrushes were all bloody.

Finally the soldier nodded and then he said in perfect Romani: Thank yourself, Uncle, that you and your daughter are alive. Now walk on and do not look back.

Grandfather put his head on my shoulder and tried to clean the lapels of his jacket. Hold my elbow, he said, but do not look at my face.

Slowly he put one foot in front of the other on the steep, slippery stones. At the door of the streetwalkers, he leaned down and commenced to cleaning the toothbrushes in a puddle. A fly settled on the balding spot at the top of his long hair. He looked up and said an old thing, but in a new, weary way: Well, I guess the horses didn't shit, too bad.

~

I got married when I was fourteen. Petr and I had a quiet linking of hands under the trees. Stanislaus had picked him out for me. I had no choice. He was older than a rock, slow to walk, quick to sleep, but Petr was hailed as a violinist amongst our people. He was big-shouldered and still full-haired. And Conka was right, he could make his violin stand up and play, it still had rosin, we laughed at that, although I wept on the morning when the sheets were checked. The women all asked me about it, Eliška did not stop, but for a long time Petr's rough hands didn't lose their charm for me and, besides, I wanted to make my grandfather happy, that has always been our way.

I do not care for your protests, he said to me, but from here on, now that you're married, with no exception, you will just call me Stanislaus, do you understand?

I watched Stanislaus walk away to sit in a rough-hewn chair by the bushes. He fell asleep with a bottle of fruit wine in his jacket pocket, and, when he woke, it had spilled across his shirt. What's my name? he said. I laughed at him. Not much of a name, he said. I unbuttoned and changed his shirt. He fell asleep again. Petr walked across and righted Stanislaus in the chair.

Further along, down among the caravans, the wedding music began. Our names were called, the sound of my own so strange alongside Petr's.

The rest of the day still shines in my mind, but in truth it is not my own marriage that I remember the most now, daughter, no, it was the wedding of my heart's friend, Conka, that was, in the end, the most splendid affair of wartime. Her young husband, Fyodor, came from a family of wealth. He seemed to smile out loud as he walked along. The marriage was announced far and wide. Curfew was defied, and our people came, some on trucks, some on foot, some on horses, already tuning their instruments, and the harps had been dug up from the ground and cleaned, tuned, rosined. He wore silver bands of coins around his waist. Most everyone had visited the tailorshop in Trnava where the young man behind the counter liked us—he took the risk and made clothes without the fancy price of other tailors who didn't want us in their shops anyway.

Stanislaus picked out a thin tie and he put the Marx pin underneath one flap so that when he danced the badge jumped around. His jacket was light blue velvet. My own skirts were tripled over, the top one made of silk—better clothing than I had worn for my own wedding just a month before.

Petr had me sit at his right-hand side all the way through Conka's ceremony, and I did not leave, except to sing songs, my favorite was the one about the drunken man who thought he had seven wives when in truth he only had one, though he called her a new name each night of the week. It was a funny tune and my husband rose to his feet in pride, in his hat and waistcoat, and played alongside me. He tucked the violin against his shoulder, raised his bow with one hand, gripped the neck with the other, and a shadow of joy smoothed his brow.

We watched Conka and the sparkle of her as she stepped under the new brooms we held aloft. A few cars were lined up along the hedges, their lights shining. The white skin of the linden blossoms spun and caught and scented the ground. The moon was a half-cut apple above us, and just as white. The best animals had been slaughtered and the longest tables laid out leg to leg, filled with hams, beef rump, pig ears, hedgehog. Lord, it was a feast. Earthenware jars full of plum brandy. Vodka. Wine. So many candles had been hollowed out from potatoes that there were not enough insects to gather round them. Conka and Fyodor stood opposite one another. A few small drops of spirit were poured into their palms and they drank from each other's hands, then a kerchief was tied around their wrists. Afterwards they threw a key into the streambed and were wed. Conka unbound the kerchief and tied it in her hair. Feather blankets were laid out on the ground. We sat under the stars and we put a few coins in the bottom of a bucket so the money would get bigger under the moon. No Hlinkas came, no farmers walked up with pitchforks, it was the most peaceful night imaginable, with hardly even a raised word about dowry, mistrust, sin.

Men kept their blackened hands behind themselves so as not to dirty Conka's dress, and even Jolana's little Woowoodzhi, who was born strange, danced. It seemed to me that the night could have go on for more than the three nights it did; we were blind with happiness.

It was my first night drunk—I had not been allowed to drink at my own wedding. I whispered to my husband, Get rosin on your bow, Petr, and we went off into the night, that's exactly how it happened and, although I know that a wall to happiness is expecting too much happiness, it still makes me smile.

~

While there were times that I yearned for a softer face to touch, or a neck without folds, it was never shameful to think that I slept content with my neck at the crook of Petr's arm. He lay under the covers with a string vest on. I suppose I began to think that I too had suddenly grown older beside him. Between one moment and the next, čhonorroeja, I had grown a lifetime. The younger boys looked at me and made jokes that I should not buy any green bananas for Petr. They each had the eyes of Bakro, my suitor, but I did not gaze their way.

Stanislaus had settled on Petr as my husband because he

knew that I would still be allowed to guide the pencil, even when the war was over. Few others would ever allow their wives to put words on a page. I had gone far beyond the first *dloc dloc*, but I wrote in Slovak. Romani never looked right to me on paper, though it sounded beautiful in my head. I never wrote in front of Petr, nor did I read in his presence, what use would it be to bring mockery down on him? But I had fallen in with books, they were friendly to me in the quiet hours. For a long time, I remember, the only book I had was *Winnetou, I,* penned by a German whose name I can't recall. It was a book given to simplicities. Still, I walked out in the forest and read it enough times to know it by heart. It was about Apaches and gunfighters, a volume for boys. Finally I was given a different volume, *The Lady of Čachtice,* which I loved—it was cracked and torn with so much use.

Stanislaus was given a copy of Engels by some men who worked in the salt mines. It was a dangerous thing to own and he sewed the pages inside his coat. I read the parable of the master and the servant, and while it didn't make much sense, it was the other voices, the Kranko and the Stens, that I truly liked. One day Stainslaus found a Bible printed in Slovak and said it was a handbook for revolutionaries, a notion I tested and began to like since there were ideas in there that made sense.

And yet, still, it was really only song that held me, our own song, which kept my feet to the ground.

New laws came upon us, even harsher than before. We were no longer allowed to travel at all. We stole back to Trnava and lay camouflaged in the forest, eight kilometers out. The chocolate factory was making armaments. The smoke drifted over us. We were joined by some of the settled Roma who left the town when their husbands were hung from the lampposts by way of reprisal: the law was ten villagers for every one of theirs. The mayor of the city gave the fascists the cheapest lives and what was cheaper to them than their Gypsies and, of course, Jews? On one steel pole eight were hung and left for the birds. For years afterwards no man or woman would ever take that street again, it was known as the Place of the Bent Lamppost.

Conka had a bruise on her neck where Fyodor had been rough with her on the last night before he went into the hills to join the fight. Something in her sagged. She walked around like a sheet on a string between trees. She sang: *If you love me drink this dark wine.*

Vashengo joined the partisans who were making noise in the hills. Stanislaus would have gone too, but he was older and his body was giving way. Still, he gave shelter to anyone who came in our direction: fighters from the Czech lands, refugees from the workcamps, even two priests who strayed our way. There were rumors of American fighters in the hills. We hid the caravans, yet twice they were spotted and shot at with bullets by passing Luftwaffe planes. We went in and fixed the shattered wood, picked the glass from broken jam jars. We carved more hovels in the mudbank, shored the roofs up with valki brick, wove reeds in the trees so the area couldn't be spotted by planes. We found frozen potatoes in the fields. Petr hollowed out the last of each potato with a spoon and filled it with sheep fat from a pot. He rolled a tight strip of cloth or string, until it was thin, then stood the wick inside the sheep fat and waited for it to harden. It did not take long and soon we had candles for the inside of our shelters. If we were hungry we ate the potatoes, though they tasted of burn and tallow. We killed a deer and, inside it, found a fawn.

The weather worsened. Sometimes the hovels flooded, carrying what little we had away, and then we commenced building once more. We were stuck by the riverbank, living like so many of the settled ones.

When Vashengo came back down from the hills, we were not too surprised to hear him singing "The Internationale." Grandfather walked with him down by the water and they returned, arms around each other's shoulders. Vashengo took off again, carrying two belts of silver to buy munitions. The songs we sang became more and more red, and in truth who could blame us—it was what Grandfather had predicted for many years. The only thing that seemed right was change, and the only thing that would bring change was good and right and red, we had suffered so long at the foot of the fascists. We were joined then by even more settled Roma, they came and lived in the forest with us. In years gone by we had sometimes pitched battles with the settled ones. They thought that we held our noses in the air, and we thought that they drank furniture polish and were wedded to Hoffman's tincture, but now the fighting between us stopped. We were too few to be divided. We boiled snow for water, searched the forest for food. We killed a badger and sold the fat to a pharmacy in the village. We had more pride than to eat the horses, but the settled ones ate whatever they could find, and we turned our eyes and let them.

News came over the radio: the Russians were advancing, the Americans too, and the British. We would have taken any of them. I woke one morning and the last of the fascist planes had just broken the sky. We were at the riverbank, and we watched as our caravans were riddled with bullets for the last time.

When we went in to repair the damage, we found Grandfather. He had gone in to find silence to read his book. It lay open on his chest. I lay down beside him and read the last forty pages aloud to him before I put coins on his eyes and we carried him out. Boot, who had grown tall and was back from the war, said how light my grandfather had become. I put the Marx book in my grandfather's coffin, under the blanket, along with cigarettes wrapped in grapevine, so that he could pull them out in the unknown. His boots surprised me as much as anything; he had sewn the seams back together with fishing wire. I wanted to undo them and take them, but we burned most of everything he owned to warm him for his journey. The flames shot up and the ground outside began to steam. Some burned trees stood in the grove, they looked like dark bones in the ground. Petr and I went to sleep with our feet pointed towards the embers. No singing was done for three days and lit candles were put upon the stream. Six weeks later, we knew that he was gone for good, though I still wore the colors of mourning.

Certain things will take the life from you.

I took a trip to the lake one day, alone, and plunged myself in. The water made my skin tight and my body became a part of the drifting. I stayed for hours, trying to go deeper, right out into the center, to see if I could touch what had fallen through. My hands reached out and the further I went, the cooler it got, and the pressure on my ears was like a voice with no sound. When I opened my eyes, they burned. The longer I stayed underwater the more I struggled, but then my lungs could take no more and I felt the speed of my own rising weight. I broke the surface. My hair was pasted down onto my shoulders and I felt my necklace drift away from me. I went underwater again, longer this time. I was quite sure that I was going to drown. They were all still there, I felt them—my mother, my father, my brother, my sisters—but who can set a lake on fire? On the shore, I sat with my knees to my chest and two days later, when I returned to the forest, much to Petr's relief, we took care of the very last of my grandfather's possessions. Sparks rose yellow into the air. I put my fingers to the ground and left my thumbprints there. Go ahead, horse, and shit.

That was the birth of me, it always will be.

I am no longer afraid to tell you these things, daughter: it was how they happened.

Even as a young girl, I always wanted too much.

The war ended, I think I was almost sixteen. The Russians liberated us. They came in, loud and red. Vashengo and the partisans came down from the hills, and flowers were thrown at their feet. Victory parades were held. The wooden shutters of shops were thrown open. We went to the city to make money playing music. We stayed in a field on the far side of the river. In the mornings we went to the railway station where Petr played his violin. Conka and I sang. *Do not blame your boots for the problems of your feet.* Huge crowds gathered and money was thrown into a hat. Some of the Russians even danced for us, hands clapping, legs outstretched. Late in the evening, as the money was counted, I wandered with Conka through the station. We loved the whine of the engines, the hiss of the doors, the movement, so many different voices all together. What a time it was. The streets were crammed. Bedsheets were hung from the windows, Russian sickles painted on them. Hlinka uniforms were burnt and their caps were trampled. The old guard was rounded up and hanged. This time the lampposts did not bend.

The gadže tugged our elbows and said, Come sing for us,

Gypsies, come sing. Tell us of the forest, they said. I never thought of the forest as a special place, it was just as ordinary as any other, since trees have as many reasons for stopping as people do.

Still, we sang the old songs and the gadže threw coins at our feet, and we raised ourselves on the tide. Giant feasts were held in the courtyards of houses that had been taken back from the fascists, and the loudspeakers pumped out music. We gathered under megaphones to hear the latest news. The churches were used for food stations, and sometimes we were allowed to stand first in line, we had never seen that before, it seemed a miracle. We were given identity cards, tinned meat, white flour, jars of condensed milk. We burned our old armbands. Under the pillars of a corner house a market was in full swing. The soldiers called us Citizens and handed us cigarette cards. Films were shown, projected on the brick walls of the cathedral—how huge the faces looked, čhonorroeja, on that wall. We had been nothing to the fascists, but now our names were raised up.

Cargo planes flew over the city, manned by the parachute regiment, dropping leaflets: *The new tomorrow has arrived.*

Out in the country, the leaflets caught in the trees, settled on hedges, and blew along the laneways. Some landed on the rivers and were carried downstream. I brought them to the elders and read them aloud: *Citizens of Gypsy Origin, Come Join Us.* The farmers no longer called us a pestilence. They addressed us by our formal names. We listened to a radio program with Romani music: our own harps and strings. We sang new songs, Conka and I, and hundreds of people came down the roadways to listen. Photographers with movie cameras pulled up in jeeps and motorcars. We waved the red flag, looked down the road into the future.

I had hope right up until the end. It was the old Romani habit of hoping. Perhaps I have never lost it.

Many years later, I was to walk up the granite steps and pass the fluted columns of the National Theater, in a new pair of shoes and a black lace blouse with patterned leaves, where I listened to Martin Stránský read my own song aloud. You do not know what you are hearing when you hear something for the first time, daughter, but you listen to it as though you will never hear it again. The theater held its breath. He had little music in him, Stránský, for a poet, but afterwards the crowd stood and cheered, and a spotlight swung around on me. I hid from it, sucking on stray ends of my hair, until Stránský put his fingers to my chin and tilted it upwards, the applause growing louder: poets, council members, workers, all waving program sheets in the air. The Englishman, Swann, stood in the wings of the theater, looking out at me, his green eyes, his light-colored hair.

I was taken to the inner courtyard where huge wooden tables were laid out with an assortment of wine and vodka, fruit, and bowls of cheese. A flurry of formal speeches.

All hail to a literate proletariat!

It is our revolutionary right to reclaim the written word!

Citizens, we must listen to the deep roots of our Roma brothers!

I was guided through the crowd, so many people pushing towards me, extending their hands, and I could hear my own skirts swishing, yes, more than anything I could hear the sound of cloth against cloth as I went out into the quiet of the street, it was one of the happiest times I remember, daughter. From inside the theater I could still hear the hum from the people, they were on our side, I hadn't heard anything quite like it before. I walked out in the cool air. A sheen of light was on the puddles, and night birds arced under the streetlamps. I stood there in the silence and it seemed to me that the spring of my life had come.

I was a poet.

I had written things down.

England–
Czechoslovakia

1930s–1959

THE ROOM WHERE I LIE is small but has a window to what has become an intimate patch of sky. The blue of daytime seems ordinary, but on clear nights it is made obvious, as if for the first time, that the wheel of the world is not fixed: the evening star spends a tantalizing few moments hung in the frame. The shrill gabble of birds on the rooftops comes in odd rhythms and, from the street below, I can almost hear the engine of my motorbike ticking. The rattle of the road is still in my body: one final corner and the bike rolled out from underneath me. Strange to watch the sparks rising from the tarmac. I slid along, then smashed into a low stone wall. In the hospital they did not have enough bandages to make a cast—they splinted my leg and sent me home.

I have given up searching, but it is impossible to think that she is gone, that I will never see her again, or catch the sound of her, the grain of her voice.

Just before the accident, near Piešt'any, a raw gust of February wind blew off my scarf. It snagged on a row of barbed-wire fencing by a military range, fluttering there a moment before falling to the ground. Zoli gave me the scarf years ago, but I could see no way of retrieving it and feared what might happen if I tried to climb the fence. The scarf blew back and forth, like most everything else, just beyond my reach.

Thirty-four years old—a shattered kneecap, a heap of overcoats, a pile of unfinished translations on the table. From the hallway comes the squeaking of floorboards and the soft slap of dominoes. I can hear the mops dipping in bleach, the keys in the door, the incantations of solitary men and women home from work. Christ, I'm no better than all those numberless mumblers of Ave Marias—how I used to hate confessionals as a child, those dark Liverpudlian priests sliding back the grill, bless me, Father, for I have sinned, it has been how many decades since my last confession?

My father once said that you can't gauge the contents of a man's heart by his greatest act of evil alone, but if that's true then it must also be true that you can't judge him without it: mine was committed on a freezing winter afternoon at the printing mill on Godrova Street, when I stood with Zoli Novotna and betrayed her against the hum of the machinery. Since I've done little worse, or measurably better, in the days before or since then, I'm forced to admit that my legacy to the world may very well be this one solitary thing that's with me now almost every breathing moment.

There are those of us who haven't yet told our stories, or refuse to tell them, and so we become them: we hide away inside the memory until we can no longer stand the shell or the shock—perhaps that's me, or perhaps I must tell it before it's forgotten or becomes, like everything else, something else.

~

Memory has a heavy backspin, yet it's still impossible to land exactly where we took off. My mother was a nurse from Ireland, my father a dockworker from Slovakia. Mam hailed from a little seaside village in Donegal. She was forever tilted sideways by the notion that pain was inevitable, chance was cruel, and all human ingenuity should go towards the making of a good cup of tea. My father emigrated to Britain in the early years of the century when he changed his last name to Swann, but didn't alter his soul; in later years he described himself as a Communist, a pacifist, and a Catholic in no particular order.

Home from the docklands, he used to put a dark thumbprint on the bread in order that I would know where it came from.

From a young age I was hooked on the plot of my father's homeland. We sat together on crates in the coalshed searching the radio bands. In the laneway behind, my friends played football. My father spent hours trying to tune in to the long-wave broadcasts from Bratislava, Košice, Prague, while the ball thumped against the wall. Only at odd moments did the weather allow the radio a crackle from the beyond—we leaned forward and our heads touched. He wrote it down and later translated for me. At night, my prayers were in his native tongue.

When the Second World War struck, it didn't seem at all unusual that he took off to join the partisans in the Czechoslovakian mountains—he said he wanted to become a medic and that he'd carry stretchers, that wars were useless and God was democratic, and, with that in mind, he'd return shortly. He left me his wristwatch and a copy of Engels in the Slovak language. I found out, years later, that he had become an expert with dynamite; his specialty was blowing up bridges. The news that he had died in an ambush came in a two-line telegram. My mother wilted away. She took me on a trip back to Donegal for a week, but for whatever reason it was not the same place that she had left behind. "Nobody lives where they grew up anymore," she said to me shortly before she died.

I was made a ward of the state and spent the last two of my

school years with the Jesuits in Woolton, walking around the edges of rugby fields in a gray V-neck sweater.

What I recall of growing up: redbrick houses, rough stones from the worked-out pit, shaved shoulders of sunlight on street corners, dockside cranes, penny sweets, gulls, confessionals, brushing gray frost from the bicycle seat. It was not exactly violins I heard when I stuck my head out the train window and bid Liverpool goodbye. I'd missed the war—a measure of luck and youth and a dose of cowardice. I went south to London where I spent two years on a scholarship, studying Slovak. I ran with the Marxists and mouthed off on the soapboxes of Hyde Park, to little success. My work was published intermittently, but mostly I sat at a small window that looked out beyond the half-open blinds at a dark wall and the faded edge of an Oval-tine advertisement.

I fell in love, briefly, with a beautiful young librarian, Cait-lin, from Cardiff. I bumped into her on a ladder, quite literally, while she was shelving a book by Gramsci, but our politics didn't match and Caitlin sent me packing with a note that her life was too dull for revolution.

In my flat, the skyline became a shelf of books. I wrote long letters to novelists and playwrights in my old man's country, yet they seldom wrote back. I was fairly sure the letters were being censored in London, but every now and then a reply fell on the welcome mat and I brought it down to the local teashop where, amid the stains and the day-old cakes, I opened it.

The replies was always terse and clean and to the point: I burned them in the ashtray with the tip of a cigarette. But then in 1948, after a burst of ink-spattered correspondence, I was on my way to Czechoslovakia to translate for a literary journal run by the celebrated poet Martin Stránský, who wrote to say that he could well do with a new set of legs—would it be possible, he asked, to bring a few bottles of Scotch whisky in my bags?

In Vienna the small wooden huts of the Russian sector were warmed by single-bar electric heaters. The guards interrogated me over cups of black tea. I was passed from hut to hut and finally put on a train. At the Czechoslovakian border, some leftover fascist guards roughed me over, rifled through my suitcase, took the bottles, and threw me into a makeshift cell. My hands were tied and they beat the bottoms of my feet with sticks rolled in newspaper. I was accused of falsifying documents, but two weeks later the door opened to Martin Stránský who seemed, at first, just a shadow. He said my name, lifted me up, put his sleeve in a cold bucket of water, and cleaned my wounds. He was, against expectations, a small man, tough and balding.

"Did you bring the booze?" he asked.

As a youngster he had been friends with my father in an illegal Socialist youth group, and now he'd come full circle; he'd been instrumental in the Communist coup and was well liked by those newly in power. He slapped my back, put his arm around me, and walked me beyond the tin-roofed sheds where he had already taken care of the last of my paperwork. The two guards who'd beaten me and taken the bottles were sitting handcuffed in the back of an open truck. One stared down at the truckbed but the other was moving his bloodshot eyes side to side.

"Oh, don't worry about them, Comrade," Stránský said. "They'll be all right."

He kept a tight grip on my arm and helped me towards a military train. The white headlamps burned and a brand-new Czechoslovakian flag fluttered from the roof. We took our seats and I felt buoyed by the shrill whistle and the blast of steam. As the train chugged off, I caught a last glimpse of the handcuffed guards. Stránský laughed and slapped my knee.

"It's not so serious," he said. "They'll have a day or two in lockup to recover from their hangovers, that's all."

The train jolted forward and we passed through rows of tall forest and low cornfields towards Bratislava. Pylons. Chimneys. Red and white railway barriers.

From Hlvaná Station, we walked along the tramtracks, down the hill towards the old town. It struck me as medieval, wiry, even quaint, but revolutionary posters were pasted on the walls and thumping music rose from loudspeakers. I still had a slight limp from my beating, but I skipped along in the light rain, carrying, of all things, a cardboard suitcase. Stránský chuckled when it opened up—a nightshirt fell out and a long sleeve trailed the cobblestones.

"A nightshirt?" he laughed. "Two weeks of political re-education for you."

He clapped his arm around me. In a vaulted beerhall, full of drunks and hanging pottery, we clinked glasses for the Revolution and for what Stránský called, as he looked out the window towards the street, other fathers.

~

In the winter of 1950 I was sick for quite a while. When the day came for me to leave hospital, the doctor signed me out, undiagnosed, and told me to go home to rest.

I lived in a worker's flat in the old part of town. The communal kitchen, on the first floor, ran with mice. Laundry was strung up and down the length of the corridor—boiler suits, overcoats, shirts eaten through with acid. The staircase quite literally swayed under my feet. When I got up to my tiny fourth-floor room, a patch of snow lay on the wooden floor. The concierge had forgotten to fix the smashed window— a week before, in a dizzy spell, I had fallen against the pane—and a cold wind blew through. I took my bedding to the only warm part of the room, where the poppet valve on the radiator hissed. In gloves and overcoat I curled up near the valve and slept. I woke coughing in the early morning. It had snowed heavily again during the night, and the floor was already covered in stray flakes. Around the radiator pipes was a patch of wet wood. The things I adored the most, my books, lay ranged on the shelves, so many different volumes that it was impossible to see the wallpaper. Three translations awaited me—chapters from Theodore Dreiser, Jack Lindsay, and an article by Duncan Hallas—but the thought of delving into them filled me with dread.

I had bought a secondhand pair of boots, stamped by a Russian bootmaker, and, although they leaked, I liked them, they seemed to have a history. I went out into the cold streets, stepping over gutters and cobblestone, past the barracks, beyond the checkpoint.

At the mill Stránský had set up a small room where, in between printing jobs, he often sat and read. The room had no ceiling, and so one could look up to the high roof of the mill and watch the pigeons flap from eave to eave. I lay down on the green army bed he kept in the corner, and the noise of the machines rocked me to sleep. I have no idea how long I slept, but I woke disoriented, not even sure what day it was.

"Put your socks on for crying out loud," said Stránský from the doorway.

Behind him, a little confused, stood a tall young woman.

She was in her early twenties, not beautiful, or not traditionally so anyway, but the sort of woman who stalled the breath. She held herself at the door nervously, as if she were a bowl of water that would not be allowed to spill. Her skin was dark and her eyes were as black as any I'd ever seen. She wore a man's dark overcoat, but beneath it a wide skirt with a tripled-over hem: it appeared she had patched two or three skirts together and rolled the hems over each other. Her hair was tied back beneath a kerchief, and two thick plaits hung down either side of her face. She wore no earrings, no bracelets, no jangling necklaces. I rose from under the covers and slipped on my wet socks.

"Forgotten your manners, young scholar?" said Stránský as he pushed past me. "Meet Zoli Novotna."

I extended my hand for her to shake, but she did not take it. She stepped beyond the threshold only when Stránský beckoned, and went to the table where he had already taken a bottle from his jacket.

"Comrade," she said, nodding at me.

Stránský had found Zoli, by chance, outside the Musicians Union and he had been given permission, through one of the elders, to talk to her about her songs. They were a secretive bunch, the Gypsies, but Stránský had always been able to comb people out of themselves. He spoke a little Romani, knew their customs, how and where to tread, and he was one of the few they trusted. They also owed him a couple of favors—during the national uprising, he had commanded a regiment that had a few Gypsy fighters, in the hills, and had, by all accounts, saved some of them with the aid of a few bottles of penicillin.

The afternoon returns to me now as a step back into what

we all once believed: revolution, equality, poetry. We pulled up chairs to the table and sat for hours, the clock ticking away. Zoli kept her head slightly bent, her glass untouched in front of her. She rattled off a few verses of the older songs. The words were in Slovak, but there was a touch of wildness to them: she wasn't used to speaking them aloud, she'd always sung them. Her style was to quietly build layer upon layer until, by the end, the songs became sad and declamatory, tales of bitterness and treachery, the verses repeated over and over, like the falling and layering of so many leaves. When she was finished, Zoli locked her knuckles and stared straight ahead.

"Good," said Stránský, rapping on the table.

She looked upwards as a bird feather fell from the ceiling and spun silently down to the floor, then smiled as she watched the pigeons fly around the ceiling beams; some of the birds were darkened with ink.

"Do they get out?"

"Only to shit," said Stránský, and she laughed, picked the feather up, and, for whatever reason, put it in the pocket of her overcoat.

I didn't know it then, but there'd only ever been a few Gypsy writers scattered across Europe and Russia before, and never any who were part of the establishment. It was an oral culture, they had no books or written-down stories to speak of, they distrusted the unchangeable word. But Zoli had grown up with a grandfather who had taught her how to read and write, an extraordinary thing among her people.

Stránský ran a journal, *Credo,* in which he was always trying to push the limits: he was known for publishing daring young Socialist playwrights and obscure intellectuals and anyone else who vaguely amplified his beliefs. I was there to translate whatever foreigners he could get his hands on: Mexican poets, Cuban Communists, pamphlets by Welsh trade unionists, anyone whom Stránský saw as a fellow traveler. Many of the Slovakian intellectuals had already moved north to Prague, but Stránský wanted to stay in Bratislava where, he said, the heart of the Revolution could be. He himself wrote in Slovak against the idea that a smaller language was useless. And now, with Zoli, he thought he'd come upon the perfect proletarian poet.

He clapped his hands and clicked his fingers: "That's it, that's it, that's it." Leaning back in his chair, he twirled the tiny peninsula of hair in the center of his forehead.

Zoli improvised as she went along—he'd ask her to repeat a certain verse so he could transcribe it, and the verse would shift and change. It seemed to me that her words contained simple, old-fashioned sounds that others had forgotten or didn't know how to use anymore: *trees, pools, forest, ash, oak, fire*. Stránský's hand rested on his leg, where he held a glass of vodka. He bounced his knee up and down, so when he finally stood up and went to the window there were dark stains on his overalls. Late in the afternoon, when darkness lengthened across the floor, Stránský extended a pencil. Zoli took it gingerly, put the end of it against her teeth, and held it there, as if it were describing her.

"Go ahead," said Stránský, "just write it down."

"I don't really create them on the page," she said.

"Just scribble the last verse, go on."

Stránský tapped his knuckles on the edge of the table. Zoli turned the thread on a button. Her lip was bitten white. She lowered her gaze and began to write. Her penmanship was shabby and she had little idea about line breaks, capitalization, or even spelling, but Stránský took the sheet and clutched it to his chest.

"Not bad, not bad at all, I can show this to people."

Zoli pulled back her chair, bowed slightly to Stránský, then turned to me and said a formal goodbye. Her kerchief had slipped back on her head and I noticed how pure the parting was in her hair, how dark the skin between two sets of darkness, how straight, how clean. She readjusted the scarf and there was a flash of white from her eyes. She stepped towards the door, and then she was gone, out into the street in the last of the light, under the trees. A few young men on a horsecart were waiting for her. She put her nose to the horse's neck and rubbed her forehead along the top of its spine.

"Well, well, well," said Stránský.

The horsecart went around the corner and away.

I felt as if a tuning fork had been struck in my chest.

~

The next day Stránský and I were invited to an air show for journalists on the outskirts of Bratislava: three brand-new Meta-Sokols, high-technology jets, were on display. Their noses were pointed westward. It was still a no-fly zone around Bratislava, and the pilots had been forced to drive the jets into the airfield on huge trucks, which had become bogged down and had to be pulled onto the field with ropes. Stránský had been asked to write an article about the Slovak-born fighter pilots. He slinked around the machines with a general who lectured us earnestly about landing patterns, high-range radar, and ejector seats.

After the lecture, a young woman from the air force strode out to the planes. Stránský nudged me: she had a stillness at her center that might have been called poise, but it wasn't, it was more like the tension that can be seen in tightrope walkers. Her blond hair was cut short, her body slim and winsome. He followed her up into the cockpit of one of the machines and they sat for a while, chatting and flirting, until she was called away. The journalists and dignitaries watched the thin sway of her as she climbed down. She reached up and helped Stránský to the ground. "Wait," he said. He kissed her hand and introduced me as his wayward son, but she blushed and shimmied off, with just one look over her shoulder—not at Stránský, nor at me, but at the military jet stuck in the grass.

"Hey-ho, the new Soviet woman," said Stránský under his breath.

We walked across the airfield, through the giant muddy marks made by the trucks. At the field's edge Stránský stopped and wiped some of the muck off his trousercuffs. He turned, rubbed one shoe against the other and said, suddenly, as if to the trampled grass: "Zoli."

He hitched up his trousers and walked over the tire marks. "Come on," he said.

~

Out past Trnava, towards the hills, along a dirt road, through an isolated copse of trees. I clung on as Stránský brought the motorbike to a skidding stop and pointed to a series of broken twigs arranged to mark a trail.

"Around here somewhere," he said.

The engine of the Jawa sputtered. I hopped off. Smoke rose from some distant trees and a series of shouts rang out. We pushed the motorbike into the center of a clearing, where intricately carved caravans stood in a semicircle. Light came through the high pines, creating long shadows. Young men stood by a fire. One turned an axehead with a pair of tongs; another blew a bellows. A number of children darted towards us. They climbed on the bike and yelped when their bare feet touched the hot pipes. One jumped on my back and slapped me, then yanked my hair.

"Say nothing," said Stránský. "They're just curious."

The crowd swelled. The men stood in shirts and torn trousers. The women wore long-hemmed dresses and thick jewelry. Children appeared with babies clasped against their chests. Some of the babies wore red ribbons on their wrists.

"It's an adorned world," Stránský whispered, "but underneath it's plain enough, you'll see."

A middle-aged man, Vashengo, with long wisps of graying hair, strode through the crowd and stood straddle-legged in front of us, hands on his hips. He and Stránský embraced, then Vashengo turned to assess me. A long stare. An odor of woodsmoke and rank earth.

"Who's this?"

Stránský slapped my shoulder: "He looks Slovak, sounds Slovak, but at the worst of times he's British."

Vashengo squinted and came close, dug his fingers into my shoulder. The whites of his eyes had a smoky gray tinge.

"Old friend of mine," said Stránský before Vashengo parted the crowd in front of him. "He owes me a thing or two."

At the rear of the crowd, near a series of carved wooden caravans, Zoli stood with four other women in colorful dresses. She wore an army greatcoat, river boots rolled down on her calves, and a belt made out of willow bark. She held a coathanger skewered with a piece of potato. She glanced at us, strode towards a caravan, stepped up, closed the door behind her.

For a split second the curtain parted, then ricocheted back.

Food was prepared, a ball of meat served with haluški and flatcakes. "How's your hedgehog?" asked Stránský. I spat it out. Vashengo stared at me. It was, it seemed, a delicacy. I picked it up from the dirt. "Delicious," I said, and speared a mouthful. Vashengo reared back and laughed, jaunty and intimate. The men gathered and slapped my back, filled my glass, heaped more food on my plate. I washed the hedgehog down with a bottle of fruit wine, then tried to share the bottle with the others, but they turned away.

"Don't even ask," said Stránský. "They're just not going to drink from your swish."

"Why not?"

"Learn silence, son, it'll keep you alive."

Stránský sat down by the fire to sing an old ballad he'd learned in the hills. The wind blew, stirring the ash. The Gypsy men nodded and listened seriously, then brought out their fiddles and giant harps. The night tore open. A child climbed on my shoulders and began to shine Stránský's balding head with her bare foot. After a second bottle, it didn't seem to me that my corners were sticking out quite so much anymore—I opened the neck of my shirt and whispered to Stránský that I'd take whatever was to come.

In the early evening, crowds of Gypsies started to arrive from the countryside. They packed into a large white tent where a row of candles lit a makeshift stage. The benches were made from fallen logs. The singers began with raucous ballads, gamblingsongs, weddingsongs, lovesongs, eveningsongs.

When Zoli walked in, she wore a long multipatterned dress with flared sleeves. Tiny beads were sewn into the dress front, and an anthracite necklace lay at the long curve of her throat. At first she was just another one of the singers. Her body was held straight and her head almost motionless, all the movement in her shoulders, arms, hands. It wasn't until later, when the night had a coating of drunkenness and the darkness had fallen, that she began to sing on her own. No harp, no violin. Raw. Sad. An old song, long and rambling, nostalgic. The firelight flickered on her face, her eyes closed, lids blue-veined, half a smile on her lips. It was not just her voice—it was what she sang that rattled us. She had made up the song herself, a story with place names, Czech and Polish and Slovak, dates and times too. Hodonin. Lety. Brno. 1943. The Black Legion. Chimneys. The carved gateposts. The charnel houses. The bone fields.

"I told you, son," said Stránský.

When Zoli finished, the tent fell silent: only the sound of the breeze through the trees outside, ancient, unpackaged. She stepped across to a wreck of an old man—the sort of creature who could have lived shabby and mumbling in a shoebox room somewhere. He wore a half-shirt, the sort favored by musicians, with no cloth at the back. When he stretched his arms towards her, his naked skin showed. She kissed him gently on the head, then sat down with him while he smoked a pipe.

"Her husband," whispered Stránský.

I sat back on the log.

"Careful, Swann, your mouth's open again."

Zoli leaned in to the older man. He looked as if he had been tall and broad-shouldered once and he still annexed that space, though he was clearly sick. Later in the evening, he coaxed sounds from a fiddle that I'd never heard before—fast, wild, screeching. He was given an extended round of applause and Zoli supported his elbow, left the tent with him. She did not come back, but the night started up again, raucous and pure. My shirt was open to the belly button. I hardly knew what to think. Someone threw a bottle of slivovitz at me—I unscrewed the lid and drank.

In the early morning, Stránský and I stumbled towards the motorbike. The seat, the blinkers, and the handlebar grips had disappeared. Stránský chuckled and said it was not the first time he'd had unreliable Czech machinery between his legs. We climbed on, tamped our jackets down for a seat, and made our way back towards Bratislava. We approached the city, the tall brickwork adorned with arches and lintels. Rows of pigeons dozed on high ledges. Wreathed dates commemorated memory in stone. It was an old city, somewhat Hungarian, somewhat German, but on that day it felt newly and wholly Soviet. Crews were working on the bridge and, beyond that, towers and factories were going up.

Stránský's wife was waiting for us in the courtyard of his apartment block. He kissed her, skipped up the stairs, and immediately went inside to transcribe the tapes. He placed the recorder on the top of her latest cartoon. She took the drawing and smoothed it out.

"It's a Hungarian name," Elena said as she listened. "Zoltan. I wonder where she got it."

"Who knows, but it's quite a song, isn't it?"

"Maybe she got someone to write it for her."

"I don't think so."

Stránský unjammed the play lever on the recorder.

"It's naïve," said Elena. "Your mother cries, your father plays the violin. But there's a quiver to it, isn't there? And, tell me this, is she beautiful?"

"She's more beautiful than she's not," he said.

Elena cracked her husband's knuckles with a rolled-up newspaper. She stood, her hair full of colored pencils, and went off to bed. Stránský winked and said he would join her shortly, but he fell asleep at the table, bent over the transcribed pages.

~

I found Zoli again, the following week, on the steps of the Musicians Union, where she stood with her hands outstretched, fingers apart.

A crowd of Gypsies had gathered together in front of the union. There'd been a new decree that all musicians had to have licenses, but to have a license they had to be able to fill out a form, and none of the Gypsies, except Zoli, were able to write fluently. They carried violins, violas, oboes, guitars, even one giant harp. Vashengo wore a black jacket with red bicycle reflectors as cufflinks. When he moved his arms, his wrists caught the sunlight. He was trying, it seemed, with Zoli's help, to calm the crowd. A small battalion of troopers stood at the other end of the street, slapping truncheons against their thighs. Moments later a loudspeaker was passed out of the window of the union and the crowd hushed. Vashengo spoke in Romani at first—it was as if he had laid a blanket underneath the crowd. He commanded a further silence and spoke in Slovak, said it was a new time in history, that we were all coming out of a long oblivion, carrying a red flag. He would speak with the leaders of the union. Be patient, he said. There'd be licenses for all. He pointed at Zoli and said she would help them fill out the required forms. She lowered her head and the crowd cheered. The troopers down the street dropped their truncheons and the officials from the Musicians Union came out onto the steps. A small boy came pushing past me, laughing. He was wearing the yellow blinker from Stránský's motorbike on a chain.

I tried to elbow my way towards her, but she leaned down to whisper something to her husband.

I moved away through the milling bodies, past the horses and carts they had lined up along the street.

I'd already memorized the tilt of her chin and the two dark moles at the base of her neck.

In the National Library, amid the dust and the shuffle, I tried to read up on whatever little literature there was. The Gypsies were, it seemed, as fractured as anyone else, their own small Europe, but they were still lumped together in one easy census box. Most had already settled down in shanty towns all over Slovakia. They were as apt to fight among themselves as they were to pitch battle against outsiders. Zoli and her people were the aristocracy, if such a word could be used; they still traveled in their ornate caravans. No dancing bears, or begging, or fortune-telling, but they did wear gold coins in their hair and kept some of the older customs alive. Modesty laws. Whispered names. Runic signs. There were thousands of them in Slovakia. They were linked with extended groups of tin-smiths and horse-thieves, but some, like Zoli's kumpanija, moved in a group of about seventy or eighty and made a living almost entirely from music. They were written about in exotic language—no photographs, just sketches.

I shut the pages of the books, walked out into the streets, under the swaying banners and the loud grackles in the trees.

From an open window came the low moan of a saxophone. These were still vibrant times—the streets were full and pulsing, and nobody yet sat waiting for the knock of the secret police at the door.

I found Stránský swaying in the beerhalls. "Come here, young scholar," he shouted across the tables. He sat me down and bought me a glass. I lapped it up, the high idealism of an older man. He was sure that having a Gypsy poet would be a coup for him, for *Credo*, and that the Gypsies, as a revolutionary class, if properly guided, could claim and use the written word. "Look," he said, "everywhere else they're the joke of the week. Thieves. Conmen. Just imagine if we could raise them up. A literate proletariat. People reading Gypsy literature. We—you, me, her—we can make a whole new art form, get those songs written down. Imagine that, Swann. Nobody has ever done that. This girl is perfect, do you know how perfect she is?"

He leaned forward, his glass shaking.

"Everyone else has shat on them from above. Burned them out. Taunted them. Branded them. Capitalists, fascists, that old empire of yours. We've got a chance to turn it around. Take them in. We'll be the first. Give them a value. We make life better, we make life fairer, it's the oldest story of all."

"She's a singer," I said.

"She's a poet," he replied. "And you know why?" He raised his glass and prodded my chest. "Because she's called upon to become one. She's a voice from the dust."

"You're drunk," I said.

He hoisted a brand-new tape recorder, a spare set of reels, eight spools of tape, and four batteries up onto the table. "I want you to record her, young scholar. Bring her to life."

"Me?"

"No, the fucking pickled eggs there. For crying out loud, Swann, you've got a brain, don't you?"

I knew what he wanted from me—the prospect thrilled me and knocked the air from my lungs at the same time.

He spun a bit of tape out from a reel. "Just don't tell Elena that I spent our last savings on this." He wound the spool on and pressed Record. "It's made in Bulgaria, I hope it works."

He tested it out and his voice came back to us: *It's made in Bulgaria, I hope it works.*

How inevitable it is; we step into an ordinary moment and never come out again. I raised my glass and signed on. I might as well have done it in my own blood.

The equipment fitted into a small rucksack. I strapped it on my back and rode Stránský's Jawa out into the countryside. Under the grove of trees, I killed the engine and waited. The kumpanija was gone. A scorched tire in the grass. A few rags in the branches. I tried to follow the rutted marks and the bent grass, but it was impossible.

Beyond Trnava I went towards the low hills where the vineyards stepped down towards the valley. I leaned the bike into the corners, wobbled to a halt when a rifle was pointed at me. The tallest trooper smirked while the others gathered around him. I was, I told them, a translator and sociologist studying the ancient culture of the Romani people. "The what?" they asked. "The Gypsies." They howled with laughter. A sergeant leaned forward: "There's some up there, with the monkeys in the trees." I fumbled with the kickstand and showed him my credentials. After a while, he radioed in and came back, snapped to attention. "Comrade," he said, "proceed." Stránský's name, it seemed, still held some sway. The troopers pointed me in the direction of some scrubland. I had rigged a cushion in place where the seat had been stolen: the troopers guffawed. I slowly turned, pinned them with a look, then took off, scattering dirt behind me.

From the hills came a strange series of high sounds. Zoli's kumpanija carried giant harps, six, seven feet tall, and, with the bumps in the dirt roads, you could sometimes hear them moving from a distance away: they sounded as if they were mourning in advance.

When I came across her, she was draped across the green gate of a field and her arms hung down, limp. She was dressed in her army coat and was propelling herself with one foot, slowly back and forth, in a small arc over the mud. One braid swung in the air, the other was caught between her teeth. On the gate was an ill-painted sign that warned trespassers of prosecution. As I approached, she stood up quickly from what had seemed an innocent child's pose, but then I realized that she had been reading while draped on the gate. "Oh," she said, tucking the loose pages away.

She walked on ahead, calling behind her that I should catch up in an hour or two, she'd alert the others, they needed time to prepare. I was sure I wouldn't see her again that night, but when I came upon them they had prepared a welcoming feast. "We're ready for you," she said. Vashengo clapped my back, sat me at the head of the table.

Zoli stood in a yellow patterned dress with dozens of tiny mirrors glinting on the bodice. She had rouged her face with riverstone.

English, they called me, as if it were the only thing I could ever be. The women giggled at my accent, winding my hair around their fingers. The children sat close to me—astoundingly close—and I thought for a moment they were rifling my pockets, but they weren't, theirs was simply a different form of space. I felt myself begin to lean towards them. Only Zoli seemed to hang back—it was only later I realized she was creating a hollow between us to protect herself. She said to me once that I had a sudden green gaze, and I thought that it could have been taken as any number of things: curiosity, confusion, desire.

I began to visit once or twice a week. Vashengo allowed me to sleep in the back of his caravan, alongside five of his nine children. The pinch of a sheet was all I had to hold on to. The knots in the wood were like eyes in the ceiling. All the way from Liverpool to a bed where, on my twenty-fourth birthday, I rolled across to see five small heads of tousled hair. I tried to take the bedding outside but in truth the darkness didn't suit me, the stars were not what I was built for, so I slept at the edge of the bed, fully clothed. In the mornings I heated a coin with a match and put the hot disc to Vashengo's window in order to make a peephole in the frost. The children joked with me— I was wifeless, white, strange, I walked funny, smelled bad, drove a cannibalized motorbike. The youngest ones pulled me up by the ears, and dressed me in a waistcoat and their father's old black Homburg. I stepped out to mist shoaling over the fields. Dawn lay cold and wet on the grass. I stood, embarrassed, as the kids ran around, begging me to play wheelbarrow with them. I asked Zoli if there was anywhere else to sleep. "No," she said, "why would there be?" She smiled and lowered her head and said that I was welcome to go to the hotel twenty kilometers away, but I was hardly going to hear any Romani songs from the chambermaids.

As a singer she could have lived differently, with no scrubbing, no cooking, no time spent looking after the children, but she didn't isolate herself, she couldn't, she was in love with that bare life, it was what she knew, it fueled her. She washed clothes in the river, beat the rugs and carpets clean. Afterwards she put playing cards in the spoke of a bicycle wheel and rode around in the mud, calling out to the children. Each of them she named her čhonorro, her little moon. "Come here, čhonorroeja," she called. They ran behind her, blowing whistles made from the branches of ash trees. Behind the tire factory she played games with them on what they called their bouncing wall. She threw a tire over a sapling for each new child that was born, knowing that one day it would fit snug and tight.

Zoli was already well known amongst her people, settled and nomadic alike. She touched some old chord of tenderness in them. They would walk twenty kilometers just to hear her sing. I had no illusions that I'd ever belong, but there was the odd quiet moment when I sat with her, our backs against a wheelbase, a short span of recited song before Petr or the children interrupted us. *When I cut brown bread don't look at me angrily, don't look at me angrily because I'm not going to eat it.* At first she said that the writing was just a pastime—the songs were what mattered, the old ballads that had been around for decades, and she was only shaping the music so they'd be passed along to others. She was surprised to find new words at her fingertips, and when whole new songs began to emerge, she thought they must have existed before, that they had come to her from somewhere ancient. Zoli had no inkling that anyone other than the Gypsies would want to listen to her, and the notion that her words might go out on the radio, or into a book, terrified her at first.

Before their performances, she and Conka sat on the steps of her caravan as they aligned their voices. They wanted to get within a blade of grass of each other. Conka was a full redhead, blue-eyed, and she wore coins, glass beads, and pottery shards woven in a necklace strand. Her husband, Fyodor, stared me down. He didn't like the idea of his wife being recorded. I feigned bustle when really all I was waiting for was Zoli's voice to pull through, with her own songs, the new ones, those she had made up herself.

One spring afternoon, near a remote forest, Zoli walked out to the edge of a lake and undertook a ceremony for her dead parents, brother, and sisters, floating candles out on the water. Three Hlinka guards had finally been charged with their murders and had received life sentences. There was no celebration among the Gypsies—they didn't seem to enjoy the revenge— but the whole kumpanija accompanied Zoli to the lakeside, and they stood back to allow her silence while she sang an old song about wind in a chimney turning back at the last moment, never reaching down to disturb the ashes.

At the lake edge I trampled the reeds, fumbled with the batteries and clicked the lever on: she was beginning to stretch and move the language, and, like everyone else, I was chained to the sound of her voice.

Later I sat with Stránský while he transcribed the tapes. "Perfect," he said as he pulled his pencil through one of her lines. He was convinced that Zoli was creating a poetry from the roots up, but he still wanted to put manners on it. She came into the city, alone, the railway ticket moist in her fist. Nervously she twisted the hair that had fallen out from beneath her kerchief. Stránský read the poem aloud to her and she went to the window, peeled back some of the black tape from the glass.

"That last part is wrong," she said.

"The last verse?"

"Yes. The clip."

Stránský grinned: "The timing?"

Three times he reshuffled it before she shrugged and said: "Perhaps." Stránský positioned the metal. She bit her lip, then took the printed sheet and pressed it against her chest.

I could feel my heart thumping in my cheap white shirt.

A week later she came back to say that the elders had accepted it and it could be published—they saw it as a nod of gratitude to Stránský for what he'd done in the war, but we were convinced it went beyond that; we were building a vanguard, there'd never been a poetry like it before, we were preserving and shaping their world while the world changed around them.

"The incredible happens," she said when Stránský took us to a bookshop in the old town. She wandered along the rows of shelves, touching the spines of the books. "It's like not having any walls." For a while she stood next to me, ran her fingers absentmindedly along my forearm, then looked down at her hand and quickly pulled it away. She turned and walked the length of the shelves, said she could feel the words running like horses. It seemed raw and childish, until Stránský told me she'd possibly not been in many bookshops before. She spent hours wandering around and then sat to read a copy of Mayakovsky. It hadn't even dawned on her that she could own it. I bought it for her and she touched my forearm again and then, outside, she hid the book in the pocket of her third skirt.

Stránský looked at us hard and askance, whispered to me: "She's got a husband, son."

We took the train out to the countryside. The other passengers watched us: me in my overalls, Zoli in the colorful dresses that she hitched sideways when she sat down. Together we read Mayakovsky, our knees not quite touching. I recognized it as a tawdry desire, but more than anything I wanted to see her hair loosened. She couldn't do it, it was the habit of a married woman to wear her head covered, though I had begun to make sketches of her in my mind, what she might look like, how that hair would fall if unfastened, how I would take the weight of it in my fingers.

At the station she ran towards Petr who sat waiting on the horsecart, his dented hat on his knee. He looked a little confused, but she whispered in his ear. He laughed, slapped the reins, and took off.

I saw myself then at a distance, as someone else, doing things that only another person would do—I waited for them to return. The stationmaster shrugged and hid a grin. A clocktower chimed. I remained three hours, then walked the long country roads towards the camp with my rucksack on my shoulder. At nightfall, my feet bloodied, I reached the camp. The men were by the fire, cheering. A jar of booze was shoved my way. Petr shook my hand. "You look like you've been slapped," he said.

Zoli had made up a song about a wandering Englishman waiting for a train station whistle and, with the violin at his shoulder, Petr played alongside her while the crowd laughed.

I grinned and thought about punching Petr, pounding him into the mud.

He walked around camp, wheezing. He seemed to carry his sickness tucked under his arm, but when he sat, the sickness spread out all around him. After a while, he didn't have the strength to leave the caravan at all. Zoli would come back in darkness, after singing, and sit at his bedside, waiting for him to fall asleep, his cough to subside.

"How young are the girls when they marry in England?" she asked. She was on the steps of her caravan, absently pleating the hem of her dress.

"Eighteen, nineteen, some not until they're twenty-five."

"Oh," she said, "that's quite old, isn't it?"

The truth was that I didn't really know. I had for some years considered myself to be Czechoslovakian but, in retrospect, I was too English for that, too Irish to be fully English, and too Slovakian to be in any way Irish. Translation had always got in the way of definition. Listening to the radio in the coalshed in Liverpool with my father, I had dreamed myself into the landscape of his country. It was not the place I had foreseen—endless mountains, rushing rivers—but it didn't matter anymore, I'd become someone new and the thought of her held me fast. Each word she came up with sent a thrill along me—she called me Stephen rather than Štěpán, she liked the strange way it brought her teeth to her lips. She would giggle sometimes at the Englishness of what I did, or said, though it didn't seem English to me at all. I bought her a fountain pen from the market in the old town, discovered books for her to read, gave her ink, which Conka used to stain their dresses. I began to learn as much Romani as I could. She touched my arm, looked my way. I knew it. We had begun to cross that hollow that had come between us.

~

A light snow fell in early September, six months after Petr died. I strayed from the camp. On a sandbar in the river were the footprints of wolves. They plaited their way towards a final twist in the riverbank and disappeared into a light forest. She was standing by the water, listening to the small thumps of snow from the branches. I came up behind her, put my hands over her eyes. My fingers went along her neck and my thumb lay in the hollow of her shoulder. My mouth touched briefly against her cheek. She pulled away. I said her name. A sharp intake of breath as she took off her red kerchief. She had, in mourning, cut her hair quite close to the scalp. It was against tradition. She turned away and walked the riverbank. I followed, put my hands over her eyes once more. She went up on her toes in the snow, a soft crunch. I rested my chin on her shoulder, felt the press of her back against me. My hand to her waist, she breathed again, and her kerchief was wrapped around my fist. She turned, pulled at the neckline of my shirt, moved within the shadow of my shoulder, pushed the small cloud of her stomach against my hip and held it there. We went to the ground, but she rolled away. She had not, she said, seen the underside of a tree since she was a child, how strange the leaves looked from underneath. We did not make love, but in the snow she said any fool could tell what had gone on, and she stamped up and down in her shoes. She left, full of tears. The ill-fitting lid of Petr's old lighter clinked, marking the rhythm of her steps. I sat for the next five hours, terrified, but she returned, tripling her route so as not to be followed, bright with eagerness, and I forgot as we pressed against the cold bark of a tree. I could almost hear the wolves returning. The moles on her neck, a perfect dimple on her left breast, the arch of her clavicle. I traced my finger down the path of her body, pulled a ring off her little finger with my teeth. I had suffered so many fantasies over the previous few months, it was terrifying to think that this was a riverbank, not some dingy alley, where I had dreamed Zoli, afraid of nostalgia, in printing rooms, corridors, against hard machinery.

Zoli believed there was a life-spring that went down to the center of the earth and that it ran both ways but mostly it rose from the well of her childhood. It was what she talked about, in her hard country accent, her days traveling with her grandfather, the roads they had covered together, the silences. When she talked about him she took her kerchief all the way across the bridge of her nose and covered her face. She figured her skin too dark, too black, too Gypsy to be in any way beautiful, that her lazy eye somehow marked her, but it seemed to me that for those few days that the moon was rolling along the ground. I was quite sure that eventually we would be caught together, that people would know, that the children would see us, or Conka would find out, or Fyodor, or Vashengo, and we were alert enough to know that the snowmelt would finally flood the bend, but it didn't matter.

She heard an owl hooting one evening, and froze in terror, covered her eyes, said something about the spirit of her grandfather returning, shamed.

"We can't do this," she said, and she stepped off, feet snapping on the cold leaves.

The train to the city was strangely old-world, brown-paneled, the wind rattling at the broken windows.

"They'll tie your balls around your neck and knot them like a bulb of garlic," said Stránský.

"We haven't done anything. Besides, she wouldn't tell a soul."

"You're a naïve fool. She is too."

"It won't happen again."

"Don't touch her, I'm warning you. They'll pull a sheet across you. She's a Gypsy woman. She belongs to a Gypsy man."

"And is that why we're printing her poems?"

He pulled up his collar and lowered himself to his work. It was almost a relief to get out from the mill, away from Stránský and his obsessions, to get lost underneath the streetlamps of the city. He rarely called me his son anymore, but I walked taller for those few months—my chest was drawing breath from Zoli, she was filling me out. We published her first chapbook in the autumn of '53, and it was embraced by all sides, the younger poets, the academics, even the bureaucrats. She wanted it threaded, not glued, for no reason I could fathom, something to do with a horse she had once known.

Small matter, the work was now towards a longer, more lasting series of lyrics. I sat, happy, on an upturned bucket, in the street outside my flat, watching the sun rise between the old buildings.

~

There exists somewhere, hidden away, a photograph of the three of us—Stránský, Zoli, and me—taken in the Park Kultury beside the Danube on a gray afternoon. The water ripples gently. Zoli wears a long, flowing skirt and a frayed bolero jacket. I wear a bright white shirt and a Basque beret, tilted at an angle. Stránský—almost fully bald by then—wears a dark blue shirt and black tie. He has a slight stomach that Zoli used to call his kettle. My foot is up on a dockside bollard. Zoli is as tall as me, while Stránský nestles between us. My arm is firmly around his shoulder. In the background a cargo ship passes with a giant sign pasted along the hull: *All Power to the Workers' Councils!*

Even now I can step towards that photograph, walk along the edge of it, climb down into it, and recall exactly the sharp thrill of being photographed with her.

"Please don't look at me," she said at times when the spotlight caught her, but it seemed to some that Zoli had begun to develop a small fondness for the microphone.

Once, in the village of Prievidza, she was taken to the Hall of Culture, which backed out onto an enormous courtyard. The yard had been full for hours with all manner of Gypsies, waiting. The reading was given in the upstairs room where the ceiling was corniced and the rows were orderly. As the locals filed in, the Gypsies stood, bowed, and gave up their seats to the villagers, then took a place at the back of the room. Bureaucrats sat in the front row, families of the local police took the seats behind. I couldn't quite fathom what was going on. It seemed the officials had been ordered to go along as part of the policy of embracing the Gypsies. The room filled and soon only a couple of Gypsy elders remained—I thought they might fight, or start an argument, but instead they willingly gave up their places and went out to the courtyard. "A point of pride," said Stránský. They were amazed that any gadžo would want to come to hear one of theirs. "At the end of the day, Swann, they're just being polite." Something in me shifted—it had seemed to me to be part of some elaborate ritual, and I hadn't thought of such simplicity.

Zoli begged for the reading to be switched to a bigger hall, but the organizers said it was impossible, so she bowed her head and went on. She was still not used to reading aloud but she did so that evening; she spoke of a light rain in the onset of winter, and a set of horses tied to telegraph poles, a brand-new lyric that suddenly went off-kilter and she could not haul it back. She stammered and tried to explain it, then left abruptly, tearing off one of her new earrings as she went.

Afterwards she opened up the bottom-floor windows and passed plates of food out to those who had waited in the court-yard for her. Stránský and I found her later, smoking a pipe in the blue shadows of the hall, one eye closed against the smoke, fingers trembling. There was talk that trouble had flared in the local bar.

"I want to go home," she said. She put her head against the wall and I felt privy to her sadness. It was, of course, the oldest idea: home. To her it meant silence. I tried to take her arm but she turned away.

Zoli disappeared for four days then and I found out only later that she had been taken around by horsecart to all the set-tlements where she did not read for them but sang, which is what they wanted anyway—they wanted her voice, the secret of it, the one thing that was theirs.

I had printed up a poster with Stránský: it was a new take on an old slogan, and it included an approximation of Zoli's face, a drawing, not a photograph, slightly idealized, no lazy eye, just a working woman's stare and a gray tunic. *Citizens of Gypsy Origin, Come Join Us*. She liked it when she saw it first, falling from cargo planes over the countryside, landing on the lane-ways, tumbling through farmyards, catching on branches. Her face was pasted up along all the pylons and telegraph poles of the countryside. Soon her tapes were being played on the radio and she was talked about in the corridors of power. She was a new sort of Czechoslovakian woman, taken out of the margins to illustrate our steps forward under socialism. She was telling the story unlike anyone had told it before. Zoli was invited to the Ministry of Culture, the National Theater, the Carlton, the Socialist Academy, screenings in the Stalingrad Hotel, conferences on literature where Stránský stood up and bellowed her name into the microphone. She spoke five languages with varying degrees of fluency, and Stránský had begun to call her a Gypsy intellectual. A shadow crossed her face, but she didn't silence him, something in her liked the novelty.

The elders had begun to notice shifts in the outside world—the licenses came more easily, the troopers didn't seek them out to demand permits, the local butchers served them with less fuss than before. The Gypsies had even been invited to create their own chapter in the Musicians Union. Vashengo hardly believed that he, of all people, could now be served in a tavern where years ago he was not even allowed in by the back entrance. Sometimes he walked into the Carlton Hotel just to hear the porters call him Comrade. He came out, slapping his cap off his knee.

One night at the dressing room in the National Theater, Zoli turned to Stránský and said she could not read aloud, she did not have the stomach for it. Her back left a trace of moisture on the leather chair. They walked out into the wings together and looked around the curtain—the theater was packed. A glint of light from a pair of opera glasses. The dimming of the chandeliers. Stránský leveled the crowd with one of her poems and then Zoli walked onstage beside him. The spotlight made her seem at ease. The crowd whispered amongst themselves. She put her lips against the microphone and the feedback squealed. She stepped to the side and read without benefit of the mike. When the crowd cheered, the Gypsies—who had been given two rows at the back of the theater—erupted in applause. At a reception afterwards, Zoli was given a standing ovation. I watched Vashengo at the tables, filling his pockets full of bread and cheese.

On nights like these, I was background music; there was no way I could get to Zoli, there was a whispering pact between us, our goodbyes were quick and fateful, yet the dull pain in my chest had disappeared by the time I woke in the morning. I had taped a photo of her in the corner of my mirror.

When we walked beneath the trees in the Square of the Slovak National Uprising, there were always one or two people who recognized her. In the literary cafés the poets turned to watch. Politicians wanted to be seen with her. We marched on May Day, our fists high in the air. We attended conferences on Socialist theater. Across the river, beyond the bridges, we watched the swinging cranes and the towerblocks rise up in the air. We found grace in the most simple of things: a street-sweeper humming Dvořák, a date carved in a wall, the split backseam of a jacket, a slogan in a newspaper. She joined the Union of Slovak Writers and shortly afterwards, in a poem published in *Rudé právo*, she wrote that she had come to the beginning of the thread of her song.

I read to her from a translation of Steinbeck that I'd been working on intermittently. "I want to go to university," she said as she tapped the spine of the book on her knee. A part of me knew it was doomed to failure. I stammered. She sat by the windowsill in silence, scraping a bit of light from the blackened glass. The next week I bartered in the university for an application form—they were hard to come by. I slipped her the application one chilly morning but heard nothing more about it, though I saw the form weeks later—it plugged a chink in the boards of her wagon where cold air was getting through.

"Oh," she said, "I changed my mind."

Yet the prospect of her still kept me going. There was a chance that others would find out, that she'd be considered polluted, *marime,* damaged. Whole weeks would go by when we could not touch sleeves for fear of being seen, but there was an electricity between us. Alone at the mill we sat with our backs against the folding bed that Stránský had set up on the second floor, by the Zyrkon cutting machines. She touched the whiteness of my chestbones. Ran her fingers in my hair. We had no clue where our bodies stopped and the consequences began. In the streets, we walked apart.

There were other rumblings among some of the Gypsy leaders of course—Zoli was becoming too gadžo for them, her Party card, her literary life, her trips to the cinema, the Lenin museum, the botanical gardens, the box seats she was given one night at the symphony where she took Conka, who cried.

She was, they said, trying to live her life several feet off the ground. It was still considered beyond the realm for her to be seen carrying around books: some notions were impossible to defeat. When she was with the kumpanija she sewed pages into the lining of her coat, or deep in the pockets of her dresses. Among her favorites was an early Neruda, in Slovak, a copy of which she had bought for herself in a secondhand shop. She moved along, lovesongs at her hip, and I learned whole poems so that I could whisper them to her if we chanced on a moment alone. In her other pockets there were volumes by Krasko,

Lorca, Whitman, Seifert, even Tatarka's new work. When she dropped her coat to the floor, in the mill, so that we could read to one another, she immediately got slimmer.

~

Winter arrived and the Gypsies did not travel. It was a time I could not, for the life of me, understand. The tape recorder froze. The reels cracked. There was ice on the microphone. My shoes filled with frost and the blood backed away from my fingers. Zoli would not spend time with me unless others were around: we could not afford to be seen too much together.

I took the train home to my flat in Bratislava, stood under the railway loudspeakers just for the sound of things. I preferred my shelf of books to the feet of Vashengo's children stuck in my ribcage, but after a couple of days the desire to see Zoli built up again and out I went, the microphone and recorder in my rucksack. She smiled and touched my hand. A child turned the corner and she sprang away. I wandered the winter camp. Rusted scrap metal. Severed cables. Bent petrol drums. Dog bones. Punctured cans. The tongues of carriages. Whole matrices of lost things. Conka had found a scarf with patterns of roses on it. She sat, all blanketed up on the steps of her caravan, face twisted by the cold. She looked thin and bitter. The men stood around as if waiting for what might fall from the teeth of horses. I wanted nothing more than to bring Zoli to the city, settle her down, have her write, make her mine, but it was impossible, she liked it there, she was used to it, along the riverbank, she saw the dark and light of the camp as the one same thing.

Graco, Vashengo's oldest son, pushed up against me. He was younger than me, in his late teens.

"And how's the boy, how's the boy, how is he?"

At first he just threw a wild punch. Great laughter. I stepped backwards. A jab, then a hook. We were backed up against a fence. I could feel the wire strands against my legs and back. I brought my bare hands to my face. Closed my eyes. Soon I could feel my whole body being worked. I looked out from my fingers. A couple of flecks like ash floated around me. I spun out from the fence and surprised Graco with an uppercut that lifted his bare feet from the mud. The bones in my fingers crunched. A crowd gathered. Conka stood in the background, next to her husband. He raised his hand, cupped it around his mouth and yelled. Another quick punch from Graco and my eardrums rang. A high wasting whine in my ears. I was aware of all the milling bodies around me. He ducked my second jab. I fell. Graco was smiling down at me, he thought it was something majestic, something intimate. He loved the idea of fighting an Englishman, it was pure hilarity to him. For all his small size he was everywhere at once. "Get up." A jab. A left hook. Another shout. "Get up, you shit-drink." He tossed back his head to clear his locks from his eyes. I felt the fence against my back again and pulled into it, held my hands over my face. Blood through my fingers. Graco seemed to have become melancholy, like he was hitting a tree. He went on punching and the roars changed, yelping noises from the kids, the adults silent and abstracted. Conka stood beside her husband, a soft grin on her face. Graco's knuckles snapped me and my head spun. A boot came in from the outer edge of the ring and caught me in the jaw. "You and all your pale pieces." Another boot came in. A foot to my ribs. And then I realized that I was fighting for my life, scrabbling backwards in the mud, all the sounds merging, until I heard her voice going up, quiet, but nervous, and she broke the line, a few strands of dark hair between her teeth, and she shoved Graco backwards, and I had no hunger for it anymore, no desire, I stood with blood dripping from my eye and it dawned on me that Zoli, too, must have been watching all along.

She leaned in to me and put her scarf to my eye to staunch the blood and said: "They're only keeping warm, Swann, that's all."

~

I suppose that in the beginning the changes seemed negligible enough—the switch in the eyes, the hunch into overcoats, the peepholes cut into doors, the darkened windows. It was a small enough price to pay. A few isolated incidents. Raindrops, Stránský called them. You put out your hand, he said, and all of a sudden they were there, almost lovely at first. But one by one these things became a form of light rain, and then the drops began to collide, until after a while we were silently watching them come down in sheets. There was a refusal to talk unless we were in an open area, or in a hired car, or down by the water. Black Marias began to appear more and more on the streets. Soon we heard stories of folk dancers being sent off to dig canals, professors on dairy farms, philosophers folding back the cardboard flaps of orphanage boxes, shopkeepers lying facedown in the ditches, poets working in the armament factories. Signposts were sawed down. Streets were given new names. It was raining hard and we hid from it—yet it was our own rain, of our own making, and it promised to bring on a good crop, we were sure of it, so we let it fall. Already too much had been invested in the Revolution, and we weren't prepared to give in to the despair that things would not work out. It was so much like desire.

"Are you fucking her, Swann?" Stránský asked one evening when the two of us sat together at the back of the Pelikan café. The place smelled of old overcoats. I looked around, table to table, at the gray faces, watching us watching them. The truth—and Stránský knew it—was that nobody was fucking her, though we all wanted to in whatever way we could.

"None of your business," I said.

He laughed his tired laugh, lifted his glass.

I walked out and was startled to notice that we were under the gaze of a cameraman who was clicking pictures from the window of a black Tatra.

The darkness rose up like it was coming from the cobbles.

For Zoli's kumpanija, the changes had begun with Woo-woodzhi, a young man who had taken to nailing his own hand to a tree. He was a hard case, a schizophrenic. The families heaved with loyalty, and Woowoodzhi was among their favorites. His bandages were changed every few hours. Zoli brought him boiled sweets from the city and whispered night-time legends in his ear. Woowoodzhi rocked back and forth at the sound of her voice. Whenever he strayed from the cara-vans the alarm went—saucepans were banged—and the women spread out along the forest edges to look for him. The boy would often be found, hammering the nails into his hands. He never cried out, not even when hot poultices were put to his palm.

In the middle of an autumn rainstorm a tall blond nurse was driven up to the caravans at the edge of the forest. She stepped out of her car into the mud, up to her ankles. She screeched for help and so the blonde was carried, with pomp and ceremony, to one of the caravans. She was given hot tea and her shoes were cleaned. She flipped the clasp of her handbag. A badge said she was from the Ministry of Health. She unfurled a piece of paper and thrust it out. Zoli was called upon to read it.

"It's a mistake," said Zoli. "It must be."

"It's no mistake, Citizen. Can you not read?"

"I can read."

"Then you must do what it says."

Zoli stood up, tore the paper into pieces, stuffed it back into the woman's palm. It was an order to bring Woowoodzhi to the local mental institution.

"Please leave," said Zoli.

"Just give me the child and there'll be no problems."

Zoli spat at the woman's feet. A riffle of whispers went around the caravan. The woman blanched and reached for Zoli's arm, dug her fingers in: "The child needs proper care."

Zoli backhanded her twice across the face. A cheer went up around the caravan.

Two hours later the troopers arrived but all the Gypsies were gone—they had disappeared without a trace.

Stránský loved the story—the troopers arrived at the mill with an arrest warrant for Zoli and told us everything—and I had to admit it thrilled me too, but we had no idea where to find the kumpanija. We searched and found nothing, not even a rumor.

Without Zoli they were days of gnawing restlessness and gloom. Flocks of gulls argued above the Danube. I worked at the mill, attended a conference on Russian typography, then sat at home, books propped open on my chest—Mayakovsky, Dreiser, Larkin.

It was a full two months later, on a day of slanting sunlight, that Zoli arrived back. She looked different: a moving rawness. In the mill she stood amid the noise and the high clacking of machinery, inhaled the smell of grease and ink. I hurried across to greet her, but she leaned away from me.

"Where've you been?" asked Stránský from the staircase.

"Here and there," she said.

He repeated it and half-laughed, went up the staircase, and left us alone together.

She drew herself up to a height. I watched as she stepped towards the hellbox and searched through the old broken ingots, looked at all the backward letters, arranged them to form a song that she had composed in her mind, *My grave is hiding from me,* a quick and luminous poem where she said she felt locked like wood within a tree. She set the letters out on the counter and pressed her hands down on the hard metal. She said she could still feel bits of Woowoodzhi in her cuticles: he had died, she said, from a bout of influenza, contracted on the same night that the caravans were trying to escape.

"They killed him, Stephen."

"Be careful, Zoli," I said, looking around.

"I don't know what careful means," she said. "What does careful mean? Why should I be careful?"

"You've seen the news?"

In her absence, Zoli had become something of a cult figure— the arrest warrant had been torn up by no less than the Minister of Culture himself. A new tomorrow was on the way, he said. Part of it would include the Roma. Zoli was the subject of a whole new series of editorials that professed she had been painting the old world so it could finally, at last, change. They saw her as heroic, the vanguard of a new wave of Romani thinkers. One of her poems had been reprinted in a Prague-based university journal. Tapes of her singing were played again on the radio. The further away she was the bigger she had become. Now there was talk in government circles of allowing the Gypsies to halt, of settling them in government housing, giving them absolute power over their own lives. The idea of them living out in the forest had become bizarre and old-fashioned, almost bourgeois to the pure-minded. Why should they be forced to live out on the roads? The papers said they should be cut free from the troubles of primitivism. There would be no more Gypsy fires, only in the theater.

"*Allow* us to halt?" The chuckle caught in her throat.

She picked up a pigeon feather from the ground and let it fall from her fingers. "The *troubles of primitivism*?" Something in my spine went liquid. She left the mill with a bundle of papers under her arms. Down the road, she climbed onto a horse-cart which she operated on her own. She slapped the horse and it reared high for a moment, then clattered down onto the cobbles.

I walked alone down by the Danube. A soldier with a megaphone shouted me away from the bank. In the distance, Austria. Beyond that, all the places that young men had fought for, died for, millions of them, fed to the soil, and beyond that, it seemed to me, France, the channel, England, and the soot of my early years. It had been nine years since I arrived in Czechoslovakia, jittery and expectant. Someone had borrowed the jaunt from my step. I could feel it in the way I walked. So much of my revolutionary promise seemed to be slipping away, my hard grip on the world, but, still, it didn't seem possible that there would come a time when it would vanish completely.

Across the river the lights from the towers twinkled once

and then went off. The streets were lifeless, cold—the only mystery was that I expected them to be otherwise.

"Don't sulk," said Stránský when I pushed open the door of the mill again. "She's only waking up. She's going to do something that'll stun us all, just you watch."

That summer, in 1957, one of the few places we saw Zoli was the house at Budermice. It was set on parkland in the shadow of the Little Carpathian hills, a country mansion maintained by the Union of Slovak Writers. A long row of chestnut trees lined the lane. The driveway curled to a grand front entrance with marble steps. Several rooms on the top floor were kept locked and most of the bedrooms were dusty. Downstairs the union had burned the old furniture—too imperial, too bourgeois—so plastic chairs had been installed, hardtop counters, towering Russian prints. Stránský managed to get the house for the whole summer—he hated anything that smacked of cronyism, but he saw it as a time for some serious creativity. He wanted us to finish a whole book with Zoli—there'd only been a chapbook, but now a real volume, he knew, would cement her reputation: he was convinced that she had a vision that would lift the Gypsies out of their quandaries.

The lawn sloped down to a stream that was conducted through a wooden pipe the size of a giant barrel. Here and there the wooden structure was pierced to irrigate the lawn. Water arced out into the grass and onto the well-tended paths. Even on clear summer nights it sounded as if it were raining outside.

Stránský went walking with her every day—Zoli, in her skirts and kerchief and dark blouses, he in his white collarless shirts that made him look a little quixotic. They strolled past the fountains, looking as if they were whispering secrets to each other. She was at the height of her powers then, and they were working out patterns for her poems. Stránský would come to me, clap his hands together and recite her lyrics. I had seldom seen a man so worked-up, burning high, wandering around the house, saying: "Yes, yes, yes, yes!" A Steinway still sat in the main dining room, one of the last of the old artifacts, though the markings had been rubbed out. Stránský raised the lacquered lid, sat on the stool, clinked his ring finger against the ivory, and denounced the empty elegance of art without purpose. He winked and then played "The Internationale."

One night, from the staircase, Stránský took a flying leap at the chandelier. It fell from the ceiling with a crash and he lay there stunned.

"Adoration's more fragile than rope," he said, looking around, as if surprised.

Zoli came and sat beside him on the marble floor. I watched from the balcony above. Stránský was half-smiling, looking at a small cut on his hand—a tiny bit of glass was stuck in his skin. She took his wrist and pinched the glass up from the folds in his hand. She hushed him and guided his finger to his mouth. Stránský sucked out the sliver of glass.

I came down the stairs, stepping loudly. She looked up and smiled: "Martin's drunk again."

"No, I'm not," he said, grasping her elbow. He fell again. I lifted him from the floor, told him he needed a cold bath. He put his arm around my shoulder. Halfway up the stairs I had a brief vision of dropping him, watching from a height as he tumbled down.

From below, Zoli smiled at me and then she stepped outside to where she slept. She wasn't used to sleeping in a room. She felt that it was closing in on her and so she kept her bedding in the rose garden. I woke in the morning to find her dozing happily under the floribundas. She washed in the running stream distant from the house. She couldn't fathom someone taking a bath in standing water. Stránský took to bathing in a giant tub outside, just to mock her gently. He sat singing in the tub, soaping himself, drinking, and laughing. She dismissed him and wandered off into the woods, coming home with bunches of wild garlic, edible flowers, nuts.

"Where's she gone?" I asked him one afternoon.

"Oh, get the stick out of your arse, would you, young man?"

"What's that supposed to mean?"

"She's out walking. She's clearing her head, she doesn't need you and she doesn't need me."

"You've got a wife, Stránský."

"Don't be a chamber pot," he said.

It was an old expression, odd and formal, one my father had used many years before. Stránský caught me square and I stepped back from him. He squeezed my shoulder, just enough to show that he still had a young man's power.

"I'm looking after her poems," he told me. "That's all. Nothing else."

Towards the end of summer, Zoli's kumpanija showed up. Twenty caravans camped in the field right at the back of the house. The backs of the horses were shiny with sweat. I woke up in the morning and smelled campfire. Conka wore a fresh scar, from eyecrook to the nape of her neck, and one upper tooth was gone. She stepped down from her caravan in the shadow of her husband, Fyodor. She wore a yellow dress patterned with feathers. Down the steps, she suddenly had a limp and I wondered who could possibly bear the courage to live that way? Her breasts sagged and her stomach pushed against the cloth dress, and for a moment she was like something I recognized from a melancholy viewing elsewhere.

Kids ran naked in the fountains. The men had already taken some of the plastic kitchen chairs and had set them up beside their caravans. Zoli was in the middle of the crowd, laughing. Stránský too was suddenly in the thick of things. He and Vashengo drank together. Vashengo had found a case of Harvey's Bristol Cream—an extraordinary thing, how they got it I never knew, but it was contraband, and could get them arrested. They drank it down to the final drop, then started in on bottles of slivovitz.

The night rose up like something to be exhausted.

Zoli sang that week, the thorn was in her skin, and we got some of her best poems. Stránský said he could detect a new music in her, and it gave him different beats for the poems, always listening, watching. He saw her as fully authentic now, she had forged herself in a world that was not ours, a poet filled with mysterious voices that sometimes even she didn't know the meaning of. He said to me that she had an intellect that came to her like a bird off a branch, unrecognized, the images chasing each other with speed. And he swallowed the portions of abstraction and romanticism that annoyed him with other poets, allowed her what he saw as her mistakes, tamed her line length, structured the work into verses.

Still, in my mind, I can hang a painting of it in midair: Stránský, after working a whole afternoon with Zoli, walking to the wagons and sitting down, playing bl'aški with tin cards, his shirt filthy, looking like one who belonged. And there I was, standing outside, waiting for her.

By the end of the week the house was ransacked. The kumpanija had taken almost every ounce of food. The broken chandelier hung in the middle of one of their caravans.

I found Zoli sitting on a chair in one of the half-empty rooms upstairs, a crumpled handkerchief in her hand. When she saw me in the doorway she rose, said it was nothing, she had only caught a cold, but as she went past me she ran her fingers along my arm.

"Vashengo says that there are more rumors," she said.

"What do you mean?"

"Resettlement. They want to give us schools and houses and clinics." She knuckled her lazy eye. "They're saying we used to be backward. Now we're new. They say it's for our own good. They call it Law 74."

"It's just talk, Zoli."

"How is it that some people always know what is best for others?"

"Stránský?" I said.

"Stránský has nothing to do with it."

"Do you love him?"

She stared at me, grew quiet, looked out the window to the gardens below. "No," she said. "Of course not."

From outside came the sound of laughter that abruptly broke the silence, lingered, and died.

We met early the next afternoon, away from Budermice, by the wheel of an old flour mill. The water had been diverted. Zoli had tripled her path to make sure she was not followed. She had in her pocket a photograph, a shot of splintered lightning, a bright blue flash across a dark landscape. She said it came from a magazine she had found, a feature on Mexico, that someday she wouldn't mind traveling there, it was a long way, but she'd like to go. Perhaps when things were finally good, she said, she'd take off, follow that path. She quoted a line from Neruda about falling out of a tree he had not climbed. I felt exasperated by her, always turning, always changing, always making me feel as if I was looking for oxygen—how much like fresh air and how much, at the same time, like drowning.

"Stephen," she said. "You'll fight with us if we have to, right?"

"Of course."

She smiled then, and became so much like the very young Zoli I'd seen in the early years at the mill, her shoulders loosened, her face lit up, a warmth came to her. She stepped towards me, placed my hand on the curve of her hip. Her back against a tree, our feet slipping in the leaves, her hair across her face, she seemed dismantled.

There are always moments we return to. We are in them. We rest there and there is nothing else.

Later that night we made love once again in the high empty rooms of the house. A white sheet took on the print of our bodies. A bead of sweat from my forehead ran down her cheek. She left with a finger to her lips. In the morning I ached for her, I had never known that such a thing existed, a pain that tightened my chest, and yet we still could not be seen together, we couldn't ford that gap. It felt to me as if we were falling from a cliff face, perfect weightlessness and then a thump.

"If they catch us," she said, "there'll be more trouble than we can invent."

An official from the Ministry came along later that same week, a tall gray-haired bureaucrat with an air of pencil sharpeners about him. He sat and glared at the women doing their washing in the fountains. He talked with Stránský, voices raised. The cords in the bureaucrat's neck shone. A sleeve moved across his brow. Stránský leaned closer, spittle flying from his mouth. The bureaucrat went inside the house and ran his fingers over the piano. All the ivory keys were missing. He turned on his heels.

Within a few hours he was back, troopers with him. Vashengo jabbed his pitchfork at a line of six troopers. "Put it down," Stránský pleaded. The troopers backed away and watched as the smallest children picked up rocks from the gardens. Stránský came between them all, arms outstretched. The troopers left with a promise that the kumpanija would leave the next day.

The following morning Zoli sat on a horsecart. I walked across the gravel. She shook her head to keep me away. Something in me burned. I would have given it all, every word, every idea, to turn around and walk with her up the stairs into that old mansion again, but she turned sideways, and someone whipped the back of the horse. Behind her, Conka smirked. Vashengo led the kumpanija away.

I found Stránský on the steps of the big house, palms pressed tight against his temples. He seemed suddenly so very old, so full of sorrow, you could see it in his eyes: "We're drinking off their coffin lids, Swann, you know that?"

~

Stránský once wrote that only when a man dies can his life acquire a beginning, middle, and an end: up until then we are constantly unfinished, even the midpoint cannot be located. So only the final word finds the middle word and this, in a way, becomes a verse—one's death explains oneself. Stránský was the sort of man who was always going to do something that would take the floor from beneath his feet—he'd been disappearing for a long time, restless with the way things were evolving. Stalin's death, though he hardly celebrated him, had winded Stránský. The Congress buoyed him up for a while, but then came the events in Hungary in '56, the tanks rolling south, and a new series of trials in Czechoslovakia. In the Tatra Hotel he raked his wedding ring along a polished table, gave a long speech about living in the margins. He wrote a poem in a Prague journal saying that he was no longer interested in rubbing his lips with red crepe paper. What he meant, I suppose, was that the more people were given power, the more they learned to despise the process that had given it to them—the country had changed, turned sour, lost its edge. Our cures were so much less powerful than our wounds.

Stránský's old political friends stopped calling over to his flat, and his visits to the Ministry of Culture found him patrolling the waiting rooms. He stopped lecturing in factory auditoriums, clubs, rural houses of culture. In the mill, he drank heavily.

"I assure you," he said, "it's the vodka that's drinking me, but I've still two fingers left."

He spread his arms out wide in the air.

"Alcohol as biography."

He finished the bottle.

In the early winter of '58, Elena left him. His marriage had been unraveling for a while—he had started to think that he was becoming a caricature in her cartoons, a small fat man with an axe to grind. I found Stránský in the corner of the mill, framed by windowlight. I had never seen him so silent. He had punched the wall and the bandage on his hand was already stained with ink.

He stubbed a cigarette out into the cloth and pointed to two men who paced the street outside.

Over the next few weeks Stránský grew gaunt and hollow-eyed. He wandered the mill, making paper cuts in his hand. The cuts kept him awake so he could work. Sometimes he lit a match off his fingernail and inhaled the sulphur. He wouldn't allow anyone to see his new poems and we didn't ask—it was better not to. I avoided him. It was only a matter of time. He allowed me to drift. It was his form of generosity—he would not drag me down with him. The hours passed like hours pass, yet they seemed longer hours than ever before. I plunged myself into creating posters, working with other artists and designers. My skill was turning out a four-color poster on the Zephyr printer. I could do it alone, in a matter of hours. Stránský would sometimes come down the stairs in the mill and walk over the freshly printed posters. Then he would return upstairs, leaving fresh ink with his footsteps.

He still delved into Zoli's work and reworked her poems, added words and fixed rhymes, checked them with her, fired back at those who said her work was formalistic and bourgeois because of her respect for nature, that she was drawing a social advantage from pain. He thought that the purpose of her poems was not to dazzle with any astonishing thought, but to make one single moment of existence unforgettable.

The three of us were to meet one Thursday at the Carlton Hotel. Under the hotel awning we stood smoking cheap tobacco, waiting for Stránský to show up. Zoli looked radiant in a bright red dress, small beads sewn into the fabric so that when she moved they caught the light, even beneath a shawl. Stránský didn't appear. A grayness chilled the air, a sense that winter was on its way. We rounded the corner and went down by the

Danube. The ground was damp but she kicked off her shoes anyway. There was very little grace in how she did it, except that her legs were momentarily liquid as they lost the shoes. She bent down to pick them up and dangled them in her right hand.

"I haven't walked barefoot in years," she said.

A motorboat puttered up the Danube and a searchlight caught us. Within seconds she had gone up the riverside track, near where the nuclear bunkers were being built, and she was bending down to put on her shoes once more. Another searchlight caught her as she leaned. A soldier recognized her and shouted her name. The searchlight threw her distorted shadow about her and the dress sparkled. I thought then that we would never get away from the circles that held us.

She whispered to me: "We can't be seen alone, Stephen. There's too much at stake now."

I didn't believe her. I couldn't. The prospect of having nothing stunned me. The darkness seemed miles thick.

At home I fell asleep, too tired to dream: it was not yet my thirty-third birthday.

When the knock came on the door early in the morning—just as dawn was breaking over Bratislava—I knew exactly who it was. Six agents turned the room inside out. They knew all the answers to their questions already. They checked my credentials and filled in an extensive dossier. They seemed upset at how housebroken my life was, how ordinary, how sanitized.

There was no radio trial for Stránský. He was labeled a parasite for the most recent of his poems, and his confession appeared in the newspaper. I scoured it for clues to the man I had once worshiped. I kept seeing him in a cell, hoisted aloft, hands tied behind his back, a terrible splintering sound as the arms dislocated from the shoulder sockets. Rubber truncheons. Electrified baths. In the evenings I had visions of him walking along by the prison walls, chilled by the utter silence of what we had become.

I was called into the Ministry and given a tour of the punishment cells. They told me to file a weekly report about what I knew: I learned a whole new vocabulary of sidestepping.

Zoli was not arrested but instead she was brought in, for what they called a consultation. I waited near the headquarters. She emerged with her face a perfect mask, only two dark parallel streaks down her cheeks gave her away. She was driven away by motorcar, her dark hair against the beige leather of the seats. I watched the car go.

She fell, then, into a period of prolonged silence. I searched, but couldn't find her. There were rumors that she had burned every bit of paper around her. Some said she had gone to Prešov and would not be back. Yellow leaves floated on the Danube. I worked on her poems but, without her voice surrounding the words, they were not the same. Plans for publication of the book were shelved—we needed her to be around for it to have its full impact. After three months, she sent one of Conka's children to my door. The child had a message but it had been relayed through three others, and she could not remember the exact details. I asked for a letter, but the child stared at me dumbly and ran her fingers through her hair. In a rough rural accent she said that Zoli needed to talk to me, and she rattled off the names of some villages I presumed would roughly pinpoint her.

I drove Stránský's bike so hard that the engine began to sputter. I stopped under an arch of cypress trees. With a pair of old binoculars I watched Zoli at the back of her caravan, strumming a violin bow against a metal sheet, an old quirk of hers, making patterns on the metal with sugar, hordes of children gathered around her, and I stood there, and it felt as if I were gripping her neck in my hand, and the strut ran all along her body, with the strings going down to the curve in her belly, and I was chest-deep in her, lost.

~

The rumors picked up speed. If I had ransomed everything and given it to her it would still never have been enough. Her people were not able to stand outside the true bend of gravity. The force was always downwards, even if the inclination was to raise them up. There was no single hour when it came about, but things had begun to slip: more talk of Law 74, the End of Nomadism, the Big Halt. Some ignored it. Others embraced it, saw it as a way to fill up their pockets and call themselves Gypsy kings, a notion that meant nothing to Zoli and her people.

The crux of the matter was assimilation, belonging, ethnic identity. We wanted them, but they wanted us to leave them alone. And yet the only way to be left alone was to let us know what their life was, and that life was in Zoli's songs.

On the motorbike, we drove east to meet with local officials in Žilina, Poprad, Prešov, Martin, Spišská Nová Ves. In town meetings she spoke about tradition and nationhood, about the old life, against assimilation. She had written down the poems, she said, in order to sing the old life, nothing more. Her politics were those of road and grass. She leaned forward into microphones. Don't try to change us. We are complete. Citizens of our own space. The bureaucrats stared at her and nodded blankly. Simply being who she was aroused an expectation among them—they wanted her in the Gypsy jam jar. They nodded and showed us the door, assured us they were on our side, but anyone could see that they were separated from honesty by fear. Nor could we be rescued by the forces of beauty around us: we clattered down the potholed roads, through valleys, beneath the snowcapped eastern mountains, in the early mornings when small house lights still dawdled by the rivers, a smoke of mayflies drifting in the air. I opened my mouth and it filled with midges.

The journey hammered me down. A deadness in my fingers. Climbing on the bike, the day seemed to stretch out, endless. Zoli carried her clothes in a zajda blanket stretched around her back, two knots tied at her chest. She had already scarred her left leg on the heat of the exhaust pipe, but she did not stop: she applied her own poultice from dock leaves. Town to town, hall to hall. In the evening, we stayed in the homes of gadže activists. Even they had become silent. I walked around with a hollow pit in my stomach. Whole marching bands of children went through the streets wearing red scarves, shouting slogans. The loudspeakers seemed to be turned up a notch. For long stretches we found in ourselves little to say. In the corridors of community offices all over the country, Zoli tore her face down off the walls, shredded the pieces, put them in her pocket: *Citizens of Gypsy Origin, Come Join Us*.

We stayed one night in a monastery that had become a hotel. It was shoddy and ruined, full of plastic plants and cheap prints. The bites that woke me were from bedbugs concealed under a loose corner of wallpaper. Bells rang out in the early morning, calling workers to their jobs. I rose and washed my arms and face in the handbasin in the corridor, paid the plump woman at the front desk. She sat in a bright plastic chair and re-garded me, diligently bored, though she sat upright when she saw Zoli, recognizing her from the newspapers.

As we rode from the monastery, a series of thin and trem-bling images caught in the rain puddles: moving feet, windows, a small slice of steel-colored sky. I had the very ordinary thought that surely there was an easier life elsewhere. Zoli and I waited for an hour to fill up the petrol tank. The motorbike was a cu-riosity with young children on their way to school. They were fascinated by the speedometer. Zoli lifted the children and al-lowed them to pretend that they were driving. They laughed and clapped as she pushed them along, school satchels slung over their shoulders, until they were shooed off by the petrol attendant.

In the evening we reached Martin, a gray little town along the Vah River. We were refused a hotel room until Zoli showed her Party card, and even then she was told that there was only one room left, though there were four single beds in it. It was on the top floor, something she always resisted unless she was sure there were no Gypsy men beneath her—every now and then she dredged up some of the ancient ways, and it was pos-sible, in the old blood laws, to contaminate men by walking above them. She eventually managed to get a first-floor room with the suggestion that she would throw a curse on the clerk. Alarmed, he scuttled away and came back moments later with the keys. It was a form of voodoo that she used only in the worst cases. She threw her bag on the soft mattress and we left for a meeting with the local officials—three Cultural Inspec-tors who had formerly been priests.

All Zoli wanted to do was hold a hand up against the tide

that she felt was washing over her, but Law 74 had become part of the vocabulary now; the idea was that the Gypsies were part of the apparatus. Zoli pleaded with them, but the officials smiled and doodled nervously at the edge of ledgers.

"Shit on you," she said to them, and she walked out into the front courtyard, and sat with her head in her hands. "Maybe I should sing a song for them, Swann?" She spat on the ground. "Maybe I should jangle my bracelets?"

In the local market she came across a family of Roma who had been burned out of a sawmill and had nowhere to sleep. She brought them through the lobby of the hotel, eleven or twelve at least, not including children, and promised the clerk that they'd be out first thing in the morning. His jaw hung slack, but he allowed them to pass. In the room I set up a makeshift sheet around one bed so as not to be improper. I tried to leave so she and the family would have the room to themselves, but neither Zoli nor the others would have any of it. They insisted I stay in the bed. The women and children giggled as I undressed. My ankles were exposed underneath the hanging sheet—it was what they deemed immodest.

Part of the curtain fell aside and I watched as they gathered in the middle of the room and talked in a dialect I couldn't make out. It seemed they were talking of burnings.

When I woke I saw Zoli, in the predawn dark, climbing out the window. All the others had already gone from the room. When she returned she held in her hand a wet cloth that I assumed she must have wiped in the dew. She lit a candle, placed it in an ashtray, and curved her hand around it as if to shield the light from me. She leaned forward and let her black hair fall before her. She pressed the wet cloth along the length of it a number of times. She brushed it as many more times with a wooden comb, then gathered her hair, coiled it, braided it. The ceiling skipped with shadow. She slipped into the far bed.

When I stood up and walked over to her she did not move. She lay with her back to me, her neck bare. A draft flattened the candle flame. She allowed my arm across her waist. She said that there were many things she missed in her life, not least a sinewy voice that might come up from beneath the ice. I nudged in against her, kissed the back of her hair. It smelled of grass.

"Marry me," I said to her.

"What?" she said, speaking towards the window, not as a question, nor an exclamation, but something distant and unfathomable.

"You heard me."

She turned and gazed some other place beyond me.

"Haven't we lost enough?" she said.

She turned and kissed me briefly as she lowered the guillotine for a final time, and I was grateful in a way that she had waited so long. A single phrase, and yet it hit me with the force of an axe. She had put a line down between us, one I could never again cross.

Zoli rose and gathered her possessions. When she left the room, I punched into the wall and heard a knuckle crack.

She was waiting outside. I had to drive her to another town. She smiled slightly at the sight of my fist wrapped in a towel, and for a brief moment I hated her and all the bareness she brought to her life.

"You've got to drive me through the mountains," she pleaded. "I can't stand the idea of those tunnels."

And yet we were in a tunnel anyway, we knew it, and maybe we had always been. We had sped into the arch of darkness, slowed down, steered a moment in the unusual cold, until it felt right, and then we'd jolted the bike forward again, pushed against the headlong wind. We had recognized a pinpoint of light, a tiny gleam that kept growing, and the longer we journeyed in the darkness the more dazzling the light had become, ever brighter, more brilliant, and we leaned forward onto the handlebars, until eventually, like everyone, we had approached the mouth of the tunnel. Then we smashed that motorbike out into the sunshine, momentarily blinded, stunned, and we stayed so for quite a while, until our eyes adjusted and we began to blink and things came into focus and all around us were pebbles and amongst the pebbles, stones, and amongst the stones, rubbish, and amongst the rubbish, small gray buildings, and between, and beyond, pockets of gray men and women, a wasteland of them—ourselves. Instead of letting our hearts sink, we had closed our eyes once more and we had ridden that bike into another darkness, another tunnel, thinking there would be a brighter light just a little further along, that nothing would derail us, and that belief, like most beliefs, was more precious than the truth.

What is there to say?

Stránský's last words to the firing squad: "Come closer, it will be easier for you."

~

The hubs were of elm. The spokes, mostly oak. The rims were made from felloes of curved ash, joined by strong pegs, bound with iron. Many were painted. Some were badly nicked and scarred. Certain ones were rigged with wire. A few were buckled with moisture. Others were still perfect after decades. They were hauled in from riverbanks, deep forests, fields, edges of villages, long, empty tree-lined roads. Thousands of them. Sledgehammers were used to remove them. Two-man saws. Levers. Tire irons. Mallets. Pneumatic drills. Knives. Blowtorches. Even bullets when frustration set in. They were taken to the railroad yards, state factories, dump grounds, sugar mills and, most often, to the weedy fields at the rear of police stations where once again they were tagged and then, after meticulous documentation, they were burned. The troopers worked the bonfires in shifts. Small groups in the villages gathered, bringing their chairs with them. In the freezing afternoons workers broke off early to see the stacks as they whistled and hissed in the fires. At times the air bubbles popped in rackety succession. Sparks yawed off into the air. The rubber caught and threw huge flames. The iron hoops reddened and glowed. The nails melted. When the fires waned, the crowds threw on extra paraffin. Some cheered and drank from bottles of vodka, jars of čuču. Policemen stood and watched as the embers made silent passages into the air. Army sergeants leaned in and lit cigarettes. Teachers gathered classes around the flames. Some children wept. In the days afterwards, a slew of government officials rolled out in jeeps and cars from Košice, Bratislava, Brno, Trnava, Šariš, Pobedim, to inspect what had happened under Law 74. It had taken just three days, an incredible success, so our newspapers and state radio told us, generous, decent, Socialist: we got rid of their wheels.

There were horses too, of course, requisitioned and sent to the collective farms, though many were old and bony and ready for the glueyard. Those were shot where they stood.

I walked the backstreets of Bratislava, reeling, the copy of *Rudé právo* rolled up in my back pocket. I knew there was a syntax in the way I carried my body, and I was careful now not to unfold myself fully to the troopers. I stayed at home, hung shirts across the window for curtains.

Zoli's kumpanija, which had been hiding out in the forests not far from the city, had tried to flee, but they were surrounded and brought to the city. They called it the Big Halt. They were joined by other families as the roads filled. Women at the front, men at the flank. Long lines of carriages and children. Dogs snapped and kept them in line. The people were herded into fields at the foot of the new towers. The troopers disappeared and the bureaucrats came, waving files. The children were deloused in the local spa, then everyone was lined up and inoculated against disease. Speeches were given. Our brothers and sisters. The true proletariat. Historical necessity. Victory is swift. The dawn of a new era.

Flags were unfurled. Bands played trumpets as Zoli's men and women were guided towards community centers—from now on they'd live in the towerblocks. They were a triumph of what we had become. They were to be envied.

Alone in my room, I listened to the radio reports: serious and high-minded, they talked of the rescue of the Gypsies, the great step forward, how they'd never be shackled by primitivism again. One of Zoli's poems was read out on the midnight program. I didn't have the bravery to turn it off.

I went downstairs, snapped the front cable on the motorbike, took apart the chain and left the links in pieces on the ground. I wandered the alleyways, my hand trailing the lichen on the walls, paced underneath the marble arch carved with Soviet stars. Blue posters were pasted on street corners, long columns of names of those who had committed crimes against the popular democratic order. I looked down at the dismal sweep of the Danube. Citizens moved along the waterfront without motive, without volition. It was like watching a silent movie—they spoke but remained silent.

In the mill, the new boss, Kysely, was a vicious little corner-shop of a man. He waited for me with a clipboard.

I ventured down past Galandrova Street, wearing a black-belted shirt and a pin from the Union of Slovak Writers, and there she was, huddled in the shadows of the mill. She wore her overcoat and her kerchief had fallen down over her eyes. I walked up and stood in front of her a moment, lifted her chin with a forefinger. She pulled away. I could hear the noise of the mill behind us, its mechanical hum.

"Where've you been, Stephen?"

"The motorbike."

"What about it?"

"It's broken down."

She took one step back, then reached forward and ripped the pin out of my shirt.

"I tried to get out there to help you," I said. "I was stopped, Zoli. They turned me back. I tried to find you."

She pushed open the door of the mill and strode inside. Kysely, grimy and yellow-faced, was wearing one of Stránský's shirts. He stared across the machines at her. "Identification?" he said. She ignored him, stamped across the floor, and went to the filing racks. The original poster plate was there, cased in steel. She took it and threw it against the wall. It bounced on the floor and slid against the hellbox. She picked it up and began to hammer the image of her face against the ground.

Kysely began to laugh.

Zoli looked up at him and spat at his feet. He gave me a smile that froze me to the ground. I took him aside and pleaded: "Let me handle this." He shrugged, said there would be repercussions, and went upstairs, past Stránský's colored footprints. Zoli was standing in the middle of the floor, chest rising and falling.

"They'll keep us there."

"What are you talking about?"

"The towers," she said.

"It's temporary. It's to control—"

"To control what, Stephen?"

"It's just temporary."

"They played one of your recordings on the radio," she said. "My people heard it."

"Yes."

"They heard there will be a book."

"Yes."

"And do you know what they thought?"

I felt something sharp move under my heart. I had heard about the Gypsy trials, the punishments that could be handed down. The law was binding. Anyone banished was banished forever.

"If you print this book they'll blame me."

"They can't."

"They'll have a trial. They'll make judgment. Vashengo and the elders. The blame will come down on me. Do you understand? It'll come down on me. Maybe it should."

She crossed the floor towards me, her knuckle to her chin. There were only two floorboards between us. She was pale, almost see-through.

"Don't print the books."

"They're already printed, Zoli."

"Then burn them. Please."

"I can't do it."

"Who is it up to, if it isn't up to you?"

The sharpness of her voice slid right through my skin. I stood, trembling. I tried rattling off excuses: the book could not be shelved, the Union of Slovak Writers wouldn't allow it. Kysely and I were under strict instructions. The government would arrest us, there were darker things afoot. They needed the poems to continue resettlement. Zoli was their poster girl. She was their justification. They needed her. Nothing else could be done. They would soon change their minds. All she had to do was wait. I stammered, came to the end of my arguments, and stood, then, rimrocked by them all.

Zoli looked momentarily like a window-stunned bird. Her eyes flicked the length of my body. She tugged at the looping drape of skirt at her feet and toed her sandals in the ground, then she slapped me once, and turned on her heels. When she opened the front door, a cage of light moved across the floor. It sprang away as her footsteps sounded outside. She left without a word. She was absolutely real to me then, no longer the Gypsy poet, the ideal Citizen, the new Soviet woman, something exotic to fall in love with.

I understood what Stránský had understood too late—we had interrupted her solitude in order to compensate for our own.

That afternoon I stood by the new Romayon printing machine. Her poems had been set, but they had not yet been printed. I ran my fingers over the metal ingots. I placed the galley trays. I turned the switch. The metal began to roll. Its dark and constant rhyme. I couldn't now give it a meaning even if I wanted to, the cogs caught and the rollers spun, and I betrayed her.

Under the mackling hum, I tried to convince myself that with a book, a bound book, she might still be able to rescue her people—they would not blame her, or banish her, she'd become their conscience and the rest of us would listen and understand, we'd study her poems in school, she'd travel the country, her words would bring her people back onto the road, the ones in the settlements would walk up through their towns without being spat on, and she would return that dignity, it would finally come together, simply, elegantly, and we would all be given a row of red medals to wear upon our chests.

It is astounding how terrifying words can be. No act is too shallow so long as we give it a decent name.

I worked on in a sweat and a fury. A memory gaffed me. I saw those young guards who had beaten the bottoms of my feet when I first crossed the border. They sat on the back of the flatbed trucks, waiting. I felt myself back on the train with Stránský, about to move, and then I heard two clear pistol shots ring out in the air.

By early morning the first of the poems was rolling off the press. I looked up at the light in Kysely's office. He was peeking through the blinds. He nodded, raised his hand, smiled.

I climbed the stairs towards the cutting machines, the weight of her work in my hands.

~

The heart's old furniture, watch it burn. I lie here now and my leg has healed enough to know that it will never really heal. Just a few days ago, after she was banished by her own people, I went searching for her. I met some farmers in a field near Trnava. They said they had seen her, and that she was walking east. There was no reason to believe them—they were working fields that were no longer their own, and they were nervous at the sight of me. The youngest had the clipped speech of one well educated. He mumbled "Siberia" under his breath, said it could be seen from the tallest tree around, I should climb up and take a look. He struck a shovel into the ground and threw a clod back over his shoulder.

As I drove away I thought that I would, without hesitation, do that work now: go into a field not my own and strike down deep into it.

I only wish I could astonish with some last-page grace. But what should I do? Stay here and read aloud my ration book? Sit down and write a revolutionary opera?

I asked Stránský once if there would be music in the dark times, and he said, yes, there had always been music in the dark times, because that's what they mostly are, dark times. He had seen the hills of rotting corpses and they did not speak back to him.

Yet there are moments I can name and miss—I will miss the tall trees around the wagons, the way the harps sounded when the wheels moved, the soaring hawks around the lakes when her kumpanija pulled out to the road. I will miss her wandering around the machinery in the mill, touching her fingers against the smudges of ink, reciting the older songs, changing them, restoring them. I will miss the way she pinched her dress with her fingers whenever she passed a man she did not know, the slight skip in her younger step, the quiver of the two moles at the base of her neck when she sang. And I will miss the urgent swerve of her Romani, the way she said "Comrade," how full and alive it felt, and I will miss the poems though they are stacked within me still.

To be where I am now is the whole of it. The days will not get any brighter. I do not seek to imagine what echo my words will find. Kysely knocked on my door yesterday when I didn't appear for work five days in a row. He gave a thin little smile as he looked me up and down and said: "Tough shit, son, you have a job to do."

And so I am off, now, on my crutches, towards the mill.

Czechoslovakia—
Hungary—Austria

1959-1960

For a long time now the road has been deserted. Vineyards and endless rows of pines. She steps along the grass verge between the mudtracks, her sandals sodden, her feet raw. At a slight bend she is surprised by a low stone wall and, through a stand of young saplings, a small wooden hut. No horse. No car tracks. No roof smoke. She walks beyond the trees to the edge of the hut, forces the door, peers inside. Dead winter grass lies in the cracks of the planks. Pieces of winecrate, empty buckets, shriveled leaves. The door hangs off its wooden hinges, but the roof is strong and arched, and might keep the worst of the weather out.

Zoli pauses at the threshold a moment, framed between light and shadow.

A cracked sink stands in the corner, a trickle from its tap. When she opens the spigot, the pipes rattle and groan. She holds her hand under the drip for it to pool and fill, then drinks from her palm, so thirsty that she can feel the water falling through her body.

She bends to remove her sandals. The layers of flesh tear and flap. The skin smarts most at the edges where the dead meets the living. She swings one foot up into the sink but, in the solitary drip, can only massage the dirt deeper into her wounds. Zoli pushes the bunched skin back into place, crosses the floor, leans against the wall, lays her head on the floor, cold against the side where her jaw aches.

She sleeps erratically, woken at times by the heavy rain and the wind outside, making the trees swing and rear and canter. The noise on the roof sounds to her like a drum she was once given as a child—it is as if she has stepped inside the hollowness of it.

From the darkest corner of the hut, she hears a series of skittering noises. Across the narrow expanse a single brown rat looks at her with curiosity. Zoli hisses the rat away but it returns with a mate. It sits on its hindlegs, licking its forepaws. The second darts forward, stops, touches its long tail against the face of the first, draws a lazy circle with its body. Zoli hammers her sandal on the ground. The rats twitch, turn, return, but she slaps the shoe off the metal windowframe and the rats scamper to the dark corner. Zoli fumbles in the hut to collect leaves, sticks, and bits of crate. She builds them into a small teepee, shakes out the cap of her lighter, cups her hands around the kindling, blows it to flame. When the rats peek out again she slides lit spears of twig across the floor, one after the other, bouncing shards of light. The twig ends burn slowly, scorching the wooden boards.

She waits, head slumped against the wall—how strange this desire to stay alive, she thinks, how easy, with no integrity nor purity, simply a function of habit.

In the morning she wakes panicked. The rats are nowhere to be seen, though fresh pellets lie in patterns beyond her feet.

A gray reef of light climbs up and around the window. From the top of the pane to the bottom, she watches a raindrop slide. An acute wave of nausea hits her. She presses her thumb against her lower jaw. Her mouth feels riven, her jaw huge. The pain shoots along her jaw, to her neck, her shoulderblades, her arms, her fingers. She reaches for the tooth with the tip of her tongue, rocks it back and forth, waiting for the roots to snap. The tooth shifts in her gum, but does not lift. She heaves again, dryly, nothing in her stomach anymore. I have been many days on the road, she thinks, and have not eaten a single thing.

At the judgment, three nights before, the congress said that she was weak, that she did not have the strength of body or mind, and they sentenced her to Pollution for Life in the Category of Infamy for the Betrayal of Romani Affairs to the Outsiders.

She wonders now if she has discovered what it means to be blind: she can see nothing before her that she wishes to enjoy, and little behind that she cares to remember.

~

It happened so quickly and she accepted it without question. She was ushered into the center of the tent and made to stand. They checked for metal in her hair that might absorb the ruling. The elder krisnitoria sat in a half-ring on crates and chairs. Five coal-oil lamps were placed in a semicircle around them. They stood and invoked the ancestral dead, the lamplight flickering on their faces as each spoke in turn, an even pitch of accusation. The crossing and uncrossing of feet. The blue curl of tobacco smoke.

Vashengo stood and asked if she understood the charges. She had betrayed her people, he said, she had told of their affairs, brought unrest down upon them. He spat on the ground. He looked like a man in a state of gentle decay, water left stagnant in a pail. Zoli pinched the front of her dress, felt the weight of pebbles sewn in her hem. She talked of settlement and change and the complicated sorrow of the old days, of which she had often sung, of the hewers of tin and the drawers of water, of stencils of smoke and fire that tightened the skin, of patterns and snapped twigs, of the sound of wood against the land, of roads and signs, of nights on the hills, making from broken things what was newly required, how the gadže used words, delegations, institutions, rules, of how she had misunderstood them, how they had hastened the dark, of brotherhood, decency, tower-blocks, wandering, of how these things would be felt amongst the souls of the departed, of wisdom, whispered names, things not to be repeated, of her grandfather, how he was waiting, watching, silent, gone, of what he had believed and what that belief had become, of water turning backwards, banks of clay, snowfall, sharp stones, of how they could still only call her black even after she had been soaked in whiteness.

It was the longest speech she had ever made in her life.

A riffle of whispers went around the tent. As they conferred, Vashengo lit a cigarette with brown hands and studied the lit end deeply. Another cough and a silence. He was the one designated to speak. He still wore his cufflinks coined from red bicycle reflectors. He lit a match off his fingernail so that it looked as if fire was springing from his hand. He sat, tunneling mud from his boot with a stick, gripped his nose between his thumb and forefinger and blew, wiped his hand on his trousers which were lined, on the seam, with oval silver studs. He stood up, neck cords tight, walked towards her. The sound of his voice was redundant, for she knew the punishment already. Vashengo slapped her face with the back of his hand. Something gentle lay in his slap, but one of the rings on his fingers caught her jawbone. She turned her face in the direction of the blow, kept her head to her shoulder.

Nobody would ever eat with her now. Nobody would walk with her. If she touched any Romani thing it would be destroyed, no matter what value: horse, table, dish. When she died, nobody would bury her. She would not have a funeral. She could not come back, even as a spirit. She could not haunt them. They would not talk of her, they could not even mention her: she had betrayed the life and she was beyond dead, not Gypsy, not gadži, nothing at all.

Zoli was told to close her eyes as Vashengo ushered her out of the camp. Her late grandfather's breathing came in behind her: in it, the sounds of years. The other elders did not touch her, but instead they guided her with the sound of their boots. All the children had been taken inside. She glanced at Conka's caravan, the chopped wheels making it list sideways. A corner of the curtain trembled and a half-shadow shot back. If I could take all my foolishness and put it in your hands, piramnijo, you would be bowed over for the rest of your life. None of the other women were looking out: they had been told not to, otherwise they too would feel the hand.

It was close to morning and a thin line of cloud had appeared on the eastern rim of the sky. In the distance stood a few warehouses, more stray towers, and an emptiness of hills, stretching beyond. No place seemed more or less sheltered than any other. It was then that she had begun to walk.

~

In the morning she stands, gripping the doorframe, staring out at the puddled vineyard, the terraced slopes, and the mist of middle-distance where a sheet of gray hangs across the low Carpathian hills. She has, she thinks, become unused to such a clean silence: only the wind and the rain and her own breathing. For an hour she waits for the rain to slacken, but it doesn't, so she hikes her belongings, pulls her scarf over her head, and walks out into the downpour.

She stops and pulls the sleep from her eye, eats the small yellow deposit from the tip of her finger.

Close to the road, she clambers over a stone stile towards the pine forest. Raindrops bell down from the branches and fall to the forest floor. She bends to fill her skirt pockets with brittle needles, pinecones, dry twigs, and carries them all, bundled in her zajda, back towards the hut.

At the doorway she throws the bundle in a heap to the middle of the floor. She shakes the lighter for fuel—enough for a week or two perhaps—and builds the fire using broken wine-crate. When it is lit, she drops the pinecones into the flames and waits for them to crack open. She touches her swollen jaw, quite sure the seeds will break her bad tooth and dislodge it altogether, but when she bites down into one, her front tooth quivers.

I will not lose my front teeth. Of all things, I will not lose those.

She hunkers down, eating. What might it be like to stay like this forever, she wonders, moving back and forth between forest and hut, over the empty field, through the colorless rain, eating pine seeds, watching the flame crackle? To lie on the floor and slip down into the boards, to wake again in silence, saying nothing, recalling nothing, with not a soul in sight, to have her name pass silently into the walls of the hut?

Zoli feels her stomach churn. She gathers the folds in her dress, shoves open the door and hurries to the stone wall. She pulls down her undergarments, the cold grass brushing against her skin. She steadies herself against the wall, one arm draped around the rock. Her stomach gives. The stench of her insides. She turns her head to her shoulder, away from the filth.

A huge brown dog stands lantern-eyed at the far end of the wall. The dog raises its head and howls, the rheumy folds of skin above its eyes shaking.

Zoli hikes her dresses, slips on the top stone of the wall. The stone scrapes the length of her knee. Her feet slosh in the muck. By the time she reaches the road the dog is already nosing in her filth and raw seeds.

She pulls her overcoat tight around her and hurries down the road, sandals slapping, away from the hut. She crosses another stone wall and sits with her back against it, chest heaving. Small swallows scissor soundlessly through the trees. No signs of houses or horsecarts. She rests awhile and recleans herself with wet grass, wipes her hands clean, swings her legs over the wall.

A larger road, this, blacktopped, long, straight.

The rain stops and she walks the shining tarmacadam in a spell of lavish winter sunlight. Her sandals squelch and rub her torn feet. I am, she thinks, a twenty-nine-year-old woman walking like one already grown old. She touches her chest with the fingers of her right hand and stretches her spine long. Her coat feels wet and heavy and an idea comes, almost comforting in its simplicity—I should just drape it over my arm. Lightheaded, she negotiates the middle of the road. All about her are long rows of vines, sheds from the collectives, and, in the distance, the mountains standing simple against the sky.

At a bend she stops to look at a lump in the roadway behind her. A thing, a person, a body, in the road. She pulls deep into the brambles. How did I step past a body in the road? How could I possibly miss it? She pushes herself further into the hedge, branches crisscrossed in front of her. How did I fail to see a dead person lying there? She waits for a sound, any sound—a vehicle, a rifle shot, a moan—but nothing comes. She hooks her fingers around the strand of bushes to look again: the body lies flat and dark and prone in the roadway.

"Idiot," she says aloud to herself.

Zoli climbs from the bushes and wearily trudges back to pick up the dropped coat. It lies on the roadway in a sprawl, one arm outstretched as if pointing in another direction.

~

A rumble of engines as she passes the gates of a collective farm. Zoli pulls herself down into the long ditch grass. The engines grow loud until they are almost upon her, and she is surprised to see truckloads of young Czechoslovakian troopers going past, rifles held across their chests, faces darkened with shadow, cheeks hollowed as if they have been blown out with tiny explosives. Not a word from them. Staring ahead in the cold. All these young men, she thinks, hardened by long wars and short memories. The same ones who took us down the road, who sprinkled petrol on the wheels, who led the horses away to the farms, who sat outside the National Theater the night Stránský read my poems. The same ones who saluted me at the all-weather posts as I passed in the snow. One of them once had a copy of *Credo* rolled up in his uniform pocket.

She shivers as the squadron sprays by, leaving tire tracks on the wet of the road.

A sudden sound startles her: like gunfire at first but she turns to see geese rising up by the hundreds from the fields, cutting a dark vee against the sky.

Pollution for Life. In the Category of Infamy. It seems possible now to Zoli that she is walking in some terrible otherness, that she is not out in these wet winter fields, cast off from everything, but instead she is standing at the point where she was, long ago, before the poems, before the printings, before Swann, before Stránský, and for a moment she is like one who believes that to continue a good dream you must lie in the exact same place you fell asleep, so she might somehow be able to drift back into days that once had been, where there were no poems, just songs, a step back into the ordinary territory of the ago, before the gatherings and the meetings and the conferences and directives, before the flashbulbs and the microphones, the openings and ovations. To become nothing at all, she thinks, a mind capable of nothing, a body capable of nothing, an escape backwards to a time when things were half-considered, inconsequential.

She had only meant for it to be good, for it to pierce the difference between stars and ceilings, but it did not, and now the words were shaped, carved, placed—they had become fact.

I have sold my voice, she thinks, to the arguments of power.

~

Caution, No Entry. She pulls aside one of the boards and peers inside. A tiny concrete shrine, only big enough to kneel in. All of the religious paraphernalia has been removed and the stone arch of the altar carefully drilled out. She searches for a candlestub left by some Citizen. A couple of gray feathers lie amid the dirt piles, and a spider toils in the upper rafters, moving towards a small sliver of leaf at the edge of the web.

The bracket pops in the top of the wooden boards as she squeezes her way inside.

She sits awhile in the driest corner. A holy cross is scratched in the front wall of the shrine, and she puts her finger to her lip, touches the cross, then places her head on her bundled zajda and dozes in the safety of the shrine. How many travelers have passed over this cold floor? How many incantations? How many people beseeching God to make two plus two not equal four?

She is woken later, startled by the sound of an airplane. Outside, the brightness stings her eyes. A line of jet-smoke in the sky.

By early afternoon beads of sweat shine on her forehead and a dizziness propels her. I must find a stream to plunge my head into, some moving water to take this fever away. But she can find no sound of running streams along the road, only bird-song and wind among the trees. She reaches a small tarmac road where a pile of chainsawed trees lie stacked like corpses. She turns as a large truck approaches, muck spraying up from the wheels. The horn blares long and loud. She stands, unmoving, as the truck bears down. The hum of the tires. The grill almost upon her, silver and slatted, light and dark. The horn blasts yet again. She closes her eyes and the wind sucks her close. Spray from the wheel splatters her face, and the driver screams out the window as the truck passes no more than a half meter from where she stands. She watches it go. The truck grows smaller against the road, a last light twinkling from its roof as it rounds a corner.

It would, she thinks, have been just as easy to have stepped out in front of it.

She returns the way she came and sits under a giant syca-more, pulls a fistful of yellowed grass from the ground and puts it in her mouth against her aching tooth. She removes her overcoat and ties the arms together around her waist. It was Swann who gave her the coat a year ago. He had returned from Brno with a whole cardboard box of them balanced precariously on his motorbike. He had bought them for the kumpanija and had even found small sizes for the children. He could not understand her when she said no, that she did not want them, that she'd just as soon walk around with a yellow armband, or a truncheon stuck in her back. Swann sat in the wooden chair by his window, perplexed: "But it's not charity, Zoli, it's just a few coats, that's all." He remained silent then, tapping the glass pane, his light hair framing his face. She crossed the room and said: "I'll take one each for Conka's children." He brightened and sifted through the pile to find the right sizes. "One for you too," he said, and put it around her, and as he touched her shoulders, he said that he had found a consignment of red shirts also. What strange laughter had come to her then, the idea of the whole kumpanija wandering down the road in the exact same cheap red shirts.

Yet what was once funny turned out to be inevitable; what was once strange was, now, finally, true.

Zoli feels as if she is carrying the sandy-haired Englishman on her back. Impossible to shuck him. She wonders how long she might walk before the weight of him drags her down, again, to the ground. He told her once that she looked like a Russian poet he had seen in photographs: the dark eyes, high forehead, her hair swept back, her tall body, her complicated stare. He brought her to the National Library and showed her the poet, Akhmatova, though she could see no resemblance. She had always thought herself dark, simple, black, yet in the photos the Russian woman looked white, heavy-eyed, and beautiful. Swann read to her a line about standing as witness to the common lot. He had asked her if she would marry him and she was stunned by the simplicity of his plea. She had loved him then, but he did not know the extent of the impossible. In the printing mill, at the end, he was not able to hold her gaze. He had not printed the poems yet, but she knew he would. What else had she expected? Where happiness was not a possibility, the illusion of it was always more important. Wasn't it Swann who told her once about a bird, a glukhar, that went deaf with its own mating calls? Both of us with that inextinguishable need to make noise, she thinks. If only I could have known. If only I could have seen.

Zoli wonders now if Swann is searching for her now. If he is, she thinks, he will not find me. He will seek and seek. He will wander the ends of the earth and return with nothing, not even a name.

Zoli clambers over a gate, down a hill, through a muddy field, where some irrigation pipes are laid out on the ground. She tries to figure a way to make it across the field: a maze of tubes and muck with a barbed-wire fence at the far end. The vast concrete sleeves have sunk a little in the mud, and the only way to cross is to walk along the top of the pipes, arms held wide for balance. She slips, her leg in the mud up to her ankle. She lifts it out noisily, cleans her sandal on the rough edge of the pipe, kneels down into the opening and looks into the hollowness of it, imagines her breath traveling all the way around the field, circling and returning, added to by the grasses and the muck.

"Hey, Gyp."

A muffled shout. She is sure it must be distant, but it comes again. She turns, startled. Behind a hedge on the hill, four children sit crouched and staring. Three retreat immediately, turning their backs to flee, but the oldest remains steady, facing her. "Hey, Gyp," he says again. Brownish hair and a broad band of freckles across his nose. Mudmarks across the front of his trousers. A stare in his eyes so much like Conka's youngest. He is wearing a jacket so big that he could fit two more boys inside.

The other children top the hill and call back to him. He lets out a long arc of spit which lands a meter in front of her, then turns and gallops up the slope.

They will bring back the adults, thinks Zoli. Cite me for trespassing. Bring a sergeant to arrest me. Fingerprint me. Find out who I am. Take me back to the city. Place me in front of my people again, shame me, humiliate me. Banish me once more.

She scrambles across the pipes and up the hill, each step a half-step backwards into the last.

～

A wooden stake scrapes her ankle and she stops in midfurrow, looks up, catches sight of a wooden roof. So here I am. I have walked all day and have come full circle, and am back in the vineyard once again. I could just as easily be anywhere else. I have spent another day walking, and what else is there to do? Nothing else. If there has been a pencil beneath me it would have made great, useless circles.

She stumbles past the young saplings, pushes the door of the hut open. On the floor lies the small round scorch mark of her fire from the night before. She nudges a piece of scorched winecrate with the sole of her bloody sandals. From the floor a small light twinkles, a shard of mirror no bigger than her palm. Zoli wonders how she had not noticed it yesterday. She lifts the shard to her eyes and sees immediately that her jaw has swollen terribly. The whole of her right cheek is puffy, her neck bloated, her right eye almost shut. I must deal with the tooth now. Be done with it. Pull it out.

In a corner she finds a single boot, the lace still intact. It is against all custom to touch the boot, another small betrayal, unclean, taboo, but she yanks at the lace until it pulls through, scattering small flakes of dried mud. She rubs the lace in her fingers to warm it, holds it beneath the dripping pipe to moisten the fabric. She makes a loop in the string, reaches into her mouth, hooks the tooth and draws in a sharp breath, yanks hard upwards, tries not to dry-heave. She feels the roots being dragged up from the bottom of her jawbone. Eyes full of tears. Blood falling now from her mouth to her chin. She wipes it away, head to her shoulder, closes her eyes, hauls again. Darkness.

The tooth rises and tears and for a moment she sees little Woowoodzhi, feverish against a tree, a nail perfectly inserted between his handbones, and he is gone, then back again, feverish once more, and she tugs harder, his small face dissolving.

A sound rips through her jawbone like the tearing of paper, and the tooth lifts.

~

In the morning she feels for the gap with the edge of her tongue. The wound is large and she wonders if she should try to sear it shut, sterilize it with her lighter. She rises to rinse her mouth out in the trickle from the tap. She lifts the tooth from the sink, dark and rotten at its base, the roots clotted and fibrous.

On the wall above the sink, there is a perfect trapeze of light from the rising sun. She watches it crawl, like something breathing, until another long shadow passes within the box of light, and Zoli drops the tooth with a clank.

A farmer stands in the field outside, the rheumy-eyed dog at his heels. A face like a Hlinka guard: thick eyebrows and small eyes and a neck with skinfolds. A long burlap sack lies at his feet; a shotgun clasped alongside his leg. He taps the gun against his high rubber boots, then hitches it to his waist and steps forward, moves out of the range of the window.

Zoli hears the clicking of dog nails, the turn of a boot at the entrance. She waits for him to come in, push the door open, put the shotgun to her neck and take her while the dog watches. The same dog, she thinks, that nosed in my own filth. She slides to the floor, brings her knees to her chest, tries to hold her breath. No movement, no sound, and she goes to the doorway. Her fingers reach around the frame and she pushes it gently, waits for the click of the gun or the thud of his fist in her face. The door swings open further and she peers around the frame.

Small acts of kindness.

Outside, the farmer has left two bread rolls and a tin cup, half-filled with black tea. So what if others have drunk from it? I will drink it anyway. She picks it up and sips, and for a split second she wonders if it has, perhaps, been poisoned.

She drinks the rest quickly, tucks the tin cup into the pocket of her skirt, touches the bread against her lips and inhales its freshness.

From the window, the farmer and dog are nowhere to be seen. Zoli rips a chunk of the bread and puts it in her mouth, then tongues it into her gum to soak up the last of the blood. At the window, only the same emptiness of trees and vineyard. She wipes a coatsleeve across her brow. Her forehead is dry and un-fevered now, and in the shard of mirror her face has already begun to lose its swelling. Did I walk all day yesterday or did I just dream it? She digs deep in the fabric of her pocket, finds a pine nut and rolls it in her palm. In what sort of chance universe have I been brought back to a place where there is a waterpipe and a loaf of bread? In what curious conjunction of fever and road have I been allowed such generosity?

She eats half the farmer's bread and places the remainder in her zajda. Then, with a start, she remembers the rats: they will nibble right through the cloth to get at the least crumb. Zoli shunts upwards with one foot on the windowframe and places the remaining bread on a crossbeam. She pushes it further along the beam with a twig. No good, she thinks, the rats will follow from beam to beam, she has seen their like before. She goes up on her toes and knocks the bread down from the beam. With her headscarf, Zoli loops what is left of the loaf, then reaches up to tie the strange-looking bundle from an iron nail in the ceiling beam.

For a long time she will recall herself by this: the loaf of bread, the ancient scarf, the spin of both in the air.

~

Years ago Conka got hold of a radio, one that used a wind-up handle. It worked for no more than thirty seconds at a time and then the signal faded, but in the middle of a wet afternoon, when the kumpanija was traveling near Jarmociek, a recording came over the radio, a broadcast from Prague. The horses were hauled short near a small stream and were taken to be watered. Everyone sat listening to the radio, silent while Conka's husband wound the handle and Zoli's voice came through.

Later, while the horses were shaking out their manes, the

youngest, Bora, climbed up on Zoli's lap and asked how was it possible for her to be in both places, inside the radio and on the road, at the exact same time. She had laughed then, they all laughed, and Conka pushed her fingers through Bora's hair. But something lay behind it, Zoli knew, even then: both places at once, radio and road, impossible alongside the other.

～

She wakes to the smallest one turning, face twitching. The other follows, fluent, waterlike. Nose to the floor, it whips across the boards to join its mate, both grown bold. Zoli backs into the corner and throws twigs across the floor, then builds three small makeshift fires in a ring around her, flings lit pine needles towards the rathole.

She wonders what it might look like from the outside: the little wooden shed half-aglow in the darkness, tiny spears of light rolling across the floor.

The morning rises along the windowledge. A long barrier of cloud is sliced by the movement of a tree branch in the wind. She looks down the length of her body. Her skirts are torn and there are small lumps of dried dirt at her knees. Her feet, still blood-raw and filthy. She stands, lifts her skirts. It is not right, she thinks, immodest, but it does not matter, I am not what I used to be. She rips a strip of white cloth from the underdress and folds it over, places it snugly at the back of her shoe. She tests it out, stepping lightly across the floor. *Marime,* unclean, but it works well and her feet feel cushioned. She leans over again and slowly lifts her dress once more, then hears, from outside, a rapping. The knock on the door is gentle yet it takes her breath away.

Only gadže knock.

She backs into the corner and sits, looking at the fire-marks beneath her, spreads her dresses over to hide them. Two more series of triple knocks. A grunt and a whisper, then rifle fire, she is sure it is rifle fire until she recognizes the high bark of a dog. The door is slowly pushed open and the dog comes through, arcing its body. It snaps at the end of a rope, bares its teeth. Light spreads sideways into the hut. The farmer and a woman stand in the doorway, made into portrait by shadow.

The woman holds the shotgun and the farmer hovers behind her. Zoli wonders how they have made their silent approach, then notices that the dog has been muzzled: the contraption is hanging down in the farmer's hand.

The woman stands gray-haired, sturdy, much older than the farmer. She wears a housedress many sizes too small. Her breasts swing low to her belly. She shouts at the dog to quieten. The dog whimpers and the hair roaches momentarily along its back. The woman looks around, finger still on the trigger of the gun. She glances at the burnt twig-ends and the small teepee of ashes, the one empty sandal in the middle of the floor.

Spreading back the loop of Zoli's skirts with her foot, she bends down and examines her face.

The long hairs on the woman's chin, the flare-out of her nose, the tiny twitch of her mouth, the smokeblue of her neck, the very green of her eyes, narrow, like the wick-slot of a lamp.

She tilts the gun, lifts Zoli's chin. "We have laws here," she says. "We have curfew." The barrel touches, cold, against Zoli's throat.

"Are you going far? Hey. Gypsy woman. I am talking to you. Do you hear me?"

"Yes."

"Are you going far?"

"Yes."

"Where?"

"I'm not sure, Comrade."

"Are there many of you?"

"Just me."

"The first snow in a blizzard comes from nowhere," says the woman.

"It's just me, only me."

"If you're not telling me the truth I'll tell the troopers."

"It's the truth."

"I can swallow hot rocks easier than I can the word of a Gypsy."

The woman turns to the farmer with some silent gesture. He grins at Zoli, shuffles outside. A brief darkness until the door creaks open once more. He stands under the frame, carrying a plate covered with a towel. He grins again, leans across, exchanging the plate for the shotgun. The woman sighs, lifts the towel from the plate, and spreads the food on the floor in front of Zoli: cheese, bread, salt, and five homemade biscuits. A small dollop of yellow jam sits on the side of the plate with some butter. The woman hesitates a moment, takes a knife from her dress pocket, and lays it sideways on the edge of the plate.

"You can't stay here," she says, flattening out the edges of the tea towel with a picture of a cathedral on it. "Do you hear me? You cannot stay."

The farmer lumbers outside once more and comes back carrying a wicker-bound wine jug. He sets the jug on the floor, stamps his boot, and yanks the dog by the rope-leash.

"It's just a little something," says the woman. "Go ahead, eat. Drink. The milk is fresh."

The farmer crosses the floor and reaches up for the lace and bread hanging from the ceiling, then looks across into the sink where Zoli's tooth sits in the metal drainhole.

"My son doesn't speak," says the old woman. "He's mute. Do you understand?"

The farmer stares at Zoli, the grin splayed from ear to ear.

"He came home yesterday waving his arms. I didn't believe him, trying to tell me there's a woman out walking in the rain. But he was up early this morning, cooking. Supposed to be hunting goose but he's cooking breakfast instead. Burned the first four batches. Jesus of sweet heaven. He's never once cooked before, never in his life, not even for his mother. Cooking for a Gypsy. I slapped him. Look at the size of him. I slapped him. But there's one good thing I like about your people. You steal a chicken, you steal a chicken. The others, they come in, they steal all your chickens and don't even call it stealing. I am sure you know what I mean. I'm too old for double-talk. I suppose they'll put me in the cold ground for it. You go ahead and eat now. There are no five-year plans on that bread."

Zoli pulls the plate towards her. The edge of the tea towel rumples.

"Are you not hungry?"

The woman rises from the floor and takes her son's elbow: "Let the woman eat in holy peace. Look at her. She wants to eat in peace."

"I bow deeply before you, Comrade," says Zoli.

The woman blanches: "I don't expect you to be here when we return."

"No."

"Nor to ever return."

"No."

"I wish you a good journey. You can take the knife, the jug. The towel if you like it."

"I kiss your kind hands."

"I would not have used them," says the woman.

She guides her son towards the door of the hut and the dog follows, head bent low. They leave the door swinging open and the farmer turns slowly to look behind, his sloping walk, the tap of the gun against his leg. What curious destiny has brought him along the road, thinks Zoli, not once, but twice in his tall and lumbering silence?

They make their way towards the line of the trees and a gap in the stone wall, the farmer still looking fondly over his shoulder.

He grins and extends his hand: in his palm rolls the white and dark of Zoli's gone tooth.

～

Zoli watches as mother and son become pale shapes against the land. She reaches out for one of the biscuits. It still holds, at its center, a touch of warmth. She smears the jam with her finger. The milk runs cold against the back of her throat. The butter she eats on its own, in one go. She wraps the shard of mirror in her pocket, carefully swaddling the tip so it will not pierce her, slides the knife into her rope belt, twisting it so that it hangs like a gewgaw. She folds the towel with its cathedral piercing a false blue sky. The plate she will leave behind.

She turns to take a look at the small hut—the laceless boot, the bent grass between floorboards, the scorch marks—and she touches her left breast. For the first time since judgment, Zoli feels a pulse of strength: she will return now to the city and leave nothing behind, not even a trace.

As she moves out, across the stone wall, onto the tarmac, she has the sudden feeling that if a truck screams down the roadway now she will undoubtedly be able to stand out of its way.

2

ZOLI SHAMBLES DOWN the footpath, in the shadows of the pines, under their tall, lamenting sway. She moves against the current of the river until she reaches the Red Army Bridge, wind-bitten and vapory in the morning. Behind her, chains of smoke rise from the outlying factories and, further still, the curve of distant hills against the sky. The Danube shines, skeins of oil floating on the surface. A wheat barge, toiling upstream, lets out a high whistle.

Across the river sits the old town of Bratislava: the castle on the hill, the chimneys, the cathedral.

Zoli hobbles out from under the steel girdings, over weeds sprouting from cinder and muck, up the grassy embankment. At the top of the bank, the wind blows cold and fast. Early traffic thrums past and the bridge shakes. Two men labor with a broken-down car, one at the rear, the other at the driver's window, guiding the steering wheel.

Zoli pulls her kerchief tight across her face.

On the far side of the bridge she cleans her hands in a small puddle and dries them on a lamppost poster, a Russian circus announcement, red and yellow with curled Cyrillic. Two trapeze artists swing at the top of the poster, blond women stretching out towards one another in the air. Rain has bubbled underneath and swollen their bodies. At the bottom of the poster, a ringmaster, a hoop on fire, and a dancing bear. How I used to love them, those dancing bears in their roped circles, heavy-

pawed and majestic, brought from far away. They came lurching through Trnava square, red-hatted and shit-smeared, into
the shadows cast down from churches. The music was wound
by the carnival man on the painted box, and the tambourine
was struck and we shouted for our favorite songs: *I have two
wives, one of them sober, one of them drunk, both of them I love
the same*. Old men stood away from streetcorners, shopkeepers
closed their doors, and women stood up from pail and rag. All
around the square was the hum and bustle of merchants, with
the local crier, the policemen, the schoolchildren.

Zoli edges her finger along the paper to where it bunches at
her fingertips.

She turns from the lamppost, crosses the road onto a small
pebbled footpath. A squeal of brakes as a car swerves towards
the footpath. She turns quickly. A shower of mud. The car horn
beeps as one of the men from the bridge leans out and leers at
her.

"Shit on you," she says quietly when they are far enough
away. She wipes the muck from her cheek.

At the underpass, swarms of men and women from the early
shifts walk towards work, their shoes slapping against the pavement. Most of them wear identical blue hats of the armament
factory, and, as they descend, they merge into the same stream
of color.

Across the square, past the bare winter trees, she passes the
Carlton Hotel, where men in the dark overcoats of the security
police trundle back and forth. She shudders at the thought of
stepping inside: the silver door handles, the huge paintings, the
gilded frames, the beveled mirrors, the curving staircase. How
foreign it is now, the columns, the pillars, the plastic plants in

the windows. There used to be applause when I entered the front rooms. They would hold their cigarettes to their mouths and squint. The soft-faced women would nod and whisper. Always the feeling that they were looking right through me, past me, anxious to be with anybody but themselves. The way they smoked, as if it would never belong to them. How loud it was when stepping from the carpet to the tiled floor. Something galloping under my ribs. Looking for Swann, his familiar face. He used to arrive hours beforehand just so I'd not feel nervous, waiting there with his hat tapping against his thigh, a copy of *Rudé právo* rolled up in his pocket.

A low swing of sadness in her belly, Zoli crosses away from the hotel and up the hill, into the short and vaulted alleyways of the old city. A banner is strung between lampposts: *Citizens, We Must Conserve Bread*. It flaps and twists in the breeze, and, as she gets nearer, one end of the banner snaps, curtsies a moment, falls to the ground, and sags in the cobblestone puddles. She steps over the slogan, walks on, hand trailing the lichen on the walls.

Quieter here, darker: the light gone out of things.

She moves along the rutted path, in the shadows, hidden especially from the troopers. If she dawdles they will stop her, cock their rifles, question her, the mud on her overcoat, the dark bloodstains on her ankles, and then bring her to the nearest all-weather post. Flip open the gray cover and examine the raised stamp of her Party card, the thumbprint, the details: 169.5 cm, black eyes, black hair, distinguishing feature a lazy left eye, a 2 cm scar on lower right lip, chin dimple, poet. She used to sign her name with three Xs, and the most perceptive of them used to ask her why. If she replied at all she would simply shrug her shoulders, making them more difficult, more prob-ing, more insistent: "But how can you be a poet and sign XXX?" Often the whole transaction would have to wait for confirmation over the radio: "That's Comrade Novotna, you idiot, let her go."

Past the flaking wall of an old city monastery, sandals slap-ping against the cobblestones. The monastery has long been gutted. What remnants of incense, stained glass, wax candles? What small ruby flames still burn behind pier glass? She looks up to see a number of narrow window slots in the upper reaches of the building, near the timbered roof. Birds fly in the win-dows, wings held together, and flare out again seconds later into the sky.

In the drizzle, she notices a group of young boys standing in her path. Their ease, their nonchalance. At the end of the line, one boy toes at the carcass of a dead pigeon. The boy is white-skinned. Red-shirted. Hair shorn close. He flicks the pigeon with his boot and it sails a moment in the air, thuds on the cob-bles with a spray of tiny feathers. Zoli pulls together the folds in her dress and steps over it. Heart quick and thumping. She hears a whistle behind her, and then the sound of footsteps.

Even when the bird hits her in the back of the head she does not turn.

Past the granite steps and fluted columns of the National Theater. Raindrops fat on the pavement. She can almost hear the voice of Stránský reading her poem aloud to the large crowd, the gray suits, the white shirtfronts, the lifted caps. All that applause. Her name was shouted out to the rafters, but it didn't seem real, it was as if it had been recorded and a button had been pressed in the watchers, and her name was part of their routine. Yet she had bowed in front of them, she had accepted the applause, she had eaten and drunk with them, shook their hands, took their astonishment, allowed it. How long, she wonders, can I remain in the city before someone spots me and tries to make a triumph of me once again? Before they line me up and snap their photographs? Before they ask for another pronouncement? Hell's fire on them, they will not hear me now, they can feed the flames with flutes, I will not bow a second time, no.

She rounds the corner of the theater, beyond the ironwork fence, past the dead winter gardens. In the tenements, gnarled women stare out from behind high windows, their bodies lost to brickwork. At a roadblock she stops cold: four troopers stand scanning the street, billyclubs banging into their hands. Traffic passes by in a muted rumble. Some pedestrians are waved through, raw-looking girls in headscarves and soiled white uniforms. Zoli bends to adjust her sandals, accustomed now to the mess of her feet. She waits until the troopers put their hands up in front of a dark automobile and lean in either window, billyclubs prodding. Breathe softly. Easy. No sudden movement. Beyond the roadblock she goes, careful not to glance at them.

A voice: "Hey, you."

A young soldier taps the butt of his rifle on the cobbles, his voice full of snarl: "Where to, Auntie?"

"Nowhere."

"Nowhere?"

"Just past the market a little way, Comrade."

"That's nowhere?"

"Just up the road a way."

"Identification."

She unties the knots, hikes the zajda from her back and deliberately sifts through the bundle. "Shit," he says, holding his nose. The toe of his boot stamps down hard on the cloth. "Go on, woman, out of here."

The tin cup punches at her spine when she lifts the bundle. Shit on you too, she thinks. Who are you to say I'm filthy? Who are you to ask where I am going? She turns the corner and spits into the gutter. Paris, you idiot, I am going to Paris. Do you hear me? Paris. She has no idea why the city comes to mind, but she strikes her fist against the left side of her chest. Paris. That's where I'm going. Paris.

At the top of the road she slows again, a stitch in her ribcage. A line of forgotten laundry is strung from one side of Galandrova to the other, the wet shirts moving in the wind as if waiting for men to inhabit them. Under the trees, beyond the warehouses, past the printing mill, she goes, staying close to the shadows. She can already smell the ink and hear the sound of the rollers—the fumes make her head reel momentarily.

Swann will be in there now, she thinks, printing government posters behind the blacked-out windows, his fingers stained, his shirt askew, the machines churning around him. *We Salute Our Persecuted American Negro Brothers. Solidarity with Egypt. Czechoslovakians for African Unity. We Must Struggle, Comrades, Against Ignorance and Illiteracy.*

And the one with her face, changed slightly, no lazy eye: *Citizens of Gypsy Origin, Come Join Us.*

~

At the top of the stairs she grips the rail, pauses, walks briskly down the communal corridor. Cambering floorboards. Broken plaster. A faint smell of mold and dust. She walks high-toed, shushing her squelching sandals, turns the door handle, and backs carefully away as it swings on its creaking hinges.

It is a room tuned to Swann—the dark linoleum curling where it meets the wall, a half-empty pewter jug of old čuču on the bedside table, the windowframe rattling in the weather, Marx and Engels each in many different languages. Gramsci, Radek, Vygotsky. Some volumes with their spines taken off, others re-stitched. On a single wall hook hangs a ratty shirt, faded and anonymous. On the floor, orange peels curled and ambered with age. Three fire irons, but no fireplace. The huge pile of overcoats from Brno in the corner. Swann has set up a simple chair for looking out the small window onto the street, four sto-ries below.

From the room above, transistor music filters down, muffled and worn, shot through with the hammering of steampipes.

She flips through the books open on the table—Dreiser, Steinbeck, Lindsay—and rifles through their Slovak equiva-lents, handwriting spidery and blotchy with ink. She pushes the books off the table in one quick sweep. They land cantered on the floor. Beneath the desk lie four containers from the printing mill. She yanks them out and turns them upside down. Pages and pages of Swann's work. Dozens of issues of *Credo*. A few obscure journals from Prague. Some letters. A book about Jack London. A collection of Mayakovsky's poetry. How many times have I heard that name, late at night when the two of them worked in the printing mill, the metal letters scattered all around them? Their laughter as they quoted the poems back and forth. The hollow of desire in my stomach, and another hollow, there, shame. I liked to watch him then, enjoyed it, it seemed so easy. The way he carried his body, the slope of his shoulders, the crackle of his voice. The lines going between him and Stránský, chains, and, later still, the same with my songs, speaking them to one another, quoting them back and forth, taking them, bending them, praising them, making them theirs.

She rips another container out from under the table where it clangs against the leg. A sudden pop of glass. Zoli wheels around but the window is intact and there is nobody at the door, no sound along the corridor. Losing my mind. Imagining things. She turns again and feels a coldness run along her fingers. She looks down, perplexed. Her nails and fingers are stretched out, blue, and for a moment she looks at her hand as if it can't possibly be hers. She rights the fallen inkwell and picks up the pieces of glass scattered near the radiator. The dark liquid gullies in the gap between the floorboards and the hissing pipe.

Zoli wipes her hand on the floorboard and the wood streaks with ink. Her thumbprints on the cardboard, the table, the books themselves. She empties the third and fourth containers into the middle of the floor. Yet more journals and translations, nothing else. She looks up at the sad petals of green wallpaper hanging just below the ceiling. A great pain in her eyeballs, like the pressure of swimming in deep water. Easing herself up from the floor, she catches her finger on a stray piece of inkwell glass. She sucks the splinter out, the ink heavy at the end of her tongue. Stránský, she remembers. Budermice. A cold thread pulls the length of her spine.

She kicks over the table and then she spots, against the wall, a black cardboard trunk with metal latches. Inside, the poems are neatly stacked on top of each other, tied with thick elastic bands, in phonetic Romani and Slovak both. The newer poems are crisp and straight-edged but the older ones have yellowed over the years. So be it. Soon they will be dust.

She hunkers over the suitcase. All the dates, towns, fields, and settlements where they were recorded have been carefully labeled. *By what is broken, what is snapped, I create what is required. When the axe comes to the forest the handle doesn't say I am home. The road is long with sorrow, everywhere twice as wide. They broke, they broke my little brown arm, now my father he cries like the rain.* They are, she realizes, the first thing she has read since the judgment.

She crosses towards the sink and stacks the poems over the drainhole, rubs her thumb along the wheel of Petr's old lighter. The curl of Petr's thumb along it, broad, slow, bringing it to life. Pipesmoke curling out. Him watching Swann. The days slowly slipping away from him. The coughing. The thought that he would soon be gone, spirit. Wandering around, hiding, waiting for Swann, thinking of him, the feel of his fingers over my eyes.

The high flame singes her eyebrows and she steps back, lifts some of the pages from the sink and begins again with a smaller scatter of poems. They take easily. She uses a fork to prop up the edges of the pages, to air them underneath. She inhales the scent as the poems burn and curl. Small pieces of ash float and fall. Zoli toes them into the linoleum where they leave dark stains.

Outside, the city goes about in the cold—tramsound, bus screech, the rain slicing steadily on the windowpane. She looks down onto the alleyway below. A sudden strange thrill runs the length of her body. All the meetings, all the speeches, all the factory visits, the trains, the labor parades, the celebrations, they are gone now, all gone—and only this is mine, this alone, this burning. She turns back into the room and the smoke fills her nostrils, fragrant, taut, sweet. She lifts more poems out of the suitcase and burns them in ever larger groups, flames surviving on flames, yellow to red to blue.

My tooth, she thinks, with half a smile, the way the mute farmer carried my tooth away in the palm of his hand.

Zoli puts the lighter back in her dress pocket: the heat of it traveling through to her skin. She brushes back strands of hair from beneath her kerchief and touches something small behind her ear. A white pigeon feather. She plucks it out and lets it fall to the floor. The early afternoon seems now so far away. When the pigeon hit the back of her head she had wondered for an instant if it had recognized flight, even in death: and then she had judged the thought worthless, vain.

She closes her eyes and exhales long and hard, turns towards the door. "Shit," she says.

The tapes.

She returns and scours the room. Two umbrellas, three cigarette lighters, a snuffbox, a bottle with a ship inside it, a small square of linen decorated with flowers, a series of Soviet pins, a dozen leather bookmarks, a samovar, an English kettle. How can one man have so many useless things? She finds the tapes in a cardboard box underneath his bed—they too are meticulously dated and stamped.

The first spool falls from her fingers, unravels across the floor, long and shiny, catching light in places, as if her voice is going into the corners.

Swann was always so careful to hold the microphone close to her lips when they were out on the road. It had bothered her—not his closeness, she had liked that, it had livened things in her, sent a shiver through her—no, what truly bothered her was the idea that her songs were being taken and put back together again by a machine. When he had played the recording to her it did not sound a bit like her, as if some other Zoli had climbed inside. It captured other sounds too, the tapping of a stick on the ground, the high strike of a match, the creak of a doorframe: it seemed almost ghostly to her; things that she had never noticed in real time had suddenly acquired a weight. She had written one night, by the light of the candle, that small rivers carted up drops as they were never seen before—it was one of her worst poems, even Swann had found it tame, he suggested that it bordered on the bourgeois.

To hell with him, she thinks, to hell, with his hands held in the air, his apology, his sharp face when I slapped him, as if he should have been surprised, his stuttering when we stood in the mill and said he had done all he could do, to hell and high rivers with him.

The tape spins out and she slices it with a kitchen knife, doubling the tape over and cutting it with one quick motion, like gutting a small animal.

Fifteen spools.

Outside, the sky grows steadily darker, winter lying down upon it. Zoli takes the last spool to the window and watches the tape unfurl from her fingers, to the ground, spinning and twisting in the wind and rain. A tail of it catches on the upcurrent and floats on the air.

There go my songs. Good riddance.

She flings the last spool and the disc sails across the courtyard, smacking into the building opposite. From the street below comes a shout and then the delighted shriek of a child. Zoli leans out the window to see a young girl pulling the tape behind her.

Just then, footsteps along the corridor. A tapping on the floor—a truncheon perhaps, or a cane. She looks around, spots the pile of overcoats, steps across the buckled floorboards, and covers herself. How ridiculous. Absurd. I should stand up and walk out, past him, without a word, without recognition. Fuck you, Swann. I will stroll down the stairs and disappear in front of your eyes. Look backwards and curse you. She shifts under the weight of the coats, but then there is the sudden thought of Swann not long ago, out on the road, when they found a children's piano, fixed the pedals with bands of steel, replaced the keys with maple wood. They hung it from the ceiling of her wagon with a giant hook, and Swann had walked behind while the piano played the road, every bump and curve, the microphone held out in front of him.

A turn of the door handle. Shoe studs on the nailheads, the hissing of the radiator valve, the strange clop of his feet. A cane, she thinks. He must be walking on a cane.

A small broken sound comes from his throat as he rummages through the room. A wooden lid is lifted and banged down hard again. Cupboard doors open and close. The mattress flops sadly to the floor. Swann says something in English, a hard guttural noise. She is gripped with a nausea, her fingers clenched, neck rigid. She recalls the feel of his hand against her hip, her back against the bark, the way he rolled her hair around his forefinger, the hard taste of him at the neck, the sweat, the ink. He closes the door with a firm snap.

At the window, she catches sight of Swann rounding the streetcorner, his sandy-haired form disappearing, one of his crutches thrown aside. A long string of tape catches his ankle as he goes, dragging it through the rain.

They were my poems. They belonged to me. They were never yours.

She turns, finds a photo of herself in the corner of his shaving mirror. She tears it into pieces. On the bed she notices an open rosewood box with a silver clasp. Around it, scattered documents, and a balled-up handkerchief. Zoli waits a moment, leans down, and lifts the wooden lid, finds a panel kiltered sideways: a false bottom. Underneath that, a gold watch.

～

Things, he said, cannot wait. They have to be made. What Swann foresaw was a world raised up in an immense arc and everyone beneath it, looking up in admiration. He wanted to take hold of all that was vague and equal and give it form. He constantly rubbed his hands over his scalp so that when he was in the printing mill his hair became the color of whatever poster he was printing. In the café he would sit unaware of people looking at him, streaks of yellow and blue and red under his cap, his hands almost entirely black. He was afraid that he didn't sound Slovak enough, but he gave everything to it, listened to the workers, developed the same accent, strode out with them under their banners. After a while his arguments grew more defined, with stronger edges. It was like watching a piece of wood being carved right in front of her eyes, and she had liked the surprise of it. Certain men in the kumpanija could sculpt a spoon, or a bowl, or a bear at their fingertips—with Swann, he would sometimes create an idea and then hold it out as if it were something she could touch.

He suggested once that she always carry a book around to

defeat their notion of her. Even if she did not read it, the others would see it. That was enough, he said. Just let them see you. Astound them by writing it all down.

As if books could stop the massacres. As if they could be somehow more than harps or violins.

~

From the arch of the doorway hangs a red velvet rope-pull, the tasseled end cold to the touch. A woman in an embroidered dress answers, her feet in slippers, hair in a blue string net. She leans out the door, looks down the length of the alleyway, and in one quick movement pulls Zoli inside.

"Yes?"

"I have some things."

"I do not trade," says the woman.

A single shaft of light shines through the dark of the small house, onto a cupboard lined with large china plates.

"My grandfather was here many times," says Zoli. "Stanislaus. You knew him by that name."

"I've no idea who you're talking about."

"It was a different place then, but you knew him by that name."

The woman takes Zoli by the shoulders, turns her around, stares down at her feet.

"I have good horse teeth too."

"What did you say?"

"I am here to sell my things. That is all."

"You people will be the death of me."

"Not before you have everything we own."

"You've an errant mouth for a Gypsy."

"I've nothing to lose."

"Then leave."

Zoli measures her steps back to the doorway. The rattle of the doorknob. Silence from the street outside. The woman's voice behind her, once, twice, higher now but still measured: "And if I was interested what might you have?"

"I have told you already, the best."

"I've heard that so often even my ears tire me."

Zoli snaps the door shut and opens the giant bundle made of Swann's bedsheets. The woman feigns nonchalance, blows air from her cheeks. "I see," she says. She shakes the keys and leads Zoli through a series of dark-paneled rooms to a rear parlor where a bearded man sits on a high stool with what looks like a small jar dangling at his neck. In front of him sits a solitary game of tarock. He adjusts his stomach in his waistcoat. With an exaggerated sweep, he takes out his handkerchief and blows his nose, then tucks the cloth back in his pocket. She watches with a shiver of disgust.

"Yes?"

Zoli places Swann's wireless radio on the nicked wooden counter. The jeweler lowers his head, pushes the buttons, fingers the dial.

"Useless," he says.

He examines the underside of a picture frame, purses his lower lip: "You're wasting my time."

"And this?"

She lays Swann's gold watch upon the counter, stretching out either end of the strap.

The jeweler takes the monocle from around his neck and examines the watch, looking up twice at Zoli. On the table lies a switchblade knife with a black onyx handle. He flips open the back clasp of the watch and looks at the inner workings, a small universe of dials and cogs. He clips it back, laces his fingers, stretches his hands wide on the table. They are, she notices, ancient and liver-spotted.

"It isn't worth much."

"I'm not one who bargains," says Zoli.

"These things are English."

"I will take two hundred."

"I cannot sell them, they are foreign."

"Two hundred," she says. "No less."

The jeweler huffs: "One hundred and fifty."

He unlocks his desk drawer, takes a long leather pouch, and slowly counts the bills out, making a show of sliding the beads across a wooden abacus. He counts another ten and says with a grin: "You look as if you need it."

"It's a bad price."

"Go elsewhere, woman."

"There's nowhere to go."

"Well then, it's a good price, isn't it?"

He pushes the bills across the table, puts the wallet back in the drawer, turns the key once more, and, with a chuckle, reaches across for a ledger and makes an entry. He stands, clasping his hands behind his back.

"Well?" he says, flourishing his handkerchief.

Zoli is already halfway down the street when the jeweler comes out of his house at a fat man's trot. She can hear the flap of his shoes on the wet pavement and the high pitch of his shouts.

She darts towards the busy thoroughfare where the market is winding down. Blue tarps are being folded away and the legs of tables collapsed. A few lean fish rest in beds of salted ice. A half dozen potatoes sit cupped on a weighing machine. Swerv-

ing between the tables, Zoli crosses the marketplace, veers down
an alleyway, doubles back, sidesteps another two stalls, ducks
in behind a large yellow container.

From across the marketplace come the jeweler's shouts. In
the shadows, amid an acrid scent of rubbish, Zoli squats down,
breathing hard. She lifts her head for an instant, peeps over the
metal lip. At one of the stalls the potato-seller, heavy and white-
aproned, gestures to keep low.

I used to wear gold coins in my hair, she thinks. We were
faithful to that, we stole nothing.

The jeweler's last defeated roar drifts across to her, but she
remains out of sight until she is sure he is long gone. She stands,
taps her overcoat where she can feel the handle of her brand-
new onyx-handled knife.

She flicks open the blade and tests it on the thread of her
overcoat: it is sharp, honed to a point.

When you fall, thinks Zoli, you never fall halfway.

～

The rain hammers, pours, soaks: in the fluted gutters it
sluices along, carrying small rafts of rubbish down the streets.
By the river, the sparse jewelry of the bridge lights. Beyond
that, the silhouette of the giant towers where the kumpanija has
been resettled. The electricity is out in the towers again. Zoli
wonders if she might be able to catch that moment when the
electricity comes on, lighting up all eight buildings at once,
their only moment of beauty. It was Stránský who had told her,
years ago, that only poetry was capable of capturing the true
horrors of human consciousness, but she had doubted that idea
immediately, thinking that poems came on and off again only
like tower lights, no more and no less.

The towers appear small and fragile now: almost as if she might lift up parts and replace them at will.

At the foot of the bridge she stamps about in her wet clothes. Underneath her skirts she wears a pair of Swann's old trousers. His boots have been stuffed with socks to make them comfortable. In the bundle on her back, the rest of his possessions. From somewhere in the night comes the sound of a motorbike, sputtering into the distance. Figures emerge from the night fog along the river—any one of them might be Swann. How is it that he hurt his leg? Did he fall, was he beaten, was he thrown down a flight of stairs? Those days by the river. His fingers along her shoulder, his chin at her neck, his head within the shadow of hers. Watching the patterns the wolf feet made on the bank.

She shivers, curses, moves along the river's edge. The bundle on her back, soaked through with damp now, grows heavier with every step.

She turns the corner into Sedlárska, past a building site, and stops at a pile of red bricks on the ground. She toes one, rolls it over on its side. How many times, this same street, these same buildings, these same cracks in the footpath? She walks towards a squat building with two huge picturefront windows. No lights on, nobody around. She steps to the window and runs her fingers along the pane. The glass frame is so big that in the center it quivers and bounces. In the instant that she brings her arm forward she also withdraws, so that the brick is still in her hand when the glass spiders and shatters.

The last chime of the last shard falls away and silence closes around her.

Two young workers appear on the other side of the street, looking across, staring. She wonders how it is that they have seen it: a woman in a huge overcoat and headscarf and a man's black boots, in the darkness walking away from the shattered window of the Union of Slovak Writers, but what matter now? They can take me, they can do what they want—when hell freezes over I will not skate towards them.

Under the awning of the riverside cinema she stops to rest. There is a poster with a blond woman and a green-coated man behind a glass pane: *The Best Will Happen Tomorrow*. Zoli catches her reflection in the glass and marks, carefully and coldly in one glance, her hair askew under her scarf, her cheek muck-splattered, her eyes blackened with lack of sleep, the laddered boneshapes of her cheeks. She looks down on Swann's boots, their ridiculous brown weight, their long laces, their shiny eyes, stuffed with socks to make them comfortable.

It had always been, when Swann was around, the time of evening that promised most brightness. Into the dark lobby. Up the stairs. Past the waterstains on the walls. The air hard with cigarette smoke. Swann would flick a lighter for them to find their way. Through the swinging door. A few heads turned. Swann liked to think that they were already stepping into saloon territory. They stood for the national anthem, then sat against the hard-backed seats and waited for their eyes to adjust. After a few moments the first ripples began, tiny craters of whiteness, dark hairlines, bright splotches, and then an eruption of color. She could sense him relaxing, waiting for the images to flare into life: the snakefence, the basin of water with soap, the deer wading through high drifts, the hand around a whisky glass. What amazed him most was that all the films were shot in Czechoslovakia. Afterwards, when they were walking through the streets, she would push her way through the imaginary doors in the Trigger-Happy Saloon and talk of the empty buffalo fields and the temperance girls and *Winnetou, I*—she was sure that Swann was watching her more than he had watched the screen, his mouth ajar, stunned, leaning close to her.

How distant now, thinks Zoli.

Cowboy films.

The sky lightens over the city as she makes her way across the tramtracks, down towards the river in the early morning. A rusty fishing boat sloughs through the wide channel, pulling behind it a trail of smoke. She climbs the long ramp to the bridge, her back bent beneath the bundle. Zoli totals up what she has to her name: one hundred and sixty krowns, an onyx-handled knife, one bedsheet, two blankets, an overcoat, boots, a pair of Swann's trousers, three shirts, a hairbrush, a pair of thick gloves, a tin cup, and a tea towel.

Someone has inserted a bouquet of flowers into the iron-work curls of the bridge. Zoli leans against the drooping stems and looks down into the water. The wind fans across the surface, ricocheting off the far bank. I should throw something in the water, climb the railing, and leap right here. Tie a kerchief around my chin. Spread my arms out. Say nothing. Tumble. Hit the surface with my skirt above my head. Disappear into the depths. Send up a flume of spray.

She recognizes the thought in an instant: it is gadžikano, vacant, pathetic. She will not allow them such simplicity.

How stupid I was. I went to their table and kissed it in thanks. They promised to leave us alone, but they did not. How strange it was to be so liked amongst those she could never quite comprehend: the parties, the chalets, the hotel gatherings, the way they rolled her out at the conventions. Their vodka, their caviar, their sweet haluški. They packaged me up and made an eloquent ribbon of me and then they allowed me the short walk up the hangman's ramp. The noose, the trapdoor, the lever.

Lightheaded, Zoli pauses on the bridge and looks down at the river, and in the vertigo of shadow there is the sudden realization that she has not burned her poems at all; there are hundreds of them still out there, in printed copies, in the mill, in the union houses, even in the bookshops along Zelená. All she has done is burn the originals and given strength to the others.

Zoli crosses to the end of the bridge at a slow walk and stands at the junction on the far side. West, the towers. South, the road away. She pulls her arms close in against her stomach, cradles her elbows in the palms of her hands, hikes her belongings on her back, and shuffles down past the line of red dumpsters, through a hole in the barbed-wire fence. Tractors move in the early morning. Cement tankers. Men alongside the sheet-metal huts, their slick yellow jackets bright against the morning gray. One bends over a pot, stirring coffee. She moves beyond him, unnoticed. Most of the towers are inhabited now but there are three blocks still under construction. The grand experiment. They wanted the best for the Gypsies, they said— as if they could be a single throbbing organism, forty thousand people lumped into one. Running water, electric switches, heating.

You hurry on the light, she thinks, it just hastens the darkness.

Zoli ducks through another hole in the barbed wire and stops at a long wall, a distance from the caravans. Hundreds of

wagons are strewn around, still clumped together by kumpanija. At least they did not burn the carriages, she thinks, only
the wheels.

She leans forward, the imprint of the pebbles against her
hands.

In the barren squares of grass, a few of the wagons are already ringed with campfires. Pins of firelight wheel the air. One
or two dim figures move in and out of the shadows. So, some
have abandoned the towers already, taken the floorboards out,
come down to the ground, burnt what should have been beneath
their feet. A small triumph. Further along the wall, someone
has put up a lean-to against the concrete blocks. Old roofing
tin, wooden boards from the apartment floors, and an orange
highway sign. She squints to read it. *Slow: Construction in Prog-
ress.* Over the boards hang quilts and army blankets. A miscel-
lany of junk along the wall. A woman kneels to the dirt floor
and cleans it with a cloth. Around her a few children still sleep,
dark shapeless mounds, beneath their quilted blankets. Inside,
an oil lamp sits on a packing crate and a long table has been created from three boards, the light from the lamp dulled by ash.
This, then, is how they will live now: soot on the glass flute.

Zoli presses against the corner of the wall and peers into the
distance. A wreckage of a dog paddles beside the hulk of an
abandoned car, recently burned out, as if someone has died in
it. At the far end of the camp, a child rolls a barrel hoop and beyond him a man stands by the fire. She knows Vashengo by the
outline of his hat alone. Graco carries a coal-oil lamp. Milena,
Jolana, Eliška, and one or two of the children are already awake.
No Conka.

She pushes her palms deeper into the pebbled wall, favoring
one leg so her hip tilts out. She longs to tilt the other forward

and stride into the camp, but she is as separate from them now as she can ever be. She watches the flickering campfires, the cigarettes traveling at mouth level, a rimless wheel of red light moving. I would, she thinks, set fire to all my words just to travel that air once more.

Some children break the line beyond the campfires towards the wall. From where do they come? How far down the road were they driven? Zoli steps back and turns her face into the collar of Swann's overcoat. In what words will the children speak of me now that I have vanished?

High above the towers a yellow crane swings through the air. It stops for a moment, lets a bundle dangle and swerve in the middle of the air. It settles, then starts to swing once more. Zoli pulls at her zajda, brings it tight around her, and ducks back out through the fence.

It feels to her, as she walks, that she has just pulled her entire body over a region of barbed wire.

~

Hiding was part of an old language but they had not hidden well. Not this time. It had snowed and the fields lay touched with a phosphorous glow. They had been picked out easily, bright colors against the snow. The troopers arrived on motorbikes and in vans. They trudged across the fields, unscrolled a copy of the new law, then stood back, curious, when Vashengo said they did not want to go. The troopers had thought it was an easy sell. *Your own apartment. Heating. Running water.* All the magical cures. They spat on the ground and then grunted into radios: "They're refusing to come." A short time later a senior officer drew up in a large black sedan. He called Vashengo over and then asked for Zoli. She touched a pair of shoehorns above the caravan door and went out across the fields. Dogs were barking in the police vans. She sat in the car, warm air blowing into the backseats. "We're not going," she said. The officer's cheeks flushed. "I'm under orders," he said. "There's nothing I can do, there'll be bloodshed." The word had flashed a Spanish poem across her mind.

"You of all people," said the officer to Zoli, "you must know, these are the best flats in the whole of the country. Don't let there be a fight."

She sat silent, the word still trilled through her. How strange it was to touch against the comfortable leather seats and hear the word, away from poems, away from pages. *Bloodshed*.

"You can travel with us," said the officer. He turned to Vashengo, who was holding his hands in front of the dashboard vents. "You too," he said. "You can sit with us, it's warm in here, Comrade."

Zoli muttered a curse in Romani, slammed the door, and walked away. The officer rolled down his window to watch her go. From a distance away she could feel his astonishment.

Outside, in the fields, the children were at play. Sleeves of ice cold against their tongues. Vashengo came and stood behind her.

"We'll go," he said. "Peacefully. I told him to call the troopers off. And their dogs."

Something in Zoli had stalled. It was as if she had already vanished. She knew what would happen. Vashengo whistled. Eliška came out onto the steps of her caravan. She passed the word around. The children cheered—they did not know, they thought it an adventure.

Flurries of snow whirled down in the white silence. Zoli walked towards her caravan and waited.

~

Slow bootcrunch through the gravel. A shadow passes on the ground. She studies the passage of a swallow, dipping down from the towers. It alights on a series of poles laid out longways on the ground. One of the workers from the huts greets her in a high language: too formal, she knows. Behind her, a low grunt and a muted whistle. The cars begin to thin out and the streetcars pass. The cracked concrete gives way to muck and the towers disappear.

Out and away, the country begins to roll lighter and uninhabited, and in the early afternoon she stops in the shade of an old tin shelter.

She is startled to see a group of four coming down the far side of the road. A small shapeless mass at first, but then as they get closer the group clarifies—three children and a woman, carrying buckets and a few small bundles, out looking for whatever food they can find. Zoli recognizes them by their walk. The children run around the woman like small dark magnets. Two dip down into a ditch, emerge again. A shout of some sort. The figures loom like something through poor glass. The distant call of geese above them.

One of the children darts across the road to a line of willows and then all three youngsters are hauled in close to Conka's dress.

A panicky claw at Zoli's throat. She grows faintly aware of a sharp odor from her body. She blinks hard. The odor worse now, her bowels loose.

Conka and her family narrow the distance. The red hair, her white skin, the row of freckles across the eyes, the scars on her nose.

The first of them is Bora. The sound of the spit comes in advance of the moment and Zoli can feel the spray in her face. She does not wipe it away. She stands, chest rising and falling, her heart surging under her ribcage. A roar in her ears, a splintering. Never a stillness quite like this. The second child, Magda, is next, crossing with soft and measured steps. The spit is without sound or venom. It lands on the shoulder of Zoli's overcoat. A muttered curse, almost an apology. She hears the girl turn slowly away—of course, her bad foot. The last is Jores, the oldest, and he leans up close, she can feel his breath on her face, the smell of almonds. "Witch," he says. A ratcheting sound from his chest. The spit volleys into the perfect point between her eyebrows.

Another roar from the side of the road, the arc of the voice, so familiar, calling the children together. Zoli does not move. She waits for Conka. Flickering now across her mind: a hill run, a bare body dressed, laughter beneath a blanket, all those childhood things, ice across a lake, a basket of candles. Balance, she thinks, balance. In danger of losing my footing and being carried off the edge. What edge? There is no edge.

When Zoli opens her eyes the road is misted and shimmering, but there is no laughter, no shouting, no lapping echo from behind. She feels the phlegm trail along her neck. She wipes it away and bends down to the grass, passes her wet fingers along the blades. The smell of the children on her fingers.

Conka did not spit.

She did not cross the road and she did not curse me.

At least there is that.

It is almost enough.

A little further on, at the side of the road, Zoli stops short and leans down to touch a tin can—grain and old berries, a single piece of meat beside it, unspoiled. Fingers to her mouth, she inhales the smell of the younger children. I will not cry. Only once since judgment have I cried. I will not again.

Zoli bends down at the side of the road to lift the tin can and, beneath that, finds a hacked-off coin from Conka's hair.

3

THE DAYS PASS in a furious blank. The sky is wintry and fast. Soft flurries of snow break and melt across her face. She descends a steep bank towards a stream, the sun glancing off the thin ice. Whole patterns of crystals encase the river-grass. She steps to the water, sleeves her hand in her boot, and cracks the surface. She pokes around with a stick to clear the shards, touches the freezing water with her fingers.

With a deep breath she plunges her face into the water—so cold it stuns the bones in her cheeks.

Gingerly she takes off her socks. The blisters have hardened and none of the cuts have gone septic, but the makeshift bandages have become part of her skin. Zoli inches her feet into the burning cold of the water and tries to peel away the last of the bandages. Skin comes with them. Later, over a small fire, she warms her toes, pushes the flaps of torn skin against the raw flesh, attends to her wounds.

Small birds come to feed in the cold of the open riverbank: she watches which trees they fly to, what last foliage, what winter berries, then sets out to collect whatever food she can find. She discovers, in the mud, a dead sparrow. It is against all custom to eat wild birds but what is custom now but an old and flightless thing? She spears the bird with a sharpened twig and roasts it in a low flame, turning it over and over, knowing at first bite that it will not be good for her, all rot and age and uselessness. Still, in the urgency of hunger, she rips at it with her teeth and runs her tongue along where the heart once beat.

The tiny yellow beak of the bird sits in the palm of her hand and she tilts it over and drops it into the flames.

She squats over the fire, thankful for her lighter. I must, she thinks, be careful in the use of it. Soon there will be no more fuel. Small fires are unseen. Small fires can be perched above and drawn upwards into the body. Small fires ignore curfew.

She feels her stomach churn, and, in the late hours, she lies tossing, turning, under Swann's blanket.

She rises dizzy, the sun a bright disc in the trees. A tall osprey surveys her from a pine tree, his neck curved long and nonchalant, only his eyeballs moving. The branch looks built to him, a perfect blue and gray melding. The osprey turns as if bored, swings its long head to the side, pecks at its feathers, then takes off lazily into the forest.

Moments later it is on the bank, a fish in its beak. Zoli inches silently towards the fire, patiently picks up half a log, flings it. It misses the osprey but the log skitters and bursts into bright embers across the ice. The bird turns to look at her, drops the fish, then lifts its wings and bursts out over the reeds. She hobbles over to retrieve the fish; it is no bigger than the length of her hand.

"You could at least have found me a bigger one," she says aloud.

The sound of her own voice surprises her, the clarity of it, crisp in the air. She looks quickly about her as if someone might be listening.

"You," she says, looking around once more. "A big fish would have been more generous. You hear me?"

She chatters to herself as she builds up her fire. She eats the white flesh, licks the bones clean, then plunges her feet in the river once more. One more day and they will be ready. I can walk and keep walking: long roads, fence lines, pylons. Nothing will catch me, not even the sound of my own voice.

It had seemed so strange a few days ago, near the roadblock, when Paris leaped into her mind for no reason at all, but now it comes back and she tries the weight of the word upon her tongue.

"Paris."

She stretches it out, a wide elegant avenue of sound.

The following morning she builds up Swann's boots with the socks, places dry moss at the ankle of each, starts off along the riverbank, watching for the osprey, expecting it to appear, stately, serene, to do something magnificent—to come down the river on a floe of ice, or to burst from the trees, but nothing stirs.

She finds a length of oak branch with a knobbed end and picks it up, tests it against the ground as a cane. It bends under her tall weight and she shakes the stick in the air.

"Thank you," she says to the nothingness, then strikes out against the road with her new cane, clouds of white breath leaving her for the morning air.

Paris. An absurdity. How many borders is that? How many watchtowers? How many troopers lined along the barbed wire? How many roadblocks? She tries the word again, and it seems that it arrives in everything around her as the days go by, a Paris in the tree branch, a Paris in the mud of a roadside ditch, a Paris in a sidelong dog that retreats at a half-trot, a Paris in the red of a collective tractor driven distantly across a field. She clings to its ridiculousness, its simple repetition. She likes the heft of it on her lips and finds that, as she goes along, it is a sound that helps her think of nothing at all, rhythmically bumping against the air, carrying her forward, a sort of contraband, a repetition so formless, so impossible, so bizarre that it matches her footsteps and Zoli learns exactly when the first of the word will hit with her heel against the ground, and the last of the word will hit with her toe, so that she is going, in perfect conjunction, sound and step, onwards.

~

At the stillness of a crossroads, she makes out the dot of a vehicle coming towards her, a motorbike, a flash of small metal, and she takes cover with her back against the damp of a roadside ditch.

The motorbike bounces past with a tinny roar. It is Swann, she can tell by the lean of him, his crutches strapped to the back of the bike. She rises and watches him labor up the bumpy road, through small countries of light and shadow, swerving once to avoid a rabbit. The animal bounds into a field, its ears held high as if amused by the encounter.

"You will not find me," she says to his disappearing form. She strikes the cane down hard on the road as the engine sound stutters into the distance. It seems to her, in the silence, that if it weren't for Swann she could almost sleep while walking.

In a tiny village market she buys a slab of meat, some cheese, a loaf of bread. "Comrade," an old fruitseller says to her, "are there many of you?" The fruitseller watches Zoli go as she cuts across a field and doubles back around to make sure she is not followed.

Later in the evening, not far from the village, she happens upon a burned-out camp, not in runic signs but a terrified clamber.

She stops short. So this, then, is why they asked. The marks are still everywhere—in the returning grass, the ruts, the peg-holes, the mounds of earth where they hastily covered their fires. Around the camp, there is a zigzag of tires and, against the trees, a single burned-out carriage, its wheels missing. The hub of one wheel has been shoved into the earth while the rest—spokes and rim—have burned into the ground. An iron wheel-hoop, fused shapeless. Bits of melted canvas frozen against the burnt wooden boards. The tongue of the carriage pierces the muddy ground, as if it just bowed down and accepted defeat. Zoli touches the wood. One of the timbers falls with a faint snap. The dark carcass of a radio sits in a corner of the carriage. She can tell by other marks in the ground that the men had tried to carry the carriage to the forest without benefit of horses but gave up after only a few paces. No sign of bones or weapons.

Zoli tears off the burnt canvas, cuts around it with her knife. Nothing else to salvage. She touches her left breast, bows her head, moves away. All that we wanted, she thinks. All that we ended up with.

A short distance from the camp she hooks the canvas among the branches and settles down for the evening. By dark she is sure she hears something pacing in a half-circle around her camp. A wolf or a deer or an elk. Not a man. Men do not circle in that way. She sits upright and stirs the loose embers of the fire, throws on more leaves. The flames jump in the pitch-dark. She rips a piece of cloth from the sleeve of one of Swann's shirts and sets it aflame, circles her camp with the rag burning.

She remains awake until morning, knees drawn to her chest,

then dozes until a patch of wet shocks her cheekbones. Giant flakes of snow gently falling. It is as if the weather, too, wants to make a fool of her.

The snowfall makes the tree branches darkly flamboyant, pencil lines in a pale drawing. Crows gather on the branches and flap off black into the sky. She can see, in the nearby trees, an eyebrow of white on the burnt-out carriage.

"Blessings," she says aloud, for no reason she can fathom.

A reply slices the crisp air. Perhaps it is the wind in the trees, or a branch falling, but then there is another sound, and a deep bronchial coughing. Zoli hurries to gather her things and bundles them in her zajda. Frosted leaves snap beneath her feet.

A voice then.

She spins.

Two men in loden jackets lumber through the trees, axes over their shoulders. They halt and one drops his axe. Together they shout as she scrambles through the snow. The whip of a twig against her face. Her foot catches on an exposed tree root. She falls, slams into a cut-off tree trunk. She rises again, but the men are upon her, above her, looking down. One is young and fresh-faced. The other wears a shabby beard and broken eyeglasses. The younger one leers. She turns in the snow and curses them but the younger one gazes down, amused. The older reaches to pick her up and she bites at his arm. He jumps back. She shouts at them in Romani and the younger says: "I told you there was someone out here. Last night. I told you. I felt it."

Zoli scoots backwards in the snow, wraps her hand around a length of stick, but the younger one knocks it out with a swift kick.

"I bet she's the one. Look at her."

"Pick her up."

"Watch the evil eye."

"Oh, shit on your evil eye. Just pick her up."

"I bet she's the one. Look at her coat."

"Shut up."

"She was going to hit us with that stick."

"Pick her up."

They lean down together and grab under each shoulder. Zoli jams her feet hard down in the snow and leans backwards, but the men have a hold and she feels useless between them. They bring her a good distance through the woods to a clearing where two donkeys pace patiently around the front of a wooden shack.

So that was last night's noise, thinks Zoli: only donkeys.

A wafer of snow slides from the roof and plops onto the ground below. Skinned logs stand in stacked piles around the shack. A piece of cutting machinery lies against the wall. Nearby, a trundlecart. The snow is footprinted and packed: more than just two men here, she thinks.

She spits on the ground and the younger one says: "She's trying to put a curse on us."

"Don't be an idiot," says the older.

Inside, the men knock snow off their boots and lead her to a chair. The air is heavy with sweat and old tobacco. Eight wooden bunks are screwed to the wall and an unlit lamp hangs from a chandelier of antler horns in the center of the room. The floor is made of flat riverrock. A workcamp of sorts, she thinks. Or illegal hunting. She watches as the younger one latches the door shut, kicks the bottom in place.

She reaches inside her pocket, opens the blade of the onyx-handled knife and slides it along her coatsleeve, the tip of the blade against her forefinger.

The older man turns away and bends down to the stove door. He opens it and pokes with a stick. The fire rises orange in the joints of the stove and a hot ember lands on his boot. He knocks it off, takes a saucepan, begins stirring food with the same stick. A hind leg of lamb hangs like a jacket above the stove. He shaves off a sliver with a blade and it drops directly into the pot.

"There's nothing good that will come to you out here," says the man.

And as if by way of proof the younger one begins to undo his belt. He pulls it through the loops and snaps it in the air. His trousers, caked in mud, fall to the ground around his ankles, but he keeps his back turned. His underclothes are a filthy gray. Zoli slips the knife further down along her wrist and closes her eyes. A deep coughing comes from across the room. She looks up to see that the man has stepped into another pair of trousers. He adjusts the belt. His eyes sharpen. He toes a small cone of wood-dust on the floor, comes across, and reaches past her for a cup on the table.

With two fingers on his cup he raises it to drink. There is, she knows, nothing in the cup.

"What's your name?"

She slides the chair backwards but he pushes her once more into the table. A smell of resin to him.

"What's your name, Gypsy?"

"Let me go."

The younger one slams the empty cup down and leans across her, his breath smelling, strangely, of fresh woodmint. So he knows the woods, she thinks, he will not be easily fooled. She nudges the knifeblade back into her coatsleeve where it feels cool against the soft of her wrist.

"Conka," she says, immediately regretting it.

"Conka?"

"Elena. I was with my people."

"Elena now is it?"

"When the troopers came."

The younger one chuckles: "Is that so?"

"The families were taken away. The last of us were driven to the city under the new laws. We were pushed along by dogs. My husband was forced to carry a large wooden box with lacquer patterns and all our belongings inside."

She hesitates and searches their expressions—nothing.

"A huge lacquer box," she says. "He dropped it on the road. The rain was beating down like a drunk. Everyone was slipping in the mud. The dogs, they had such sharp teeth, you should have seen them. They ripped us. They took a chunk from my mother's leg. The troopers hit us with their sticks. I still have the marks. They let the leashes loose. My children got bitten. Eight children, I once had eleven. All our belongings were in that box. All my jewelry, papers, everything, inside that box. Wrapped in old twine."

She pauses again—only a slight twitch at the side of the younger's face.

"I've come now from the city. To get the box. Eight children. Three died. One stepped on an electric cable by the cypress lake. When the thaw came they were digging by mistake with metal shovels. Once there were eleven."

"A whole team?" says the younger with a grin.

She turns away and stares at the older man who smooths out the hairs of his eyebrow with his knuckle.

"We have a roof now," says Zoli. "Electric lights that come on all the time, water that runs. The new directives have been good to us. Good times are coming. The leaders have been good to us. All I want is to find the box, that's all. Have you seen my things?"

The older pushes himself wearily from the stove and sits down, carrying with him a bowl of kasha with small pieces of lamb scattered in it.

"You're lying," he says.

"A blue lacquer box with silver clasps," she says.

"For a Gypsy you don't even lie very well."

Light crawls up and around the window—no curtains, she notices, no woman's hand in the cabin. She allows the tip of her knife to press deeper into her cupped finger.

"What's your name?" says the younger again.

"Elena."

"That's a lie."

The older man leans in, serious and gray-eyed. "There was a man out in these parts riding a two-stroke Jawa. An Englishman. He was looking for you, says you've gone missing. Says he's been searching all over. We saw him by the forest road. He wants to take you to a hospital. He looked like he should've been in the hospital himself, driving around with a broken leg. Hadn't shaved in a while. Said your name is Zoli."

He slides the bowl of kasha across the table, but she does not touch it.

"I really need to find the box. It has so many precious things inside."

"He said you were tall, with a lazy eye. He told us you'd be wearing a dark overcoat. That you might have a gold watch. Roll up your sleeve."

"What?"

"Roll up your fucking sleeve," says the younger.

He steps across and hikes her coat, wrist to elbow. The knife falls with a clatter to the floor. He stamps on it, picks it up, tests the blade with his thumb, then turns to the older. "I told you. Last night. I fucking told you."

The older leans in further to Zoli: "Do you know him?"

"Know who?"

"Don't play us for fools."

"I know nothing about a watch," says Zoli.

"He said it was his father's. A precious timepiece."

"I don't know what you're talking about."

"He asked for petrol for his motorbike. He didn't seem much of a threat. He spoke a funny Slovak. He tried to tell me he grew up here, but I know better. Is it true, then, what he says? How did you get a man's name?"

Zoli watches as the younger one cuts the hairs on his arm with the knife, whistling at the sharpness of the blade. The older takes off his cap, something soft and compassionate in the lift. His graying hair, a little damp, lies pressed against his scalp. When he leans forward she notices a small scapular swinging at his neck.

"It was given to me by my grandfather," she says finally. "It was the name of his own father."

"So you're a real Gypsy then?"

"You're a real woodsman?"

The older laughs and drums his fingers on the table: "What do I say? We're paid by the cubic meter."

So, she thinks, a workcamp for prisoners. They remain out here, all summer and winter. Minimum security. Morning until night, sorting wood, gauging it, chopping it, weighing. She watches as the younger rises and goes to the door where he takes an oilskin cloth out of the hanging pair of trousers. He unties a string from the cloth and produces a set of playing cards, slides them across the table to Zoli.

"Our fortune."

"What?"

"Don't be a God-fearing idiot," says the older, slapping the cards off the table.

The younger one retrieves them from the floor. "Come on, tell us our fortune," he says again.

"I don't tell fortunes," says Zoli.

"It gets lonely out here," says the younger. "All I want is my fortune told."

"Shut up," says the older.

"I'm just telling her it gets lonely. Doesn't it? It gets real lonely."

"I'm telling you to shut up, Tomas."

"She's worth money. You heard him. He said he'd pay us money. And you said——"

"Shut up and leave her alone."

Zoli watches as the older goes to a small bookshelf where he takes down a leather volume. He returns to the table and folds back the cover.

"Can you read this?" he says.

"Christ rides!" says the younger.

"Can you read it?"

"Yes."

"For fucksake!"

"Here's where you are now. Right here. It's an old map, so it looks like it's Hungary but it's not. This is where Hungary is, along here. The other way, over here, is Austria. They'll shoot you before they lay eyes on you. Thousands of soldiers. Do you understand? Thousands."

"Yes."

"The best way to make it through is this lake. It is only one meter deep, even in the middle. That's where the border is, in the middle. They don't patrol it with boats. And you won't drown. They may shoot you but you won't drown."

"And this?"

"That's the old border."

He closes the book and leans in close to Zoli. The younger looks back and forth, as if a language lies between them that he will never understand.

"Ah, fuck," he says. "She's worth money. You heard what he said. A reward."

"Give her back the knife."

"Shit."

"Give her the knife, Tomas."

The younger skids the knife across the floor and sighs. Zoli picks it up, backs across the hard stone floor towards the door, pulls down the handle. Locked. A brief panic claws at her throat until the older man steps across, leans forward, turns the handle upwards, and the door swings open. A blast of cold wind.

"One thing," he says. "Are you really a poet?"

"I sang."

"A singer?"

"Yes."

"Same thing, no?"

"No, I don't think so," she says.

All three step out into the stinging light of the morning. The oldest extends his hand.

"Josef," he says.

"Marienka Bora Novotna." She pauses a moment: "Zoli."

"It's a funny name."

"Perhaps."

"May I ask one thing? I was wondering. I think I've seen your photograph once. In the newspaper."

"Maybe."

"I ask only then—"

"Yes?"

"How have you come to this?"

He looks beyond her, eyes distant, and she realizes then that it is not a question she is called upon to answer, rather it is something he is asking himself, or some old self standing in the distance, amid the trees, and he will ask it again, later, when he feels the hard roll of axe handle in his hand: How have you come to this?

"There are worse things," says Zoli.

"I can't think of them, can you?"

She turns her face towards the distance.

"Hey," says the younger, "what are we going to say to the Englishman if he comes back?"

"Say to him?"

"Yes."

"Perhaps," says Zoli, "you will tell him his fortune."

~

At the top of a hill she looks north and south—Bratislava and its towers long gone now, not even a hint of them on the skyline. She is pleased by the silence as it reverberates from horizon to horizon. There are days when she walks great distances and the only sound she discerns is the swish of her own clothing.

At a lonely farmhouse she crouches behind a barn, listening. She crosses to the huts and undoes the string that holds the hasp. A few scrawny hens eye her from behind the wooden slats. When she reaches in, one erupts from the box with a long squawk and flies past her. Illegal, of course, to own chickens— they must belong to a family nearby. She reaches in a second time, keeping the gap in the door tight. In the uproar the others take to the air and she lunges and grabs one by the wing. She holds it in the well of her skirt, and breaks the neck with a simple twist, follows with a second. From the nesting boxes she fills her pockets with eggs and wraps them in the cathedral tea towel.

She unwinds a long piece of thread from her coat, ties it around the neck of the animals, and places them together at her belt, where they bounce against her thigh as she walks, as if still alive and protesting.

Hunger has made me original, she thinks: the chicken-stealing Gypsy.

Three afternoons later it occurs to her from roadsigns that she has already crossed the border into Hungary. She had expected a concertina of barbed wire to mark it, or a high concrete watchtower, but maybe it was just a hedge or a furrowed field or the little village where they spoke both languages. Perhaps it was when she crossed the shallow streambed in the forest, snow falling and trees darkly waving. It startles her, the ease with which she has crossed from one place into another, the landscape wholly alien and yet so much the same. The other border, East and West, she knows, will begin in a matter of days and it strikes her, as she walks, that borders, like hatred, are exaggerated precisely because otherwise they would cease to exist altogether.

The first of the wooden watchtowers appears on stilts like a tall wooden bird. Two soldiers perch within it, scanning the horizon. Here, Hungary. There, in the distance, Austria. She creeps along, half-bent to the earth, her body porous to every noise. Before her, the haze of mist drifting off the marsh. The air is cold, but lines of sweat run along her shoulderblades. She has stripped her bundle down to the barest needs—only a wickerjar of water, some cheese, some bread, the tarp, a blanket, her warmest clothes, the stolen knife. She backs a good distance away from the watchtowers, settles in the grass far from the dirt road, feels for a dry place to lie down.

No more movement, thinks Zoli, until nightfall.

She tracks the sun awhile across the sky, through the woven shapes of the branches above, until the last of the mist has burned off. How strange to try to sleep in such light, but it is important to rest, and to keep warm—there can be no fire.

Afternoon birdcall wakes her. The sun has shifted southward, red at its edges. She lifts her head slightly at the sound of an engine, and sees, in the distance, a squat truck with a canvas back trundling along the forest line. The voices of young soldiers, Russians, carry through the forest. How many dead bodies lie along these imaginary lines? How many men, women, children shot as they made the short trip from one place to the other? The army truck passes along the edge of the trees and away, and, as if by design, two white swans break across the sky, their shapes laboring above the treetops, quartering on the wind with their necks craned, apparitions not so much of grace as difficulty, with the gunneling sound that comes from their mouths, a deathcall.

Other people, she knows, have had reasons to cross—for land, or nation, or desire, but she has no reason, she is empty, clean, raw. Once, as a child, traveling with her grandfather, she had seen a hunger artist in a village west of the mountains. He had set himself up in a cage and made a spectacle of his starvation. She watched him as his ribs grew clearer, stronger, almost musical. He lasted forty-four days and he looked so much like an old man when they took him from the cage that she was surprised to see him given, at last, a plate of crumbs and a drink of milk. This is how I am, she thinks: I have made a spectacle of myself, and now I am taking their crumbs. It is still possible to turn around—there is nothing to prove. And yet I have come this far, there is no more reason to return than there is to advance.

Zoli shifts slightly on the blanket. I should sleep, build up my strength, pull myself together, free my mind, become clear.

By early evening it seems to her that the darkness has begun to lift itself out of the earth, overtaking the grays and yellows of the marsh floor. It rises to the top of the trees and shoulders against the last patches of light. She considers a moment that it is, in fact, more beautiful than she has ever created in words, that the darkness actually restores the light. The trees more dark than the dark itself.

She bundles her belongings tight and rises up from between the logs. This is it. Take it now. Go. She taps her left breast, begins moving, hunched, carefully, deliberately. Windnoise in the grass. A shape in the distance catches her eye, another watchtower, this one camouflaged with leaves and bushes and almost immediately she hears some dogs in the anonymous distance. She strains to hear what direction they are heading but it is hard to tell with the wind.

A high chorus, getting closer. Trained bloodhounds maybe. The sound of men's voices, joining the clamor. At a distant watchtower, two soldiers jump from the last rungs of the ladder to the ground, their rifles pointed at the sky, moving out at a trot. So this is it. I should just stand and raise my arms and have them call the dogs off. Why gibber? Why beg? And yet there is something about their excitement, a tension to their voices, that makes her wonder. She crouches down into the grass. The headlights of a truck on the far road light up the marshland. A second truck, a third. The dogs only a short distance away now. The lights paint the grass silver, spectral.

It is then she sees a brown flash along the road. Ten or twelve of them. Antlered, majestic. Dogs snapping behind them. A shout of grim confidence from a soldier and then a yelp of joy.

Deer. A whole herd of them.

Sweep left, she whispers, sweep left.

She hears the soldiers whooping under the clamor of the dogs. Her fate, she realizes, is within the swing of a deer foot. Swing away from me, away.

The herd passes through the forest line behind her. Over her shoulder the soldiers follow, shouting.

She races forward and through a low ditch. Water sprays upwards and she skews a moment on the slick mud before gaining her footing once more. Beyond the ditch, a line of trees. A light sweeps the landscape. She ducks into the shelter of a single cypress tree, slides down behind it, pauses for a breath and looks about in terror before lurching onwards. Her wet shoes make sucking sounds against the earth. She punches her way through a brake of long grass. The thorns of a bush rip her hands. She hears another dog's barking and then a high yelp. Have they finished their chase? Cornered their animal?

Her breath wheens fast and uneven. Her lungs, scalded. I must get now to the lake. A quarter kilometer perhaps. To the water edge.

Zoli rolls her shoulders from her overcoat, and drops it on the ground. I will not fill my pockets with water, no.

Four searchlights tilt and sweep across her. She drops to the soft earth, face in the dirt. The lights stencil the marshland. In the distance the hounds are being held back from the deer and the laughing voices of the soldiers carry through the night. The deer with its belly split open, surely, the guts steaming on the ground.

Zoli ventures forward again, the bracing cold pulling at her skin, her heart, her lungs tight.

The merest luck, she thinks, has preserved me.

Slovakia

2003

THE BOTTLES WERE EMPTY, the ashtrays full. They had cheerfully slapped his back, sung for him, even fed him the last of their haluški. They had gazed at pictures of his child and posed for their own, by the fire, standing tall and fixed. They had laughed at the sound of their own voices on the tape recorder. He even played it for them in slow mode. They had accepted all his money, except for fifty krowns in a hidden pocket. They'd played him like a harp, he thought, but he was not fazed; he even felt for a while that he had a bit of the Gypsy in himself, that he'd been inducted into their ways, a character in one of their elaborate anecdotes. They led him this way and that about Zoli, and the more krown notes he laid on the table, the more their stories loosened—*she was born right here, I am her cousin, she wasn't a singer, she was seen last month in Prešov, her caravan was sold to a museum in Brno, she played the guitar, she taught in university, she was killed in the war by the Hlinkas*—and he felt like a man who'd been expertly and lengthily duped.

He promised Boshor that he'd come back when he discovered anything more about her, maybe the next week, or the one after, but he knew he'd never return. The young girl, Anděla, picked up the china cups from the table and smiled at him as she backed away—she wore his wristwatch high on her arm. He had even, towards the end, watched the cigarette foil being used to languidly clean a gap in Boshor's teeth.

He tapped his pockets. Everything was intact. Car keys, tape recorder, wallet. Boshor shook his hand and grasped his arm in affection, pulled him close. They almost touched cheeks.

Outside, the shadows lay gray on the settlement. The kids cheered when he pushed open the shack door. Robo was sitting on a cinder block, carving a piece of wood out of which had come the figure of a woman. The whittled chips lay in white patterns at his feet. Robo skimmed off the last bark edge and handed him the statue, leaned in and said: "Don't forget, mister, fifty krowns." He smiled and put the statue in his pocket: "Just get me to the car." The other kids pulled at his jacket sleeve. He leaned down and mussed their hair. He felt happily torn by the desolation; he'd survived it, he was safe, secure, out in one piece. The bands of sweat at his waist and armpits had dried. He had even begun to fret that his car was pointed in the wrong direction, that he would have to reverse it all the way up the dirt road, or execute a three-point turn with all these little kids around.

"This way," said Robo, "follow me."

He moved through the muck and made signposts in his mind to come back to later, random thoughts, notes to scribble down in a journal: The children's clothes are strangely clean. No running water, no taps, no pylons. Electricity is pirated. A girl with eight piercings in her ears. Two huge rubber rings used as jewelry. Not many young men in their twenties or thirties—possibly in prison. Man in bright pink jacket. Chess pieces strung as a windchime. Old woman using broken television as a seat. Immaculate white cloths flapping on the washing line.

He was passing by the last of the shanties when Robo let go of his arm and moved back into the shadows. He felt immediately that he had been dropped.

A bare-chested man. Small. Barefoot. A bottle scar on one cheek, almost a perfect circle. A tattooed teardrop on the other, beneath his eye. He held the engine of a motor scooter in one hand and his chest was slathered in fingerlines of grease. The journalist turned quickly to look for escape, but the tattooed man took his elbow and pulled him towards a shack. "Come here, come here." A curious high tinge to the voice. The tattooed man deepened the grip around the journalist's forearm, and then, as if from nowhere, a young woman in a yellow dress appeared at his other elbow. She bowed, a small wren of a thing, her hands folded as if in prayer.

"I'm sorry," he said, "I have to go."

He tried backing discreetly away, but the tattooed man was gentle, insistent. The ragged edge of a sackcloth doorway was drawn back. He bumped up against a rough wooden pole. The shack seemed to shake.

"Come on, Uncle, sit down."

Shapes grew out of the darkness. Three children sat on the bed as if placed there for show.

"I really must go," he said.

"You've nothing to worry about, Unc, I just want to show you something."

The children made room on the pine-pole bed. It was strung with rope. On one end lay a folded white eiderdown and a cushion for a pillow. When he sat, the ropes sagged and the poles shifted. The tattooed man's hand lay heavy on his shoulder. The journalist looked around. No windows. No carpet. No wall hangings. Only a row of empty shelves on the far wall.

He turned away and there, swinging from the ceiling, hung a huge zelfya scarf, a hand peeping out of it.

"Food," said the tattooed man. "We need food for the baby."

The tattooed man ran a finger along the lip of a little Russian-made fridge, and then swept a lighter around the emptiness. He said something in Romani to the woman. She squeezed up onto the bed. Her smile was wide, though two of her lower teeth were missing. She edged closer, ran her hand along the buttons at the front of her dress, put an arm around the journalist's shoulder. He pulled back and smiled again, thinly, nervously.

A rat tiptoed across the zinc roof.

The woman opened her top button and then, with a sudden flick of her fingers, reached inside her dress. "Food," she said. He turned away but she squeezed his shoulder and when he turned back he saw that she had her breast out in her hand, the whole of it, milky at the nipple and striated with sores. Oh, Jesus, he thought, she's turning tricks on me. Right in front of her children. Jesus. Her breast, she's giving me her breast. She held it between her middle fingers and began to keen, incanting something in a low, desperate voice. She squeezed the nipple again. He stood up and his knees gave way. A hand pushed his chest. He thumped back onto the bed. Her breast was still out and she was pointing to the sores.

The tattooed man reached up to the hanging bundle and raised his voice: "We need food for the baby, the baby is so hungry." And then, out of the bundle came a tiny bag of bones, wrapped in a Harley-Davidson T-shirt.

The child was placed in the journalist's arms. My own baby would cry, he thought. She is so light, so very light. No more than a loaf of bread. A packet of flour.

"She's beautiful," he said, and he went to put the baby in the woman's lap, but she folded herself against it, curled up tight, put her chin to her chestbone. She moaned, closed the button of her dress, hugged herself, and her moans rose higher.

A fly settled on the child's top lip.

The journalist took one hand from the baby and patted his pockets. "I've nothing with me," he said. "If I had anything I'd give it to you, I swear, I wish I had, I'll come back tomorrow, I'll bring food, I promise, I will."

He swished the fly away from the baby's mouth and watched as the tattooed man slapped his fist into his palm, and he knew for certain now that they were prison tattoos, and he knew what the teardrop meant, and all seemed suddenly cold. A ball of emptiness swelled in his stomach, and he stuttered: "I'm a friend of Boshor's, you know."

The tattooed man smiled sharply, then stood up in the center of the hard-packed floor. He reached for the baby, took it in his arms, kissed it on the forehead—a slow, careful kiss—and then dropped it in the zelfya. He stretched his arms wide and said, as if there were coins in his voice: "There's a cash machine up by the supermarket, friend."

The hanging bundle swayed in the air, back and forth, a slowing timepiece. The tattooed man pulled the journalist up from the bed, put his arm around his shoulder, held him close. It was as if they'd competed in some vast athletic competition together, wrapped themselves in the flag, the anthem was ringing out, and thousands were cheering all around them.

"Come on, friend, follow me."

The sackcloth was pulled back from the doorway and the hard light stung the journalist's eyes. He looked back at the woman, passively smoothing the eiderdown. A platoon of flies was now buzzing around the baby. The sackcloth curtsied across the open frame.

In the raw camp air, the tattooed man laughed. Robo appeared from the corner and began walking at the head of their shadows. "Don't forget, mister," Robo whispered. Everything seemed tightened down. A pressure on his ribcage. A pulse at his temple. The tattooed man stayed close by his shoulder, careful to bring him across the bridge, all exaggerated safety.

"Don't put your foot here, friend, that's a bad one."

For a moment he thought he still had the child in his hands, he tried to cradle it, but his foot caught on a swinging plank, and the tattooed man grabbed him by the lapel, hauled him back, and touched the soft swell of his waist: "You're safe with me, friend."

He cast his eyes up towards the distant village: a church-tower peeping up above the trees and the clock ringing for a quarter to five in the afternoon.

They walked towards the car, the kids swarming around them. Robo shuffled behind. It was silent, their pact. He ferreted in a hidden pocket for the money and backhanded it to Robo, fifty krowns. Robo yelped and broke away through the crowd and disappeared into the trees. The tattooed man stopped to watch Robo go.

"Robo," he said, closing his eyes as if weighing something extraordinarily heavy on his lashes.

The journalist fumbled in his pocket for his keys. The man stood behind his shoulder, breathing against his neck. The doors unlocked with a click and then the tattooed man vaulted across the front hood, landed in the passenger seat with a soft plink as his skin hit the plastic.

"Nice car, friend," said the tattooed man as he clapped his hands together.

"It's a rental," said the journalist, and he was amazed as he drove away, reversing through the crowd of kids, that the tattooed man leaned his head on his shoulder, like some lover.

At the bend in the road, near the fridge, he turned the car around, beeped, waved out the window to the children. His stomach heaved. He shoved the car into gear. The kids waved as the car wheels caught, cheered as mud flew in the air. The hedges shot by. They passed the women still washing sheets in the river. The tattooed man popped out the ashtray and began picking through the smoked butts.

"I won't gyp you," he said as he smoothed out the crushed end of a cigarette, and the journalist felt as if he had been chest-kicked by the word, as if it meant nothing at all, like fly or shit or sunrise.

The road widened and curled up the hill. The tires gripped hard on the tarmac. His knuckles turned white on the wheel. He had no idea what he could do to get rid of the tattooed man, but then—in sight of the town—it struck him. That's it, he thought. It was simple, honest, elegant. He would go to the supermarket and buy baby formula, yes, baby formula, and milk, and cereal, and tiny jars of food, and some clean bottles, some ointment, some rubber nipples, a box of diapers, a tub of baby-wipes, even a doll if they had one, yes, a doll, that would be good, that would be right. Maybe he would throw in a few extra krowns. He would emerge from the supermarket laden down and at ease.

He leaned back and steered the wheel with one hand, but when he rounded the corner towards a low row of shops, the tattooed man turned to him as if he had divined his intention and said: "Y'know, they don't allow any of us into the market, friend." His skin plinked away from the plastic of the seat. "We are forbidden, there's none of us allowed."

The wheel bumped against the curb.

The tattooed man was out of the car before it had even stopped. He vaulted the hood again and opened the door before the key was out of the ignition. "Cash machine," he said, pointing. "Over there."

The journalist cast about for a policeman, or a bank official, anyone. A few teenagers sat brooding on a low brick wall. Under their swinging legs, the faded graffiti read: "Gyps go home." The tattooed man tightened his grip and they crossed to the machine.

"Stand back," the journalist said, and was surprised to see the man shuffle backwards.

Some of the teenagers laughed and one wolf-whistled.

"Stand back or there's no money. Do you hear me?"

The teenagers laughed again.

He shielded the numbers from view as he punched them into the keyboard. The high beeps of the machine sounded out. Behind him the tattooed man was moving foot to foot, biting his lip. The cogs rattled and the levers whirled. Two hundred knowns came out in twenty-krown notes. He ripped them from the rollers, turned, walked four steps, and thrust the money into the tattooed man's hand.

"The baby is so hungry."

"No," he said, "there's no more."

He was seven steps from the machine when he heard the receipt cough out from the wall. He froze, then turned and jogged back to get it, crumpled it in his fist.

"Five hundred please, five hundred, she's so hungry."

The journalist patted his wallet again to make sure nothing had been lifted.

"Please, Uncle, please."

He pulled the handle of the car door, his hands slippery with sweat. The keys shook as he shoved them into the ignition. The engine caught. He locked all four locks simultaneously.

The tattooed man pressed his face up against the window. His mouth was moist and red.

"Thank you," he mouthed, his breath fogging the glass.

The car lurched forward and a wave of cool air enveloped him. "Fuck," the journalist said. He swung out onto the road. "Fuck." The light was fading. In the rearview mirror he saw the tattooed man striding off in the direction of the supermarket, swaggering as the electronic doors opened. The man entered the market with a small skip of his feet and his head disappeared amongst the shoppers.

The car clipped the curb and the moist face print dissolved from the window.

As he drove along the winding road towards the highway, looking back down on the settlement, the journalist felt what he thought was a sadness, or an ache, or a desire, and these thoughts heartened him, warmed him with their misery, and he pretended that a part of himself wanted to slide down the bank, wade through the filthy river, give them all that he owned, and walk home, penniless, decent, healed, return their ancient dignity by leaving, by the riverbank, his own.

He drove on, then reversed once more, got out, and stood on the hill overlooking the settlement. The satellite dishes looked like so many white mushrooms: he used to go wandering in Spissy Podhraide for those.

The last of the light winked on the metal roofs. Some children rolled a bicycle wheel through the mud, stepping in and out of their own lengthenings, shadows of shadows.

He narrated a brief line into his tape recorder and played it back to himself: it was empty and stupid and he erased it.

A brief spit of low cloud went across the sun. He lifted his collar against the breeze and he looked down again, towards the camp. The man with the tattoos was returning across the bridge. He was carrying a flimsy plastic bag, bell-shaped, heavy, and he was looking down into it. He swayed across the rickety planks, one leg slower than the other, concentrating hard, mouth to the bag, breathing in and out, in and out, breathing. In the other hand he held a half-gallon can by a thin wire handle.

The tattooed man tottered a moment on the bridge and then he was gone, into the warren of shacks, out of sight.

The breeze blew cold across the hillside. "Paint thinner," said the journalist to himself and then he repeated the line into his tape recorder.

He stepped towards his car, slid into the seat, threw the recorder down beside him. With an empty inner thud, he realized that he didn't know the tattooed man's name, that he'd never asked for it, had not been given it, did not require it, the transaction had been nameless, the man, the woman, the children, the baby. He rubbed his hands on the steering wheel and looked down at the recorder. It lay, running, the tiny spools turning in the silence.

"No name," he said, and he clicked the tape recorder off, stamped the clutch, and shoved the gearstick hard into first.

He turned on his headlights in the dusk, and drove away from the settlement, insects smashing against the windscreen.

Compeggio,
Northern Italy

2001

It struck me early this morning, while lighting the first of the kerosene lamps, how strange it is to be so much at peace and yet still nothing certain.

The lamplight filled the room. I opened up the rolltop drawer of the old desk, shook the fountain pen awake. The ink splotched the paper. I went to the window and looked out. Enrico used to tell me that it takes a great deal of strength to get the snow out of the mind—not so much the path out from the mill down to the road, or the blanket the length of the valley, or the mounds backed up against the road, or the whiteness of the village, or the patches of sheer ice high in the Dolomites—it is the snow in the mind that takes the most getting used to. I failed to put any words on paper, so I pulled on a pair of his old shoes and walked down into the village. There was nothing about, not a footprint except his own—which were my own—and I sat on the steps of the old pastry shop and wondered about what you asked, about how a road could ever have brought me to such a place.

Before the village began to stir, I walked back up the winding road to the millhouse, in the still-dark. I put wood on the stove and turned on the other two kerosene lamps. The room was warm and amber. All I could hear was your father's voice in everything, even his shoes had left a wet mark on the floor.

~

Things in life have no real beginning, though our stories about them always do. Seventy-three winters have passed now across my brow. I have often settled by your bed and whispered to you of distant days, have told you of the young girl staring backwards, of your great-grandfather, and what happened to us in the Shivering Hills, of how we crossed and recrossed our land, of how I sang and what happened to me and those songs. I could never have known what would become of the pencil in my fingers. For a good while, in that previous life, I was celebrated. They seemed like the best of years, but they did not last—maybe they were not meant to—and then came the time when I was banished. In my new life, I could not bear the thought of my old poems. Even a flash of them across my mind brought a coldness to my spine. I had already made a little grave for them, the day of my judgment back in Bratislava, when I walked out from beneath the towerblocks and away. I promised myself that I would never write again, nor would I try to remember the old poems. There were times, of course, when their rhythm flitted across my mind, but for the most part I closed them off, pushed them away, left them behind. If they returned to me at all, they returned as song.

In all those years I never dared put a pen to paper, and yet I must admit that once or twice, after I met your father, I found myself stirred. I sat waiting for him to come across the mountain, or to walk up the mill road, or to appear at the window, and I thought that perhaps, in the silence, I should crack open the cap on the fountain pen, remove a page from his blank journal, and put down my simple thoughts. Yet it scared me. It reminded me of too much and I could not do it. It seems strange now after all these years, and to you, čhonorroeja, it might seem ridiculous, but I feared that if I tried to give written meaning to my life that I would once again lose what I had gained. There were these mountains, these silences, your father and you—these were not things I was willing to part with. Your father bought me books but he never asked me to write. The only person he told about my poems was Paoli, and he said that Paoli would not have known a poem unless you had him drink it. Both are gone now, Paoli and your dear father, and you are elsewhere, far away, and I have grown old and stooped and even happily gray, but in the face of your questions it strikes me now that I have no reason to fight it anymore, so I sit down at this rough-hewn table and attempt once again to put pen to paper.

Forty-two years!

When a bird breaks the line of the window it surprises me almost as much as a word.

I am sorry now that I burned your father's belongings, and I know I should have kept them for you, but in grief we do such foolish things. He told me once that he wanted his body brought to the summit where he could look down on both countries, Italy, Austria, so he could contemplate the memory of a life spent dragging cigarettes, tractor parts, coffee, medicines, from one side to the other. He said he was content for his body to be left up there for the hawks and the eagles and whatever else wandered his way—he almost relished the idea of becoming part of the buzzards, he called them the most Tyrolean of birds. In the end I could not do that, dearest heart, the thought of leaving him there was far too much, so I took all of his possessions, except one pair of shoes made from his old suitcase, and burned them not far from the millhouse. I lay down in the place of the burning, an old form of mourning. What I loved most of all were the shirts he wore, most especially the woolen ones, do you recall them? They were patched and repatched and patched again. He had learned, when he first moved to the mountains, to darn the elbows with needles, using single strands of birch twigs sharpened to a point. He joked that he was glad that I was going to burn his shirts, but it would not take long. I came back days afterwards and searched in the scorched earth for the buttons and the metal beltloop from his jacket, but the fire had burned everything down.

There is an old Romani song that says we share little pieces of our hearts with people and the further we go along, the less we have for ourselves until there is not enough left to go around and that's called traveling, and it's also called death, and since it happens to us all there's nothing more ordinary than that.

~

In Bratislava I burned my poems. I walked down the swaying staircase into the bright light of day carrying another man's possessions—his boots, his shirts, his radio, his watch. I could see nothing for my future. I was twenty-nine years old. I was cast off. So much of my life had been taken from me and yet I did not want to die.

I went out to the towerblocks for one last look. Eight shadows fell from the eight blocks, thick and dark across the ground where the children played. The caravans tilted sideways where the wheels had been ripped off. I turned away and began my terrible walk, all the way south through the small villages of Slovakia. They were the worst days of all, and often in the mornings, when I woke up in the forests, I was surprised—not so much at the notion that I had slept, but that I was alive at all.

I struck out west and crossed the border into Hungary where the only relief that came to me was the idea that I would not, now, be followed by Swann. He could not cross the border. That part of my life was behind me and I moved on to forget it. Snow came, thick in the wind. I bundled into my blankets. Villagers stared at me as I passed. I am sure I looked wretched, all skin and bone and rags. Some were kind and brought me bread, others asked where the caravans were. I selected a point in the snow's distance—a tree, a cliff, a pylon—and walked towards it. At a deserted farm, I filled my pockets with bonemeal from a feeding trough and later boiled it and ate it without thinking. The paste clove to the top of my mouth. I was eating the food of animals. I slept one night in a large cave, the roof tonsilled, the folds in the stone like curtains. Soldiers had carved words in the rock, names and dates, and I wondered how could wars extend so far? In the corner I found an old tin of meat, cracked it open with a rock, ate with my fingers. The truth is that I no longer, then, considered myself a Romani woman at all. They called me Gypsy, yet I was not even that. Nor did I think of myself as one who had read books or sung stories or written poems—if anything I thought of myself as only a primitive.

For days I kept myself low to the ground, then I waded into the lake which is, I suppose—if there is to be a beginning—the place where my life in the West began.

Even at this very moment I can feel the cold wall of water as it rose against my chest. All night long I waded through the lake so freezing cold that my feet burned. There were no rocks on the bottom of the lake and it was hard to walk, but I kept my arms high, and for once I was glad of my height. Some water plant wrapped itself around my ankle and I tried to shake it off, but lost my balance. Soon I was dripping wet from head to toe. I did not expect the rolls of barbed wire the Austrians had put down, so when I got nearer the edge of the lake I had to step over. At first I thought I was just bumping against another lake plant, but then I felt my skin ripping. My legs were sliced and bloody and yet I thought then that I was not made up of flesh or muscle or bone, I was made up of strength and it would take me onto land. I had been walking since early nightfall and all was silent. The only light was the sweep of searchlights along the frontier.

I was sure that, when dawn broke, the Russian soldiers would find me an easy shot against the light.

Stupidly, I had brought with me only bread and it had gone sodden in my pockets and drifted out into the lake. A few damp crusts were all that remained. What foolish things cross our minds at these times, daughter, the worst of times, and I thought that I would keep on going for just a glass of milk, and the prospect of this kept me wading, perhaps it was because when I was young, and traveling with the kumpanija, we were told that milk would keep our insides clean. I stumbled on, my mind unsteady. The shore seemed to retreat and for a while I thought maybe I was walking in one place, as in some awful dream, with the sandy underbottom accepting my steps one after the other, but I finally managed to wrap a blanket around my hands and pushed on. I got over the last of the underwater wires and collapsed on the ground. The searchlights swept along the shore in cones and the trees were ghost-shaped.

I stooped low and went to a marsh hole not far from the lake, lay back against the wet of the soil, and looked down upon the rips of flesh from the barbed wire. I searched my pockets for the last of the soggy crumbs and ate, trying to savor them in my mouth. The light crept up. In front of me was more marshland and surely more wooden towers with soldiers. I would do what I had done on the other side of the border—wait for the hour just before darkness, then stumble through until I found a friendly person or a farmhouse.

I was told as a girl that death always came with the hoot of an owl. I have never clung to old superstition, čhonorroeja, my own grandfather dissuaded me of such things on the road to Prešov, but I think what kept me alive that dark morning, strange as it might seem, was that I did hear an owl as he hooted long and hard, and it shocked me awake because I wanted to see in what sort of body death would arrive. It seemed to greet me with birdsong and insect noise. Something burst out of the nearby grass and I looked up to see a pheasant a little way up in the air, taunting me. How delicious it would be to catch her in my bare hands, wring her neck, and eat her without even use of a fire. I searched in the earth for anything at all to eat, even an earthworm, the most unclean of things, but there was nothing, and I sat, my body chattering in the cold. I had sewn Petr's lighter into my dress pocket. I tore it out and tried to flick it alight to warm my hands. No flame.

~

I woke under glaring light. A shadow fell across me and a white face looked down. I still to this day do not know how they found me, though I was told that I was discovered half-dead in the marsh and indeed they treated me like one dead at first.

The nurse shone a flashlight in my eyes, took hold of my jaw and said in German: Keep still. She pushed my head back onto the pillow and whirled away saying: She bit me, the little savage. I did indeed and did it well, and I would do it again, daughter, if I had to. I was sure straight away that they would arrest me, beat me, send me back to Czechoslovakia. Three nurses gathered, I could smell their sharp perfume. One grabbed hold of my cheeks, the other used a brown stick to hold down my tongue, and the third shone the flashlight into the back of my throat. The fat one wrote on a chart. The tallest took a little jar of something from her pocket and they passed it around one to the other, inhaling the fumes. It has always fascinated me that the gadže cannot smell themselves, I find it strange that they do not know how unusual their soaps and foods and bad odor, but some people only have an eye for others and never themselves. They held the jar to their noses and coughed and said how much I stank. The nurses made a telephone call and asked for some assistance, then said: We're taking her down to the showers.

Believe you me, that is when hell's fury was let loose—all I had heard for a decade was talk of poverty, strikes, and persecution, of the ordinary people in the West beaten down, of how we were hounded, of how little had changed since the days of the fascists, of how the streets were strung with reams of barbed wire, and in my delirium it was possible to believe that in the West they had begun their showers again. Who would deny that if it happened once it would not happen again? There is nothing so terrible that they will not try to repeat it. I shouted in Romani that they would not take me to their showers, no! I would not let them take me! I pulled back the sheets and ripped the drip out of my arm. They whistled for the guard but I was already out of the bed. A siren went off. The tall white-haired nurse tried to stand in front of me, but I shoved her backwards, stumbled to the door, pushed it open, I do not know where the strength came from.

Three men in uniform appeared at the far end of the corridor. One banged his billyclub on the wall. I backed into a room. Light came through one small window. Outside, through the haze of glass, was a patch of green. I squeezed out and landed in the grass. A number of tents stood squat on the ground. Beyond them, a few wooden buildings where smoke rose from the tin-pot chimneys. I heard someone shouting in Hungarian and another language I didn't recognize. I ran down the dirt road, past the tents, towards the gate, but the men in uniform were standing there wearing white armbands. They put up their rifles and said, with half a smile: *Halt.* A single red-white-red wooden barrier lay across the road. I could see long flat plains and in the distance huge mountains, with clouds halfway up them, capped with snow against the blue sky—so this, then, was Austria and the West, what a strange way to see it, through an open gate, with nurses shuffling in the dust behind me, and a rifle pointed at me.

Along came a tall gray-haired woman with four soldiers trailing behind her. She had the air of a bureaucrat but she stood in front of me and said: This is a D.P. camp, don't worry.

Her voice was calm. We're here to help you, she said. She took another step forward.

Displaced persons, she said.

When I tried to break the line of soldiers, one of them caught me in the shoulder with the end of his rifle. The woman knocked his gun aside and said: Leave her alone, you brute. She bent down to me and began whispering that I would be all right, not to fret, she was a doctor, she would take care of me. Yet I did not trust her—who would? I pushed away from her, began to walk towards the red and white gate, my head held tall, my body straight.

Okay, said the woman, put her in cuffs.

They brought me to a gray building where the nurses undressed me. A few soldiers stood outside the shower room and although most of them looked away, one or two came to the small window and looked inside. I sat on a hardbacked chair under the stream of water, while the nurses rubbed me fiercely with hard soap and brushes on long broom handles.

I tried to hide my nakedness. On and on they went about how I wore no breast support, about how I smelled, and that there was no smell on earth like a Gypsy, but still I said nothing. Near the end of the shower one of the soldiers put his pink tongue against the glass and licked it. I curled into myself and closed my eyes. They threw me a towel, then led me to another hospital room where they razored my hair. When I looked down on the floor there were some white larvae moving through the clumps. I had no feeling. It was my hair, but so what? It hardly mattered, it was just another ornament. Since a young age I had cut it off many times, always against custom. They sprayed me with a white powder that made my eyes itch. I did not allow them to know I could speak a little German, but I understood their words and believe me they were not talking of me as a flower that had sprung from the earth.

I had escaped an old life and was caught in a new one, but I could have no sympathy for myself, it was of my own making.

I was brought back to the ward. The doctor put her stethoscope to my chest. She said I was being held for my own safety, she would look after me, I was protected under international treaties, there was no cause for concern. She had the confident voice of one who did not believe a single word she was saying.

Her name was Doctor Marcus, from Canada, and she spoke German like she had just shoved a fistful of stones into her mouth. She said she would give me medical quarantine for a month or two, but after that I would have to apply for refugee status and then I would be allowed the status of the other displaced people. On her desk Doctor Marcus had some of my possessions: my Party card, my knife, some paper krowns wrinkled from the lakewater, and the coin Conka had given me, still wrapped in strands of her fine red hair. I reached out to get my possessions but she dropped them in a large paper envelope and said that they would be returned when I began to comply. She spun the coin in her fingers, dropped it in the envelope, and closed the clasp. A hair had fallen onto the desk.

Are you willing to talk to me? the doctor asked.

I pretended again that I was mute. Doctor Marcus spoke into an intercom system, instructed them to bring in the translator, an enormous heap of a woman who asked me question after question, in Czech and Slovak both, who I was, how I got a Party card, what had happened to me, how did I cross the border, did I know anyone in Austria and, of course their favorite question, was I really a Gypsy? I looked like one, they said, I dressed in colorful rags like one, but I did not seem like one. I sat still with my hands in my lap. The translator told me to nod yes or no to her questions. Are you Czech? Are you Slovakian? Are you Gypsy? Why have you come in from Hungary? This coin is an unusual coin, isn't it? Is this your identity card? Are you a Communist? I sat still. The best way around her was silence. When they were finished, the translator threw her hands up in the air but Doctor Marcus leaned forward and said: I know you understand us, we only want to help you, why don't you let us?

I lifted the single strand of Conka's hair from the desk and they took me off to quarantine.

~

So much time was spent in the white rooms of the hospital that I began to think back on all that had happened. My voice is strong now when I recall this, but back then I was a weak and terrified thing, and I stopped in every corner I could find, real or not. I did not want the roads of my childhood to return, I attempted to put them out of my mind, but the more I did so the more they appeared.

We used to make potato candles, Conka and I, we hollowed them out and lit the thin walls of potato with light, and in winter Conka loved to skate with the lit candles in her hands, tree to tree, they kept her hands warm. She had a pair of skates her father had made from old boots and knifeblades. Sometimes the lights went out when she turned on the skates, or skidded and fell, or sometimes the ice sprayed up and put out the wick-flame. Above us the stars swung. These and other things returned to me while I lay in the Austrian bed—I sometimes felt as if I were still out on the ice. I heard cracking and saw hands reaching up for me. I could hear boots in the forest and there stood Swann and there stood Vashengo and there stood Stránský, rifling through a sheaf of papers and, behind them again, a row of bureaucrats and nurses and officers and guards. I turned and thrashed about in the bed, but the pictures returned harder, faster, with the insistence of things impossible to shake.

Doctor Marcus arrived at the end of my bed every noon, her stethoscope twinkling in the light, a row of pens in her pocket, one with a Canadian flag, and although she looked not a bit like

Swann, I could not help thinking that she was like a sister to him, with her light hair, hazel eyes, her oval face.

You don't have to suffer, she said. There's no point. Why don't you tell me your situation and then I can help?

It was like an old song, a children's rhyme, I had heard it so often, it was as if she had taken the words of a bureaucrat and put them in a child's mouth.

I know you can talk, she said. The nurses heard you. On the first day, you were screaming in a language they didn't recognize, surely it was Gypsy, am I right, was it Gypsy?

I turned away.

Some people think you're Polish, she said.

Then she leaned in even closer.

But I think you're from outer space.

That almost made me smile, yet when Doctor Marcus left I stared at the ceiling, and the more I stared, the more it pressed down on me.

They did not know my name let alone my anguish.

Later in the day Doctor Marcus came back and shone her flashlight into my eyes and wrote something on her chart. Pills were given to me with water, white tablets with orange writing. I had the strange thought that I was swallowing words and Swann's face kept coming to my mind. I had lost a tooth in my journey and the orange pills fitted perfectly in the gap. I spat them out when the nurses left, dropped them down a hole in the top of the metal bedstead.

I don't think that even now I can find the proper words to describe the feeling of having left my life behind. I was suspended in empty air like a shirt from a branch. Every time I turned in the bed I would see an old road, the lane at the back of the chocolate factory, or the road to the schoolhouse near Prešov, or the high path to the forest above the vineyards; small flashes that burst out green and yellow into my mind. I turned to the other side of the bed and more flashes came. I was at a strange bridge. I did not know how wide it was. I tried crossing it. I stood in the dark waving at what was, a second ago, the bright sky. Leather straps were buckled down across my chest. They put a piece of rubber between my teeth. The child I was came back to me, hovered above me, her lazy eye looking down. After a while I recognized that the child was Conka too, but her hair was hacked off. She sat watching things retreating into the distance. Strange noises came, nothing like melody. A line of trees went out of sight. A tent flapped in the wind. The nurses hovered over me and a needle went into my arm. I turned away and tried to rattle the orange pills from the bottom of the bedstead. I would have taken them all in one go. They were terrible days, they could not have been worse.

The doctor finally said she would not give me any more pills or injections. She barked at the nurse to put her arm under mine and allowed me to walk through the ward. I stood and swayed. Walking helped cure some things and for the next few weeks they fed me well and all my lacerations healed, my hair began to grow back, and my feet were carefully tended to. They replaced the bandages three times a day, using a soft creamy medicine that smelled of mint. They allowed me to mark my sheets—I did not want to share my bedclothes even if they were to be washed, I made it clear by holding on to them and wrapping them around my wrist.

Doctor Marcus said let her keep them, they're only sheets, it's a small price, she will open up soon.

But I said to myself that I would not open up, I would make

a little place for myself in my mind, I would close its door, settle behind it, and I would not step across to open it again, ever.
I walked around and around, like a clockhand. After a while my
feet began to recover and my legs felt strong. Doctor Marcus
came in and said: Oh, what rosy cheeks we have today. I
thought that I should give her one of Stránský's old lectures on
Marxism and the historical dialectic, and then she wouldn't
think me such a broken paltry thing wandering around her hospital floor, but in truth I never really thought about the days
with Stránský or Swann—no, it was more my childhood that
kept coming back to me, the touch of Grandfather's shirt, nine
drops of water in the ashes, looking from the back of the wagon
while the caravan bounced, and I think now that these thoughts
were there to protect me and to make sure that I kept myself intact, although at the time they almost drove me to an edge I did
not recognize.

You can die of madness, daughter, but you can also die of
silence.

~

There is a quiver in my fingers and the hairs on my arms
still rise when I put voice to these things. I dress in the dark
these days, remove the glass chimney from the kerosene lamp,
take the lid off the firebox, crumple the paper, drop it in, strike
a match, wait for the flame to catch, then bring the same match
to the stove. I have been spared another night to come into this
day. Soon I hear the ticking of the metal and the char-sound of
wood, and it becomes light enough to see and the room comes
alive.

I had, today, a strange thought as I walked down all the way
to the village. It was just past noon and the light seemed to sus-

pend the street, full of years somehow. I walked along the road, towards Paoli's old shop. I kept my eyes down on the pavement and watched the feet of people as they went past. The bell clanged when I went in—it is still one of the few shops where the old ways have held. Paoli's son Domenico was behind the counter, lighting candles to put on a table.

It was then that it flashed in front of my eyes, a simple thought and yet I still cannot shake it. For a brief second, I saw Conka. She wore a scarf and her hair was bundled beneath. She stood near the bottom of the towerblock where I had left her long ago, in Czechoslovakia. Her children were grown and gone. She wore a dark dress and her hands were shoved deep in her pockets. She walked towards the towerblocks, but the lift was broken, so she began to climb the stairs. At first I thought that she was looking for firewood, that she was going to rip up the floorboards from the flats, carry the wood down and burn it so she could cook a meal for her family. But all the doors to the flats were locked. She climbed higher, going from floor to floor. It grew dark. She got to the top of the towerblock, reached into her pocket, and took out a potato candle. From the other pocket she took out a match. She fumbled awhile to light it, but finally the wick took. It sat there, flickering on the top wall of the flats. She watched it a long time and then she reached forward and pushed it off the edge and down it went, through the air, aflame.

Why I thought this I still do not know. Domenico took my arm and told me to sit down on the corner stool in the shop, my hands were trembling so. His brother, Luca, the smallest of them, carried my groceries home, relit the kerosene lamp for me. He asked me if I would be all right and I said yes, I would. He asked for you and I told him you were in Paris, that you send letters, you live in an apartment, that your work is good and healthy and keeps your mind sharp.

Paris, he said.

I am quite sure his eyes sparkled—you are not forgotten, čhonorroeja.

He bid me goodbye and he spotted the pages on the table, but I am sure he thought nothing of them. I could hear him whistling as he went down the hill.

～

After a few days in quarantine I could stand it no longer and I called on Doctor Marcus and said to her in German, Am I a prisoner? She stared at me as if I had just somersaulted twice through the air. She said, Of course not, no. I told her that I was ready to go. She said it was not that simple and why hadn't I talked earlier, it would have been much easier. Why do you say that I am not a prisoner? I asked again. There are certain rules we must adhere to for the good of everybody, she said. Is this not the free West? Pardon me? she said. Is this not the democratic West? What an interesting thing to say, she said. Tell me why I am being held prisoner. There are no prisoners here, she replied.

I told her that I wanted to be released immediately, that it was my right, and she sprang back indignantly that she would do her very best, and she could promise me that at the very least I would be allowed out of the hospital if I helped them with information. Be thankful, she said, for what you have.

They always ask you to be thankful, čhonorroeja, after they have locked you up. Perhaps they also ask you to kiss them when they throw away the key.

My name is Marienka, I told her.

The chair scraped as she pulled it up closer.

Marienka, she said, that's a beautiful name.

Is it? I asked.

She blushed.

Doctor Marcus took down my strange story on her white notepad. My German was not good enough, nor did I want to speak in Slovak, so I spoke to her in Magyar. The translator was a pious young man from Budapest who wore a giant crucifix at his neck. I did not call myself Zoli for fear of two things, their laughter at my name and the chance that the word would take wing and they might find out exactly who I was.

The story was simple. I had been born in the Hungarian lands. I was abandoned by my husband and I wanted to join my children who were living in France. They had left in '56, but I could not go since I was arrested and beaten. I got out of jail and went back to my settlement which was near the border. My people had never cared about borders. Once it had been one giant country and we still treated it that way. The Party card was something I had found on the ground near a dump by the border. I saw Doctor Marcus pale with doubt, so I circled back and told her that I'd inserted a picture of myself into the card and that one of my family was an accomplished forger. Doctor Marcus shrugged. She said: All right, go on, go on. For a little gaiety, I said I'd taken a bus from the city of Györ but the bus broke down and I bartered for a bicycle. It was my first time riding such a machine. I wobbled down the road and farmers laughed at me. I slept in abandoned farmhouses, ate nettle soup, and made a borscht from sour cherries. I threw away the bicycle when I got a flat tire. Doctor Marcus began smiling then, and as the story went on she became triumphant and scribbled everything down as fast as she could. I began to like this person I was creating, and so I said that I had stolen a second bicycle, except this one had a giant basket on the front and, of course, I had borrowed some chickens, tied them down in the basket, feathers flying, and had lived on them until I made my break for freedom.

You can make them swallow any lie with enough sugar and tears. They will lick the tears and sugar and make of them a paste called sympathy. Try it, čhonorroeja, and you might feel yourself dissolve.

I cannot explain why so many of them have hated us so much over so many years, and even if I could, it would make it too easy for them. They cut our tongues and make us speechless and then they try to get an answer from us. They do not wish to think for themselves and they dislike those who do. They are comfortable only with the whip above their heads, yet so many of us have spent our lives armed with little more dangerous than song. I am filled with the memory of those who have lived and died. We have our own fools and evils, čhonorroeja, but we are pulled together by the hatred of those who surround us. Show me a single patch of land we did not leave, or would not leave, a single place we have not turned from. And while I have cursed so many of my own, our sleight of hand, our twin tongues, my own vain stupidities, even the worst of us has never been amongst the worst of them. They make enemies of us so that they do not have to look at themselves. They take freedom from one and give it to another. They turn justice into revenge and still call it by its old name. They expect us to see the future or at least to rob its pockets. They shave our heads and say: You are thieves, you are liars, you are filthy, why can't you just be like us?

This is the truth of how I felt then, daughter, and so I said to myself that I would be like them only for as long as it took to get out of the camp and move on elsewhere.

I was transferred from the hospital into the camp, given blue status, on a day of sunlight. Doctor Marcus reeled off a long list of rules. I would be permitted to go to the nearby town two days a week, but I would not be allowed to beg or tell fortunes or any of the other things they expected us to do, they were against local rules. I could leave at eight in the morning and had to be home by curfew. They would give me a ration book and I could deposit it in the camp bank. No drinking alcohol, she said, or relations with men, and beyond the camp walls I was not allowed to fraternize with the guards.

Before I left the hospital the nurses pretended they'd found another louse in my hair just so they could shave it off. They pulled the razor hard across my scalp.

My other clothes had been burned, but what could I do, mourn for them?

I was taken to the storeroom. I found a long scarf to put over my scalp and I was given new sandals to parade around in, brown with a shiny brass buckle. I chose some Portuguese dresses in splendid yellows and reds, but when I put them on I caught a glimpse of myself in the mirror and I looked so much like my old self that I turned around and chose a long gray dress donated by the people of the United States. I was given my useless money and Party card and even my onyx-handled knife. I burned the card right away. I opened the envelope to see Conka's coin sitting there. I kissed it and thanked my dear lost friend for not spitting at me, and yet for giving her children the dignity to do so.

Doctor Marcus escorted me to a special room at the far end

of the wooden barracks. Only the very youngest children were about and they trailed behind me, laughing, pulling at my sleeve. Some of them were kicking a ball made from a pig's bladder and their high voices split the air. The women looked out from the kitchens. Most were Hungarians. I felt a tenderness for them since I knew they had been here since they walked across the border in '56, four years before. Someone had written on the wall in Magyar: *We have left behind the raincoats, pray for us.*

When we turned the final corner towards the last barracks, near the wire fence, I stopped cold. A woman, dark, long-skirted, sat on the steps nursing a young baby. She put her hand to her mouth in surprise, handed her baby to another child, and came to touch my head.

Lamb of heaven, she said, they shaved off all your hair.

I cannot tell you, čhonorroeja, how low my heart dropped at the sight of this woman, and I knew almost immediately that I would have to escape, not only because I was polluted, but because eventually they would know, they would feel it from me, I tell you the bare truth, a Rom always knows, and I would bring the shame to them too. She took my hand in hers and gave me a slab of bread. I cannot do this, I thought, I am a traitor. And yet what was I betraying? What was left of my old self to betray? How distant I felt from the Zoli who had spent many hours in the rooms of Budermice, and the ringing phones of the writers' union, and the pulsing machines of Stránský's printing mill, and the shining chandeliers of the Carlton Hotel, and all the other places I met Doom and put on her shining jewelry.

Now here was bread being put in my hands by a dark sister, jabbering in our sweet and ancient tongue.

Her name was Mozol. She grabbed my elbow and pulled me inside the dark barracks—her blankets, several bundles, a series of mats unrolled on the floor—and pointed at a fat man sleeping under a hat, on a tattered couch. That's my husband, Panch, she said, he's lazier than a bad sin. He snores even when he walks, I tell you. Come, come, I will show you around. We are rich with room. None of the gadže want to be with us, so we have the whole barracks to ourselves, can you imagine?

She touched my cheek then spun me around and dizzied me with her voice: Lord above, I kiss your tired eyes.

With Mozol all I had to do was nod and listen. She put one and two words together, and soon they made ten thousand. Her endless jabberjaw filled my ears, but it felt as if a salve had been put at the raw points of my mind. She showed me around the barracks, led me through the camp towards the shop where I could use the ration slips. On and on Mozol talked, I am not sure she ever paused for breath. Her husband couldn't get a word in either. He called her his little nightingale, but even then she would drown out his voice with her babble. Mozol had seven children and was working on her eighth, and if there was nobody around to talk to she would have talked to her own belly.

All hardships, čhonorroeja, have a streak of laughter in them.

Those few days are welded into me now and I cannot speak of them quietly. I took on a life I did not know. I was no longer a poet nor a singer, or one who read books, not even one who traveled. I woke in the same place each day. I put a saucepan of coffee on. I aired the mattress, beat it with my bare hands. I ate with Mozol's family around their three-legged pot. I was privy to their yarns and confidences. I had never had such a life before.

I swapped out my clothes for a few of the Portuguese dresses once again. I caught sight of myself, colorful, in the windows of the offices. My hair grew, and I sewed the coin in the strands. My old language bore me to the window.

You may ask why I did not leave, move out from the camp under cover of darkness, and keep moving, why I brought the secret shame to Mozol's family, why I never told them who I was and what had happened to me. The fence surrounding the barracks was so low that a child could have climbed it, but we were scared of what lay outside. The awfulness of the camp was less than the fear of what lay beyond. And I will also tell you this: there was a terrible plague of insects one day a few weeks after I left the camp hospital, grubby little things with small yellow wings. I got up early one morning and found a good many of these insects clinging to the wall. They had lost their way, and had clung there until dead, held fast by their tiny claws, stiffened into their last moment. I went to wipe the dead ones away, but as soon as I did one of them, just one, came out of its stiffened pose, and I bore it on a cloth to the open window with the one bit of life still left in it.

And so, for a while, I allowed myself to live under the awning of my own people once again. An invisible hand had reached in and turned my heart a small notch backwards.

~

In the camp I had taken one great big year of breath and held on to it. I did not attempt to escape.

Mozol and I began to collect flowers, which we sold in the

marketplace near to Domplatz. At home in the barracks we buried our money in the corner behind the stove. Mozol had spent twelve years in the camps, her children had been born there, and she dreamed of nothing more than leaving, but she needed a country to take her in, and who would sponsor the Gypsies when they thought of us as something less than human? But one morning she came running up to me and thrust a paper into my hand, a Canadian insignia stamped on it. Doctor Marcus had told her what was in the letter. I opened the envelope, took a glance, and then announced myself happy indeed. Mozol gazed at me. How did you know what the letter said? she asked. My spirits dropped. How did you know what the letter said, my heart's friend? I looked to the ground. I almost told her that I had read it, daughter, that I could indeed read and write, that all along I had brought the shame to her, but I caught myself. I walked across the high wire then, saying I was able to feel what was in the letter, it trilled through my toes, it was intuition. She looked at me doubtfully but I spun her around in the dust and she began to laugh. She was on her way to Toronto, but within a few days another note came to say that she and Panch would have to pay for a portion of their own passage. The nurse who read the letter aloud had a shine in her eyes when she read it. The fare was enormous, it would have bought them a patch of land. Mozol could not understand. Surely I can go by train, she said. To Canada? said the nurse and she laughed.

Mozol lay in her wickerbound bed crying. Bit by bit she began to descend, if you can imagine, into silence. She said that Jesus had wept for everyone, but the gadže had put a roof in the sky and yelled down destruction so his tears could not refresh us. I have never really believed in God or a heaven or any of that loud ranting, but I believed in it for her, it is what she wanted. She ran rosary beads through her fingers and I called back our old prayer: *Bless these bits, these bridles, these reins, keep these wheels firm to your solid ground.*

Later that week we were sitting on the steps of the barracks. An ant crossed in front of me, carrying another ant bent double. I pressed my hand to the cool earth. The ant stopped at my hand and looked for a way around but then climbed my fingers and took the body of the dead one across. I leaned down and blew it gently off my finger.

We fall out of rhythm with our earliest ways. There were so many times when I had forgotten my old life, I even forgot I was polluted, or maybe I had just put a rag on the blade, and in some ways I had begun to think of myself as Mozol's sister. The decision had no fear. Sometimes you make up your mind about something without knowing why. I knew the town well. I did not like what I was about to do, daughter, but I had forced myself not to think about it. I cut the nerve that twitched in me and went to the dump at the edge of town. Some piles of rubbish were smoking from early fires. Ash and dust wheeled in the air. I rescued the door of a thrown-away cupboard, yellow with flaking paint. I tore it from its hinges and gauged its weight. I carved a set of maple leaves and a griffin on either side of the door —ridiculous, of course, but I did not care.

I fashioned two grand rubber earrings from parts of a discarded carburetor.

In the early dawn, I found a Spanish scarf in the collection of camp clothing. I tied it around my head, went out the gate, and wandered along the streambank at the rear of the camp. I picked pebbles from the water, the smoother and more polished the better. The pebbles clacked in my pocket as I made my way into the center of the town, carrying all my materials. Gusts of wind encouraged me along. I passed through a cobbled square. How strange the light was, it filled everything up, yet nothing seemed to cast a shadow. I kept expecting to have trouble, but found none. A woman on her own did not present too much of a threat. I wandered until I settled on a narrow alleyway just off the long Odenburger, not far from the railway station. I was struck by the stillness of the alley, though many were passing on foot. I found two broken concrete blocks in an unpainted doorway, set the door on top, put a blanket underneath, and sat down with my head bowed. I said to myself over and over that I was a traitor to everything, even myself.

Nothing happened. A smell of cabbage wafted out from a nearby restaurant. I could hear the buzz around me, the restaurant workers gathering at the door to watch, to smoke, to point. Austrian women in long brown coats passed with their heads cocked indifferently, but I could sense an excitement they did not want to betray. I listened to the sound of their shoes as they turned, nearly always six paces beyond. Just a moment's hesitation, and then they moved on. I had settled on silence as a form of communication, as good as any. A young man hunkered down on the ground in front of me and held out his palm. I placed the stones in his hand and asked him to roll them across the table. I told him to be calm, that he had nothing to be afraid of. Take my hand, I said, but do not look into my eyes. His own hands were smooth and unlined, his arms were thin and his shoulders narrow. His face, though, was generous, and on his wide nose were the red marks of one who usually wears eyeglasses, so I said to him that I had a strong feeling that he had left something behind, perhaps it had something to do with distance. He shook his head, no. Well, then, I said, maybe it has something to do with sight. His mouth twitched. Yes, he stuttered, and he took the glasses from his pocket, put them on. I had a hold on him already. It was nothing more or less mysterious than that. I touched the scattered stones one by one and incanted some gibberish above them.

I thought of myself then in a poor reflection of what I used to be and yet it did not disturb me. I felt at ease with the sham, and I began by asking: The heart or wealth?

The question meant nothing, yet seemed to have the right weight.

The heart, the boy replied immediately. I made the sign of the cross on his palm. He rolled the stones a second time. He had been through dark times, I said. Yes. He was searching now for a different place. Yes. Some of it, I said, involved flight or movement. His eyes lit up and he leaned in closer. A city or town, I said, not far away. Yes, yes, Graz, he replied. There had been dark things in Graz, I said, and he had held on to the hand of someone. Yes, he declared, and his eyes grew big. He said that he had a friend named Tomas who had died after the war, he had stepped on a tram line and his foot had been caught and he was killed, the tram bearing down on him, unstoppable. I closed my eyes, then asked him to roll the stones across the board again. There was awful sorrow at the death of Tomas, I said, and here I furrowed my brow. It was something to do with trains. Yes, yes, he told me, it was a tram! Tomas was suffering, I said, from something during the war, some awful moment, it had something to do with his uniform. Yes, you're right, the boy whispered, he had wanted to desert. He wanted to leave the army, I repeated, and he was afraid of what would happen, the disgrace. Yes, said the boy, his Uncle Felix. I stared into his eyes and told him that there were other secrets too, and here I deepened my brow. I touched the boy's cold hands and said, after a long silence, the name uncle Felix. But how do you know, said the boy, how on earth do you know that name?

I wanted to say that some things are more important than the truth, but I did not.

From this distance of four decades it may seem that I was not scared, but I can tell you now that my blood was coursing triple time, for I kept expecting troopers to round the corner, or some dead family spirit to lean in from a doorway to see what had happened to me, how I had betrayed all that I had ever known. I had no name for what I had become, it did not exist in either pain or pleasure.

Still, the less I talked, the more the boy talked, and he was not even aware of what he was telling me. They never remember what they have said, čhonorroeja, instead they wait for the wisdom which you have borrowed. He gave me his answers and I repeated them back and made them mine, he had no idea of my trickery. I could have dressed the dead in bearskins and taught them how to dance and still he would have believed that they were there to console him. His voice became low and even. I said to him that he should carry bread in his pocket as protection against bad luck and that in the spirit world everything was fine for his good friend Tomas. I talked of goodness and purpose and vision. Keep things close to your heart, I said, and they will be a power. The boy stood, reached deep in his pocket and took out a whole handful of coins, which he laid on the wooden board.

You cannot understand what this means to me, he said.

I pocketed the coins and hurried back to the dump. I found an old chair and set it up in the alleyway and by noontime I had four customers, each of whom paid successively more, relegated as they were to their own peculiar dooms.

There are times I must admit that I had a little giggle at the foot of their foolishness. Once a trooper came by, slapping his truncheon at his thigh. For all his snarl he could have been a Hlinka, but I rolled the riverstones for him and filled him with folly about his good life, and he promised that he would leave me alone as long as I did not make too much of a fuss. I told him he should wear socks of a different color for good luck and the next day he walked past me, flicked a quick look at me, raised his trouser legs, one after the other, brown and blue, and marched on.

A number of weeks went by and I lost myself in the telling. Word of my talents spread. Many young men in particular came to visit me. I could see that something inside them had gone soft and loose and hopeless, but when they talked about it they briefly forgot it. I filled them with promises of cures and good days to come. I made a cross of wax mixed with charcoal and wrapped it in hair. I sewed two yellow buttons together and tied them on a stick. These I called my little corpses and I set them up around me; such ridiculous charms only gave weight to my words. They paid me good money for such foolishness and I sat watching the shadows reach out for other shadows as the idiots rolled a few riverstones across a cupboard table. I had no mercy for them, it was not my pocket they were reaching into.

Mozol almost cried her eyes out onto her breast when I gave her all the money.

In the height of autumn, 1961, Mozol left on a canvas-covered truck. Her few possessions were stacked high in the air and her children still higher upon them. Her husband was spread out over them to keep them from falling, but was already sleeping. She smiled, clasped my hands, and looked me in the eye. For many years I would remember that look, how close I came to telling her the truth. I stopped her several times as she gathered her possessions together and said: Mozol, I must tell you something. But she said, I am too busy, tell me later. I am quite sure she knew, she kissed my forehead when she left, then put my hand against her heart.

There is no single goodbye for us, chonorroeja. Ačh Devlesa. Dža Devlesa. One is staying. One is leaving. Stay with God, go with God.

I saw the white mountains and how they lay against the sky, and I am not ashamed to tell you that the sight was terrifying.

You'll be next Marienka, said Doctor Marcus. She walked back towards her clinic with her hands tight behind her back.

How lost I felt then, daughter, how very alone.

Only people with desires can be fooled, and I had none. My friend was gone. The next morning I put on the same clothes that I had worn for months, took my makeshift table, and prepared to go into town. But then I caught a glimpse of myself in the glass and let me tell it to you straight, daughter, I knew that in my shame I had lost every shred of dignity that I had ever worked to own. I do not seek to make a complicated dance of it, I had done these things for a purpose, but now the purpose had disappeared. I looked at myself and saw nothing that shored me up on the left shoulder and little to shore me up on the right. The worst burden in life is what others know about us. But maybe there is one burden even worse than this. It happens when they don't know about us, it is what they think about us when, in silence, they force us to be what they expect us to be. Even worse is how we become it and I, chonorroeja, had become it.

I went down past the cathedral to Franz-Liszt Street. No sound came from the high shuttered windows. I set my things around me. The people gathered and I gave them all bad omens that they accepted and wore like masks. The next day, I walked beyond the red-white-red barrier like there was nothing unusual at all, but instead of going down by the dump road I went towards the mountains.

~

Last night I woke thinking Enrico was here. I rose and flamed the lamp but found only these pages. Out the window, I could see way down into the valley. What is it about the cold that sharpens the edges of everything? Enrico used to say that the emptiest days are the loveliest.

Do you, daughter, recall the sight of your father coming home after a foray across the rocky part of the northern mountain when he had cut himself from a fall off a small cliff? He was carrying animal medicines then—steroids, hormones, injections to sell on the other side. He had packed them solid into a giant rucksack, had even filled his pockets and socks, and then he trudged off to Maria Luggua. A blizzard blew up, a curtain of snow opening and closing around him. He was edging his way around the point in the mountain where not even the goats ventured. He stepped off into nothing but air, and his fall was broken only by an outcrop of rock. He landed in a drift and he looked down to see that his leg had been ripped open. He contemplated the animal injections but didn't know which might help him with the pain. He had to dig himself out with a small folding shovel strapped to the side of his rucksack. The blood filled up his snowboot. He could only recognize where he was by the feel of the trees—the further down he went on the slope the less gnarled the bark became. When he reached home, he dropped the rucksack, and simply said: Put the kettle on, Zoli, I'm freezing.

He pulled off the snowboot, put it by the stove and said it had been a very bad evening for a walk. He had been gone three whole days.

I can see him now, his thin nose, his wide mouth, the lines grooved deep in his face, his eyes half-closed against the glare of the snow.

When the new trade laws came in, there was no longer any need for medicines or cigarettes or coffee or seeds to be brought across the mountain, and he had always refused to bring dynamite for the Tyroleans who were blowing up pylons and causing havoc. He stopped his trade, just as suddenly as he had started, and he seldom walked the mountain anymore, except on festive days, and he made his living instead at the millhouse, and when the millhouse went the way of everything else, he bought it, moved with us in here, kept the wheel running, and did whatever handyman jobs he could find around the valley. Two or three times a day he stood in the doorway, looking out over the weather above the mountain. He could have walked out blindfolded and still found his way there.

I have loved your father, pure and simple; his and yours are the only lives I have never betrayed.

The first truck to ever give me a lift belonged to a fruit farmer. He wore a black suit. His cheeks were red and newly shaven, his eyes bloodshot. He knew that I was running from something, but at first he did not say a word. I sat tight in the seat as the gears clanked and the engine rumbled into life. The farmer asked where I was going and when I didn't answer he shrugged and said he was on his way to the market a few towns down the road and I was welcome to join him so long as I did not make a fuss. I feigned being mute once again and the farmer sighed deeply as if it were the oldest trick, which it was, and one that has always failed me, as much as looking over my shoulder.

Scared of something? he asked.

The hedges shot by, trees and windmills, and I realized just how strange it had been to have walked so far, things being so much different at speed. I still did not recall how I had walked in the haze after the judgment. I kept that part of my mind blank, I could not face it, how I had crossed the border first from Slovakia and then from Hungary, and then to Austria. Nor did I think of where I was going. Paris seemed as good, or as ridiculous, a place as any.

After a while it began to rain. The windscreen wipers were broken but the farmer had made a rope that he could pull from inside the truck. He showed me how to do it with exaggerated movements and it made me happy, this small task. I tugged the rope from one side of the dashboard to the other. The fruit farmer complimented me, but I noticed that he had opened his window and was smoking furiously. So he thinks I smell, I thought. I wanted to laugh. I rolled down my window and felt the cold wind blowing. We went west in open country under the shadow of the mountains. The road was long and straight and the trees snapped to attention. The mountains lay white and enormous in the distance. It was curious to me that the closer we came to them the further away they seemed to drift. The farmer drove with one hand on the steering wheel and looked across at me every now and then.

You know those Russians put another satellite up in the air? he said.

I had no idea what he was talking about, nor for what reason he said it.

You can see them at night like small stars moving, he said.

I made a complicated series of hand gestures and finished by scrunching my fingers down into the palm of my hand, like grinding a tooth that might once have laid there, long ago. The fruit farmer shook his head and sighed. He steered with his knee and lit yet another cigarette. Two streams of pale blue smoke came from his nostrils and then he leaned across and passed the cigarette to me. I shook my head, no, but another voice said take it, Zoli, for crying out loud take it. He shrugged and held the cigarette near the window, and I watched as it reddened and burned down. Sparks flew from his fingers. The smell of tobacco made my head spin. That was one of my first lessons about the West—they do not ask twice. You should always say yes. Say yes before they even suggest that you might say no, say yes even before they ask you to say yes.

The road sped beneath us. For the first time I began to think I was truly in a different country. I turned to look at a family collecting blackberries at the side of the road until they became small dots in the distance. Tall silos gave way to church steeples and, near the outskirts of a large town, the farmer pulled into the roadside verge. Right, here we are, he said. He climbed out, lifted a tarp and handed me some apples. I've always had a passion for the traveling life, he said. I nodded. Just steer clear of the Kieberer, he said, and you'll be all right.

For whatever reason I forgot my mute ways and asked: What's a Kieberer?

He did not blink an eye and said: The gendarmes.

Oh, thank you, I said.

He laughed long and hard and then said: I thought as much.

I felt my body tighten and I yanked the door handle, but he threw his head back and laughed again.

He drove the truck alongside me as I tried to walk away along the verge of the road. Traffic was zooming past and blaring their horns. To one side was a grazing field, the other a stoneworks. When I quickened my pace the fruit farmer quickened too. He was rolling tobacco with two hands and steering the truck with his knees, but then he brought the truck to a halt, sealed the paper with his tongue, leaned out the window and gave me two hand-rolled cigarettes. I took them straightaway.

I'm fond of escape stories, he said.

He clanged through the gears and drove off in a cloud. I stood watching and thought: Well, here I am in Austria, with two hand-rolled cigarettes and a man waving me goodbye from a battered fruit truck, if ever I had four guesses of where I would be after so many years, all of them would be wrong.

～

That night I found some lovely gardens, dense and private, to sleep in. A hard breeze was approaching, announced in advance by the clapping of house shutters. Rain came and I huddled against a wall. I woke to find that I had spent the night beneath a monument to war. Stanislaus used to say that wars were fought especially for the carvers of stone, and I thought about the truth of that, when in every small village of Europe you can see Christ or Soldier hammered out in stone. But who, on a battlefield, čhonorroeja, wants a monument? Who, in the middle of his fighting, thinks he will one day be in the hands of a mason?

I cursed my old poems and went down to the town square—I did not even know what town I was in—and told a series of fortunes for a paltry sum that brought me enough for a train ticket. A shiny train stood on the tracks. Questions rattled in my mind. Where could I go? How could I break a border without a passport? What place might accept me? I tried pushing these thoughts aside. I would buy a ticket west, that was all. I was halfway through the queue at the ticket window when two gendarmes appeared. One lifted my chin with the cold end of his truncheon. He turned and whispered to his colleague. I had a fair idea that they would make their own statue of me, so when the gendarme looked over again, this Gypsy woman was gone once more, on foot.

You do not cross the mountains in Austria, you follow the valleys and the rivers. It is like you are held in the clasp of a breast, not always a kind breast, but one that will guide you along anyway.

My river was the Mürz, clear and leaping. I walked for many days, hugging the bank. On the floodplain there were a few small huts where I could lie down and sleep for a few hours, sometimes on swales of straw. I watched the circles of a hawk swooping down for food in the tilted grass. I made a canopy above my head with sticks and an old cloth bag to keep out rain and sunshine. When I was forced to move from the riverbank and follow the direct line of the road, there were always a few kind drivers who brought me a distance down the valley. I knew that I was going west by the fall and rise of the sun. Flocks of wild geese flew overhead, and I saw myself as one who lagged behind their formations. In places the road became wide and ambitious with more lanes than I had ever seen before, although, where possible, I still kept to the small backways or the riverbank. Voices rang out from steepled churches. Laughter and good smells spilled from restaurants. In the smaller villages, some of the Austrians taunted me—Gyp, thief, Black Pharaoh—though just as many raised their hats in greeting, or sent their children after me with cheese, bread, cake. A boy put me on a scooter and promised to take me around a railway tunnel but he did not, he simply rode his scooter up and down in front of his friends who jeered and taunted. I pretended to put a spell on him and he stopped—they are so fearful, sometimes, of their own invented fears.

Once I passed a burning house in the night with the family outside. I returned and gave to them what little food I had, some bread, some strips of chicken meat. They did not throw the food to the ground as I expected, they just huddled down, prayed, and thanked me, and it struck me then that the world is as varied in goodness as it is in evil.

I had acquired the confidence of a blind woman—I could have stepped down the road with my eyes fully closed. I was following the grass along the busy way to Kapfenberg, Bruck, Leoben, when the mountains began to rise, higher even than the biggest of the Shivering Hills. I paused at the path heading south, and the other heading north, and took, like many times before, the wrong one. I walked north along a different river, the mountains crowding in closer, the trees on the cliff faces above me, steep rocks held back by giant nets. The traffic whizzed past and it was then that I saw signs for a tunnel, a red sign with a white border. Nothing petrified me more—even when I was a child I refused to go into such darkness. I looped backwards and tried to find a smaller road, but there was no way around. In a roadside petrol station I made inquiries of an old man who said that there were roads that would lead me over the mountains, but I would surely perish. The safest way to get through the tunnel was with the Lastwagenfahrer, the truck drivers.

They lined up behind the petrol station and talked across from truck to truck in languages as coarse as they were varied. I was not sure if they would look kindly on a Romani woman traveling alone, but the truth is that I was so deeply scared of the tunnels I would have done anything to avoid walking through them. For two days I turned and returned to that station before I bought myself, to my shame, a bottle to put me under a spell. The bottle was labeled with green vines and tasted of cough mixture, but it gave me courage to walk in amongst the drivers time after time. I climbed into the trucks, brought my knees to my chest, stared straight ahead. There were many tunnels, of course. Often they were only just being built and we would sit for hours, but the drivers, up until the last, were good to the core. They gave me cigarettes and sometimes the last of their food. They showed me pictures of their children and one allowed me to take the small statue he cherished of Saint Jude. Later I sold it, to my shame, for food. At the end of each tunnel I got out of the truck to clear my head and bid goodbye to the men who often told me that I could go further with them if I wanted. But my spirit had been put in my feet, čhonorroeja, and I felt safe there, and wanted to walk again, and I thought, Am I cursed to this?

I kept my head down and for the most part I still stayed in the valleys and slept in the abandoned sheds down on the valley floor. At times I balanced on narrow tree trunks laid across streams so I could find shelter in a light forest. When I approached the tunnels I bought myself a bottle and went then to wherever the trucks might stop.

It seemed to me that there were two different worlds, that of trees and that of engines: one seemed clear, the other dark.

Sometimes when I got to a village there would be a few of our own people on the outskirts. For my own safety—I did not want to talk to my own for fear of polluting them—I could easily shoo the children off with curses. I remember, though, a settlement on the edge of a small town in the plains beneath the central Alps. A few young boys could be seen through the low trees. I did not want to be seen by any adults, but a woman came over from a well carrying water and she greeted me first in German and then Romani. Her dialect was hard to fathom, but in her delight she dropped the bucket and blessed me three times and then took me to their camp. I could not get away, she had such a grip on my arm. The children danced around me, tugging at my clothes. I became so caught up with them that I sprinkled a metal sheet with a pile of sand and used a saw to show them how the sand jumped. They giggled and rolled about in joy. The women cooked me potato pancakes and filled my cup with fruit juice, I tell you the truth, there was never such generosity.

Five girls were brought out to dance. They wore identical green dresses with corded sashes of white tied around the waist. Listening to the music, I was happy, but imagine my raw fear, daughter, when they announced that there were three of our own from near Trnava who had been staying with them for some years now. They would be back in the evening from their work in an automobile factory. I tried to break away but could not, the force of their friendliness was too strong. They even gave me some old clothes and washed my own for me. I feared for the evening and, sure enough, when the men came along, the first word that came out of their dark mouths was Zoli.

Nobody had called me this name in such a long time that it had the strength of a slingshot.

And yet they did not cower or retreat, nor spit or curse me. Instead they raised my name to the air. They were of settled folk from out near the chocolate factory, but they had left shortly after the war. They had seen me singing a few times but did not know of my time as a poet. It was soon clear to me that they knew nothing of what had happened in the judgment, nor even what occurred in the last few years to our people, the re-settlement, the laws, the burnings. They had been turned back at the border several times now, these men. They still knew routes across the Danube, they would get back eventually to Slovakia they said, there was no other place they wanted to be. One always loves what is left behind—and I feared I would break their hearts if I were to tell them the truth about what had been done to our people, although I knew that sooner or later in the evening the questions would come to me, deep hard questions that I would be called on to answer.

The mind can do anything it wants. All along I had blocked out song, it was a denial that came from deep inside. The choice to forget is a way of surviving. Yet at that moment I knew that, to survive, I had to sing once again. The people crowded around me, a lantern was turned on, bottles were passed. I knew I would never sing one of the songs I had written down—that was the pact I had made with myself—but I could sing the old songs, the ones I had known as a child. I took a deep breath. The first notes were awful. The people cowered. Then I relaxed and I felt the music move through me. *When I cut brown bread don't look at me angrily, don't look at me angrily because I'm not going to eat it. The old horse is standing though he is not sleeping, he always has a watching eye, a watching eye, a watching eye. If you have the money you can think what you like.* I do not suppose that you will doubt it when I say that there were tears in the eyes of the people that evening and they hugged me to their hearts like I was their very own sister. I thought, I am polluting them and they do not know, I am bringing shame down upon them and they have no idea.

It brought a sharp knife to my heart and yet what was I to do? How many small betrayals would there be for me? It is rules not mirrors that steal away our souls.

They danced that night, the firelight catching the red thread in their black dresses. In the morning, when I stole away, I allowed myself to sing a few of the songs as I went. They surprised me with their beauty and carried me along. Once or twice I would hear some of my own songs in my head, those I had written down, but I forced them out, I did not want them.

The road hooked west. A family stopped for me and the man jerked his thumb and told me to get into the back with his children. The children unrolled the window and I felt the warm wind blowing on my face. There were nose prints of a dog on the rear window, but no animal. I did not ask, though I could see tearmarks on the faces of the children, and I had an idea that they had lost their pet. Red, I thought. To gladden them I began to hum the tune of the old horse song. The man turned in his seat and gave a small smile, though the mother kept looking straight ahead. I sat back and hummed some more and he said he liked the humming and I surprised myself with song. My voice tipped out into the wind and back over the hundreds of roads I had already traveled.

When the man dropped me off outside a café the children cried, and the mother gave me money. The father pinched his hat by the crown, tipped it to me and said that he always had a warm heart for the outdoor life. In the tanned leather of his face, he smiled.

You sing well, he said to me.

I had not heard these last words in such a long time and I mouthed them in the distance as I left the town for the hinterland. Later I sat, lit myself a fire, and watched the riverspiders on the water. They moved quickly across the surface, uncanny, ancient, leaving no circles nor ripples, as if they were part of the water itself.

~

It was many days later, and some towns further on, that I met my final truck driver.

He pulled the truck over to the side of the road, near a laneway, where some boys were playing, and said that a little kiss would not go astray. I said to him that I would tell him his fortune, but he said to me that he knew it already, it was plain to see, it was there in front of his eyes, it involved a little kiss. His face was greasy and shining with sweat. When my hand hit the doorhandle he grabbed the other and he said yet again that a little thanks was needed. I yanked the handle but he clamped hard on my neck and pushed me down, his thumbs deep in the hollow of my throat. I prayed for all my strength and hauled back my fist and blackeyed him, but he just laughed. Then he gritted his teeth and hit my forehead with his. Things went black. I saw myself then as Conka's mother, her fingernails as they were pliered out. He ripped all the buttons off what I wore and his hands went to my second dress and he tore that open too. It is no long story, what I tell. I watched his hands. He went soft-faced and gentle for a moment, and said: Come on, woman, one little kiss. I knew then, as he was stroking my shoulder and the side of my face, that what I had stolen was what would save me.

The blade went into his eye socket with an ease not far from butter.

I was out of the truck, hauling all that I had, and he was stumbling around, shouting the whore took my eye out, she took my fucking eye out. Indeed the knife was in his hand and his eye was a bloody mess. Some boys gathered around him and began to shout and then they pointed at me excitedly. I ran down the narrow laneway, looking for a turn. I passed a wooden shed and pulled back one of the rotting boards, crept through. Fresh shards of wood fell to the ground where I pulled the plank back and I knew I had left a marker for them to follow, but I had no time. Loud footfalls in the alleyway. Inside the shed were piles of broken slates, some farm machinery, and a blue automobile. I tested the door handles but they were locked tight. I hunkered down at the back of the car and pulled the silver latch. The trunk flew up. I flung my bundle of possessions inside, then looked about in terror and climbed in. I held the lid of the boot so it would not close. From the shed came the ripping of a plank. The boys shouted and banged around. I heard them tug the handles and I was quite sure I was finished.

When I think of it now it was such bare stupidity, but when they left the shed—one shouting that he had seen me running across the fields—I lay back and cried, čhonorroeja. Would things always be like this? I pulled the lid of the boot down but lay part of my blanket over the latch so it wouldn't shut me in. I curled up against the dark.

In the morning, I woke as the boot-lid bounced up and down.

~

My ordeal with the onyx knife did not land me in prison, as you might expect. The man who found me in his car wore a smart collar and tiepin. He stared in at me, then slammed the lid of the boot down. As we drove, I could hear him muttering amid the rattle of what must have been rosary beads. I was sure he would lead me to the courthouse, or to the officials, or to yet another camp, but when the boot was opened up, an hour or more later, a young man in a black suit and white collar looked down on me. I blinked against the light, clutched at my torn clothes.

All yours, said the man with the tiepin.

I was terrified, but the young priest guided me along the pebbled path towards a house. I had heard much about priests, and knew how easily they turn into bureaucrats, but something about Father Renk stopped me from running. He sat me down at a small table in the kitchen of his house. He was a young man, with a little badger streak of gray at the temples. He'd known many Gypsies in his life, he said, some good, some bad, he did not make judgments, but how in the world did I end up in the back of a motorcar? I began to invent a story but he said, sharp and sudden: The truth, woman. I told him the story, and he said that indeed the police probably were searching for me, but not to worry, I had been driven a good distance away. He had dealt with displaced persons before, in the nearby Peggetz camp.

There's a bed if you want it, he said. He showed me the stairs to a small room at the top of the house where I would be allowed to sleep. In return I was asked to clean the floors of the church, to keep the sacristy in order, and to attend his services—simple daily tasks that were more difficult for me than they should have been. In the end I stayed for three months and I still recall those days, how unusual they were, full of cloths and dishes and furniture polish. For all my worldliness, the simple mechanics of a vacuum cleaner stumped me and I had never before used bleach. I made holes in the young priest's shirts. I left an iron sitting on a tea towel and burned the ironing board, but Father Renk found it all amusing. He sat in the kitchen and watched me and chuckled and once even took the vacuum himself, singing as he guided it down the hallway. There were long cold mornings spent listening to his homilies about peace—he stood at his altar and said to his parishioners that we must live together in fellowship, one and all, that it was a simple thing to do, black, white, Austrian, Italian, Gypsy, it did not matter. How little he knows, I thought, but I did not say a word, I went about my cleaning duties and kept my head low.

One night he saw me, not kneeling, but sitting at the altar. He sat across from me in the front pew and asked what it was I was searching for. To go across the mountain, I replied. He said it was a good proposition but only God knew where it would take me to. I replied that God and I were hardly friends, though the Devil seemed to like me sometimes, a notion which made him turn to the window and smile.

Over the next few days Father Renk made several phone calls, until one morning he said to me: Pack up, Marienka, come on. Pack what? I said. He grinned and put money in the palm of my hand, then drove me south through beautiful countryside, past villages where people waved at the priest's car. On the underside of a bridge was a sign: *One Tyrol.* Up we drove, through bends that seemed never to end, hairpins and switch-backs, so that it felt like I might turn around and meet myself. With every meter there was something new to take my breath away—the mountains sheer and gray, a flock of sheep taking the whole mountain road with ease, the sudden shadow of a buzzard darkening the roadside grass.

We stopped in the little village of Maria Luggua where Father Renk walked the twelve stations of the cross, blessed me for my journey, and then left me in a village café with a man who hardly looked at me from over the rim of his cup.

Across the mountain? he said in German, though I could tell straightaway it was not his language.

I nodded.

There are two things in this part of the world, he said. God and money. You are lucky that you found the first.

He had never taken a person across before and he did not cherish the idea, and would only do so if I could carry a sack on my back. I knew nothing about smuggling, or contraband, or taxes, but I said I could carry my weight and more in order to get to Paris. He chuckled at me and said, Paris? Of course, I said. Paris? he said again. He could not stop himself from laughing and I thought him a detestable thing in his leather waistcoat, with his stringy hair and his lined face. It's the wrong way, he said, unless you want to climb the mountains for another year or two. He drew a map for me on the back of his hand where he showed me Paris and then he showed me Italy and then he showed me Rome. I am not a fool, I said to him. He drank his small dark coffee and said, I'm not either. He stamped his cigarette out on the floor, rose, and didn't look back.

Down the street, he finally turned and pointed at me and told me that my luck only ran as far as my friendship with the priest.

Over the other side of the mountain and that's all. Do you understand me? he said.

Three sackloads of syringes were what he carried the night he brought me across the border. He did not, in the end, allow me to carry anything. We silently set out along the valley floor, the moonlight blue on the riverstones. We waded through a high meadow where the grass reached above my waist. He had instructed me that there were two types of troopers on either side of the border, and they were strung along the hills at various intervals. The Italians, he said, hated him most of all. You know you could be arrested? he said. I replied that it was hardly a new prospect for me, I knew the difference between a door and a key. We stopped at the edge of a forest. You're full of pepper, aren't you? he said. He shook his head and sighed, then looped a string around my waist which he tied to his own belt. He said he was sorry to have to treat me like a donkey but in the darkness I could get lost. The string was only long enough to stretch out and touch his shoulder. He was surprised that I kept pace with him and only once or twice did the string tighten around my waist. Halfway up he turned and raised his eyebrows and smiled at me.

His shirtfront pulsed, but I thought little of him yet, čhonorroeja, there was no skip yet in my heart for him.

The moon disappeared, the darkness was full, and there seemed more star than sky. We stayed away from any of the paths or dirt roads that ran up the mountainside, and instead we kept to the trees, feeling the hard pull of our legs against the steep ground. He grew at ease with the silence between us and only once on the ascent did he turn quickly at a noise. He put his hand on my head and forced me to hunker low. Far off, in the trees, two flashlights shone beams at a steep ledge, the lights sweeping the rock. It struck me that we might have to climb, but we turned sideways, and went quietly through the forest, and away. The climb grew ever upwards until the trees stopped. A long run of rocky scree loomed in front of us. Be careful with the rocks, he said, they're slippy. We went onwards, cresting the mountain, but, just over the top, he turned and said that the tough part was still ahead of us, the carabinieri had a grudge against him, and they would like nothing more than his capture.

For the descent he untied the string and shifted the weight of the contraband on his back. The water grew louder the further down we went, following the course of large gray boulders. Rain began to fall and I slipped in the mud. He lifted me. He said he knew that sooner or later my balance would become undone, but I had no idea what he meant.

Are you not scared of troopers? he asked.

·I built the sentence slowly in my mind to lay the full impact of it on him, as it was something Stanislaus had been fond of saying a long time ago, and I wanted to leave one good thing with this strange man, Enrico, and so I said in German: I would happily lick a cat's arse, my heart's friend, if it got the taste of troopers out of my mouth.

He reared back and laughed.

I stayed that night in the hut he had built. He had made latches on the door from the remnants of tires and the planks were stained with black tar. The windows were small. Only one piece of furniture looked out of place—a rolltop desk crammed with papers, some of them watermarked. He gave me blankets and a carafe of cold mountain water, stacked a few provisions on the table, and said I was welcome to all of it, smoked meat, dried vegetables, matches, condensed milk, even a lantern. He left the hut, still in the darkness, to complete whatever business he had in the village of Sappada and the door clicked behind him.

I had crossed yet another border and was now in Italy.

The sight of the bed filled me with happiness and I fell crosswise on it from one corner to the other. Outside, the river babbled in its fastness. I quickly fell asleep. I knew he had come back in, for I saw the mark of wet bootprints upon the floor. It must have been hours later, for the light was intense and yellow, when I heard the rattle of his breath in a nearby chair. He mumbled some words in Italian to what he thought was my sleeping form and then he left again, shutting the door gently behind him.

All of this is to tell you, čhonorroeja, that the idea of going any further no longer pulsed in me. There is an old Romani saying that the river is not where it starts or ends, but it seemed that I had certainly come to the crest of something, I had thrown away the idea of Paris, and the shape of my walking had changed. I replaced the blankets, packed the food he had left me, kissed the table in thanks, then walked out of the hut. I followed a valley road for five full days. I could not help but bring my mind around to Enrico, how he had not questioned me about anything at all and yet it had not seemed a lack of curiosity or a dislike. The further I got from him, the more he came back to me. He once said to me, in later years, so much later, that the reason life is so strange is that we have simply no idea what is around the next corner, and it was an obvious idea but one most of us had learned to forget.

On a rainy day in the mountains, I heard the sound of rolling tires. He pulled up behind me in a ruined jeep, called to me, and said perhaps I was a little tired, and I said, yes, and he told me that I was welcome to get into the jeep for shelter. I said it hardly looked like shelter since there was no roof. He shrugged and said: You can always pretend. I looked out over the mountains, then walked across, got in the seat beside him. Dry, isn't it? he said. We turned around in the road, with the rain lashing us sideways. I huddled down against the blowing heater. The road opened up before us and I suppose this is where my traveling story ends.

We went to Paoli's café where Paoli looked across the counter, shook his head, grinned, and told us to sit.

I asked Enrico why he had not asked me anything about being a Gypsy and he asked me why I had never asked him anything about not being one.

It was perhaps the most beautiful answer I have ever heard in my life.

~

We knew each other slowly, in terror and excitement, drew apart, stepped backwards. Sometimes I caught sight of him in the dim lamplight and he seemed closer to the shadows than he was to me. We clasped in an awkward embrace and sat for a long time without moving, but the distance grew shorter, unfolded, and the desire never wore itself out. It seemed to me that the world had tried me and finally showed me joy. For a long time we found in ourselves little to say and we learned to be together without speaking. The moment we lived in was enough. During the night he slept with my hair across him and

I watched his ribcage move up and down. The mornings came and he stepped to the stove, brought it to life. There was a spot of soot where he had touched my cheek. At night I told him of Petr, of my days with Swann and Stránský, of what had happened between us—he simply sat and listened until a sharp line of windowlight opened the morning.

When he left, sometimes for days on end, I would wait up without ever sleeping. I was not sheltered from despair, and there were times I wondered how in the world I could survive in such a place, days I was sure I would just walk off into the hills, disappear, keep moving, to no particular place, or purpose, but then he came back and the light opened up again, and it seemed to me that happiness had returned, unasked. It was hard to remember what waiting had once meant.

There were all those years I had spent in the caravan—strange, when I looked out, not to see any horses.

Enrico was not an easy nor a simple man. He did not like where he had come from and he hid it for a long time. It had never struck me that wealth could fester, but Enrico fought his. I finally learned that his was a family of famous judges and lawyers, of wealth and renown, even sympathy. He tried to leave it behind, the fine houses of Verona, the open spaces and courtyards, the white statues in the garden, but I suppose when you leave something behind it will always follow you. What Enrico belonged to was nothing more or less than the mountains. He had already gone, at a young age, through a series of jobs in hotels, chairlifts, restaurants, but he really only wanted to be alone in the peaks, and so he had found a hut on his country's side of the border, sheltered by a hill and trees kept small by winter. He built the hut using money from odd jobs. He had few visitors and was known by some as Die Welsche, the stranger, though in truth he himself said that he was just a citizen of elsewhere.

Enrico knew he would stay in the mountains the day he gave his leather suitcase to the local cobbler and asked him to make a pair of shoes from them.

He lived beyond the reach of most people and grew to enjoy what Paoli called his fine idleness. He was liked, your father— he brought his medicines across the mountain, kept himself quiet, and had no time for the bombers who wanted to level the telegraph poles in the name of Tyrol. He stayed away from his family, sought nothing from them, and went hungry when it was time to go hungry. He did not use this as a badge of sacrifice, he was no saint, far from it. He said years later how stupid it had been to deny their existence, and yet it was my own difficulties that eventually forced him back to his family.

I had been in his hut for just three months when the carabinieri came up the road. Fresh uniforms, white belts, epaulets. It was like watching the approach of sadness. Don't say a word, Enrico whispered. They marched in, put me in handcuffs, stood me at the door, and then gave your father a good beating in front of my eyes. Afterwards he took the first train he could back to Verona, in his old clothes and white bandages, and, though he never told me what he gave in return—it was the first time ever he had asked a favor of his father—he returned with a document that released me from the clutches of the carabinieri. Within a few days a car arrived with a court officer and handed me a blue passport, said it was compliments of the Italian government. He left without another word. I asked Enrico what it had taken for this, but he shrugged, said it was nothing, that what was an ordeal for me was an easy task for him. Yet even then I knew that it had taken some of the life from him— the carabinieri had never before known where, nor which family, he came from. It also pierced some of the Tyroleans who doubted him now, but Enrico said it was not his choice to care, I had the passport and that was enough—a man would always be traitor to one thing if he truly believed in another.

He laced his boots and continued his work, smuggling goods across the mountains. He knew that if ever they found him he would spend his time in jail—he would not ask for a second favor. It eventually happened one spring and he was away for a three-month stretch. I thought my heart would scale the walls of the hut, čhonorroeja. I lay awake listening to you climb in my body.

And so it happened.

One afternoon, Enrico lifted a fine suit from a wooden chest, blue with very thin pinstripes. He held it up to the light and said: I hate this thing. He rolled it in a ball and wrapped it in brown paper. We're going to Verona, he said. He had bought me a fine dress though it was two sizes too short and it showed my new size. It is hard to forget the oldest of customs, blood laws, territory, silence, but he would take no part in them. He put his hand to my stomach and grinned like a fool. We were driven to Bolzano by Paoli who whistled all the way. On the train Enrico ran his hands together nervously, and then all of a sudden tried to explain his family, their history, but I hushed him. Right there in the carriage he dressed in the suit, the dark tan of his neck sharp against the pale white of his body. We sat, the countryside clicking by. Once or twice he stood and laughed out loud: Here I am! he said. Here I am, going home!

A few hours later we were walking down a wide laneway together. The house in Verona put me in mind of Budermice, the light so clean it felt like it had been wrung through water.

It was the occasion of Enrico's brother's wedding and so his family was there, some outside on the lawn, others drinking on the veranda, the women arguing in preparation for supper. His father grinned and smashed a glass when we appeared. His brothers cheered. His mother, your grandmother, was a refined woman—but not so refined, čhonorroeja, that she couldn't eventually tell me so. I held my dark head high and took it in my stride, I was not going to hide in the corners.

A feast was spread out on giant silver plates, glasses of the best wine, trays of the freshest olives, the finest meat, the most colorful and exotic of fruits. I thought to myself this was just a flicker and I was going to enjoy it, who knows how long it might last. Enrico stayed close to my shoulder. He said, Here's Zoli. Nothing more. I was glad—with him, my name was enough. More wine flowed. An opera singer stood up for an aria. We applauded and Enrico's father winked across the tables at me. He took my hand afterwards and walked me through the grounds and said that he would never know his son properly, but he had also never known him to put on such a suit, he was glad for it, something in him had shifted. You're a good influence, he said with a grin. Enrico's mother glared at us from across the lawn. I dared to smile at her and she turned away. Enrico and I were given rooms at opposite ends of the house, but he entered through my doorway late that night, drunk and singing, and fell asleep at the end of the bedspread. He woke in the morning with his tongue dry and his head thumping, and said we would be greeted at death together so why should we wait—it was his way of saying he wanted to marry.

On the train journey back, we stepped across a line while the train was still moving and he clasped me to him, that was all the formality he wanted.

~

It is only a few years ago now, 1991, I think—the label of years seem so little to me now—that the Wall fell, though perhaps it has never been a wall so much as an idea grown away from its own simplicity.

We walked down from the millhouse to Paoli's shop, Enrico and I, and we watched the television pictures from Berlin—how strange to think of those young men using hammers to break apart the bricks at the exact same time as Paoli cursed his little coffee machine that never worked. The scenes from Berlin seemed to me so much the work of my grandfather and his strong hatred of cement. Paoli kept the coffee shop open late that night, and your father walked me home with his arm across my shoulder.

Will you ever go back? he asked.

Of course my answer was just another disguise for yes. There were many nights when I had dreamed myself into the wide open spaces of my old life and the people who were now just shadows. Each year he would ask me again and so, four years later, your father borrowed just enough money for the trip from his brother in Verona. You will recall the time—you stayed with Paoli's family while we took the train all the way from Bolzano. We went clear across two countries and stopped in Vienna, your mother grown old in her headscarf, your father in his threadbare suit. The streets were so clean that they surprised me with the occasional piece of litter, a cigarette butt, a bottle cap. We bought our tickets for Bratislava but stayed one

night in what was once a fine hotel on a street near the railway
station, Kolschitzkygasse, where the streetlamps seemed to
curtsy. There was a mirror on the dressing room table over
which I draped the bedcover in order not to look at our reflec-
tions. We lay completely still. Your father had bought me an
array of colored beads, which I intertwined around my waist
for a belt, it was the closest I wore to the clothes of my old life.
I cinched down on the beads and could hear the glass chipping
as I tightened. The hotel was two lifetimes old. The dim hum of
elevator cables sounded and the front desk bell clanged. There
was cornicework high in the corners. Molding a handspan beneath the waterstains. I made pictures from the collision of
stains and created my old self there. I still was not sure if I could
ever make the journey back to the place I had been a child.

Enrico did not say a word when I stepped down off the train
the following day and shook my head, saying: Sorry.

He turned his hat inside out and punched a small dent in it,
and I knew full well that he was thinking of the money he had
borrowed. We walked through the city of Vienna like two old
piano notes floating, and later that evening took a bus out to the
countryside for an hour or more, to Braunsberg. We walked up
the hill overlooking the Danube and in the distance I could see
the towers of Bratislava standing gray against the skyline. It
looked like a thing made of child's building blocks, my old
country. The river curled away from it. The wind blew strong.
Enrico squeezed my hand and did not ask me what I was thinking of, but I turned away, I did not know an answer. It seemed
to me that our lives, though mostly gone and getting smaller,
were still large with doubt. The distant towers went in and out
of cloud shadow. I held Enrico's arm and leaned against his
shoulder. He spoke my name and that was all.

I could not go back there, not then, I could not make myself cross that river, it was too difficult for me, and he walked me back down the steep hill with his arm around me, and I thought us both a part of the silence.

The next morning we stood in the train station. I was tempted to make the journey as I watched the letters clacking on the signboards, but instead we took the train in the direction of what I could, I suppose, now call home. Your father laid his head against my shoulder and slept, he sounded for all the world like an old horse wheezing. Later he found me a berth on the train and put me to sleep and he climbed up beside me. That whole journey back to Italy, I wondered what I had missed, or what, perhaps, it was better to have missed. I feared my old country would be the same, and yet I also feared it would be terribly changed. How can I explain that there are times we hold on, even to the terrors? But if I speak the truth, it would have been the lake that I would have visited, along the road to Prešov, the dark groves where we played the harps, and the small laneway where we danced at Conka's wedding—those days shone in my head like a bright coin.

～

There are times I still miss the crowded days and being old does not shelter me from sadness. Once I was guilty of thinking that only good things could happen; then I was guilty of thinking they would never happen again. Now I wait and make no judgment. You ask what it is that I love? I love the recollection of Paoli each time I hear the shop bell sound. I love the dark coffee brewed up by Paoli's daughter, Renata, who sits at the counter in her dangling earrings and painted fingernails. I love the accordionist, Franz, in the café corner shielding his bad teeth with his hand. I love the men who argue about the value of things they don't really like. The children who still put playing cards in the spokes of their wheels. The whistle of skis. The tourists who climb out of their cars and hold a hand to their eyes and then climb back in again, blind. The blue wool mittens of the children. Their laughter as they run down the street. I love that in the orchards the fruit trees grow out of mud. I love the stroll through woods in autumn. The deer walking up the narrow switchbacks, the lowering of their heads to drink, the black center of their very eyes. I love the wind when it blows down from the peaks. The young men in open ragged shirts down by the petrol station. The fires that burn in homemade stoves. The brass catches worn on the doorway. The old church where roofbeams lie noiselessly in rubble, and even the new church, though not its mechanical bell. I love the rolltop desk where the papers have not changed. I love to recall when you were one year old and you took your first steps and you fell on your bottom and cried, surprised at the hardness of the wood floor. The first stomp of your tomboy foot. The day you came in with the firewood and stood in the doorway, almost taller than I, and you said that you would be leaving soon, and I asked where and you replied to me: Exactly. I love the dawn of all these questions, they come around again and again and again. I love the winters that have crossed me and even the angry weather that has passed over us all, and our times of silence on those days when Enrico was not home, when I was left to wait for the click of the latch and he came in, shaking snow or rain or pollen off his boots.

It is good, daughter, to be prepared for surprise. This is a place where a slant snowfall can arrive at any time—even in summer I have seen flakes fall, followed by gales of light and dark. It is strange to think how far my life has come, having discovered enough beauty that it still astounds me.

~

Enrico once told me of a time when he was just a boy, no more than five years old, the sort who was told to wear navy-blue calzoncini and long white kneesocks. He ran around the courtyard of his Verona home, its beautiful garden with large ferns and white brick and fountains and giant pots of towering plants that his mother's gardener tended to. In the far corner of the garden there stood a large brass statue of three chimpanzees: one with its hands over its eyes, one with its hands over its ears, one with its hands over its mouth. Beneath them was a small well of a pond where water gurgled in and out. Enrico used to sit there and pass his days.

I sometimes still see myself as a child and how much I was loved and how much I loved in return and in my childish heart I was sure it would never end, but I did not know what to do with such love and I relinquished it. I put my hand over my mouth, my ears, my eyes, but I have come around again, and I still call myself black even though I have rolled around in flour. I have always been with my people even though they have not been with me.

He never much asked me about my past, your father, so I told him willingly, I always thought that he, and you, were the only ones to whom I could trust these words of mine, the dark ink of what they have said.

SINCE BY THE BONES THEY BROKE WE CAN
TELL NEW WEATHER: WHAT WE SAW UNDER
THE HLINKAS IN THE YEARS '42 AND '43

What sharp stones lifted our wheels,
What high skies came to rest on the ground.
On a golden morning the river turned
And two uniforms appeared at our backs.
We asked by what roads we could escape—
They showed us the narrowest one.

Don't go looking for bread, dark father,
You won't find bread under breadcrumbs.

The spring died at the furthest corner
And our song went into the mountains
Where it sounded along the ridges
Then put on a twice-removed hat.
We called this song the quiet
But it came answering back.

Some days we went looking for the sky
But, Lord, it was a long walk upwards.

Land of black forests we grew from you.
We found the sun in your branches,
Warm shelter in your roots,
A shirt, a hat, a belt in all your moss.
Now it is raining and raining so hard,
Who can make our black ground dry?

The hour of our wandering has been
And passed and been and passed again.

They drove our wagons onto the ice
And ringed the white lake with fires,
So when the cold began to crack
The cheers went up from the Hlinkas.
We forced our best horses forward
But they skidded, bloody, to the shore.

My land, we are your children,
Shore up the ice, make it freeze!

The women came to their windows
To see what was up the road ahead.
They threw out the fire's ashes
So that some might rise in the wind.
The darkest birds of winter
Told others not to follow behind.

The snow fell large and white
And buried our wheels center deep.

How soft the road underfoot,
The branches gray and bare.
Light through light in the treetops
Warned other light not to return.
We had been everything to the forest
Except enemy and danger.

How many times the trees bowed
In our long and dark marching.

They loaded the railway trains
Until the springs went flat.
We heard the moaning of Gypsy children
Too hungry to sleep or dream.
Even those who stayed alive
Found a grave in each survival.

In all the white fields and forests
Old sorrows called out to the new.

At the gate two wooden poles,
Out of which nothing could be carved,
Not a spoon, a moon, nor a Gypsy sky,
Not a swift or an owl or another flight.
We went through them single file,
Our faces turned to the sky.

Who could tell the time from the stars
If the roof was an inch from their eyes?

A child's black fingers descended upon a moth
That descended upon a candleflame.
The winter was closing in
Cold and fast and blue.
We dreamed of a better place
Just above the roof of the pines.

Yet some small splinter of shade
Was nothing but another shadow.

We carried the streams of streams through seasons.
What sorrow and terrible wailing were heard
In all your lonely downcast corners,
Auschwitz, Majdanek, Thieresenstadt, Lódź.
Who gave them such places, O Lord,
Right on the edge of black forests?

We were taken in through their gates,
They let us up through their chimneys.

Gentle mother, make no friend
With the snake that even the snakes hate.
You ask why this song doesn't speak
To you of dreams and of opened gates?
Come and see the fallen wheels
On the ground and deep in the darkest mud.

Look at our fallen homes
And all the Jews and Gypsies broken!

But don't leave behind the dead,
With whom we shared our hunger.
Don't let the snakes go free
Of what they wanted us to be.
Icicles eaten from the wire in winter
Will not freeze our tongues with weight.

We are watching still, brother,
The bend in the distant corner.

The bell that has been pealing
Is not the bell you heard before.
We will tear it to the ground
And use the old forged brass.
It will take us back around
The long five-cornered road.

I speak from the mossy earth to you—
Sound out your mouth's violin!

The song of the wandering is in all the trees
And is heard in the last stars of daybreak.
It ripples in the bend of the river
Turning backwards towards us again.
Soon you shall see nothing in the chimney
Except silence and dim twilight.

The sky is red and the morning is too—
All is red on the horizon, Comrade!

Old Romani mother, don't hide your earrings,
Your coins, your sons, your dreams,
Not even inside your golden teeth,
And tell this to hell's dark brother:
When he goes collecting
He won't take any more of us along.

Who has said that your voice will be strange
To those who have risen from you?

Sun and moon and torn starlight,
Wagon and chicken and badger and knife,
All the sorrows have been heard
By those who suffered alongside us.
You who were sad at evening
Will be happy now at dawn.

Since by the bones they broke
We can tell new weather.

When we die and turn to rain
We shall stay nearby a little while
Before we go on falling.
We shall stay in the shade of the mossy oak
Where we have walked
And cried and walked and wandered.

Zoli Novotna
BRATISLAVA, SEPTEMBER 1957

Paris

2003

SHE DESCENDS THE TRAIN in the amber light of after-noon, shading her eyes with her hands. Her daughter steps from the shadows, looking tall, short-haired, lean. They kiss four times and Francesca says: "You look beautiful, Mamma." She dips to the ground to pick up the small bag at Zoli's feet. "This is all you brought?" They link arms and walk out under the wide ceiling of Gare de Lyon, past a newspaper stall, through a throng of girls, out into the sunlight. At the corner they hear the shrill beeping of a car horn. Across the road, a young man in an open leather jacket clambers from a car. His hair is cut close, his shirt ambitiously undone. He rushes across to Zoli and his stubble bristles against her cheek when he greets her.

"Henri," he says, and she rests for a second against a lamp-post, winded, the name so close to that of her husband.

Francesca half-skips around the front of the car and helps Zoli into the front seat. "Does he speak Italian?" Zoli whispers, and before her daughter can respond, Henri has launched into a speech about what a pleasure it is to meet her, how young she looks, how marvelous it feels to have two such beautiful women in his car, two, imagine, two!

"He speaks Italian," says Zoli with a soft chuckle, and she closes the car door.

Francesca laughs and hops in the backseat, leans forward with her arms around the headrest to massage the back of Zoli's neck. She has not, she thinks, been so carefully touched in a long time.

The car jolts forward and merges into traffic, swerves around a pothole. Zoli puts her hands against the dashboard to brace herself. The streets begin to branch and widen and clear. Out the window she watches the quick blip of traffic lights and the flash of billboards. I have arrived in Paris so many times, she thinks, and none of them ever like this. They speed through the yellow of a traffic light and down a long avenue shaded by half-grown trees. "We'll show you around later, Mamma," says Francesca, "but let's go home first. We've a nice lunch ready, wait until you see how many cheeses!" It is a thing her daughter seems to have invented for her, that she is a lover of cheese, and she wants to say, That's your father, not me. Zoli puts her hand on Henri's forearm, asks him if he likes cheese, and he finds it funny, for whatever reason, she is not entirely sure, and he slaps the steering wheel as he turns a sharp corner.

They slow down, past kiosks and storefronts strange with foreign script. A number of Arab women in dark headscarves emerge from a shop, only their eyes apparent. Further up the street, a black man wheels a trolley of jackets across the road. Zoli turns to watch. "So many people," she says. "I never expected it to be like this." Her daughter unbuckles her backseat seat belt so she can whisper: "I'm so glad you're here, Mamma, I can hardly believe it."

Henri taps the brakes and the car jolts. "Put your belt on, Francesca," he says. A silence descends until Zoli hears the soft fall of her daughter's body against the rear seat and a long exaggerated sigh.

"Sorry, Franca," he says, "but I'm the one driving here."

How odd it is to hear the nickname of her daughter from

this young man. How extraordinary, in fact, to be here at all, in this small car, in these thrumming streets, on a sunny Thursday afternoon when back in the valley they will be cutting grass on the lower slopes.

They negotiate a few more winding side streets and pull in next to the curb under a row of low trees by a pale stone building studded with blocks of ancient red marble. They climb out of the car and walk through the front courtyard. Henri puts his shoulder to the giant ironwork door. It creaks and swings, revealing a black and white tiled floor. They walk towards an old elevator, but Zoli veers off to the stairs, explaining that tunnels and elevators are not for her, that they make her claustrophobic. Henri takes her elbow and guides her towards the elevator's intricate grillwork. "The stairs are so steep," he says. Zoli reaches back for her daughter's hand. She is afraid now that she will dislike Henri, that he is one of those who is almost too happy, the sort who forces his opinions of happiness on others. A sharp look appears on his face, and he goes ahead, alone, in the elevator.

Mother and daughter stand wordless in front of each other. Francesca drops the bag on the first stair and takes Zoli's face in her hands, leans over and kisses her eyelids.

"I can't believe it," says Francesca.

"You'll be glad to get rid of me in a day or two."

"Want to bet?"

They laugh and climb the stairs, stopping on each landing for Zoli to get her breath back. She has the clammy thought that they will have arranged their home for her, that they will have laid out a bed and perhaps a night lamp and they will have cleaned and ordered things out of their usual places, perhaps even put up photographs for the occasion.

On the fourth floor, Francesca hurries ahead, opens the door, throws her keys onto a low glass table.

"Come in, Mamma, come in!"

Zoli pauses a moment on the threshold, then slips off her shoes, steps in. She is pleasantly surprised by the apartment, its high walls, the cornices, the crevices, the oak floorboards, the woodcut prints along the hallway. The living room is bright and open with high windows and a piece of artwork she immediately recognizes as Romani, vibrant clashing colors, odd shapes, a settlement of sorts. A photo of Enrico sits on an old wooden shelf made from a slice of railway sleeper. A dozen other photos accompany it. Zoli runs her fingers along the hard tar on the shelf, then turns and examines the rest of the room.

In the center of a glass coffee table sits the leaflet for the conference, in French, odd words shoved together. The leaflet is slick and professional and not at all what she expected. She should, she knows, pay attention to it, comment on it, compliment it, but Zoli wants nothing more than to ambush it with silence.

A row of books sit under the table and she lifts one, photographs of India, and deftly lays the leaflet underneath, its edge sticking out so it doesn't look hidden. Her daughter stands over her with a glass of water, and tenses slightly at the sight of the covered leaflet.

"You must be tired, Mamma?"

Zoli shakes her head, no, the day seems bright and open. She runs her fingers along Francesca's blouse: "Where's that cheese you promised me?"

They pass the lunch in idle chatter, the train trip, the weather, the new layout of Paoli's shop, and as the afternoon lengthens, a heaviness bears down. Her daughter brings her to the bedroom, where the sheets on the double bed have been freshly changed, and a nightgown has been laid out with a shop tag still on it. Francesca snips the tag from the back of a nightdress and whispers that her boyfriend will be staying elsewhere for a few days, and that she will sleep on the couch, no protests allowed. She folds back the covers and fluffs the pillow and guides her mother to the bed.

Zoli feels briefly like a pebble that, having lain around for quite a while, is quickly tossed from hand to hand.

"Have a good nap, Mamma. And I'm not going to say anything about bedbugs."

"I wouldn't even feel them."

She wakes to darkness, disoriented a moment. A harsh whispering issues from the kitchen, the voices low and urgent. She lies and listens, hoping they will quieten, but Henri curses, and then she hears the slamming of a door, the slide of grooves in a kitchen cupboard, a rattling of cups. Zoli looks around the room, surrounded by the possessions of others, cosmetics on the table, photographs in frames, a row of men's shirts in the cupboard. In her mind she goes through the three rooms of her own millhouse, how the four doors creak, how the curtains jangle on the rings, how the stove leaks a little light, how the lantern flickers. Curious to have taken a train here and arrived so quickly, somewhere so unfamiliar, as if the journey has failed her by such ease. She lies back down on the bed. A surprising stillness to the room—no sounds of traffic, or children playing outside, or neighbors with their radios.

"You're awake?" says Francesca. She has put on some light makeup and she looks exquisite as she steps gracefully across the room. "Are you ready for dinner, Mamma? We've booked a little restaurant."

"Oh," says Zoli.

"Henri's gone to get the car. Do you like him, Mamma?"

Zoli wonders a moment what there might be to like, so quickly, so abruptly, but she says: "Yes, I like him very much."

"I'm glad," says Francesca with a chuckle. "I've been with worse, I suppose."

They embrace again. Zoli swings her legs off the side of the bed, narrows her mind, forces it upon her arms and legs, stands. The nightdress comes up over her head. It takes an effort not to sway. Francesca turns her back and flicks on a small lamp on the nightstand as Zoli puts on her dress. Foolish not to have brought more clothes, but she wanted to impress that it would only be for a few days, no more, that she would not be part of the conference, that she would just sit and watch and listen, if even that.

Her daughter hitches the dress at the shoulders.

"Are you all right, Mamma?"

"I wouldn't know I had it if it didn't hurt," says Zoli, and a smile loosens over her face.

At the door there is a series of three gold locks she had not noticed earlier. Three. And one hanging chain. It strikes Zoli that she has never lived in a place with locks on the door.

"We should take the elevator."

"No, čhonorroeja, we'll walk down."

Outside, in the darkness, the engine of the car purrs. Henri waves them over with the sort of grin that already seems to throw out opinions and confidences. She will try hard to like him, she tells herself. He has, in any case, a fine name—so much like Enrico, though the sound is not as round or as full—and he is handsome in a measured way. She slides into the front seat and pats his arm.

"Onwards," Henri says abruptly, and they drive off through a light rain.

By the time they reach the center of Paris, the rain has let up and the streets shine wet and black under lamplight. Elegant statues and houses, each angle planned, each tree thought out. Boats along the Seine dimple the water. Zoli opens the window to hear the rushing of the water, but receives only traffic.

At the restaurant there are engraved mirrors behind the bar. Wood and heavy glass. Waiters in long white aprons. She is given a menu and it strikes her with a start, how absurd, a menu in French, but her daughter says: "I'll help you, Mamma." So many things to choose from, and nothing amongst them simple. She sits in a mild haze, listening to her daughter and Henri talk about their jobs, social work with immigrants, of how there is always a heartbreaking story, how it is hard to believe, in a civilized society, that these things still go on, day after day.

Zoli finds herself drifting, watching the movement of the waiters in the background, their intricate steps. She circles her fork around the edges of her wineglass, but snaps herself back when Francesca touches her hand: "Did you hear me, Mamma?"

It is, she knows, a story about an Algerian man and a hospital and flowers by someone's bed, but she can't quite locate the center of the story, and has to catch up. She surmises that the man sends the flowers to himself, and it seems to her not so much a sadness as a triumph, sending flowers to his own bedside, but she doesn't say so, she is caught up in the caughtness of her daughter who has a tear at the edge of her eye, which she brushes away.

A waiter arrives bearing three large plates. The dinner unfolds and Henri seems to sweep in behind Francesca, as if he has started driving the table, taken the front seat, lowered the pedal. He rattles on, in a high voice, about the plight of the Islamic women and how nobody takes them seriously at all, how their lives are defined by the narrowness that others bring to it, how they have been poisoned by stereotype, that it's time for people to open up and listen. He is, thinks Zoli, the sort of man who knows in advance all that, for him, is worth knowing.

Dessert arrives and the taste of coffee fills her with sadness.

She wakes in the backseat of the car, startled a moment as Henri points out the Arc de Triomphe. "Yes, yes," she says, "it's beautiful," though the car is sandwiched in traffic and she can hardly see it at all. They swing past a tower and then zoom along the quays. Henri clicks on the radio and begins to hum. Soon they merge onto a highway and it seems like only moments later when Zoli is being brought up in the elevator. She panics briefly and reaches for the buttons but her daughter catches her arm and strokes her hand. "It's all right, Mamma, we'll be there in a flash." A strange word, it seems, and the light actually flashes across her mind as if invited. She feels her daughter support her indoors. Zoli flops to the bed with a little laugh: "I think I drank too much wine."

In the morning she rises early and kneels down by the couch and combs her sleeping daughter's hair, the same way she used to comb it when Francesca was a child. Francesca stirs, smiles. Zoli kisses her cheek, rises, and searches in the kitchen for breakfast items, finds a card on the fridge with a magnet attached. She runs the magnet over her own hair and suddenly Francesca is there behind her with a phone to her ear: "What are you doing, Mamma?"

"Oh, nothing, Franca," she says, and it's a name so close to Conka that it still manages, at times, to hollow out Zoli's chest.

"What's the magnet for?"

"Oh, I don't know," says Zoli. "No reason really."

Her daughter begins chatting rapid-fire into the phone. There is, it seems, a seating issue at the conference and some rooms have been overbooked. Francesca clicks down the phone and sighs. In the kitchen she opens a can of coffee beans, grinds them, fills a contraption with water. So much white machinery, thinks Zoli. She can feel a slight tension between her and her daughter, this is not what she wants, she will not embrace it, conference or not, and she asks Francesca how she slept and she says, "Oh fine," and then Zoli asks her in Romani. It is the first time they have used the language, it seems to stun the air between them, and Francesca leans forward and says: "Mamma, I really wish that you would speak for us, I really wish you would."

"What is there for me to speak of?"

"You could read a poem. Times have changed."

"Not for me, čhonorroeja."

"It would be good for so many people."

"They said that fifty years ago."

"Sometimes it takes fifty years. There's going to be people from all over Europe, even some Americans."

"And what do I care for Americans?"

"I'm just saying it's the biggest conference in years."

"This thing makes good coffee?"

"Please, Mamma."

"I cannot do it, my heart's love."

"We've put so much money in. It's huge, people from all over the world, it's a mosaic. They're all coming."

"In the end, it won't matter."

"Oh, you don't believe that," says her daughter. "You've never believed that, come on, Mamma!"

"Have you told anyone about the poems?"

"No."

"Promise?"

"Mamma, I promise. Please."

"I can't do it," says Zoli. "I'm sorry. I just can't."

She places her hands on the table, emphatically, as if the argument itself has been tamped beneath her fingers, and they sit in silence at a small round kitchen table with a rough-hewn surface. She can tell her daughter has paid a lot of money for the table, beautifully crafted, yet factory-made all the same. Perhaps it is a fashion. Things come around again and again. A memory nicks her. Enrico used to spread his hands out on the kitchen table and playfully stab a knife between his fingers, over and over, until the wood at the head of the table was coarse and pitted.

"You know, Franca, this coffee is awful, your father would roll over."

They look at each other then, mother and daughter, and together they smile broadly at the thought of this man now slid briefly between their ribcages.

"You know that no matter what, I am still polluted."

"But you said it yourself, Mamma, that's all gone, it's over."

"That's gone, yes, those times, but I'm still of those times."

"I love you dearly, Mamma, but you're exasperating."

Francesca says it with a smile, but Zoli turns away, looks towards the kitchen window. No more than a meter away is the brickwork of a neighboring building.

"Come on," says Zoli, "let's go for a little stroll. I'd like to see those ladies I saw yesterday, near that market, maybe we'll buy some headscarves."

"Headscarves?"

"And then you can show me where you work."

"Mamma."

"That's what I'd like, čhonorroeja, I'd like a little stroll. I need to walk."

By the time they reach the front courtyard of the apartment, Zoli is already wheezing. A few grackles fly out from the trees and make a fuss above them as they walk along the cracked pavement, her daughter busy with a mobile phone. There is talk, Zoli knows, of the cancellations and registrations and mealtimes and a dozen other things more important than the last. It strikes Zoli that she has never once in her life had a telephone and she is startled when Francesca snaps hers shut and then open again, holds it out in front of them, clicks a button and shows her the photograph.

"Older than a rock," Zoli says.

"Prettier though."

"This young man of yours . . ."

"Henri."

"Should I get the linden blossoms ready?"

"Course not, Mamma! It gets so tiring sometimes. They just want you to be their Gypsy girl. They think during breakfast that you will somehow, I don't know . . ."

"Clack your fingers?"

"I've gone through so many of them, maybe I should get an accountant."

They sit in the sunshine awhile, happy, silent, then walk back arm-in-arm to Francesca's car, a beetle-shaped thing, bright purple. Zoli slides in the front seat, surprised, but gladdened, by the disorder. There are cups on the floor, papers, clothing, and an ashtray brimming with cigarette ends. It thrills her, the complicated promise of a life so different. On the floor, at Zoli's feet, she sees one of the colored fliers for the conference. She studies it as the car lurches forward, trying hard to figure out the wording. Finally her daughter says, as she shifts the gearstick: "From Wheel to Parliament: Romani Memory and Imagination."

"A mouthful," says Zoli.

"A good mouthful, though, wouldn't you say?"

"Yes, a good one. I like it."

And she does like it, she thinks, it has force and power, decency, respect, all the things she has ever wanted for her daughter. The wheel on the front of the flier has been distorted so that a Romani flag, a photograph of an empty parliament, and a young girl dancing appear through it. The edge of the flier is blurred, distorted, and the colors are lively. She bends down, picks it up, knows her daughter feels heartened. She flips it open and sees a series of names, times, rooms, a schedule for dinners and receptions. She will not, she thinks, go to any of these.

In the flier there are photographs of speakers, one a Czech woman with high cheekbones and dark eyes. The thought of it gaffs Zoli a moment—a Czech professor, a Rom—but she does not let on, she closes the flier, clenches at a bump in the road, and says: "I can't wait."

"If you speak I could arrange something, on gala night, maybe, or the last night."

"I'm not made for galas, Franca."

"One time you were."

"I was once, yes, one time."

The car winds out to the suburbs of Paris and in the distance she can see a number of small towers. She recalls the time she stood on the hill with Enrico, overlooking the landscape of

Bratislava. She feels, tenderly, the touch of him, inhales his smell, and sees—she does not know why—the ends of his trousers flapping in the wind.

"This is where you work?"

"We've a clinic out here."

"These people are poor," says Zoli.

"We're building a center. We've got five lawyers. There's an immigration hotline. We get a lot of Muslims. North Africans. Arabs too."

"Our own?"

"I have a project going in the schools in Saint Denis, one in Montreuil as well. An art thing for Romani girls. You'll see some of the paintings later, I'll show you."

They park the car in the shadows of the towers. Two young boys roll a car tire along a pavement. The ancient games don't change, thinks Zoli. A number of men stand brooding against the gray metal of a shuttered shop, brightened with graffiti. A cat stands high-shouldered and alert in the shop doorway. An older boy hunches down into his jacket, aims a kick at the cat, lifts it a couple of feet in the air, but it lands nimbly and screeches off. The boy raises the flap of his jacket and then his head disappears into the cloth.

"Glue," says Francesca.

"What?"

"He's sniffing glue."

Zoli watches the young man, breathing at the bag, like the pulse of a strange gray heart.

A thought comes back to her: Paris and its wide elegant avenue of sound.

They link arms and Francesca says something about the unemployment rate, but Zoli doesn't quite hear, watches instead a few shadows appear and disappear on the high balconies of the flats. She smoothes down the front of her dress as they walk across a stretch of scorched grass towards the door of a low office building propped on cinder blocks. The door is locked with a metal bar. Francesca flips out a key and fumbles at the lock, opens it, and the door swings open when the metal bar is pressed. Inside there is a row of small cubicles with a number of people working in them, mostly young women. They raise their heads and smile. Her daughter calls for a security guard at the far side of the cabin to go and lock the outside door.

"But how do we get out?" asks Zoli.

"There's another door. He guards that one, and we lock the front one."

"Oh."

She hears the clicking of computer keyboards die down and sees a number of people rising from their desks, their heads popping above the low corkwood walls.

"Hi, everyone!" shouts her daughter. "This is my mother, Zoli!"

And before she can even take a breath there are a half dozen people around her. She wonders what she should do, if she should hold her dress and bow, or whether she might have to kiss them in the French way, but they extend their hands to shake hers and it seems that they are saying how nice it is to finally meet her, *finally* like a very small blade between her shoulders, she intuits it from the Italian, and she hardly knows in what language to speak back. They crowd her and she feels her heart going way too fast. She looks around for her daughter, but can't find her, in the faces, how many faces, Lord how many faces, and the word *eiderdown* slides across her mind, she does not know why, she feels her knees buckle, she is on a road, she is around a corner, but she catches herself, shakes her head, returns, and suddenly her daughter is there, holding her aloft, saying: "Mamma, let's get you some water, you're pale."

She is brought across to a brown swivel chair. She leans back in it: "I'm all right, it's just been a long journey."

And then she wonders, as she takes the glass of water, in which language she has said this, and what, if anything, it has meant.

"This is my cubicle," says Francesca.

Zoli looks up to see photographs of herself and Enrico, standing in the valley on a summer afternoon. She reaches out to touch his face, dark with sun. There is also one of Francesca as a child of eight, a kerchief on her hair, standing outside the millhouse, the turn of the wheel slightly blurred. Did we really live this way? she wonders. She wants to ask the question aloud, but nothing comes, and then she snaps herself back, pinches her wrist, and remarks how nice the office is, though clearly it is a temporary structure, cramped, leaky, tight.

"What were you saying about eiderdowns, Mamma?"

"I'm not sure."

"You're pale," Francesca says again.

"It's just a little hot in here."

Her daughter clicks on a small white fan and directs it at Zoli's face.

"I have always had some paleness," says Zoli, and she means it as a joke, but it's not a joke, nobody gets it, not even her own daughter. She reaches forward and turns the fan off, and can feel Francesca's warm breath on her cheeks, can hear her saying: "Mamma, maybe I should take you home."

"No, no, I'm fine."

"I'll just make some phone calls."

"You go ahead, čhonorroeja."

"You don't mind? It's just a few calls, that's all. A couple of other things and then I'm all yours."

"Headscarves," says Zoli for no reason that she can recognize or discern.

When they emerge through the back door, there is a group of young boys swinging along, carrying a giant radio on their shoulders. They wear baseball caps turned backwards and wide baggy trousers with brightly colored shoes. The beat of the song, loud and jarring, is not entirely foreign and Zoli thinks that she has heard it somewhere before, but perhaps all songs come around to the same song, and she wishes for a moment that she could walk with the boys, over the hill of rubbish to the cluttered construction site, just to figure out where exactly she has heard it before.

"Drive me around, Franca," she says.

"But you're tired."

"Please, I want to drive around."

"You're the boss," says her daughter, and it's meant as something sweet, Zoli knows, though it comes out barbed and strange-sounding. They round the back of the makeshift cabin and her daughter stops short. "Oh, shit," she says as she leans over the hood of the car, pulls back the windscreen wipers. "They took the rubber," she says. "They use them for catapults. That's the fourth time this year. Shit!"

A pebble lands at the back of the car and rolls on the tar.

"Get in, Mamma."

"Why?"

"Get in! Please."

Zoli settles in the front seat. Her daughter leans against the car, her breasts against the window, and Zoli can hear her talking urgently into the phone. Within moments the security guard is out, his radio crackling. Francesca points at a number of children scampering away in different directions. The security guard bends down to Zoli's window: "I'm very sorry, Madame," he says in a broad African accent, then walks wearily towards the construction site.

"Can you believe that?" says Francesca. "I'm going to get you out of here."

"I want to see it."

"What is there to see, Mamma? It's not exactly the valley. Sometimes the gendarmes won't even come in here. There's a few vigilante groups now, they keep it quieter. Mamma, don't you think—I shouldn't have brought you out here, I'm sorry."

"And where are ours?"

"Ours?"

"Yes, ours."

"Block eight. There's a few out near the highway too. They've built little shelters for themselves. They come and go."

"Block eight, then."

"It's not a good idea, Mamma."

"Please."

Francesca shifts the car into gear and drives past the shuttered shops, pulls up at a series of yellow bollards. She points across a gray courtyard at the buildings, six stories high, where laundry is strung from balconies and shattered windows are patched with thick gray tape.

Zoli watches a tiny girl running through the courtyard, carrying a folded red paper flower stuck on the end of a coat-hanger. The girl picks her way across the gloom, past the hulk of a burned-out van, and begins to climb a set of black railings. She twirls the coathanger above her head. The folded flower takes off and she jumps and catches it in midflight.

"How many live here, Franca?"

"A couple of hundred."

The figure of an enormous woman looms out onto a balcony. She leans over the railing—the fat of her arms wobbling—and screams at the little girl. The child darts into the shadow of the stairwell, pauses, flicks her wrist, and the paper flower takes off again in the air, and then she is swallowed by darkness. Zoli feels as if she has seen her before, in some other place, some other time, that if she spends long enough she will recognize her.

The girl appears on the top balcony, where she skips along and is suddenly dragged into the doorway.

"I'm sorry, Mamma."

"It's okay, love."

"We try to help as much as possible."

"Go ahead, horse, and shit," says Zoli, and the engine catches and the car pulls away.

By the motorway Zoli catches sight of the camp, strung out along a half-finished piece of road. The doors of the caravans are open and four burnt-out vans stand nearby, their front bonnets open. Three barechested men are bent over one engine. A teenage boy drags a stick in the dirt; behind him, a wake of pale ash. Some older men sit on chairs, like stone figures quarried. One of them dabs at his mouth with a flap end of shirt. Smoke rises from sundry fires. An array of shoes are strung on a telephone wire. Tires lie strewn around an upended wheelbarrow.

They pass in a raw, cold silence.

Zoli stares out at the blur of the cars, barriers, low bushes, the quick whip of white lines on the road.

"Who are all these people tonight?"

"Mamma?"

"At the conference, who are they?"

"Academics," says Francesca. "Social scientists. There are Romani writers now, Mamma. Some poets. One is coming all the way from Croatia. There are some brilliant people about these days, Mamma. The Croatian's a poet. There's a man from the University of—"

"That's nice."

"Mamma, are you okay?"

"Did you see that wheelbarrow?"

"Mamma?"

"Someone should turn it the right way up."

"We'll be home soon, don't worry."

In the apartment she falls asleep quickly, hugging the pillow to her chest. She wakes in the afternoon, the room silent. In the adjacent bathroom she drinks deep from the cold-water tap. She dresses and lies on the bed with her hands on her stomach. She could stay like this, she thinks, for quite a while, though she would need a view, maybe a chair, or some sunlight.

In the early afternoon Henri comes breezing through the door. He stops at the sight of her, as if he'd forgotten she'd be there. He is dressed in crisp white trousers and a light blue shirt. He clamps a phone to his ear, smiles broadly, blows her an air-kiss. Zoli has no idea what to do with the gesture. She nods back at him. This is his room, she thinks, these are his shirts, his cupboard, his photo frames, one of which she herself inhabits.

In the bathroom, she sprinkles some water on her face and readies herself for the living room. She is glad to hear the sound of Francesca's voice, from the kitchen, talking about some catering accident. Henri, it seems, is on the lookout for a band of musicians, drunk somewhere and due to play at tonight's opening tonight.

"Scottish," he shouts into the phone, "they're Scottish, not Irish!"

Across the room Francesca winks at her, circling her hand in the air as if to hurry her phone call along. In the background the television is on, mute. Zoli sits at the coffee table and flips open the photographs of India. The dead along the Ganges. A crowd in front of a temple. She turns a page as Henri begins clicking his fingers frantically, first at Francesca, then at Zoli. "My God, my God, oh, my God!" he says as he slams the phone down and turns the volume of the television up high. On the screen he appears tight and nervous. The camera sweeps away from him to a group of young girls in traditional costume, dancing. The screen flashes with the title of the conference, then back to the dancing girls once more.

Francesca sits on the couch beside Zoli and when the report is finished she takes her mother's hand and squeezes it.

"Well, did I foul it up?" says Henri, combing back his hair with his fingers.

"You were perfect," says Francesca, "but you might have been better if you'd taken off that straitjacket."

"Hmm?"

"Just joking."

Mother and daughter lean into each other, hands clasped. Light slides through the curtains and seems to spread itself out at their feet.

"Well, you might have just loosened it a little," Francesca says, and then she lays her head on Zoli's shoulder and both of them laugh together as one.

"Well, I think I did just fine."

He turns on his heels, stomps back to the kitchen.

The two women sit, foreheads touching. It seems to Zoli the perfect moment, unbidden, unforced. She would like to freeze it all here, rise up, leave her daughter on the couch, in the warmth of laughter, walk through the apartment, pick up her shoes at the door, stroll down the stairs, through the quiet streets, and leave all of Paris frozen in this one moment of strange beauty, floating through the city on the only moving thing in the world, the train, heading towards home.

~

Zoli showers by sitting on the edge of the bath, facing the rain of it. The water mists her hair. She hears stirrings in the bedroom, the fast shuffle of feet, the quick closing snap of the door. Henri's voice is harried, looking for his cufflinks. She can hear Francesca insisting that he hurry up and leave. There is silence from Francesca and then a long sigh.

Zoli closes her eyes and allows the water to fall along her body.

The front door closes with more than its usual noise and then she hears a gentle knocking on the bathroom door.

"Coast is clear, Mamma."

They dress together in the bedroom. Zoli keeps her back turned though she catches a glimpse of her daughter in the corner of the mirrored armoire, the skin taut at her waist, the brown length of her leg. Francesca wiggles into a blue dress and a pair of high-heeled shoes.

Zoli leans against the armoire, closes her eyes to the reflection: "Maybe I should skip it, čhonorroeja, I'm a little tired."

"You can't skip it, Mamma, it's the opening night."

"I feel a bit dizzy."

"It's nothing to worry about, I promise."

"I could just stay here. I'll watch for Henri on the TV."

"And die of boredom? Come on, Mamma!"

Her daughter fumbles in a drawer, then stands behind Zoli and drapes a long necklace over her throat. "It's an old Persian piece," she says, "I found it in the market in Saint Ouen. It wasn't expensive. I want you to have it."

Francesca's hand touches, soft, against the pulse of her throat.

"Thank you," says Zoli.

On the drive over—through a maze of highways and overpasses—Francesca drums on the wheel, saying how it was nearly impossible to find a hotel for the conference. "We had to drop the word *Romani* and change it to *European,* just so they'd let us in." She laughs and wipes a smudge from the windscreen with the end of her shawl. "European memory and imagination! Imagine! And then we had to put the word back in, of course, for the flier, so the hotel tried to pull out. We can't have Gypsies, they said. We had to threaten a lawsuit and then the prices rose, we almost had to cancel. Can you believe that?"

The car loops in front of the hotel, palm-fronted, glassy, glossed over with a high cheapness.

"And they wanted to know if there'd be any horsecarts!" She unbuckles her seat belt before the car stops, laughs hard, and hits the steering wheel and, mistakenly, the horn, so that the car seems to arrive angrily at the curb. She flips open the seat belt across her body: "Academics on Appaloosas! I mean, what century are we living in?"

Zoli hears birdsong and it takes a moment for her to realize that it is being piped through loudspeakers. So much the world changes, so much it stays the same. She passes through the revolving doorway, treading slowly so that for a moment the electronic door almost hits the back of her ankle. She inches forward and the door goes with her and she feels as if she is moving through a millwheel.

"I hate those doors," says Francesca as she guides Zoli along the corridor, past a series of small signs, to where a giant version of the flier sits outside a large brown-paneled conference room.

Zoli recognizes some faces from Francesca's workplace, their wide-open smiles, and indeed a few of her own—a Rom always knows—she can tell in the swirl of faces, the eyes, the quick glances, the happy grasp of shoulders. My language, she thinks. She can hear it in snatches, like a bird in a room, one corner to the other. It feels as if air has entered her legs. She sways. A glass of water is thrust in her hand.

Zoli sips the water and feels a flush of emptiness. Why the fuss? Why the worry? Why not be back in the valley, watching the sun sink beneath the windowframe?

Across the hallway she sees Henri pumping hands with a tall man in a banded white hat.

"That's the poet," whispers Francesca. "And across there, that's one of our big donors, I'll introduce you later. And that girl's from *Paris-Match*, a reporter, isn't she gorgeous?"

All the faces seem to blur into one. Zoli wishes for anger but can't dredge it up. She wants to reach out and grasp whatever she can find, a fencepost, a rosebush, a rough wooden railing, her daughter's arm, anything.

"Mamma?"

"Yes, yes, I'm fine."

A bell rings and Francesca guides her along the corridor into the ballroom where circular tables have been arranged with shining cutlery and folded napkins.

Laughter sounds through the hall, but a gradual silence descends at the sound of knives tinkling against glass. A speaker stands up at a podium, a tall Swedish man, and his speech is translated into French. Zoli is lost, but happily so, though every now and then her daughter leans across and whispers the context of the speech in her ear—a sharp sense of our own experience, memory as a funnel, understanding Romani silence, no access to public grievance, the lack of preservation, the implicit memory at the heart of all things. They seem like such large words for small times, and Zoli allows them to wash over her as applause ripples through the room.

She watches her daughter walk onstage, swishing up in her beautiful blue dress, to give a brief welcoming speech in Romani and French both, and to outline the three days of conference, the Holocaust, the Devouring, Lexical Impoverishment, Cultural Values in Scottish Balladry, Police Perception of Belgian Roma, Economic Stratification, and, at the core, Issues of Romani Memory. How proud she is, she says, to see so many scholars, and so much interest at last: "We will not be made to stay at the margins any longer!" A great cheer goes up from the tables, and there is talk then of names and sponsors and donors and although Zoli has begged her not to mention her name she does so anyway, and it feels as if the room has hushed and the air has been sucked out to fill the space. There is a brief round of applause, brief, thank God, and no spotlight. Henri grabs her hand and squeezes it, and really all she wants now is to be back in the apartment, lying on the bed with her hands folded across her stomach, but it means so much to Francesca, all of this, she must remain, stand side by side with her daughter, and what does it matter anyway? It is such a small thing to give. She feels a small shame at the walls of her heart. I should stand and applaud her. I should sing out her name. All I have been is small against this. Petty, foolish, selfish. Zoli hikes the hem of her dress and stands, applauds as her daughter comes down the steps on her high heels, a beaming smile, a triumph.

They nestle in to one another. This is what I have, thinks Zoli. This is my flesh and blood.

Onstage the Scottish musicians begin to break the skin of the evening and the music fills the room—mandolin, guitar, fiddle. Laughter sounds out all around and movement blurs the hall. Waiters. Hotel staff. Tall men with leather patches on their sleeves.

Zoli leans back in her chair, touches her throat, and is surprised by the feel of the new necklace against her skin. She barely remembers putting it on. How long, she wonders, since she wore something like this? She closes her eyes to Enrico. He strides up the hillside, towards the mill. His coat is thrown off his shoulders before he even enters. He kicks the mud off his boots and closes the door.

Go, violin, she thinks, go.

The pulse of the music rises. Under the table, she releases one foot from its shoe. The air feels cool against her toes. She lifts off the second shoe and stretches backwards and feels a light tapping at her shoulder. A voice from behind. Her name. She turns in the chair and fumbles to get the shoes back on her feet. Her name again. She stands. He, the visitor, is fleshy, wiry-haired, mid-forties or so—something about him open and full, a wide smile on his face. He stretches out his hand, plump and soft.

"Dávid Smolenak," he says. "From Prešov."

The air around her suddenly compresses.

"I do have the right person, don't I? Zoli Novotna?"

She stares at the row of pens in his waistcoat pocket.

"Are you Zoli Novotna?"

It is the first time she has heard Slovak spoken in many years. It sounds so acutely foreign now, out of place, dredged up. She has, she thinks, been transported elsewhere, her body playing games, her mind tripping her up.

"Excuse me," he says. "Did I get the wrong person?"

She scans the room and sees the rows of faces at table after table, animated with music. She stammers, shakes her head, then nods, yes and no.

"You had a book? In the '50s?"

"I'm here with my daughter," she says, as if that might account for her whole life.

"It's a pleasure," he says.

She wonders what pleasure it could possibly be, and feels a flush of heat at her core.

"Prešov?" she says, as she catches the edge of the table.

"Would you have a minute, maybe?" he asks. "I'd love to talk to you. I read your book. I found a copy in a secondhand store in Bratislava. It's amazing. I've been to the settlements, Hermanovce, places like that. They're quite a sight."

"Yes," she says.

He balls up his fist, coughs into it, and says: "You're hard to keep track of."

"Me?"

"I ran into you first when I was reading some articles about other writers, Tatarka, Bondy, Stránský, you know."

"Yes, yes," she says, and it feels to her as if all of the windows have been closed all at once.

"I didn't know you were going to be here," he says, almost stuttering. "I assumed . . ." He laughs the sort of laugh designed to fill spaces. "If it wasn't for Štěpán, I wouldn't have known anything."

He lights a cigarette and moves his hand in a coil of blue smoke. Zoli watches the smooth trajectory of the cigarette to his lips, and the movement of his hands in the air, the quick fingers. It is as if the words come out in odd streaks from his mouth—talk of Slovakia, the plight of the Roma, what it means now to European integration, and suddenly he is in Bratislava, he is talking of a towerblock called the Pentagon, graffiti in the stairwells, dealers in the dark shadows—what sort of dealers? she wonders—and something about an exhibition, about Stránský's poems being resurrected, a strange word, she thinks, Stránský would not like it, no, the very thought of him billowing through the gardens at Budermice, resurrected.

The journalist touches her elbow and she wants to say, No, please leave me alone, leave me be, I am in a garden, I am walking, I am not where you think I am, I am gone, but he is off again on a tangent about a poem, one of her old songs, something about the trunk of a linden tree. He was searching out Stránský, he says, and discovered *Credo,* and then a chapbook, they were odd, these poems, rare, beautiful, in a dusty back issue, and when he went searching for the book he was told it could be bought in the secondhand shops, there was a small cult around it, that she is seen as a voice, a new voice from old times, and he has been looking, searching, digging, and then he says the name again, *Štěpán,* how he helped out when he finally got in touch with him. He crushes the cigarette into a saucer on the table. The smoke rises and she watches it curl. *Štěpán,* the journalist says yet again, and then he mentions something about a photograph taken at the piano of the Carlton Hotel, the clarity of it, the beauty, and she wants more than anything just to lean over and to pour water on the smoldering cigarette, to extinguish it, but the more she watches it the more the smoke rises in stutters.

"Swann?" she says.

"Yes."

"Stephen Swann?"

"Yes, of course," he says.

Zoli drags the chair across the carpet, lowers herself into it. She reaches for a glass of water, puts it to her lips. She does not know whose it was, yet she turns it a half-circle and takes a sip. Taboo to drink from someone else's glass, but the water feels immediately cool at the back of her throat.

On the far side of the room a pale face comes forward into the light.

"In the reception," the journalist says, or seems to say, but his voice feels blown sideways, past her, beyond. It is as if there is a rush of air at her ears, the words make no sense, they are just bits and pieces. The journalist leans forward, earnest and podgy-eyed, his breath stale with cigarette smoke: "I met him today."

He goes to his knees in front of her, arm on her chair, and she can feel the weight of his other hand on her wrist.

"Ms. Novotna?" he says.

She rises to her feet and there across the room, standing like a silent sadness sunk down, is Stephen Swann, staring back at her.

Zoli thinks a moment that she must be wrong, that her mind has slipped an instant, that she has found his face in someone else, that the mention of his name has brought his face to another, that the dizziness has misled her, that time has just shifted and fractured and landed in shards. The man—is it Swann?—looks directly across at her, one hand down by his side, a wooden cane in the other. He is dressed in a fine gray suit. His hair, or what remains of it, is gray. A shiny bald pate in the middle. Heavy lids frame his eyes. His face is thin, his brow furrowed. He does not move. Zoli looks about her for some escape. Her breath sounds to her like someone drowning. She casts about for her daughter again, grasps the back of the empty chair. Go away, she thinks. Please go away. Disappear. The music from the stage is loud, powerful, and the extended pull of a bow across a violin makes her shiver.

"If you'll excuse me," she says to the journalist.

"I was just wondering if we could have a word—"

"I must go."

"Later perhaps?"

"Yes, yes, later."

The man across the room—it is Swann, she is sure of it—has begun to move in her direction, stiff and lopsided on the cane. His body moves in the folds of the suit, which creases and uncreases, like some strange gray animal.

"All of us, we'll get together," says the journalist.

"Of course, yes."

"We'll meet here?"

She stands suddenly and faces the journalist, stares into the round outline of his face, and says sharply: "You must excuse me, please."

From the corner of her eye she watches Swann, his neck a

sack of sag, vanishing into the folds of the jacket. She thinks for a moment of curtains disintegrating on a rail. "Don't come here," she whispers. She pushes the high back of a chair out of her way. Three tables away. "No." She grabs the cloth of her dress and bundles it in her fingers. "Disappear," she says quietly. "Leave." Two tables, and then he is standing in front of her and he says his name, quietly, softly, "Štěpán," as if he is finally and entirely Slovak, as if he always has been, but then he corrects himself, maybe remembering something so old it has been carved from a tomb: "Stephen."

"I know who you are," she says.

"Zoli, can we sit?"

She wants, in that instant, nothing more than a wicker chair faced to the sunset in the valley and to grow old and dead, that's what she wants, she would like to be in the valley on that brown wicker chair, yes, dying in the shadow of Enrico.

"No," she says.

Swann tries what surely wants to be a smile, but is not. "I can't tell you how . . . I am . . . I . . . ," he says, as if he is trying to recall a Slovak word he might never have known. "So happy." His words make a hollow imitation of his face. He takes a pen from his pocket and stares at it, nervously inverting it, his pale hands twitching. "I thought something had happened to you, I thought maybe you were, I thought maybe, all these years . . . it's so good to see your face, Zoli, so very good. May I sit, please, may we sit? How did you—"

"No."

"I want to say something. Please."

"I know what you want to say."

"I have something I've wanted to say for years. I thought you were—"

"I know what you thought."

He clears his throat as if to speak again, some knowledge, some good word, but it does not come, it seems caught in his throat, and he cannot disguise his shaking. He lowers his head and his eyes accumulate shadow.

She steps sideways and she does not know why or from where, but in her hand she has picked up a small metal spoon. She thinks of placing it back on the nearby table but she doesn't, she pockets it, and she is sure then the waiters are watching, or the journalist, or the security guards, and they have seen her, she has stolen a spoon, that they will come across, accuse her, they will grab her forearm, say, Excuse me, come with us, show us the spoon, thief, liar, Gypsy. She can hear the thump of Swann's cane behind her. In front of her, a thick crowd—the young Croatian poet surrounded by women, the workers from her daughter's office. Swann shuffles behind her. The sound of his cane.

She would like the people to part like water but she cannot get through, she must tap them on the shoulders. They turn and smile and their voices sound to Zoli as if they're speaking from inside a tree. She slides past, her nerve ends stripped clean.

At the far side of the room, Francesca watches, a small frown on her face, confused, but Zoli shakes her head, gives a wave, as if she is all right, not to worry, čhonorroeja, I'll be okay. She pushes the last chair aside. Out the door, into the corridor, fast now, around the corner.

He's gone bald, she thinks. Old and bald and wearing a suit a size too big. Liver spots on his hands. White knuckles. A silver-tipped cane.

She hurries towards the entrance, through reception, out the revolving door, where the concierge skips towards her. "Taxi, please," she says in Slovak first, then Italian, and she feels as if she wants to tear at her tongue, remove all these languages. The concierge smiles and raises his hand, his glove so very white against the red of his uniform.

Zoli is halfway in the taxi and halfway out when she realizes she doesn't have any money, and she thinks how absurd, climbing into this car, in a land she doesn't know, going towards a room she doesn't know, with no coins to take her there. "Wait, please," she says to the driver.

In the hotel glass, the reflection startles her, her gray hair, the bright dress, the shrunken bend of her back. To have come all this way and see herself like this. She pushes back through the revolving doors. Far down the corridor she sees Swann—he looks as if he has spent his life turning in every wrong direction he can find, and, for a moment, she sees him as that man on the motorbike, with a rabbit hopping in front of him, swerving to avoid it, his crutches strapped on the back, light and dark moving over the fields.

She hurries down the corridor, ducking through the kitchen to the amazement of a young man chopping carrots into tiny slivers. Someone shouts at her. Her hip glances off the edge of a metal table. She follows a young waitress carrying a large silver tray out of the kitchen, into the hall again where she stops a moment, breathes deeply, looks for Francesca in all the faces, their confusion, their joy, their music.

"Mamma?"

Zoli shuffles across and takes her daughter's elbow. "I need some money. Some French money."

"Of course, Mamma. Why?"

"I need to get a taxi. I need to go home. Your home. Hurry."

"What's wrong?"

"Nothing, precious heart."

"Who was that man you were talking to?"

"That was Swann," she says. She is surprised at herself. She wanted to say: Nobody. To shake her head and shrug. To cast it off, pretend indifference. To stand there, a picture of ordinary strength. But she doesn't, and instead she says it again: "That was Stephen Swann. He has some journalist with him."

"Oh, my God."

"I just need some money for a taxi."

"What did you say to him?"

"What did I say? I don't know what I said, Franca. I need to go."

"What's he doing here?"

"I don't know. Do you know?"

"Why would I know, Mamma?"

"Tell me."

"No," says her daughter. "I didn't know."

"Just give me the money, please. I'm sorry, I didn't mean that. I beg of your sweet eyes, Franca."

She sees a light sweeping over the valley, a bird through treetops, a road rising white in front of her eyes, then she feels herself sway. Francesca takes her elbow and places the other hand tight around her mother's waist. The rush of hotel wall-paper. The quick glint of light on glass. Fingerprints at the low corners of the windowpanes. Swann is leaning against the wall, framed by two cheap prints, his chest heaving. The journalist stands beside him, head bent, scribbling in his spiral notebook. Swann looks up as they pass. He raises his hand again.

320

"Don't turn," says Zoli. "Please don't turn."

They move towards the revolving door and the sound of taped birdsong. Francesca presses money into her hand.

"I swear, Mamma, I had no idea. I swear on my life."

"Just take me out to the taxi."

"I'll go with you."

"No. I want to sit alone."

She catches a brief waft of her daughter's perfume as she slides into the backseat. "Keys!" shouts Francesca, and Zoli rolls down the window, takes the key ring in her palm.

She can see Francesca mouthing something as the taxi pulls away—I love you, Mamma—and in the rear of the reception area, shuffling, trying to get through the crowd, is Swann, rail-thin, quivering. He looks like the sort of man who can't afford to leave, and doesn't want to stay, and so he is doing both at once.

Zoli sits back against the warm plastic of the seat and looks out to the alarming beauty of the sky as the taxi swings away from the hotel.

~

She takes the elevator without a second thought, places her head against the cool of the wooden panel, and recalls the noise of his cane, the shine of light on his forehead, the contours of his brow.

For a long time she forgets to push the button.

The chains clank and she rises. The elevator opens on another floor. A young woman and a dog step in to take her place. She walks the final flight of stairs. Turns the key in the door. Negotiates the long corridor in the dim light. She drops her dress to the floor and the metal spoon tumbles out of her pocket. Her underclothes fall behind her. She stands naked in front of the long mirror and gazes at her body—a paltry thing, brown and puckered. She reaches up and unloosens her hair, lets it fall. All the ancient codes violated. She walks into the living room and picks up the photograph of Enrico from the shelf near the window, takes it from the frame, returns to bed, lifts the covers, curls up under the sheets with the photo just beneath her left breast.

She wishes for a moment that she had waited to hear the things that Swann might have had to say, but what would he say, what could he say, what would ever make sense? Zoli closes her eyes, grateful to the dark. Patterns passing, crystal patterns, snow now, gently settling. There are no days more full than those we go back to.

She wakes to the sound of people coming into the apartment. The clicking of bottles and a hollow boom of an instrument in a case being banged against a wall. She sits up and feels the photo pasted against her breast.

"Mamma."

She is startled to see Francesca at the end of the bed, curled up, knees to her chest. The room seems familiar now, almost breathing.

"You'll take the life from me, precious heart."

"I'm sorry, Mamma."

"How long have you been there?"

"A little while. You were sleeping so well."

"Who's there? Who's that? Outside?"

"I don't know, that asshole is bringing people here."

"Who?" says Zoli.

"Henri."

"I mean who's with him?"

"Oh, I don't know, just a group of drunks. The bars are closed. I'm sorry. I'll kick them out."

"No, leave them be," says Zoli. She pulls back the sheet and shifts sideways on the bed, puts her feet to the floor. "Can you give me my nightdress?"

She stands with her back to her daughter and pulls the dress over her head, rough against her skin.

"You were sleeping with Daddy?"

"Yes, how silly is that?"

"Just silly enough."

A series of shushes come from the living room, then one clink of a bottle cap falling to the floor, rolling across the hardwood, and a series of stifled laughs.

"Mamma, are you okay? Can I get you something? Hot milk or something?"

"Did you talk to him? Swann?"

"Yes."

"And he said he was sorry, didn't he?"

"Yes."

"Did he say what he was sorry for?"

"For everything, Mamma."

"He's always been an idiot," says Zoli.

The low sound of a mandolin filters through the apartment and then a harsh piece of laughter, followed by the faint pluck of a guitar.

"Come here beside me."

Her daughter swings longways across the bed, spreads herself out, takes a piece of Zoli's hair and puts it in her mouth. In so many ways, her father's child. They lie side by side in the intimate dark.

"I'm sorry, Mamma."

"Nothing to be sorry for."

"I had no idea."

"What else did he say?"

"He lives in Manchester now. He got out in '68, the whole Prague thing. He says he thought you were dead. There were bodies found along the border. He was sure that something bad had happened to you. Or that you were living in a hut somewhere in Slovakia. He says he looked for you. Searched all over."

"What's he doing here?"

"He said he likes to follow things. To keep in touch. That it was a hobby. He still uses the word Gypsy. Goes to a lot of conferences and things. The festival down there in Santa Maria. All over the place. He says he owns a wine shop."

"A wine shop?"

"In Manchester."

"Nobody lives where they grew up anymore."

"What's that?"

"Just something he said to me once."

"He said he was heartbroken, Mamma. That's what he said. That he's been heartbroken ever since."

"He lives alone?"

"I don't know."

"Swann," Zoli says with a slow, sad laugh. "Swann. A capitalist."

She tries to imagine him there, amid a row of wooden racks, learning to count prices, the bell on the doorframe tinkling. He stands and greets the customer with a small bow of the head. Later, stooped, he shuffles to the corner shop to buy his half-liter of milk and a small loaf of bread, then goes home to a small house in a row of small houses. He sits in a soft yellow chair and

looks towards the window, waiting for the light to disappear so
he can have his evening meal, wander off to bed, read the books
that will make up his mind for him.

"He wants to see you again, Mamma. He said that his ideas
were borrowed, but your poems weren't."

"More of his horseshit."

"He says he has some of Stránský's poems too."

"Did he say anything about Conka?"

"He fell out of touch with everyone. They were made to
stay in the towers, that's all he knows."

Francesca's body stretches away from her as if, in their hud-
dling, they might be able to extend each other.

"And the other man, the journalist?"

"He'd like to talk. That's what he said. He found an old
book of yours, and went searching. He was just curious at first,
enjoyed the poems, he said. He'd like to talk to you. Tomorrow."

"You can talk to him for me, Franca. Tell him something."

"Tell him what?"

"Tell him I've gone somewhere."

"You're going home, aren't you?"

"Of course I am."

"What will I tell him?"

"Tell him that nothing is ever arrived at."

"What?"

"Tell him that nothing is ever fully understood, that's what
I'd like to say."

A peace descends between them now, a quietness that trav-
els across the sheets. Her daughter hikes herself onto an elbow,
a little hill of shadow where her hip juts out.

"You know what he wanted to know? Swann. At the end?"

"Tell me," says Zoli.

"He was a bit embarrassed. He kept looking at the floor. He said he just wanted to know one thing."

"Yes . . . ?"

"Well, he wanted to know what had happened to his father's watch."

"That was his question?"

"Yes."

Zoli watches as a small bar of light moves along the wall and down. Someone passes in the corridor outside and a series of shushes sound from the living room. She closes her eyes and is carried away on the notion of Swann resting on one small fixed point of an ancient clockhand, as if it all might come around again, as if it all could be repeated and cured. A single gold watch. She wonders if she should feel pity, or anger, or even amusement, but instead she locates the pulse of an odd tenderness for Swann, not for how he was, or what he has become, but for all he has lost, the flamboyance of what he had once so dearly believed in, how absolute it was, how fixed. What must it have been like for him, to break the border one final time and to move back to England? What must it have been like for him to return empty, to be back with less than he had ever imagined leaving with? Swann, she thinks, did not learn for himself how to be lost. He did not know the meaning of what it was to turn and change. She wishes now that she had kissed him, that she had taken his slack face in her hands, touched her lips against the pale forehead to release him, to let him walk away.

Zoli lays her head against her daughter's breastbone and feels the breath trembling through Francesca's body.

"You know what I want to do?" Zoli says. "I'm going to see him tomorrow. Then I'd like to get on a train and go back to the valley. I would very much like to wake up quietly in the dark. That's what I'd like."

"You're going to tell Swann where you're living?"

"Of course not. I couldn't bear the thought of him coming there."

And then Zoli knows for sure what she will do: she will take a taxi to the train station, stop off first at the hotel, move under the birdsong, call Swann's room, stand in the reception, wait, watch him shamble across towards her, hold his face in her hands for a moment, and kiss him, yes, on the forehead, kiss him. She will allow him his sorrow and then she will leave, take the train, alone, home to the valley.

"I'm happy there," says Zoli.

A note jumps out from deep in the apartment, a hard discordant thing moving through the air, surrounded a second later by a new one, as if testing the old one, until they start to collide, rising and falling, taking air from each other.

"Idiot," says Francesca. "I'll tell him to shut up." Her body pulls taut, but Zoli taps her hand. "Wait a moment," she says. The music rises and draws itself out, quicker, more turbulent.

"Get dressed," says Zoli.

"Mamma?"

"Let's get dressed."

Laughter bursts out with the music now and the smell of smoke filters along the corridor. The women step away from the bed. Their clothes lie scattered in the darkness. They fumble a moment: a nightgown, a blue dress, a high-heeled shoe. Francesca's arm gets caught in her sleeve, and Zoli helps it along. She strokes the side of her daughter's face. They stand together at the bedroom door.

"But you're in your nightdress," says Francesca.

"I don't care."

They cross the wooden floors of the corridor and a sharp silence fills the room when mother and daughter appear. Henri stands, wide-eyed, with a thin joint at his mouth. "Oh," he says, swaying on his feet. Scattered around the room are the Scottish musicians. One of them, tall and handsome and curly-haired, stands and bows deeply. He stubs out his joint in a flowerpot. Francesca giggles and looks across at her mother. How glorious, thinks Zoli, how joyful, that it is all, still, even on this night, so unfinished.

Zoli nods to them and simply says: "Smoke away."

The musician looks around, a little startled, fishes his joint from the pot. He straightens it, lights up, and laughs.

"What happened to the music?" says Zoli.

She used to play the sugar upon the metal, she recalls, in those old days when she gathered children at the back of her wagon—she would place a sheet of siding on a wooden saw-horse, sprinkle the sugar on the sheet, sometimes salt, or, if nothing else, seeds. She teased the violin bow along the very edge of the plate until the metal began to hum. The sugar jumped and swerved and found its own vibrating patterns: standing waves, circular clumps, solitary grains, like small white acrobats. Afterwards the children clamored to lick the sheet clean. She had loved those maps, their random patterns, their odd music, the way the children clapped the sugar into place. She had never thought of them as anything new or unusual, although she heard that others called them chladnis, sound charts—the sugar settling at the points where there was least sound—and she thought, even then, that she could have looked at the metal sheet and found a whole history of her people painted there.

"Go on," she says. "Play."

The curly-haired one strikes a note on the mandolin, a bad note, too high, though he rinses it out with the next, and the guitarist joins in, slowly at first, and a wave moves across the gathering, like wind over grass, and the room feels as if it is opening, one window, then another, then the walls themselves. The tall musician strikes a high chord and nods at Zoli—she smiles, lifts her head, and begins.

She begins.

ACKNOWLEDGMENTS/AUTHOR'S NOTE

WE GET OUR VOICES from the voices of others. I am enormously indebted to a number of people who have helped me research, refine, and radically change the structure of this novel over the past four years. I can claim no familial link with the Romani culture—it is, I suppose, the novelist's privilege to play the fool, rushing in where others might not tread. I have scavenged from all over and am indebted to so many sources that it would be impossible to list them all. Our stories are created from a multiplicity of witness.

The following artists and writers have inspired me—Ilona Lacková in *A False Dawn: My Life as a Gypsy Woman in Slovakia* (University of Hertfordshire Press); Milena Hübschmannová; Bronisława Wajs (Papusza) and Jerzy Ficowksi. I have found enormous help in the work of Ian Hancock from the Center of Romani Archives at the University of Texas. The Romani language and orthography are only now in the process of being standardized. As Hancock has written, the word "Gypsy" is intently disliked by some Roma and tolerated by others. The persistence of the use of "Gypsy" lies in the fact that there is no single Romani equivalent universally agreed upon. Time and scholarship is changing this. I have used certain spellings and constructions determined by geography, history, and political affiliations that were current at the time when the novel takes place, sometimes purposely confused. The choices and mistakes are purely mine.

The story of Zoli was suggested to me after reading the extraordinary study *Bury Me Standing: The Gypsies and Their Journey*, by Isabel Fonseca. *Zoli* is loosely inspired by the life of Papusza, the Polish poet who lived from 1910 to 1987. Zoli's poem in this novel is original, though it takes some of its form from the poetry of Papusza and others. Despite published reports to the contrary (including some statements attributed to characters in this novel), there have been many Roma poets in Europe down through the years—their work has been careful and loving, even if consistently ignored.

I would like to give very special thanks to Laco Oravec and Martin Fotta and everyone else at the Milan Šimečka Foundation in Bratislava who, over the course of two months, helped me negotiate the contemporary Romani experience. The novel would have been impossible without their help. I can think of no better guides, nor no better hosts than the people of the settlements that I visited in eastern and western Slovakia. The following know their own role; I only wish I could give them deeper thanks: Richard Jurst, Robert Renk, Valerie Besl, Michal Hvorecký, Jana Belišova, Anna Jurová, Daniela Hivešová-Šilanová, Zuzanna Bošelová, Mark Slouka, Zdenek Slouka, Thomas Ueberhoff, Dirk Van Gunsteren, Thomas Bohm, Manfred Heid, Tom Kraushaar, Francoise Triffaux, Brigitte Semler, Martin Koffler, Barbara Stelzl-Marx, and the various people of the Roma camps and housing estates that I visited.

In New York I want to give sincere thanks to Lorcan Otway for all his advice and scholarship. Thanks to Hunter College and the Hertog fellowship program. A deep bow to Emily Stone, my research assistant. Gratitude also to Roz Bernstein, Frank McCourt, Terry Cooper, Gerard Donovan, Chris Barrett Kelly, Tom Kelly, Jeff Talarigo, Jim Harrison, Aleksandar Hemon (for the music!), Bill Cobert, and all at the American Irish Historical Society. The book is dedicated to all at the New York Public Library, including the scholars at the Cullman Center, but a specific thanks goes to Marzena Ermler and Wojciech Siemaszkiewicz, and of course to Jean Strouse, Pamela Leo, Adriana Nova, and Amy Aazarito.

Amongst the many, many authors whose writings I have found very helpful are Will Guy, Eva Davidová, Emilia Horváthová, Michael Stewart, Alaina Lemon, David Crowe, Donald Kenrick, Tera Fabianová, Cecilia Woloch, Jan Yoors, Margriet de Moor, Louise Doughty, Václav Havel, and Walter Starkie, to name but a few.

Last, but never least, my thanks to Allison Hawke, Daniel Menaker, Kirsty Dunseath, and Sarah Chalfant.

Zoli

COLUM McCANN

A Reader's Guide

A Conversation with
Colum McCann and Frank McCourt

Frank McCourt: I was saddled with the quintessential miserable Irish childhood. You enjoyed the opposite, didn't you? What sort of life does a writer need these days in order to carve out a career in novels?

Colum McCann: That's where I envy you, Frank! You had something to write about from the beginning! I had to carve stories out of nothing! Seriously, though, you're right. There's advantages and disadvantages to both. I grew up in a safe, sub-urban Dublin household. My father didn't drink. My mother stayed at home. I remember when I came home from school at lunchtime, she would be waiting for me. She used to cut the crusts off my lettuce-and-tomato sandwiches. It was a tiny ges-ture, but representative. I was blessed in so many ways. They looked after us well. We ate together at the family table. We went for walks on Sunday afternoons. And we were sur-rounded by books. When I think about it, there were thousand of stories in our house. Of course it wasn't all simple and hunky-dory. It never can be. But it was close and it will always be home.

It's interesting to contemplate the notion that writers are not necessarily born, but that they make themselves—from the stuff of desire, of community, of the need to listen. There's never just one way to tell a story. That would be acutely boring. But for me I have no desire to write about my upbringing. Two hundred blank pages. What is it they say? Happiness writes white.

FM: You make these wild imaginative leaps. For *This Side of Brightness* it was a homeless man living in the subway tunnels. For *Dancer* it was a gay, Muslim-born ballet icon. Anyone can tell from a quick glance that you're not homeless and, let's face it, neither of us really look like dancers, so where do these stories come from?

CM: My stories come from images and then I end up building worlds around them. The story of Rudolph Nureyev stemmed from a story I heard that took place in the flats of Ballymun, where a young boy caught a glimpse of Nureyev on his family's first television, out on the balcony of a high-rise project. He was holding the TV, and I was awestruck by the notion that a seven-year-old Dublin boy was carrying the world's greatest dancer in his arms. I wanted to explore the idea that we all have stories, that stories are the ultimate human democracy. It doesn't matter how white you are, how poor you are, how straight you are, how far-flung you are, we all have stories and the deep need to tell them. That's the door I've been knocking on for quite a while now. That's my current obsession—the thought that stories are the only true human currency.

FM: Zoli is in some ways your most "foreign" character, a woman, a poet, a Rom, an exile, an Eastern European. How did you discover and maintain her voice?

CM: Zoli broke my heart a number of times. It certainly was the biggest leap I had ever made. But I'm interested in compassion and clarity and making new worlds available. Or at least, making old worlds visible—I mean visible in literary terms. To do that I had to try to be honest to her voice. There were occasions when I would have to sit for a long time—weeks on end—waiting for her voice to come. She was elusive. Strangely enough, though, now that I've finished the book I can call back her voice in an instant. I can close my eyes and she's right there. Many people have written to me to say that they can still hear her echo in their heads.

FM: Growing up around Limerick, we always had our tinkers, our travelers, our Gypsies. I know they're ethnically different to the Roma, but they seem to share some similarities.

CM: Yes, we had our travelers in Dublin too. They always seemed to embrace mystery. And we had so many clichés in place. You know, when we were growing up, my mother used to say to us: "You be good now or the Gypsies'll come take you away." Years later I was in a settlement in Slovakia where I heard a mother berating her son. I turned to my translator and asked what was going on. He said: "Oh, she's giving her son a hard time. She's telling him that if he doesn't behave the White Man will come take him away."

I thought I had suddenly come some full strange and lovely circle. We doubt one another. We distrust. We have the same stories.

The travelers are Ireland's oldest minority group. There's been a long history of anti-traveler prejudice. There's about

30,000 travelers in Ireland. Around the world there are something like twelve million Roma. But the hatred is often the same. And the tarring brush paints both groups as secretive, immoral, dishonest, filthy, uncouth, nomadic, predatory—the list is endless. You repeat something long enough, it becomes the truth. Let me tell you this: In all my time with the Roma I was never hassled, never robbed, never pushed away. I suppose in the end I was the one who was robbing from them. I went there with all the prejudices intact and came away a changed person. That's what I want the book to do too. It's a lofty aim, but why not aim high, since most of our flights of desire fall short, anyway? I believe in the social novel. People ask me why I didn't write about the travelers. I don't know. It wasn't the right time for me. It wasn't the story I wanted to tell. I had found this Polish poet, Papusza, and she took my breath away. It was her story that Zoli was modelled on. It probably would have been easier to tell the story of the travelers. At least I would have had some geography in place. As it was, I had a mad time just researching this book. I started from point blank nothing. And I had to build from there.

FM: Zoli is a survivor. And she survives primarily on her wits, but in the end she survives and endures by her use of language, her songs, her poetry. Is there a message behind this?

CM: As much as there's a message behind anything, I suppose. Language is at the fulcrum of all that we do. Language and memory. Nobody knows that better than you. That was at the heart of *Angela's Ashes*.

FM: Some of what amazes me is that there is still very little literature available about the Roma, but there are anywhere from ten to twelve million Gypsies living in the world. Why are there not more stories told?

CM: There's a kaleidoscope of reasons I suppose. Firstly they have traditionally been an oral culture. Very little was written from within—until recent years, that is. Until Romani scholars began to say that one of the ways of combating cliché is not by silence, but by speech. And then there's the ability, or inability, of the non-Roma to listen. We need to learn how to listen to the stories that are there, and to have a deep-rooted empathy within us. We need to destroy our own stereotypes and build from the ground up. Because we have so many stereotypes. And they can commit murder, these stereotypes. They can fly fascist flags, they can spit, they can sterilize, they can kill.

And I come back again, as I often do, to John Berger's line: "Never again will a single story be told as if it were the only one." Stories must be told from all angles. Those who try to own them are those who abuse power. Do I believe that literature has power? Certainly. I have to believe that. And every writer who has ever lived under a tyrannical government knows that a lot better than I do.

FM: Ireland is in the midst of a huge economic boom. Some of that means that the Roma are coming in from Bosnia, from Romania, from Slovakia, along with thousands of other immigrants. Ireland is in the midst of a cultural boom, or bust, depending whom you talk to. You started writing about other cultures at a young age. Do you think you were, in a way, writing the history of your country in advance?

CM: Well, I don't know. I do think writers anticipate things, though they're not necessarily conscious of it. Fiction suggests trends and then has to come around, afterwards, and re-interpret them.

I will tell you this, though. I remember writing a story called "Fishing the Sloe-Black River." It was a magic realist story about emigration, women fishing for their sons. I thought at the time that it was cutting edge. And I never thought it would be anything but that. However here I am, almost twenty years later, and that story strikes me as decidedly quaint now. It seems so old-fashioned. It's strange. Life is gloriously unfinished. We never know what it's going to deal us.

FM: Great steps have been made in Ireland in recent years. Why not write about those? Why bother with what you call the "small, dark anonymous corners"?

CM: Because I suppose every story is a story about Ireland. To expand the consciousness of what it means to come from that little, dark, shadowed country and then to realise that it's not dark and shadowed at all. As Whitman says, every atom belonging to me as good as belongs to you.

FM: You, Sebastian Barry, Colm Toibin, Roddy Doyle, and Joseph O'Connor have all wandered from Ireland for subject matter. Is modern Ireland becoming too rich for your taste?

CM: Well, it's become too expensive, that's for sure! I can't recognize it when I go home. I think the new emigration (as a problem) is the problem of return. It's not so hard to leave anymore. It's hard to go back. Brodsky talks about the notion of not being able to go back to the country that doesn't exist any-more.

Also, I think we're at a time when a lot of us are looking out. We will have to look quickly inward again and write the Irish novel from within. But there's nothing wrong with being out-side for a while. It gives us perspective. I think we're getting ready to jump back in, feet-first. I know I want to. I want to go in and take it all on. Just when everyone starts thinking that I'm not an Irish novelist at all, I want to go back and find the voice of my land. Because that is where my voice came from. And I have a deep love and appreciation, and maybe a healthy dose of skepticism, of and for Ireland.

FM: And the next project is . . . ?

CM: That said, it's a New York novel that has 9-11 implications, though it's set in 1974. And it's about joy and technology and faith and all those crazy things. After that, the Irish book. Jesus, that's looking into the future, isn't it?

For further information, readers can go to colummccann.com

Questions for Discussion

1. Many Romani scholars have argued that the portrayal of Gypsy communities in the mainstream media is partly responsible for ongoing negative stereotypes. McCann opens the novel from the point-of-view of a journalist who seems to be sympathetic toward Zoli, but as the novel progresses the journalist's attitude seems to be benign but superficial. What does the journalist represent?

2. What do we, as readers, learn on a deeper, more substantial level about the life of the Roma from Zoli's story?

3. Zoli's story—even when raw and terribly sad—is told in smooth, bold, simple strokes, almost as if she is whispering in our ears. The Roma are known for having a predominantly oral culture. How much do you think that Zoli (and, by extension, the author) value the art of intimate storytelling?

4. Zoli is asked by a little girl how she can be both "on" the radio and on the road at the same time. "But something lay behind it, Zoli knew, even then: both places at once, radio and road, impossible alongside the other" (p. 151). How can old traditions survive in the modern world?

5. In the 1940s and '50s, Zoli becomes a poster girl for socialism. But then the socialists try to put her and her whole culture in the "Gypsy jam jar" (p. 119). As a result, her own people blame her for what happens. Soon, she is betrayed on all sides. Is Zoli a prophet of sorts? Are prophets inevitably doomed to banishment?

6. Stephen Swann falls in love with Zoli. At times he believes that the love is fully requited, but is he just deluding himself? Is he a reliable narrator?

7. "We had interrupted her solitude in order to compensate for our own," says Swann (p. 128). Why does Swann feel so lonely and outcast before Zoli's banishment? Is he a forerunner of a certain type of international wanderer? Is he at heart, ironically, what some people might have called a "gypsy"?

8. Is Zoli a poet or a singer? Or are they the same thing?

9. When McCann first embarked on this novel he says he knew "little or nothing" about the Romani culture. What was your own experience of the Gypsy way of life? Has it changed now after reading the novel?

10. Not the least of McCann's achievements is the realism of the voices of his characters. How does he achieve the verisimilitude?

11. "One always loves what is left behind," says Zoli (p. 258). Is our view of Romani life solely based on some sentimental folk memory of something that does not exist anymore? Will

ignorance prevent the embrace of true cultural diversity? Or will memory and/or poetry carry it through?

12. This epic story encompasses the twentieth century's battles with fascism and communism and idealism. Yet it comes back to the fundamental search for home. How much do the politics of our times define where our true homes are?

13. The epigraph quotes Tahar Djaout: "If you keep quiet, you die. If you speak, you die. So speak and die." How much faith or strength do you think Zoli would put in these words?

14. Zoli says "I still call myself black even though I have rolled around in flour" (p. 277). What do you understand her to mean by this?

15. Zoli triumphs in Paris. It is a small, personal triumph, a journey toward joy. Will that joy extend itself through the rest of her days? Do you think her poetry will now be rescued and sung by others? What happens to Zoli after the final page?

Suggested Further Reading

In the Skin of a Lion by Michael Ondaatje

A Long Long Way by Sebastian Barry

What Is the What, by Dave Eggers

The People's Act of Love by James Meek

Bury Me Standing: The Gypsies and Their Journey
by Isabel Fonseca

PHOTO: © JAMES HIGGINS

COLUM MCCANN is the author of a number of other works of fiction, including *This Side of Brightness* and *Dancer,* both of which were international bestsellers. He was featured as the "Next Great Novelist" in *Esquire* magazine's "America's Best and Brightest" (2003). He is the winner of the inaugural Ireland Fund of Monaco's Literary Award, the Rooney Prize for Irish Literature, and a Pushcart Prize, and he was recently inducted into the Hennessy Hall of Fame for Irish Literature. McCann's books have been published in twenty-six languages. His short film *Everything in This Country Must,* directed by Gary McKendry, was nominated for an Oscar in 2005. He lives in New York City with his wife and children.